KISSING MADDIE

Maddie stood just in front of her hide curtain, wrapped in a fur robe, unbound raven hair spilling down to her waist. Sam stared back at her. Waited.

"I heard a sound," she whispered.

He cleared his throat. "Just me. Takin' a turn bathin'."

"I didn't mean to intrude. Can I get you anything?"

He answered without thinking. "You can scrub my back if you've a mind."

Crossing the room, she knelt behind him. He handed her the bar of soap over his shoulder.

Sam heard the soft swish of Maddie lathering her hands, felt the first tentative touch of those hands. Her stroking hands moved across his shoulders, down to the waist, their touch firmer now, slow and exploring.

He had half a mind to tell her to stop; the rest of him wasn't cooperating. All too soon, her hands fell away on their own. But she stayed put.

He rose out of the tub, taking her with him. In a single move, he stepped out in front of her, pulling her tight against him. He buried his face in her freshly washed hair, breathing deeply of her own unique scent. She made a sound—not of protest, he was sure—encouraging Sam to lift his head, find her lips, drink deeply of their sweetness.

The kiss lasted a good long time.

Books by Pamela Quint Chambers

SAMANTHA'S HEART
THE BRIDE QUILT

Published by Zebra Books

THE BRIDE QUILT

Pamela Quint Chambers

Zebra Books
Kensington Publishing Corp.

http://www.zebrabooks.com

ZEBRA BOOKS are published by

Kensington Publishing Corp.
850 Third Avenue
New York, NY 10022

First Printing: June, 1999
10 9 8 7 6 5 4 3 2 1

Printed in the United States of America

In memory of my mother-in-law
Theda Eleanor Bates Chambers
1912–1997
who loved books all of her life and
who was inordinately proud that her
daughter-in-law wrote a few.

Chapter One

Monday, 17 February 1845
The town of River Valley, in the Midwest

"Madeline?"

"Madeline, you haven't heard a word I've said."

"Madeline Genevieve Preston, wake up over there and come join us. Thelma's just been relating the most delicious bit of gossip. It's about your intended," Thelma's sister Janet taunted.

Madeline stared out through the lace curtains of the parlor's front window, oblivious to both the dreary, chilling sleet turning the clay road to impassable mire and the teatime chatter going on around her. Lost in troubled thoughts, she awoke with a start when Janet, having risen to join her, pinched her upper arm—hard.

"I should think you'd be avidly interested in what Thelma has learned about Elmer Chester, since it concerns you as well."

"What concerns me?"

Madeline absently lifted her right hand to the chignon at her nape to assure herself that every last hair lay neatly coiled inside the handwoven net.

"You're not wearing an engagement ring," exclaimed Janet, aghast.

Madeline tilted her nose high. "Most likely because I am not engaged to marry anyone."

"Thelma heard that you were," asserted plump and pregnant Susanna White, taking another rich petit four from the china serving plate Madeline herself had hand-painted. "She says Elmer Chester proposed on Valentine's Day, this Friday past—how wildly romantic—and that you accepted."

Madeline offered a brief, mirthless laugh. "Papa's partner offered 'a merger' between us last Friday, yes, but the occasion was hardly romantic since Mr. Chester is older than Papa, weighs not an ounce under three hundred pounds, and has already buried one young wife no more than seven months ago.

"In addition," Madeline hastened to add, least there be any doubt as to the man's unsuitability, "Mr. Chester has absolutely no imagination, no sense of adventure. To him, an evening's excitement would consist of two biscuits with his supper stew instead of one, or mutton on Tuesday rather than roast chicken."

"Oh, but she didn't die," Thelma corrected smugly.

"Who?"

"Elmer Chester's first wife. *That's* what I've been trying to tell you. The honorable Mr. Bank President Chester is no widower. He's a *grass* widower. His wife ran off with the butler!"

"To escape her dreadfully dull old husband, I'd wager. Well, I for one have no intention of becoming the second

Mrs. Chester, no matter how Papa might insist. I have other—"

Madeline bit her lower lip, mindful of her near slip. No one must know the desperate lengths to which she intended to go to avoid Papa's highly unsuitable arrangement for keeping his lifelong friend and senior partner happy.

"Other what?" asked Maureen Talbot, newly engaged to Gabe Sidwel, her eyes aglow equally with happiness and conspicuous curiosity.

"Other goals. Other expectations. Other hopes for my future, and my life. You and Thelma were allowed to select the men whom you've promised to wed, and Susanna and Janet are already married to those of their own choosing; why cannot Papa understand that I must be permitted the same freedom?"

"Probably because you have turned down so many suitors already that your father fears you will be destined for the life of a spinster unless he takes matters into his own hands," came Susanna's tart retort.

"I'm not yet twenty."

"I was sixteen when Bill and I married," chimed Janet.

"You believed yourself so in love you couldn't wait any longer," Madeline reminded her, without adding that the childhood sweethearts now had two screaming, quarrelsome toddlers to chase after and possibly another on the way, as Janet had today confided. "I myself have never found a person with whom to share the porch swing for two consecutive evenings, let alone the rest of my life."

"You are too particular," said Maureen. "Look at me and Gabe. I know his ears stick out so that they glow translucent if the sun strikes them just right, and that our poor offspring will probably all have a mouth full of horse-sized teeth like his, but he is kind and affectionate and a good provider. And he will love me with an unswerving devotion for the rest of our life together.''

Had Madeline been an individual given to hugging, now would have been the time to cross the room to the tea table and offer Maureen a hug in support of her pronouncement; as she was not, she managed the barest of smiles.

"I am happy for you, Maureen, for all of you." She glanced from one to the other of the faces turned her way, as familiar as her own. "By your examples, I am all the more certain I *must* not marry old Mr. Chester. It would be just my bad luck to meet the fellow capable of sweeping me off my feet the moment the vows were exchanged. Then where would I be? My decision not to marry Papa's partner stands, and if he continues to insist, I shall . . . I shall . . .''

Again she almost betrayed herself to her dearest friends and was dismayed at how easily it might happen should this vein of conversation continue.

"You'll what?" they chorused, expecting some secret to be shared, as they had always shared them since earliest childhood.

She forced what sounded, to her, like genuine laughter, gay and carefree. "I shall lock myself in my bedroom and hide the only key until Elmer Chester passes on to his reward—which shouldn't take any time at all given his ponderous capacity for over-indulgence. Have you heard that Annabella Maxwell and Raymond Butler also recently became engaged?" Miss Maxwell was the town flirt with a less than sterling reputation, always good for a half-hour's gossip.

"*I've* heard," Thelma whispered conspiratorially, "that they *have* to get married, and that Anabella's not even certain Ray's the father."

"Well *I* heard . . ." interrupted Susanna, and so the

teatime gossip whisked away elsewhere, as Madeline had intended.

She followed the flow of conversation more closely this time, not only to avoid its coming around to her again, but in an attempt to keep from dwelling on the monumental predicament into which she'd gotten herself. With characteristic impetuousness, she had rashly committed herself to the only recourse presenting itself in time to avoid marrying Papa's persistent partner. Not at all certain she hadn't jumped out of the frying pan into the fire, she grew more convinced by the hour that she had made a terrible, irreversible mistake; and that she would very soon be forced to follow through with it along a path taking her far and forever away from everything she knew and everyone she loved.

Late that evening, alone in her room, she paced the floor, a copy of the document she had signed on impulse Saturday afternoon crushed in her hand. Though she had reread it countless times, Madeline could find no flaw that might free her from her written promise to become a mail-order bride destined for far-off California.

How innocently she had attended the lecture with her parents, given by a Major Eben Vance, lauding the beauties and the virtues of the fertile land of lush California. The charismatic military man waxed eloquent over exotic vegetation and vistas of mountain and ocean unmatched anywhere else on earth. Here rugged men of sturdy pioneer stock had laid claim to thousands of acres from which to carve their fortunes and their dynasties. All this bounty lacked only courageous, adventuresome women to bring home and family and gentility to the burgeoning communities all over a great and wondrous land. Major Vance's goal, and that of the stoic, taciturn Indian guide at his side, was to take those women, those brides, safely overland the thousands of miles to their glorious destinies.

His mission lay in offering every unencumbered female of marriageable age at the assembly the opportunity to join his expedition, to be among the first of those to write their names in the history of the far West as trailblazers, each in her own right. Sign-ups were limited to the first ten ladies on this premiere journey; all others would need to wait for subsequent offers of a similar nature. And, warned the major, once this maiden trip had been success-fully completed, one might have to wait months, years, to find vacancies upon such a list again.

Papa and Mama were disgusted, having anticipated an edifying lecture on the Western Frontier only to receive a charlatan's pitch for women for hire. But Madeline thought this surprising new practice both a practical and a clever way to solve the problem of an enormous scarcity in the wild and wonderful new West. And an excellent opportunity for the half-dozen young women she watched flock around Major Vance at the conclusion of his lec-ture—all day laborers and household help, they appeared to be, each one eager to sign. She found herself struggling with an almost irresistible urge to be among their numbers. Only her father's firm grasp upon her elbow as he ushered her and her mother briskly toward the door at the back of the auditorium kept her from signing up.

The crisp winter chill awaiting them out of doors should have awakened her senses to the foolish decision she'd almost allowed herself to act upon. Instead, an opposite response gripped her, arousing an even greater desire to go. A surge of panic at being left behind so overwhelmed her that she made the excuse of having left her favorite gloves on her seat in the auditorium, and turned back. She pushed her way through the crush of people. Most everyone cleared her a path, seeing her for a person of social position by her dress and demeanor alone, allowing her to gain the front row uncontested. She received the same attention from the major himself, whose steely gray eyes, identical in color to his dramatic mane of silver hair, glittered the instant he spied her. Without preamble, he thrust papers into her hands. Without another thought, or the foresight to read them through, she signed his copy and hers. Those same papers she now held crumpled in her fist.

"I simply won't show up tonight. Let Papa deal with the legalities should there be any."

Hearing her own words spoken aloud, she realized she was behaving like a coward, speaking so bravely to her friends of avoiding marrying Elmer Chester in one breath, refusing to follow through with the only viable solution presented to her in the next. Where were her courage, her pride, her self-respect when she most needed them?

"I shall go."

Decision made, sudden, unexpected excitement burst full-blown within her. Taking care to be quiet about her preparations, she lifted her satchel off the high shelf inside her armoire and stuffed possessions inside willy-nilly. Time was of the essence. Major Vance had warned he would depart on the morning train at dawn, with or without all those who had signed on. He'd have little trouble finding other willing souls between here and Independence, Missouri, the stepping-off place into the vast wilderness beyond, to take the places of those of faint heart.

Finding her satchel insufficient for her needs, Madeline dumped the contents out of her copious knitting bag and loaded that, too. From her handkerchief drawer, she drew every cent remaining from Papa's generous monthly allowance, thanking fortune that she had not spent it as quickly as she had received it this winter, the weather having been on the whole too inclement for shopping expeditions. She stuffed the roll of bills into her plum-colored velvet reticule beneath a half-dozen of her loveliest lace-trimmed, embroidered handkerchiefs. From her jewelry box, she chose an assortment of modest necklaces, bracelets, brooches, and earbobs. Her smallest vial of smelling salts, comb and brush, and a handful of hairpins followed, and lastly her small pocket Bible. The bead-trimmed bag was now so full she could scarcely pull the drawstrings tight, but there wasn't one item she dared eliminate. One never knew what one might require in a given situation.

Madeline rifled through her wardrobe until she located an outfit she considered most suitable for extended travel, a violet merino coat dress, high in the neck, with a moderately sized cape and the fashionable new elbow-length Hungary sleeves over puffed undersleeves, tight at the wrists. Because the cape was removable, the dress would do in all temperatures. For coldest weather, she chose a street-length cloak in the latest French style, of serviceable wool. Its color was a slightly darker shade of violet, all of her wardrobe consisting of shades of purple from deepest indigo to lightest lilac, to compliment her violet eyes, raven hair, and the porcelain-pale complexion of which she was inordinately proud. She spent little time fussing over her ablutions; the grandfather clock in the downstairs hall struck three times as she tied in place her prettiest heliotrope bonnet with matching dyed feathers.

With everything in readiness, including herself, she approached the most difficult task of all, penning a letter to her parents to leave propped against her pillow for the maid to find in the morning. Time being of the essence, she kept it simple and to the point, telling them succinctly that she loved them, not to worry as she was safely in Major Eben Vance's competent care, that her decision was based as much on an overwhelming need to experience life beyond River Valley as to escape the loveless marriage they'd urged her to undertake. And finally, that she would write at the first opportunity.

The clock chimed four times as she let herself out the front door, so heavily laden with satchel in one hand and sewing bag and reticule in the other that her shoulders bowed under the weight. But her resolve remained strong and anticipation lightened her steps. She had set her feet irrevocably upon a path leading to the greatest adventure of her life, for a purpose so noble, so patriotic, as to be the stuff of legends in the making. Destiny called her to the far distant promised land of sunshine and bounty, and she had answered. She could scarcely contain her soaring expectations for the adventure upon which she was about to embark.

On April 1st, fittingly All Fool's Day, Major Vance's small, bedraggled party arrived, not in warm and sunny California, but to a cluster of log shacks high in the Rocky Mountains—a stockade, or a trading post at best, certainly nothing more, aptly named Luckless, as were the eleven new arrivals themselves. A hand-lettered sign nailed to the trunk of a towering pine stated:

LUCKLESS, CO. TER.:
POPLACION 3 1 13
ALL MALE N PROUD V IT

Below this, another elaborated:

H O T E L, GEN. STOR, HOR HOUS N SALOON

A thick swath of black paint resembling an arrow pointed to the largest of the half-dozen log structures in the tight clearing with forest crowding in close at every turn. To

this their small group moved as one, seeking shelter from
the relentless downpour of countless days' duration—one
more in a series of disastrous mishaps that had plagued
Major Eban Vance and his mail-order brides from the
very beginning of this ill-conceived, poorly prepared-for
journey. The major himself, as it turned out, had neither
the knowledge nor the practical skills for the undertaking.
His guide had proved woefully ignorant as well, as had
each and every one of the women, none of whom possessed
any applicable training whatsoever.

Immediately upon their party's arrival in Independence,
wiser men than Vance himself—wagon masters, experienced guides, seasoned travelers—issued dire predictions
of the folly in beginning a cross-country journey in mid-
February. No one, but no one, with a brain in his head
left before the first of May, when the last of the snow had
melted in the mountain passes and spring rainstorms had
ceased turning the trail to miring muck. Eben Vance paid
the warnings no heed, nor did he give ear to the future
brides' collective pleadings, dismissing them as the vagaries
of easily frightened females. He remained convinced that
the first party to start, arriving ahead of the others, would
be the most richly rewarded. Positive the warnings came
from those who hoped to beat him to the lucrative Pacific
shore, the major set his scout to procuring needed supplies,
as well as the wagons and horses to carry them. When he
unexpectedly ran low of funds, he turned to his passengers
for assistance, discovering that only Madeline carried more
than a few pennies in pocket change, and leaving her with
little more.

The journey, ill begun, went from bad to worse thereafter, horrendous beyond one's most terrifying nightmares. Weather which in the first days had been balmy—
bolstering the ladies' faith in their chosen leader over the
sages' advice in Independence—turned foul before they'd

traveled more than a hundred miles. Too late, however, to turn back, the major insisted, without losing every cent of his investment and making a future attempt impossible.

Downpour turned to blizzard, and roads became mud-holes, knee-deep. Known trails ceased to appear, some buried beneath snow, some existing only on the crude map the major carried. Supplies ran dangerously low, quantities vastly underestimated for the given circumstances. The two wagons broke down repeatedly, finally irreparably, and had to be abandoned. Horses grew weak from lack of food and overwork, dropping dead in their tracks one by one. Somewhere in the Rockies, the ten women and two men became hopelessly lost; one young woman, the frailest to begin with, took ill and died and was left buried beneath a mound of rocks as the others moved on.

Eight weeks into their fearful journey, near dusk on April 1st, Major Eban Vance's exhausted assemblage arrived at this outpost high in the mountains with little more than the rags that remained of their clothing on their backs, their cracked and worn-out boots on their feet, their stomachs as empty of nourishment as their pockets were of cash.

Their arrival, however, was greeted with an exuberant, boisterous welcome by the completely male population of Luckless, a motley collection of mountain men, trappers, and traders. Within the blessed heat of the single, all-inclusive business establishment, the members of the Vance party found themselves wrapped in warm woolen blankets, fed stew and hard biscuits until satiated, offered ale all but Madeline indulged in to the point of inebriation—or beyond, as in the case of the major and his guide, along with every citizen of this godforsaken settlement, to the last man. The young ladies grew giggly and silly and alarmingly compliant to the lewd advances of a roomful of women-starved drunks. Madeline, cheeks flaming, slapped away more than one exploring meaty paw, finally leaping off the rough plank seat altogether when she felt a hand sliding over her thigh, simultaneously pushing her skirt waistward and reaching boldly for her most intimate, private femininity.

"Major Vance!" she implored of their self-designated leader. He lifted his drunken head from the impromptu pillow he'd made at the juncture of Coralee's generous breasts, not at all pleased with the interruption. "Major Vance, I must insist that we women be allowed to retire to whatever accommodations you have arranged for us before something untoward occurs."

Further angered by her strident tone, one she'd frequently been forced to use with him on the trail, the major barked, "Your accommodations are up to you, Miss Preston. You need look no further than the fellow seated to your right or your left, as have the other young ladies, to find a warm bed and a hot body for the night. Now leave me be so I may enjoy mine."

Knowing it useless to attempt to reason with this man, with whom she'd disagreed by the hour since the very first moment of their disaster-fraught journey, Madeline observed the debauchery rampant around her, appalled, the supper she'd so recently consumed with such desperate relish a leaden weight in her stomach. Hands layered protectively at the base of her throat, she backed out of the light of the solitary lantern swinging over the long plank table around which everyone had gathered, into the shadows beyond. Headed surreptitiously toward the door, away from the bold scrutiny of those unfortunate enough to be without female companionship, Madeline pondered her fate and her future, trapped as she was, penniless and possessionless, in an unrelenting, savage land with only her body with which to bargain for so much as a place to sleep. And not a single male present to choose from who wasn't sotted and crude and filthy to the point of probable insect infestation.

If only Papa had not insisted she marry old Elmer Chester, none of this—ah, but that was water under the bridge and too often brought to mind these last miserable weeks! She found herself in this predicament because of her own actions, and no one else's, and it would be only action on her part that would see her through her present difficulties. Suddenly, too weary, too sore of body and mind to think beyond where to bed down, Madeline prayed the fellow who'd welcomed them into this establishment, offering respite and refreshments without questioning their ability to pay, would as willingly provide her private rooming somewhere, anywhere away from this rowdy crowd.

Before she could act upon her decision to investigate the possibility, the door beside her burst open so violently that she scarcely had time to jump out of the way before it bounced off the wall, missing her by a mere fraction. Cold and rain blew in. Shouts from one and all protested the invasion. The door slammed shut, revealing a terrifying pair—an upright-standing bear and a wolf crouched at its side, teeth bared.

"Got a room for the night?" growled the bear, only a man in a bear-hide robe after all.

"One's all I got to spare, an' that's m'own," declared the fellow behind the plank and upended barrels comprising the counter at the far side of the room, distinguishable from the others only by the filthy apron tied around his considerable girth.

Madeline comprehended nothing beyond the discovery that a single private room existed, and that *she* must have it, no one else. With inspiration born of desperation, she recalled the last object of value remaining to her, the birthstone ring she'd worn without removing since Papa gave it to her on her sixteenth birthday. Without a second thought, she slipped it off a starvation-thin finger as she hastened across the room, coming up short just behind the bear-like newcomer. His four-legged companion lifted its lips in an ugly smile, emitting a low warning for her to advance no farther. Nothing, however, not even a wild beast threatening life and limb, could keep Madeline Preston from claiming the blessed solitude of a room to herself alone, not after the indignities she'd suffered these last several weeks.

"*I* would like that room, if you please, sir. I have this ring with which to pay for one night's board, if you'd be so kind as to accept it in payment." She extended the bit of jewelry on an open palm for his examination. Her courage did not extend to stepping any closer to the growling beast, be it dog or wolf.

The aproned fellow squinted at her offering, his stubbled jaws ruminating around a juicy plug of tobacco that dribbled out of the corners of his mouth and down his whiskered chin in twin tracks.

"Mebe I will an' mebe I won't, li'l lady. How many 'sides yerself lookin' to share the room an' willin' to pay fer th' privilege?"

Madeline straightened her spine, lifted her chin high, hoping to convey her status of superiority.

"Only myself."

"An' you, mister?" the proprietor asked, turning away his head, but not his squinting, small-eyed stare, to expectorate a stream of brown fluid somewhere in the vicinity of his feet, hopefully, but not likely, into some form of containment. "You plannin' on sleepin' alone? Gotta charge by the head, man er beast."

"Plan on payin' cash money for Wolf and myself an' the five others in my party waitin' outside."

The proprietor slammed a hammy fist down on his

counter so hard that the board bounced on its barrel supports.

"Sold t' th' highest bidder. Mister, ya got yerself a room fer the night."

Disappointment a keen, bitter taste in her mouth, Madeline convulsively squeezed her fingers closed around her meager offering, fighting back tears. Not quite ready to admit defeat, she lifted her chin a notch higher.

"Sir, how dare you let your last room to this ... this person instead of a lady in need, no matter what he is willing to pay?"

"Did 'n' done, lady." The barkeep glared at her with pure dislike. He bobbed his head sharply, once, toward the fur-robed stranger. "Mebe this here fella'll let ya share with him 'n' his friends fer the price of that pretty li'l ring of yers," he suggested with a wink.

Her rival for the room turned his head slightly in her direction over one shoulder. Beneath his fur hood, she saw only his piercing dark eyes—as cold and as deep as a moonless winter night—and a portion of his wind-reddened nose, all else hidden behind salt-and-pepper hair, from bushy beard to untrimmed mustache and thick, winged brows. Unkempt strands hung too long over a high, broad brow. One could not tell where the animal pelts he wore ended and his own began. Madeline shuddered involuntarily.

"Share accommodations with this man? Not if his were the last lodging on earth, freely and willingly offered."

Madeline spun on her heel and marched away, not hearing the mountain man's response except as a deep rumble, which caused the proprietor to roar with laughter. At her expense, she had no doubt. She sought a far corner where lantern light failed to reach, a place where the owner of this sorry establishment stocked his supplies for sale. She breathed deeply of new leather, oiled steel, malty flour, and lye soap, finding the mingled odors a welcome change from the reek of unwashed humanity, bad cigars, and spilt spirits.

No one objected, or even seemed to notice, when she arranged a place for herself behind a wall of crates upon a bed of colorful, patterned woolen blankets, with one rolled for a pillow and another to cover her aching, weary body. Snuggling deep, she felt as if she'd discovered heaven. Though she could not shut out the noise, scant minutes passed before she dozed.

Despite abject fatigue, Madeline slept fitfully and awoke long before dawn, as she determined by unrelieved darkness and blessed silence broken only by a chorus of muted snores from behind log partitions. She sat up, prepared to rise and slip out for some very necessary ablutions before anyone else ventured up and about. The creak of leather hinges alerted her to someone entering through the front door. She held her breath and waited, she knew not for what.

"I told you no one was here at this hour."

Madeline recognized the low, conciliatory tone Major Vance used to silence what he considered ungrounded apprehensions. Whoever was with him made not the slightest effort to be quiet.

"Then, where th' bloody hell *is* that female what fancies herself a lady? I want t' have me th' gal I bought an' paid fer an', by gum, I mean t' have 'er, *now!* flat on'er back, sittin' an' standin' an' every other way I kin come up with. Find 'er fer me, Vance 'fore I skin yer scalp off'n yer head an' sell it t' th' first redskin what heads m' way."

Heart hammering so hard in her chest that it hurt, Madeline scrunched down and prayed for invisibility from the massive mountain man's detection. Unbelievably, it must be herself for whom he searched—this reeking beast with a patch over one eye hiding who-knew-what horror, a tobacco-stained beard striped black and white like a skunk, and a fleshy-lipped leer displaying a half dozen rotting teeth. As she had so lightly predicted safely back in her parents' front parlor, she had indeed thrust herself out of the frying pan directly into a fire, to a place one would flatter by calling a hell on earth. She made herself as small as possible, screwing her eyes tightly shut, and prayed as if her life depended upon it, believing with all her heart that it very well might.

Oh, dear, sweet, merciful Lord, save me from this fate worse than death to which my impetuous folly has brought me.

Madeline curled into a tight ball on her sleeping pallet, threw her cover over her head, and lifted one edge only high enough to clearly hear the major's next words, which chilled her even more than the trapper's.

"Never fear, sir. You can be certain Miss Preston is somewhere in camp. She is far too intelligent to run off into the wilderness all alone, without provisions."

"Smart er stupid as a post, means nothin' t' me. All's I want is a wife t' see t' my needs—all of 'em—'n' that's what I paid ya good cash money fer. If'n we cain't find this'a one, give me another'n. Makes no never mind."

"All the other girls are spoken for, and glad to be done with their travels for good and all. I intended to take them all the way to California as brides for a woman-starved land. But you men pay well. And the ladies won't budge."

There was a pause. Madeline could almost hear his characteristic shrug, dismissing the problem as summarily as he had so many others on the trail. "In a couple of days, with fresh supplies, my guide and myself will head back east for another batch. Hopefully, we'll have less bad luck and far better weather on the next westward attempt."

The trapper chuckled coarsely. "An' if'n ya don't, yer always more'n welcome t' stop off here with 'em agin. Let's you 'n' me go check that smokehouse out back. Ain't in use right now. Mebe m' gal's hol' up out there. Gotta warn ya, Vance, we don' find 'er, an' soon, I mean what I says about liftin' yer scalp. That, er get m' good cash money back from ya. Mebe both.''

"Spare me my scalp, sir, and I'll gladly refund twice— thrice—what you paid and still have plenty left over for profit."

"Done 'n' done."

The men guffawed together in some warped male cama- raderie, departing as they'd come in, without disturbing anyone but herself.

Madeline extracted herself from her smothering co- coon, taking deep, steadying breaths. The chilling conver- sation she'd overheard by sheer good fortune galvanized her into action as nothing else could have. She had believed the disastrous overland journey thus far almost beyond enduring, but this latest catastrophe was simply unconscionable. She would die before she'd submit to that uncouth monster to which Major Vance had sold her.

The only solution, of course, was to attempt precisely what those two, discussing her, declared she dared not. She must run away. Into the woods. A fearful choice, but not nearly as frightening as staying. She had absolutely no money to buy her freedom from her prospective husband; there was nothing she could say or do to remain unwed— except as in some unthinkable lesser capacity than married.

She had survived eight weeks on the trail, despite Major Eban Vance's inept bunglings. Surely she had acquired sufficient abilities to survive on her own. Some small good fortune had placed her alone, in the dark solitude of pre- dawn, within a well-stocked trading post. She would make sure she left this loathsome place far better prepared than at her departure from Independence all those weeks ago. And, thank that same good fortune, she still had her birthstone ring, the emerald surrounded by diamond chips, with which to pay for her purchases.

She worked quickly and quietly, picking and choosing from the proprietor's limited stock. She found no knapsack among his stores, so used a discarded flour sack; her heavy woolen cape should serve to keep her warm, both to wear and to sleep beneath—spring-like weather must commence any day now, as soon as the rains passed. For her ring's estimated worth, far below its actual value, she chose easily carried foodstuffs requiring little preparation before consumption out of hand. Water from fresh mountain streams she counted on to provide her only beverage, as in the recent past.

With everything in readiness, Madeline pulled her ring off her finger one last time to set it on the rough plank counter. She eased the front door open, eliciting only one faint squeak from its leather hinges, and slipped outside. No one seemed to be about in the pearly darkness before daybreak, not even the pair who searched for her.

The rain had stopped, the air taking on a soft freshness promising a fair, balmy day. Encouraged by that promise, Madeline set off, scurrying from the scant cover of one tall pine to another, ever alert for any sign of humanity.

Certain that when she was finally determined to be missing, the hue and cry would take whoever sought her back along the way they'd come, she went in exactly the opposite direction, straight uphill, into the thickest of the surrounding forest. She would travel thusly for a day, maybe more. When she was thoroughly convinced her passage had gone undetected, then and only then would she circle back downward far beyond the den of perdition so appropriately named Luckless, and head straight for home.

Chapter Two

Well out of sight of the crude settlement, Madeline paused to ease the stabbing stitch in her side. She perched on a granite boulder, at first concentrating only on taking one steadying breath after another. As the tempo of her heartbeat returned to normal, she looked around, attempting to get her bearings, aware of a welcome warmth on her shoulders, a mild breeze lifting wisps of hair off her flushed cheeks. Tilting her face to the sun, she breathed in the heady scents of coming spring—rich, damp earth, pungent pine, the sweetness of some early bloom. Everywhere around her, birds sang of courtship and conquest. For a few precious moments, with her eyes closed and her senses attuned, it was as if she had indeed been transported to that land of verdant lushness and year-round summer that had been her goal—far-off California. This fair, mild spring day, after so many of dismal cold and rain, if nothing else surely represented a blessing on her desperate flight.

Much encouraged, Madeline retrieved the sack of provis-

ions from the ground beside her and rose, better prepared
to continue her journey. A quick glance in all directions
suggested no one route superior to any other. Uncertain
which way led uphill and which down, what might be north
or south, east or west, she recalled one of the few bits
of useful information their guide had been capable of
imparting, that moss always grew on the northernmost side
of trees. Taking as her cue this fragment of knowledge,
Madeline set off in what she felt confident must be a north-
easterly direction, north to take her as far from Luckless
as possible, east because home lay east of these fearful
mountains.

Pressing onward, over and around obstacles, checking
the location of green lichen against gnarled gray bark
at regular intervals, Madeline further evolved her plans,
congratulating herself on her ingenuity and her self-
reliance. She would continue thusly until the pattern of
sun filtering through the trees onto the spongy carpet
underfoot cast few shadows, indicating midday. Then,
heading straight eastward for an hour or so, she'd at last
turn southeastward until she picked up the wagon trail
Major Vance had followed before losing his way, confident
she could not fail to do far better than he had.

At what she determined to be noontime, Madeline
paused beside a spring-fed stream, now swollen and swift
with melted snow. She scrubbed her face and hands with
a bit of fabric torn from one of her lawn petticoats, regretting the damage to the garment despite its soiled, trail-
worn hem. She comforted herself with the thought of all
the lovely new things Papa would lavish upon his only
daughter and solitary offspring with her Prodigal-like
return.

Thoughts of Papa and Mama and home brought the
sting of quick tears to her eyes. She sniffed, blinking away
evidence of unwelcome weakness to search through her

sack for luncheon selections—rubbery dried apple slices from one brown paper parcel, salty crackers from another. Water so cold it made her teeth ache as her only beverage, she sipped from cupped palms as she knelt upon the rocky shore.

"What would Papa and Mama think of their darling daughter now?" she asked her rippling reflection, appalled at her appearance as much as the quaver in her voice.

Her hair had not seen attention in weeks, her comb having been lost early on. Spit baths were, at best, furtive, hurried, and inadequate. Since the day her journey began, she'd worn the same dress, though the violet merino ensemble grew limp and shapeless, its color faded until scarcely distinguishable, and stained beyond saving with perspiration, food, and filth. Madeline rocked back on her heels. Her offensive image disappeared from view, but not from mind. At her sides, her hands clenched into fists, sandpapering her raw, blistered palms with grit from the rocky earth beneath her.

"I will not be weakened by these temporary hardships and setbacks. I absolutely refuse to fail."

Newly resolved, Madeline scrambled to her feet, caught up her pack, and strode purposefully on her way.

All too soon, the terrain grew considerably rockier, the vegetation scarcer, the trees twisted and stunted. Though she'd become accustomed to the thin air of the mountains, she found herself gasping. Pausing to look back the way she had come, she saw that she'd climbed far higher than intended. Below her lay endless miles of pine-covered ranges, black with deepening shadows interspersed with brightly scattered patches of rose and red and orange from the setting sun, like an enormous crazy quilt blanketing the land as far as the eye could see. Madeline lingered, mesmerized by the sight, understanding quite suddenly how the earliest explorers in the vast new America must

have felt on viewing similar scenes. Perhaps she was the
first to stand just here, on this very spot. What a humbling
thought! And what a frightening one, for it only enforced
the reality that she was completely and utterly alone in this
untamed wilderness.

"And you might very well be stranded alone atop this
mountain after dark if you don't soon cease your musings
and hasten upon your way," she scolded herself aloud.

Cringing at the thought, Madeline hurried downward,
south and east, finding her progress impeded by an increasingly hazardous descent as darkness fell over the Rockies,
swiftly and completely. She'd forgotten how quickly the
light of day faded this early in the season. She must not,
under any circumstances, allow herself to be so careless
again.

Barely able to see one foot in front of another, the next
instant her feet flew out from under her. Flat on her back,
sliding downhill at an ever-increasing speed, she rode an
avalanche of shale, never slowing in her unstoppable
plunge. She caught at shrubs and saplings to no avail,
tearing up the weaker by the roots, shredding her palms on
those which held fast, plummeting toward certain disaster.

She came to an abrupt halt, slamming with jarring
impact up against the bulk of a railcar-size boulder. Gingerly lifting herself into a sitting position, Madeline took
inventory for possible injury by touch alone in the moonless black of nightfall, considering herself incredibly fortunate to have survived relatively unscathed.

Unfortunately, as she quickly learned to her dismay,
her sack of provisions must have flown out of her hands
sometime during her tumble. Her cloak also proved to be
missing, and she dared not add yet another folly to her
growing list of blunders this day by stumbling around in
the dark looking for either.

Madeline almost gave in to tears at last. Fearing she'd

be unable to stop once she began, fearing more that her sobs would turn into wild wailing she could not control, in all likelihood drawing to herself the attention of some night-stalking predator, she suppressed the urge.

Pressing back against the boulder that had stopped her fall, she pulled her knees tight against her chest and rested her forehead atop them on crossed arms, overwhelmingly weary all at once.

If she could sleep, in the morning things were bound to look much better—at the very least, considerably brighter! She'd locate her cape and her supplies and be on her way, far less heedlessly than today. In a few days, three at the most, she would reach Fort Farewell, the last outpost before barbaric Luckless. There she had only to place herself in the care of the fort's commander, who'd see that her journey homeward proceeded far more swiftly and smoothly than the hellish one into this treacherous land.

No sooner had she dozed off, it seemed, than an earsplitting howl rent the silence. Madeline jerked awake, heart thudding so hard that her body shook. Another howl responded, and another, and another, until the eerie cries came from everywhere around her. She could not tell which were real and which echoes, but she knew the fearsome beasts from which the horrid sounds issued. Wolves. Huge, carnivorous demons of the night, they preyed upon those of lesser strength and guile, be they other wild creatures or one defenseless human.

Their ceaseless cries bounced from one precipice to another, closer and closer with every call. Madeline clamped her palms over her ears in an unsuccessful attempt to shut out the fearful racket, certain she saw the evil yellow gleam of almond-shaped eyes at every turn. Instinct urged her to flee, and her last shreds of common sense warned of certain disaster, if not death, should she dare leave this questionable shelter for the dark unknown.

Curling into a tighter ball, she prayed fervently for protection, for salvation, from this endless nightmare into which she'd thrust herself with so very little forethought. Shivering uncontrollably now from swiftly dropping temperatures in addition to her runaway fear, Madeline waited, wide-eyed, for morning.

She awoke with a start when crossed arms slipped off raised knees. Dawn had arrived at last, though no sun greeted her with the promise of another fair spring day. The opaque black of night merely gave way to billowing, smoky gray, obscuring everything a scant arm's-reach away, as if thick clouds had fallen from the sky to blanket the world, silencing sound, turning each labored breath liquid. The warmth of yesterday's sun, rather than a promise, had proven nothing more than a cruel, taunting joke.

Trembling with a chill that rattled her bones, her teeth clattering together with an audible chatter, Madeline could not recall ever being so cold. Or alone. She unfolded aching limbs and struggled to stand, stifling a pained cry. Not the smallest bit of her from crown to sole had been spared soreness and stiffness beyond any thus far endured. Hunger caused her head to swim as soon as she gained her feet. Supporting herself on a braced arm against her rocky shelter, she bent forward until the dizziness passed.

Her plight had increased, not diminished, with daybreak. If visibility reached no more than inches beyond her boot-tips, how was she to locate her pack, her cloak? Find her way back to civilization?

"What a fool you've been, Madeline Genevieve Preston, to think you'd make it out of this savage wilderness on your own."

She borrowed a few choice expletives from Major Vance's vast repertoire, experiencing no qualms whatsoever at using them loudly, with relish. As angry as she was with herself, still a frightened sob caught in her throat, shattering the silence, unsettling her all the more. There was every possibility she'd not survive to see her twentieth birthday, only weeks away, and no one hereabout but herself to know or care.

"I will not cry, I will not cry, I will not!"

She chanted the refrain rapidly over and over until she successfully quashed unwelcome emotion, a feminine indulgence she could ill afford.

"When this fog burns off, I'll return to Luckless," she decided abruptly. It was only a day's journey away, as opposed to weeks, even months to Independence.

By now the major must have surely comprehended that she would brave almost anything rather than marry the crude mountain man he'd chosen for her. If she guaranteed him a substantial sum upon her safe delivery into her grateful parents' arms, she felt certain she'd have no trouble convincing him to take her home, especially since he claimed to be headed East anyway. That she hadn't thought of this in the first place caused her to feel as foolishly impetuous and reckless as Papa and Mama frequently declared her to be.

Decision reached, Madeline became increasingly aware that the temperature had dropped another twenty degrees or more since daybreak. She'd learned enough on the trail to understand how quickly, how easily, one could succumb to the cold this time of the year, though by the calendar spring had arrived. Movement, ever onward, might well be all that separated her from a death by freezing or starvation without cloak and provisions. She dared not linger here much longer, loathe though she was to leave this scanty shelter, which felt far safer to her than the great unknown beyond the fog. No sooner had she thought this than a bit of moisture struck the tip of her nose, then one cheek, then the other.

Rain! she thought, looking up, stomach twisting into a knot. *No, not rain. Snow! Sweet Providence, no! Not this, after everything else.*

The fog had lifted a bit, but the first large, lacy flakes were floating gently downward from gunpowder-gray clouds, almost instantly transformed into angry, needle-like pellets, coming down in earnest, faster and thicker, blown sideways by gusts of frigid wind.

She'd clearly run out of time. Tempted to propel herself down the granite mountainside with all haste before snowfall obliterated all signs of possible safe passage, she forced herself to pick her way, finding dependable hand- and footholds before leaving ones already located. She avoided looking down beyond the next safe ledge or crevice. Doing so compounded the dizziness occasioned by constant, relentless emptiness gripping her stomach.

The ground leveled a bit where raw cliffs met forest. Madeline rested, catching her breath, taking inventory of the newest abrasions to her battered hands, deciding without emotion that none required immediate attention. Her nails had been torn off at the quick by unaccustomed labor long before today, and her palms bore a smattering of blisters and calluses no amount of night cream would ever banish completely. But she'd discovered strength in those hands she didn't know she possessed, and experienced an unexpected surge of pride, of accomplishment.

A faint glint of metal at her feet caught her eye, dull in the gloom, but undeniably telling of human passage. Heart in throat, Madeline knelt, scraping away snow and leaves with her ruined hands until she unearthed her discovery, rocking back on her heels.

"Sweet, blessed heaven, it's a monogrammed teaspoon.

How did this come to be out here in the middle of nowhere?"

She rubbed a thumb over the scrolled 'S' embossed on the handle, casting a hopeful glance around for further clues confirming habitation in the woods somewhere nearby, too afraid to hope, too desperate not to.

At first she dared not believe her eyes. But they saw truly! A miracle, surely, for she knelt squarely in the center of a faint but definite trail, stretching into the woods in both directions. Praise be, her prayers had been answered!

Madeline scrambled to her feet, shoving her find into her pocket. Certain salvation lay eastward, she gathered up her skirt and scampered down the faint, narrow track before it disappeared altogether beneath a blanket of white.

She broke into a clearing at a mad dash and nearly tumbled headlong off the rim of a high, rocky plateau where the trail abruptly ended.

"No! Not after raising my hopes!"

Defeated, she stood at the very edge, staring hopelessly out over distant white-capped mountains at every turn, impossible to surmount, knowing she must go on, not at all certain she had the will left to do so.

Idly her gaze traveled downward, eyes widening, breath stilled. Below, in a narrow valley carved out by a tumultuous mountain stream, lay a log structure, possibly only a small shed, but a shelter nonetheless. But how to reach that precious haven when the trail disappeared into solid rock! Or had it only been interrupted?

Renewed optimism surged. There had to be a way down, there simply had to be. It would prove far too cruel a joke for Fate to place salvation so near at hand without granting her the means of attaining it.

She giggled rather hysterically when a glance to the left showed her the travel-worn path winding its way downward

around a curve—safe passage after all. Spirits soaring as
if with the eagles forever circling high in the Rocky Mountain sky, she hurried on her way. Her problems were almost
at an end; shelter and safety lay close at hand.

How near the cabin had seemed from the plateau and
how smooth the trail into the valley! Bitter disappointment
swelling in her throat, Madeline climbed up hill and down,
slipping and sliding and falling, picking herself up time
after time after time, refusing defeat.

The storm soon grew to blizzard proportions. Her trail
finally disappearing altogether, Madeline pressed on, even
after she could no longer see where she was going and
her limbs lost all sensation. Hopes dashed, Madeline mindlessly planted one foot in front of the other, struggled
through knee-high drifts, got up when she fell, continued
onward whether it mattered any longer or not. She didn't
know what else to do, and could not bring herself to lie
down on some snow bank and wait for death's eternal
sleep to claim her.

Papa, Mama, I'm so, so sorry!

Sleep, sweet beckoning sleep, could not much longer
be denied, despite her most valiant efforts. On the verge
of succumbing, Madeline stubbed her toe and tripped,
falling forward. Outstretched arms failed to protect her
from striking her shoulder, hard, against something substantial.

*The cabin at last? What else could it be! Praise the Lord, in
spite of every obstacle thrown my way, somehow I've found it.*

Dry sobs heaved her chest as she laboriously felt her way
around from corner to corner until she reached the plank
door. Discovering the door unlocked, she kicked aside a
section of log left propped against it. Battling the weight
of snow and wind, she pushed hard. The door cracked
open enough to allow admittance. With a glad, grateful
cry, she stumbled inside, slamming the door against the

storm without. Pressing her back against the sturdy planks, Madeline slowly slid to the floor, shivering uncontrollably, willing herself not to give in to threatening tears, not now when she'd finally reached a safe haven. In spite of her determination, dry sobs shuddered through her. She wrapped her arms around her waist in a self-hug, waiting for the sensation to pass.

Some time later, Madeline struggled up from the cold dirt floor like an aged infirm. In the eerie gloom, saved from total darkness by weak wintry light seeping around the edges of the covering over the small window beside the door, she saw that the cabin consisted of one room only, no larger than Mama's back parlor, with a loft of sorts in the deep shadows of log rafters pressing so close she could almost reach up and touch them. But oh, how grandly spacious it seemed after the accommodations she'd been subjected to these past many weeks. And it was all hers, for apparently no one had been in residence for some time.

Not the slightest sign of human habitation remained within, not a single personal possession suggesting whose home it had been. On the left were a plank table and bench beneath a row of crude shelves, for the most part empty, promising little; on the right, a narrow rope bunk was built into the wall. Directly across the way, the empty hearth of a stone fireplace contained not a stick of firewood. Rubbing crossed arms with numb hands, alarmingly aware that she just might freeze to death as easily inside this shelter from the storm as without, she moved cautiously into the room, sidestepping away from the snowladen draft around the door.

Her thigh slammed up against some immovable object. A humpback travel trunk, her quick perusal revealed, possibly containing warm clothing, woolen blanket, anything to ward off the chill. Uttering a glad cry, Madeline crouched

before this source of as yet undiscovered riches. *Locked.*
Madeline slammed doubled fists on the bowed lid.

Was she to be thwarted at every turn? Was every hope
to be dashed as soon as she filled her heart with it?

"No! Not so! Every obstacle has an eventual solution.
As will this one, too. Think, Madeline, think."

She regained her feet to take a second look around in
the faint light remaining of the day. As if foreordained,
against the wall on the far side of the solitary door leaned
a hatchet. Seizing the opportunity so clearly presented,
she grabbed it up, applied its blade to the trunk's recalcitrant lock, and dispatched this latest barrier *poste haste.*
With a triumphant shout, she threw back the lid.

Scarcely able to see the contents for the gloom, she
hauled out item after item, discarding one after another—
thin cotton undergarments, linsey-woolsey trousers, cotton
shirts, books, papers. She'd all but reached the bottom
unrewarded when her hands closed around a thick, soft
object wrapped in a length of gingham within which
resided a quilt. Unfurling the found treasure, Madeline
wrapped it snugly around herself in absolute delight.

"Ahhhhh!"

For an endless time, she sat as she was, cocooned in
the coverlet, relishing the sheer comfort of the simple
utilitarian object. With body heat somewhat revived, so was
her ability to think, to search out further solutions to her
most pressing problems.

Upon the fireplace mantel of a single, rough-cut timber,
she spied a solitary candle in a pewter stand. Trailing the
quilt behind her, Madeline hastened toward her latest discovery, expectations high. And found no striker, nor a
single scrap of wood. No light. No fire. And absolutely no
idea how to go about making either possible were the
proper implements for doing so plentifully available. Fervently she wished she'd paid the slightest attention to how

her female traveling companions, all former household help, managed to start a fire from whatever they found close at hand.

Once again thwarted and thoroughly frustrated, she turned away sharply, tripping on the trailing quilt, barely saving herself from a fall. A quick cold dose of reality told her that had she fallen and seriously hurt herself, she might easily have died of her injuries here in this isolated, desolate place. Caution, above all, must be her primary prerogative from now on.

She reluctantly removed her only protection against the cold, doubling it over her shoulders, finding it all the more cumbersome and awkward, and far too short, leaving her lower half left to the elements.

Patience gone, Madeline grabbed up the hatchet from where it had fallen beside the trunk, flung the offending quilt on the crude plank table, and brought the weapon down across one folded end again and again, until she'd shortened the whole by several inches. Task completed to her satisfaction, she wrapped her makeshift garment around her, tossing the remaining remnant in the general direction of the trunk.

"There now! Much better!"

Turning her attention to the shelves close at hand, she faced yet another disappointment. Save for an iron pot and frying pan, a few pewter dishes and cups, and a rusty cracker tin, there was nothing. Absolutely nothing! Not a single food staple to appease her painful hunger, nor any sign anywhere in the close, cramped cabin of bins, or barrels, or bags containing sustenance.

Madeline sat down hard on the bench beside the table, starvation and defeat a bitter taste in her mouth, all her efforts for naught in the end. She would freeze, or she would starve, but surely she would die, alone, whereabouts unknown. And the very worst of it all was that Papa and

Mama knew only that she intended to head to California, expecting her to write upon arrival. Now she never would. She'd simply disappear off the face of the earth, to her parents' never-ending bewilderment and sorrow.

Grief-stricken for them, and for the folly of choices bringing her to this pass, Madeline staggered to the crude bed. Throwing herself down upon its bare, lumpy mattress, curling into a tight ball, she closed her eyes and waited to die.

A resounding bang reverberated through the walls of the cabin. Madeline's eyes flew open to utter darkness. Fully expecting that the cabin, under the weight of snow from the ongoing blizzard, had collapsed around her head, she threw herself off the bed onto her feet, leaving her altered quilt behind. Quaking, anticipating the worst, she cast a frantic glance around her to discover the cabin as sound as ever. Relief short-lived, she saw instead that the door had been thrust open hard enough to rattle the walls. A massive form filled the gap, so huge as to blot out any incoming light.

A bear, a grizzly, from the deep growl emanating from the beast! Heart in throat, Madeline somehow found her voice and waved her arms at this newest threat.

"S-s-shoo! Shoo! G-g-go away! Begone!"

The monster lumbered further into the single small room, uttering another fearsome growl. With nowhere to run and nowhere to hide, Madeline backed up a couple of steps, bumping into the bed, shaking so she could scarcely stand.

"G-g-go away! G-g-get out of here! Shoo!"

"Damnation, woman, there's a blasted blizzard goin' on out there. *You're* the one trespassin'. *You* get the hell out."

The beast-robed brute moved surprisingly swiftly and unerringly to the hearth, pulling something from a pouch he wore at his waist. Madeline cringed back into the shadows. Seconds later a spark flared, then a weak, wavering light in a fistful of burning twigs. Lastly the candle offered up a slender flame as he dropped the twigs into the vacant hearth to sputter and die. Candlestick in hand, he turned, face illuminated, eyes deep-set, jawbone craggy in flickering shadows. All else disappeared behind hair and fur.

"You!" Madeline cried out. "Y-y-you stole the last available room from me in Luckless, and now you would cast me out of the only shelter for miles around as well? Sir, you—you haven't a shred of common decency, none whatsoever."

A threatening grumble and a single stride brought him face-to-face with her in a circle of candlelight.

"This here's *my* cabin, woman, built log by log with my own two hands. I sure as hell ain't turnin' it over to the likes of you." The burly beast rolled his eyes ceilingward. "What're these mountains comin' to, when flatlanders start infestin' 'em, layin' claim to what they've no legal right?"

Fear dissolving into self-righteous indignation, Madeline stamped her foot.

"For shame. What a tempest in a teapot. I am only one lost soul, and cold and hungry. I pose no permanent threat to your home or your privacy."

The mountain man barked a bitter laugh, leaning in until they were all but nose to nose.

"Shoot, woman! If it was just you, I'd toss you back out in the snow without givin' it another thought. But what the bloody blue blazes am I supposed to do about *them?*"

His massive, robed arm flew outward, a thick forefinger pointing toward the doorway where wind and snow blew in freely and a tiny cluster of pale figures waited, clearly dumbstruck with apprehension. A boy and a girl perhaps in their early teens, two smaller children with nearly identical faces of twins, also a boy and a girl, and in the arms of the tallest female a squirming, blanket-wrapped bundle which suddenly emitted an infant's wail of hunger, or pain, or out-and-out indignation.

Never at a loss for words for long, Madeline instantly voiced her conclusions.

"Sweet merciful heaven, you evict the homeless *and* kidnap helpless children? You, sir, are every bit the monstrous beast you appear."

Chapter Three

"Hell's bells, woman, I didn't *snatch* 'em. I inherited 'em. Whether I want 'em or not."

Madeline's mouth fell open, then snapped shut. Finally, she managed an exhaled, "Oh! I see!"

The man's eyes narrowed. "You don't see a bloomin' thing, but I'm not takin' the time to explain it to you while we all stand around freezin' our—freezin'. You, boy, shut that damn door on your way out. There's firewood and kindlin' just outside on your left. Take that pair with you. We'll be needin' as much as you can carry. Probably more."

The youngsters scurried to do as he bade, while the oldest girl stood just inside the cabin, clutching the crying baby, tears silently streaming down her cheeks. On impulse, to avoid the beast next turning on the weeping child, Madeline spoke up.

"What would you have *me* do?"

He looked about to tell her exactly what she could do

with her offer, and herself. Clearing his throat with a rumble, he modified whatever he might have said.

"Can you whip up supper biscuits?"

His tone so skeptical that she desired nothing more than to declare herself an expert, Madeline regrettably shook her head. His grunted response evidenced that he expected as much.

The girl with the child in her arms took a forward step, speaking in little more than a whisper.

"I—I can, mister. I can make biscuits."

He tossed a quick glance her way.

"Put the baby somewhere, then, and get at it. You'll find all the fixin's in the root cellar. There, under the table. The trap door."

She scurried to comply. He gave Madeline a lengthy up-and-down perusal. "You think you can manage to fill that kettle over there with snow for meltin'?"

"Of course!"

Chin high, Madeline flounced to the shelves for the kettle, feeling the fool for not having noticed the handled trap door while alone in the cabin. With the table shoved to one side, the door in the floor lifted at an angle, braced with a length of log. Below she could see the faint outlines of untold gastronomical treasures which might have been hers hours ago had she but known. Tantalizing scents intensified her hunger to the point of unbearability, but she did as she was told, passing the three children struggling inside under the weight of armloads of logs. Food and heat, both so very near at hand! A bitter smile touched her lips at the cruel humor in the thought.

She stepped out into a world of swirling, blinding white and calf-high drifts. A cluster of trampled footprints from the children's forage were already swiftly disappearing. Scooping up the first undisturbed snow she came to, Madeline hastened back inside, happily surprised to see that a small fire already crackled and spat in the hearth.

In her eagerness to reach its warmth, Madeline stumbled over her own feet. With a growl, the man pounced to catch the kettle before the contents spilled. Madeline righted herself with effort and no help whatsoever from the inhospitable brute. Tempted as she was to call him on it, she didn't quite dare raise his ire further.

He squatted before the fire to set the kettle upon its hook, ignoring her completely though she stood mere inches away, warming outstretched hands. He held his own huge paws to the heat briefly, palms outward, long fingers splayed. When he stood, shrugging out of his heavy fur coat, Madeline quickly stepped back to join the children.

Draping the heavy garment on a peg in the wall with an economy of motion, he faced his small audience—the girl laboring over her biscuit preparations upon the plank table, the other children clumped together in the shadows just beyond the flickering light of the fire, herself near at hand—all wide-eyed and open-mouthed at the sight of him.

Without the enormous fur coat, he was still impressively, dauntingly huge, like some mythological savage. Dressed in tanned, fringed shirt, trousers, and knee-high moccasins, adorned with a massive, rattling necklace of what appeared to be beads and claws and a leather pouch strung on a strip of rawhide, he wore a portion of his dark hair in two thin braids hanging forward over his broad shoulders halfway to his waist, framing a bushy salt-and-pepper beard, and the remainder flowing down his back in waves. From his earlobes hung small gold rings.

Eyes narrowed, he tossed a glance from one mesmerized face to another.

"What the bloody blue blazes're you all starin' at?"

Each one of them flinched as if struck, even Madeline,

in spite of herself. The smaller girl let out a wail and burst into tears. Her twin stepped in front of her, his narrow chest out-thrust though his voice quivered noticeably.

"You scared Jane."

With a rumbled growl, the man retorted, "Didn't. And anybody else plannin' on takin' exception to me an' mine better recollect whose food you're goin' to be eatin' an' whose cabin's keepin' you warm an' safe from the storm. Anyone got anythin' more to say on the subject?"

He leveled his dark-eyed glare on Madeline, who'd been about to offer her opinion regarding his treatment of herself and the children, and just what he could do with his backhanded hospitality. She held to silence with difficulty.

Plainly satisfied he held the upper hand, he addressed her. "Set out plates.

"We'll be needin' at least two more loads of kindlin' each from the three of you," he told the twins and their older brother. "You, girl, got the biscuits ready for the spider? Fire's about right."

"Y-y-yes, s-s-sir."

"Ain't nobody's 'sir'." He threw another pointed look Madeline's way. "You kids can call me Sam, if you've a mind to while you're here, or Uncle, if you can't keep from it."

"And what would you have me call you?" Madeline queried, chin high, very weary of the surly fellow's endless blustering and posturing.

"Sure as hell not what you're thinkin' of callin' me. Sam Spencer's the name. Mister'll do."

She drew herself up tall. "And I am Madeline Preston. Miss Preston to you."

She thought she saw a spark of humor in his steady, brown-eyed stare.

"Maddie, then."

"Madeline."

"Madeline's a name for some dried up old spinster lady. That you?"

Madeline pinched her lips tight, painfully aware that he'd goaded her quite skillfully, a circumstance she had no intention of repeating.

He shook his shaggy head slowly, face thoughtful.

"Well, then, what with you not much carin' for Maddie, and me not particularly fond of dried-up old maids, guess what I was callin' you before'll have to do. Set the table, woman. The rest of you, get about your chores or you'll be goin' to bed mighty hungry."

Dismissing the lot of them, he turned back to the fire to drop several handfuls of something into the boiling kettle from the pouch secured on a beaded belt around his waist. Positive he meant what he said, too hungry to retaliate, Madeline proceeded to perform her task as quickly as did the others.

With a fragrant stew of unknown content bubbling on the hearth, their cantankerous host helped haul in wood to stack against the wall between the fireplace and the table, now set with a mismatch of pewter plates and bowls and cups.

"If you will tell me where you keep your flatware— knives, forks, spoons—I'll set them out."

She spoke to the man only as necessity required, and then in a tone he could not fail to notice contained both displeasure and disapproval, and a hint of condescension since, by his expression, she'd felt compelled to explain to him the meaning of the term 'flatware'.

He lifted both hands, palms out, and wiggled his fingers.

"Here's mine. The rest of you'll have to supply your own."

Madeline pursed her lips and said nothing. But she wanted to—oh, she did indeed. Instead, she strode past him to the one window in the cabin. The hide covering had been pierced at the four corners and stretched over pegs set into the window frame, easily undone. In moments, the glow of the setting sun through the dirty, imperfect pane augmented the single candle's luminescence, dispelling shadows and gloom.

At once the room reverberated with the beastman's roar, followed by scathing profanities. Two strides took him to the narrow bed where he snatched up the discarded quilt lying beside the sleeping baby, who never even stirred. He spun on them, his face behind the heavy beard a livid shade of red. In one huge paw he held aloft the altered coverlet. Clenched teeth bared, he emitted fiercer versions of his usual grunts and growls, demonstrating his rage more bone-chillingly than words. In his eyes, though, she caught a glimpse of something distinctly human, soul-deep and raw.

The children shrank back, terrified of becoming the object of the attack Madeline knew without a doubt was directed at her, and her alone. Taking courage from that fleeting look of vulnerability, she stepped forward.

"If this latest display of poorly controlled temper is in regard to that quilt, I must confess I was forced to make alterations to save myself from breaking my neck on its trailing length, or going without and freezing to death. I'm certain you can understand the necessity—"

He stepped menacingly close, dipping his head until they were all but nose to nose. His voice rumbled out deep, enraged, and hurting in the same breath.

"What I understand, woman, is you ruinin' the only damned thing I set store by."

Spinning abruptly, he yanked open the trunk, flinging the quilt inside. He spied the remnant on the floor at his feet, and with a snarl, tossed it inside too. He slammed the lid, briefly fingering the fresh scars and ruined lock with narrowed eyes.

"Any one of you lift that lid again, you're out on your ear for good an' all, no matter how freezin' the temperature or how deep the snow. Got that?"

Dead silence.

"Got that?"

"Y-y-yes, sir," chorused the children.

"You've made yourself quite clear. If the quilt is so important to you, I suppose I could attempt to repair—"

His features as frigid as an ice sculpture, his tone even colder, he pointed a raised fist in her direction, shaking it, threat clear.

"One more word an' you go *now*." His penetrating glare dared her to utter it.

Silence followed, so deep only the bubbling stew and crackling fire interrupted it. A log fell in halves, sending up a shower of sparks; each child cried out, Madeline jumped but uttered not a sound.

He grabbed his coat off its peg, exiting the cabin without explanation, closing the door with unusual care.

Had he slammed it, Madeline might have thought he intended only to demonstrate his usual bad temper; that quiet shutting left an ominous silence that the oldest girl eventually filled, speaking for them all, looking to her for an answer.

"Is—is he gone for good?"

"I most certainly hope so," Madeline replied, though in truth, she didn't. *If he doesn't come back, how will the rest of us survive?*

No sooner had the thought occurred than the door burst open in a blast of swirling snow.

"Don't let that fire die, woman!"

He withdrew as quickly as he'd come, banging the door shut only to thrust it open again immediately.

"I'm leavin' Wolf to guard you. Feed him, water him, but *don't* try to pet him."

The four-legged beast bounded into the room ahead of a closing door, stance at the ready, menacing golden eyes wary and watchful. Dog-like, he immediately shook off the snow clinging to his fur, from long nose to feathered tail, liberally spraying the room and those nearest by. Madeline and the children hastily stepped back from the onslaught, eliciting a warning growl from the animal very similar to his master's.

She spoke softly. "I believe he's trying to tell us he would prefer no quick movements."

"M-m-maybe he's hungry," the eldest girl suggested barely above a whisper.

"I'll feed 'im."

The older boy spoke for the first time, his tone as authoritative as he could manage with a voice that cracked and wobbled mid-sentence. At the challenge, daring disagreement, in his steady blue gaze, Madeline conceded for the time being.

"Please do. Then perhaps we may satisfy our own hunger in peace. Are the biscuits ready?" she asked their cook.

Eyes downcast, the girl nodded, sending her fine, fair hair flying. *She'd do far better with that hair braided,* thought Madeline, possibly a single one in back as she herself wore every night to bed. *I'll have to suggest . . . But then, what business is it of mine how the child wears her hair? A mother's responsibility, definitely not mine.* Which brought another thought to mind. What calamity could have befallen their mother and father that these children had been placed in their uncle's dubious care?

Question unanswered and soon forgotten as the mingled fragrances of meat and bread overpowered all else, Madeline watched the girl kneel beside the fire, carefully tucking her skirt under her well away from flame and sparks. With a hooked implement, she pulled out of the coals onto the hearth the footed spider containing the biscuits. Rising, she gathered pewter plates from Madeline's tidy place settings around the table, dishing up stew and biscuits for each sibling to fetch in turn. Wolf, naturally, received the first serving, on the plate which would have been his surly companion's had he stayed. Offering a plate to Madeline, her narrow, plain face—passive, submissive—gave no clue to the girl's thoughts or feelings.

"Thank you," said Madeline. "It all looks very good."

The girl's light brows rose in surprise. Madeline smiled and received a flicker of one in reply. The response, small though it was, warmed Madeline's heart, to her surprise and inordinate satisfaction. Joining the children at the table, seeing that the others had nearly cleaned their plates, hands and face covered with the evidence of their industry, Madeline forgot all else but her own consuming hunger, forgot propriety and manners, and dipped her fingers into stew thick with meat and vegetables. Imitating the children, she used a biscuit in lieu of utensils, though she cringed at the fleeting thought, "what would Mother think," only to realize she didn't care a whit. The first few bites went down without tasting. A warning roil of her empty stomach slowed her enough to relish the wild, rich flavor of the unknown ingredients, appreciate the light flakiness of the biscuits. Giving credit where credit was due, she complimented the girl on them.

Characteristically, she dipped her head. "There's more if you want 'em."

"More. More. More," chorused the others.

Rising immediately, ever the little mother, the girl saw to her siblings' needs, then held out her hand for Madeline's plate. Madeline put voice to her thoughts, alive with curiosity now that hunger had been satiated.

"As it would appear we'll all be confined in these close quarters, at least for tonight," she prefaced, "I think it would be appropriate to exchange names, and perhaps tell a bit of how we came to be here in this cabin together."

Eyeing her warily, no one advanced any information.

"I'll go first then. My name is Madeline Preston, as I earlier stated." She paused expectantly. Four pairs of identical blue eyes stared unblinkingly at her face; not a word was spoken.

"I am from a middle-sized town in the Midwest, where my father owns a bank." A silence-filled pause. "I left home with a party of ladies headed for California under the guidance of a man who, unfortunately, knew little more about reaching that goal than the rest of us. We lost our supplies, possessions, and the trail here in the Rockies. When circumstances became unbearable, I left the group behind to set out on my own, and proving to be no better at finding the way than my guide, ended up here." Tale told, she could think of nothing more to add to elicit a response from the children.

"I'm Jane," said the younger girl abruptly. "James an' me 'r' twins. We're seven, but I'm older 'n' him."

James snorted. "Five minutes don't count."

"Does so," retorted Jane confidently. That settled, in her mind if not his, she continued her introductions. "Paul's thirteen, 'n' Lucy's fourteen. We're supposed to live in Mis . . . Missouri but . . . but . . ." Words failed, her lower lip quivered, her eyes filled.

"Our folks died," Paul bit out in anger, directed either at Madeline for inadvertently making his sister cry or at his parents for passing on, possibly both. "Lucy an' me could've taken care of the kids on our own. We don't need no—"

"Paul!" Lucy interrupted.

"Mama made us promise to come live with . . . with him," Jane interjected indignantly. "We waited weeks 'n' weeks 'n' he didn't come."

"We stayed at Fort Farewell seemed like forever," her twin supplied, "It was great. The soldiers wanted to teach me 'n' Paul to shoot, but the commander's ol' wife wouldn't let 'em. She figured she was in charge of us just 'cause we stayed in their house 'til Uncle Sam come. Boy, was he surprised t' see us. Funny thing, he didn't even know we was there waitin' for him. Didn't take to the idea much neither." James nodded emphatically, his earnest young face trying in vain to mimic his uncle's displeased frown.

"He didn't like *us* much, then or now," continued Jane. " 'N' we don't like him neither. He's mean. He made us come even when it got freezin' cold 'n' snowed real hard. 'N' he never let us rest, not once. It was *awful.*"

"We're here now," said Lucy, grim-faced but resigned. Standing, she began collecting dirty plates. "An' Ma'd expect us to make the best of it. No matter what." The look she sent around the table brooked no disagreement, not even from Paul, who glared at her mutinously but said nothing.

The door burst open, making everyone jump; Sam Spencer filled the opening. Madeline rose.

"Mr. Spencer, must you always make such a dramatic entrance?"

Sound rumbled in his throat. He tossed an armload of animal furs on the floor. "Bedding. For the kids. In the loft. I'm bunkin' in the barn."

"Thank you." Something wickedly spiteful prompted her to add, "If we were to use your quilt in addition—"

His look turned as frigid as the air blowing in from outside. "If you ever so much as lay a hand on that quilt again, woman, 'less you're plannin' on fixin' it good as new, it'll give me a whole lot of personal satisfaction to toss your meddlin' hide off this mountain over the highest cliff I can find."

"Very well, I—"

"Matter's closed."

"As you wish. I merely—"

" 'Nough said!"

"All right. I—"

A rumbling in his throat made her pinch her lips tight around her failed attempt at the last word. With a straight-lipped smile of grim satisfaction, he studied the gathering around the table with an eagle's keen eye.

"See to it all the leftovers get stored below so the smell won't draw marauders."

"M-m-marauders?" Madeline quickly forgot her vow of silence.

Sam shrugged his massive shoulders.

"Bears mostly, sometimes redskins."

"Red . . . Indians?" her voice quivered in a whisper.

"Bears 'n' Indians, wow," interjected James, small face alive with hope.

"Bears're mean this time of year, an' protective, bein' fresh out of hibernation with a new batch of cubs. Grizzlies're nothing to mess with in any season. Indians is mostly friendly, though."

Madeline cleared her throat. "How does one tell the friendly from the unfriendly?"

"Friendly won't scalp you."

"Oh!" she said weakly, glad she was sitting down. "I . . . I'm relieved you've left your . . . your pet to protect us."

"Pet? Wolf? Hah! He's no pet, woman, make no mistake about that. He's just hangin' around me 'cause I saved his sorry hide when he was no more'n a pup, pullin' him out of a trap before the trapper who set it did. He'll keep you all from harm so long as he knows I want him to, as a favor."

His tone suggested his own mind might change on the subject at any time. Madeline bristled at the implied threat.

"Thank you both, then. We greatly appreciate your generous hospitality." She made no attempt to keep the sarcasm out of her voice.

Ignoring her jibe, he made a long, lazy perusal of her from crown to toe. "Wouldn't go takin' it for granted if I was you. Could be one or the other of us, maybe both, might turn inhospitable mighty fast, if someone says or does something to raise our hackles."

Thoroughly tired of his threats, idle or otherwise, Madeline tipped her chin to look him in the eyes.

"From your tone, sir, one might get the idea that your *in*hospitality has already been extended."

Humor glittered amber in his deep brown eyes.

"You catch on pretty damned fast for a city-born female. Hope you're as smart at heedin' my words."

He spun on his heel to slam out of the cabin. Madeline waited until the plank door shut tightly behind him, determined to have the last word if only for the children's benefit.

"One would have to be deaf, sir, *not* to hear you."

Inordinately pleased with herself, if for no other reason than that she heard childish giggles from the twins behind hands over mouths, Madeline hastened to help Lucy clear the table. It would never do to allow the already overburdened youngster to carry the domestic load alone, though obviously far more experienced than she herself.

"Dang-blasted female, firin' the last shot, an' damned near hittin' the bull's-eye dead on."

Sam slammed the pieced-plank barn door hard enough to make it shudder in its frame. Two strides took him to the nearest stall. Grabbing up the pitchfork leaning nearby at the ready, he pitched hay for all he was worth, until the mule, Ol' Clyde, snorted protest. From the next two stalls,

his horse, Red, and the mule he'd had to purchase at
the fort to carry the kids and additional supplies, echoed
Clyde's sentiments. Under a flurry of falling chaff, Sam
ceased his labors to lean crossed arms on the fork's handle
and stare balefully into Clyde's large, soft eyes, containing
no guile, no judgment.

"The thing is"—Sam paused to gather his thoughts—
"thing is that woman's darned aggrivatin', Clyde. An' all
the time givin' me those ... looks ... out of those ...
those purple eyes. Well, actually, more the color of early-
bloomin' violets ... you know the ones, down by the crick?
An' if that's not bad enough, there's this little black beauty
mark just to the right of her pouty lower lip ... looks just
like a tiny, black heart.

"I swear"—he raised one hand, laid the other briefly
over his heart, and caught the pitchfork before it toppled
without the mule blinking an eye in doubt—"must be I've
wintered too long on these old mountains, if I'm findin'
that shrewish, sharp-tongue harridan attractive. Shoot,
Clyde, she only comes up to here." He jabbed a finger
midway down his chest. "You'd think my stompin' around
an' my shoutin' ringin' in the rafters'd be enough to shut
up a little thing like that, but it ain't. Don't imagine anything is. Enough, that is. Well, *I've* had enough, more'n
enough to last a lifetime, matter of fact. What's the world
comin' to, Clyde, when a fellow can't even get away from
folks meddlin' in his life on the top of a mountain?"

He threw a pained glance ceilingward. "What'd I ever
do to deserve the likes of *her,* and five, count 'em"—he
held up his hand, fingers splayed—*"five* kids, to boot? A
man can't hardly live long enough to've done anythin'
that bad, cold-blooded, premeditated murder included!"

The mule's snort of protest brought Sam to his senses
like a cold bucket of water in the face, recalling how he
had come by those kids.

"My sister, Emily, passed on, her an' her husband," Sam told Clyde matter-of-factly, and sniffed.

The information, old by months, was days fresh and nerve-raw to him. The trip to Fort Farewell for needed supplies as soon as the first spring thaw permitted turned out a hell of a lot more eventful than he'd planned on. Right on top of the commander's informing him of Emily and Matt Ogden succumbing to diptheria during the winter just past came the news that he'd been willed everything and all that they held of value, their five offspring. With no one left on either side to pass them off onto, no grandparents, not even a maiden aunt, what else could he do but take them?

Seemed like he'd never be through shouldering the heavy load of family, not even half a continent away from home. When he was ten, Pa had fallen dead in his tracks right in the middle of spring plowing. Heart failed him, Doc said. Sam learned the hard way what his Pa had had to put up with, battling the sorry played-out land he inherited along with the care of his ma and young sister. At ten, Sam heaved and sweated his way up one row and down another, swearing all the way that he'd get out for good and all, just as soon the hell as he could.

If he did say so himself, he didn't shirk his duty. He took care of Ma and Sissy until Sissy up and married Matthew Ogden—another danged farmer—when she wasn't more than fifteen, and went off to live on his piece of land clear on the other side of the nearest town. Broke Ma's heart, or maybe she never got over missing Pa. Wasn't more than a few months before she was dead and buried, too. Hell, he sold that confounded farm off so fast, he was packed and ready to take off to parts unknown in a couple of weeks. He'd always had a mind to become a free trapper like those passing through Independence for parts east or west, and it looked like it was now or never to follow his dream.

Dream turned to nightmare his first winter in the Rockies. Too green to know what he was about, he found himself lost, without shelter or provisions. If he hadn't somehow stumbled into Bertie and Three Fingers' valley, he wouldn't have survived until spring. With the generosity of seasoned mountain dwellers, they offered him the hospitality for the duration of their cabin, their stores, and Bertie's daughter, Hester. Being an honorable fellow, he naturally married her first. Come spring, he claimed his own valley one mountain over, and built a cabin with their help. Before another winter rolled around, he'd become a true mountain man same as any other around, planning on hunting and trapping and living life to the fullest in the company of his bride, and offspring when they came along.

A year later, Hettie was gone, dead, and he was all alone in his cabin, so consumed with recriminations and regrets, he even denied himself the companionship of his only friends, Three Fingers and Bertie, who loved her same as himself. It took him another year to come around. Lots of times, the only thing that got him through the long days, and longer nights, was hanging onto Hettie's quilt like his life depended on it—her "bride quilt," pieced with her own two hands during the one and only summer they shared. Packed into the humpback chest wrapped in an old sheet, that quilt hadn't seen the light of day from that time to this. Knowing it was inside that old trunk kept Hettie's memory stored away safe, hidden all these years— in his heart and on his conscience—the powerful hurt finally easing to a tolerable ache.

All it took was that female chopping the heck out of Hettie's quilt, and all the memories he thought he was handling came rushing back, full-blown and crushing.

"Damn-blast it!" Sam exclaimed. Ol' Clyde blinked and snorted. "Sorry, old hoss, don't know what's got into me. Heck, yes I do. That *woman*. It's all that blankety-blank female's fault I've been ruminatin' on the past when it's better left just there, in the past. Soon as this storm's over, she's leavin'. On her own two feet or over my shoulder, off my land and out of my life, for good and all."

Chapter Four

Her face, in sleep, looked as innocent as a babe's. Near dawn, standing over his bed, which she'd latched on to, Sam took his own good time studying her. Beneath a matted tangle of raven hair were flawless, fragile features— skin like fine china, though sun- and wind-burned and flushed in sleep; delicate blue veins throbbing at her temples; eyelids faintly shadowed by the violet eyes beneath. And that blasted little black beauty mark at the corner of her lower lip demanding kissing.

Sam shifted uneasily in his moccasins and forced himself to study other, more telling details regarding his unwanted guest. The clothes she slept in, likely the only ones she had to her name, looked specially made and expensive. Her long-fingered hand, lying palm-down on the blanket covering her chest, appeared as soft as an aristocrat's; the other, spread palm-up beside her cheek, bore signs of recent hard labor. How such as her had come to be on a mountaintop in the middle of a spring blizzard was a puzzle. But damned if he cared to go searching for the answer. Double damned if he was going to make her troubles his. Emily's five kids dumped on his doorstep was more than affliction enough for the crusty old hermit he'd become, a man who cherished his privacy and his solitude.

By the Great Wakan, what'd I ever do to deserve this?

Sam threw his silent, desperate plea toward the rafters, not really expecting any answer, knowing for a fact he'd committed enough transgressions in twenty-eight years of hard living to bring this latest catastrophe—and far worse—down upon his head. That didn't mean he wasn't going to fight this latest punishment tooth and nail all the same. Starting right now!

He grabbed a fistful of the bear robe the woman had cocooned herself in and whipped it off her, onto the floor.

"Up an' at 'em, woman. You let the fire die despite my warnin', now you're goin' to have to start it goin' again."

She shot into a sitting position, wrapping her arms around her in a self-hug as soon as the roar of his voice and the cold struck her. For a bewildered second or two, her strange-colored eyes went wide with terror. Until her gaze fell on him. Then she narrowed them into a furious squint, putting a delicate wrinkle in the bridge of her small nose. He figured there was a pile of cuss words building up behind all that fury, but she only sputtered wordlessly a couple of times, too much the lady to spit them out.

"It's your fault the fire went out as much as mine," she accused him finally in a blizzard of angry words. "No one got a wink of sleep until almost morning, thanks to you, what with the children's nightmares after *your* horror stories of bears and Indians last night. The very least you can do to make amends is to see to the fire yourself. And quickly, if you will—it's bitterly cold in here."

Sam refused to accept the guilt she flung his way. He bet he was a whole hell of a lot colder out there in the unheated barn than them here in the cabin with the left-over heat of a dying fire. He didn't figure he got any more sleep than her highness.

"You ain't gettin' out of your chores with that kind of female reasonin'. If you don't pull your weight—or can't— no reason why I oughta feed an' shelter you. Mountain livin' don't allow for no shirkers an' no free rides, woman."

She bounced out of bed as if she were strung up on a bedspring. She stuck her little round chin in the air and tossed him a murderous, arrow-sharp glare. She gave in, but not easily.

"If you will demonstrate for me how to prepare and light a fire in the hearth this one time, I am certain I shall be able to proceed on my own hereafter."

He grinned with a wicked twist of humor. "I'll do better'n that for you, woman. I'll let you do the work, with me explainin' as you go."

She dipped her head briefly. "As you wish. Let us get on with it quickly, then, for it seems to grow colder by the moment." Her words trembled with the chill in the room; she rubbed her upper arms vigorously.

Sam watched her bosom bob up and down with her efforts for about as long as he could stand it. He cleared his throat with a rumbling growl, then spread one arm out in a wide swing, hand open, palm up.

"After you."

Head high, temper too, she proceeded him to the hearth, her skirts whipping back and forth over the packed-earth floor, leaving him to imagine her tight little backside swaying beneath half a dozen petticoats.

Shoot, ol' coon, you've been livin' alone too long, havin' thoughts of that nature about the likes of her.

He hustled to catch up with the blasted female just as she tossed a couple of logs from the dwindling pile into the hearth. He crouched to throw them out again with a wordless grumble of protest.

"Kindlin' first, woman. Ain't you got no common sense?"

She fisted her hands on her trim hips atop faded purple. "Mr. Spencer, inexperienced as I may be at fire starting, I at least have sense enough to know one will never locate 'ain't' in Webster's Dictionary, nor would I express myself in double negatives."

Anger rising to match hers, he figured he could've lit the fire with a bare fingertip; he rose to tower over her.

"Did you get my meanin'?"

"I—I . . . well, yes, but . . ."

"Then hellfire and brimstone, woman, who the bloody blue blazes cares about my wordin' so long's you get a fire goin' before we freeze right here where we stand? Not to mention those five kids sleepin' upstairs."

Her face softened for a flash; then the look was gone, but not before he discovered she'd taken to those kids of his. Maybe she was good for something after all. Sam hung onto his last few shreds of patience, hope flaring with the burst of flaming kindling as he taught the stubborn female how to strike stone against iron, then blow on the resulting spark until the teepee of twigs and dried grasses began to smoke. That hope saw him through showing her how to build a pile of logs on a firm foundation to get the most heat out of the fewest, cautioning her not to squander the precious supply.

"Spring storms take their own good time dyin' down, blusterin' an' blowin' for all they're worth so you won't forget to appreciate summer when it finally arrives, short an' sweet. Woodpile's gotta last 'til they run their ornery course an' give up the fight."

Swiveling on the balls of his feet as they squatted before the fire, he almost bumped noses with her. Something flopped over in his stomach, like a trout on a hook, caught and prime for reeling in. Sam jumped to his feet as though he'd been shot from his Hawken.

"Gotta get more wood."

Bolting from the cabin, he stood just outside, chest heaving, furious and frustrated, not knowing why—or not admitting to it. It was all her fault, that danged contrary female. He should've taken himself a squaw like Bertie advised him to last time a man's needs overtook him. That's all it was, for a fact, pure physical stirrings, nothing more. It wasn't that—that blasted female herself had him running out into the cold instead of lingering inside his own warm cabin, with the temperature dropping and snow coming down like there'd never be an end to it. Damned if he'd stand here like a fool, turning into a snowman on his own front stoop!

Sam grabbed up a staggering armload from the woodpile and headed inside, kicking the door shut behind him.

His throat closed tight, cutting off a warning, at the sight of her bending over to lay a log carefully atop the burning pile, her skirt dipping into glowing hot coals at her feet. Dropping his load with an ear-ringing crash, he reached her just as her hem started smoldering, knocking her forcibly out of danger, slapping out the meager flames with his bare hands before they caught and flared.

"By the spirits, woman, you tryin' to send yourself up in a blaze, an' the kids an' my cabin with you?"

He saw fury over his rough handling turn to bewilderment, then horror, as she saw her scorched skirt front and realized the fate that had nearly been hers. Sam figured about now she'd break down bawling, expecting him to take pity on her, comfort her; he should've known, as contrary as she was, that she wouldn't. Her temper blazed twice as high.

"You might have warned me of possible dangers. Look

at my skirt. It's ruined. Exposing my petticoats to—to one and all. And—and . . . did . . . did you h-h-have to . . . be so . . . so rough? I believe you . . . you enjoyed manhandling . . ." Chest heaving, she mouthed the last without breath for the words.

Sam gave as good as he got.

"Dammit, woman, if I'd taken the time to be gentle, you'd be roasted up well-done by now, an' our only protection from the storm nothin' but a pile of ashes. You oughta be thankin' me 'stead of cussin' me out. I saved your worthless hide an' blistered my hands up good in the process." He thrust both hands at her, palms up, so she could see his injuries—angry red splotches, broken, singed skin.

She tentatively reached one hand toward his, but he thrust them behind his back. Her eyes looked suspiciously liquid, but if there were tears, they didn't spill over. Her words, when they came, were so quiet, he had to lean toward her to hear them.

"Th-thank you. I am never-endingly grateful to you for saving my life."

"Never-ending, I don't need, so long's you're grateful enough to fetch a kettle of snow an' set it on the hook without burnin' yourself an' my place down. You do that an' I'll go rouse the young'ns. Uh, too late. Baby's up an' wantin' its breakfast," he deduced from the wail echoing through the rafters.

She tilted her head, eyes quizzical, smile dimpling one cheek, directly above that birthmark. "It? Don't tell me you are unaware whether you have a niece or a nephew in the child?"

Sam offered an exaggerated shrug of pretended indifference, though now she brought it up, he did wonder what Sissy'd turned out this last time. "It's a baby. Eats, cries, messes itself. Don't make no never mind what kind, 'til it's old enough to put to work."

A disapproving frown replaced her tempting smile. "One is born male or female, you know, and of equal value."

"Everybody knows—"

"It is bad enough the poor thing has no name but Baby, but to be considered nothing more than an 'it' simply because she—"

"She?" Sam made a quick, mental calculation, finding the males trailing by one, if you counted the woman here.

"Hah! I was right."

Lost in thought, it took Sam a minute. " 'Bout what this time?"

"Your attitude tells all. You dislike the female gender. Probably properly jilted by one or more ladies in the past, because of your barbaric demeanor, most likely. No wonder you live alone atop your mountain in the middle of nowhere."

Sam clamped his jaw down tight around the need to set her straight. It was none of her damned business what'd made him swear off females!

She gave him a tight, smug little smirk and a brisk bob of her head in self-satisfaction.

He growled a warning; she didn't budge an inch, her grin going all the wider, cocksure and danged irritating, saying as clearly as words, "I'm right." He bared his teeth briefly, and she chuckled. He opened his mouth to say something, he wasn't sure what, and was saved from making more of a fool of himself only because the kids came pouring down the ladder single file, the oldest girl last, squalling babe in arms. Tempted to roar at the timid girl to shut that kid up, he turned on the aggravating woman instead.

" 'Stead of standin' around palaverin', you'd've better

used the time fetchin' snow an' startin' breakfast porridge."

She looked him in the eye. "I shall be happy to collect a kettle of snow, but I do not know how to prepare porridge."

Sam grunted. "Figures."

"I—I'll do it, miss."

Lucy's faltering voice came from near the ladder.

Sam threw up his hand in exasperation. "Figured on that, too. Put the baby . . . put *her* down someplace, then, an' get to it. You make hotcakes, too? Good, I'll have me a stack, a tall one. There's a slab of bacon in the cellar, an' a jug of maple syrup for sweetin'. An' coffee, all 'round, but don't waste it."

"Is . . . is there any milk?"

"Milk?"

"F-For Baby."

Sam rubbed furiously at the muscles at the back of his neck, which had knotted up tighter than cords of drying rawhide.

"Shi . . . Shoot! Can't it—can't she eat what we eat?"

"S-s-some. Porridge, 'n' hotcakes. But . . . but . . ."

"Children require milk for proper growth and good health."

The woman stepped in for the flushed and floundering girl, sounding all prim and proper-like, echoing some lesson learned by rote in childhood, same's he had and remembered belatedly, hearing Ma's voice as clearly as if she stood beside him. Forgotten memories of home rushed him, but he stomped them down dead in their tracks before they grabbed him in a stranglehold. A guilty conscience lingered. He shoulda known . . .

He threw a glowering gaze around the room, jaw clamped until it ached. Storming toward the fireplace, he grabbed his coat off the peg.

"Where are you going?" the woman demanded.

He tossed her a glare, shrugging into his furs.

"You want milk, I'm gettin' you milk."

The slamming door reverberated behind his departure. No one spoke until its echo died.

"Well, then," said Madeline with an overly bright smile. "Shall we have our breakfast? Lucy, if you will show me what I can do to assist you, together we should make short work of the task."

Though six years Lucy's senior, Madeline could not help but feel that the younger girl far surpassed her in domestic knowledge. After bringing in a kettle of snow, all she could do was stand by and observe. Like a little mother, Lucy saw to the infant's needs first, changing her, satiating her hunger on thin porridge sweetened with syrup. Madeline was surprised to discover that, upon being unwrapped from her warm cocoon of blankets, the infant proved to be larger and less helpless that she'd imagined. She could sit up and gurgle and smile and wave her little limbs for all the world as if she were ready to rise up and join the twins at their play.

"How old is she?" Madeline asked of Lucy.

Lucy offered a shy sideways glance as she attempted, unsuccessfully, to wrap her littlest sister against the drafts with which the cabin abounded. Giving up, she set the baby down on the dirt floor. Biting back a protest, Madeline watched the child crawl toward her twin siblings sitting on the cot playing cat's-in-the cradle with a bit of string James had dug out of one bulging jacket pocket.

"Nine months."

"Nine months old? Why . . . why hasn't she yet been given a name?"

Instantly, Lucy's eyes—really a rather lovely sky-blue color—teared up; she bit a trembling lower lip of a too-generous, albeit well-formed mouth, details Madeline had failed to notice before now. Perhaps she'd mistaken the girl for unattractive based on her timid, downcast gaze, the perpetual slump to her narrow shoulders. Madeline couldn't begin to imagine the full extent of the responsibilities thrust upon this child, now only barely on the verge of young womanhood at—what was she?—fourteen. At fourteen, she herself had had nothing more on her mind than parties and pretty dresses and boys, and no chores beyond learning to perform a few light classics upon the piano and behave with proper decorum in any given social situation.

Never at a loss for words, Jane spoke up to cover her sister's awkward pause.

"Ma 'n' Pa died 'fore namin' Baby. They was awful sick, an' outta their heads, then they was gone."

Prettier in features than her older sister, a near mirror image of her handsome twin brother who would one day turn a head or two, this child's blunt boldness Madeline found far less attractive than Lucy's quiet shyness. Still, the little girl—all of them—had suffered much; each dealt with the losses according to his or her capabilities. At only seven, the child was not beyond help, should one care to . . . Madeline interrupted the tenuous thought before it, and they, made her their prisoner as surely as the storm had.

"Ah, I see," she responded lightly, suggesting, "It seems a shame she shouldn't have one. Perhaps we could choose a name for her ourselves."

Both twins shook their heads vigorously. From his position beside the hearth, attending the fire, ever-isolated from the rest, Paul spoke up for the first time. Madeline believed that his face would one day, in maturity, become strikingly handsome, if he rid himself of the sullen resistance and cocky defiance he now wore like a protective mask. Too thin, gangly, all hands and feet, he appeared awkwardly uncomfortable with his own changing body.

The glare he leveled upon her rivaled his uncle's glower, challenged her right to authority over himself and the others.

"That's for Uncle Sam to do, bein' he's in charge."

His strident tone clearly intended to put her in her place, have the last word. Madeline bit back a sharp reprimand, recalling the aggravating adult most recently influencing the youngsters' malleable minds. Another bone to pick with Mr. Sam Spencer, and not with the sullen thirteen-year-old standing beside the fireplace, feet spread and hands fisted at his sides in a silent challenge.

"So be it," she agreed. Ignoring the glint of superior satisfaction in the boy's eyes, she turned her back on him before he did likewise to her. "Shall I set the table, Lucy?"

Too sweet in nature to stand by watching a silent battle escalate between Madeline and her brother, Lucy bobbed her head. "Yes, please. And—and could you manage slicin' bacon for fryin' too?"

"Of course."

Saying she could and accomplishing the simple chore, however, were two entirely different matters. Her attempts to keep the greasy slab of smoked meat on the table with one hand and wield a large, sharp knife in the other resulted in uneven slices and shreds—and a cut on her thumb which had her yelping and sucking on her own salty blood. After which, Lucy gently took the blade from her to finish the task herself, volunteering that the nick to Madeline's thumb, already ceasing its flow, was not serious and would heal without bandaging or scarring.

Reassured, Madeline stood back, observing Lucy's continued meal preparations without interference. Every slice of bacon under Lucy's hand on the knife proved perfect and uniform. Placing them in the spider, the girl glanced hopefully toward her, then down at Madeline's scorched skirt, and set the pan on glowing coals herself, without

suggestion or comment. Madeline observed how she automatically tucked her skirts tightly under her knees, well
out of range of flame and sparks, storing the technique
away for later use, should the occasion again arise. She
knew it would, given that Mr. Mountain Man Spencer had
assigned her the chore of keeping the fire alive without
so much as a by-your-leave. She would dearly love to show
herself competent in the eyes of that infuriating male, and
in those of the children, who watched her, alternately
puzzled and pitying at her fumbling failures.

She stood at Lucy's elbow, taking mental notes of hotcake preparations, quickly losing track of ingredients and
amounts as the girl dumped in a bit of this and a dab of
that, mixing in an undetermined quantity of warm water
reserved in a cup for that purpose.

Feeling like a hopeless domestic failure, Madeline
offered, "From our cook at home I learned to whip up
the most delightful divinity you've ever tasted, and a cara-
mel flan to melt in your mouth. I have an incurable sweet
tooth," she concluded.

Rather than be impressed, the girl merely appeared per-
plexed.

"I'm sure them're mighty fine dishes for breakfast in
the city, Miss, but I think Uncle'd rather have his bacon,
'n' porridge, 'n' hotcakes, if you don't mind."

"They—that is, divinity is . . . Flan isn't . . . Oh, fiddle,
you're right, of course. Bacon, porridge, and hotcakes it
shall be." Madeline let the subject drop, feeling foolish
and frivolous in the young girl's eyes.

They waited breakfast for the man as long as the younger
ones would tolerate. Sam Spencer had still not returned
at its conclusion. Madeline stared out the window as snow
built its way toward the sill, a futile occupation, for there
was nothing to see but white on white and visibility poor
at best. It was better, however, than sitting with her hands

in her lap, helplessly watching Lucy do all the manual labor, skillfully and expediently, without her.

After a noon meal of stew and cornbread, with the promise of more of the same for supper, Madeline's boredom swelled beyond the levels of endurance. Aside from the contents of the forbidden trunk—which, she regretfully recalled, contained books she might have enjoyed perusing—there was nothing in the cabin's one room left to explore, nothing else to read, no writing materials with which to pen a reassuring letter to her parents toward the time she could reach some civilized place to mail it.

Inactivity forced her to face one of the basic indignities regarding wilderness living, which she'd not recently been able to address. Quite frankly, she . . . smelled, and not sweetly of toilette water. Hesitantly, she approached Lucy, purposefully catching her alone while the youngest three napped together on the cot and Paul stepped outside for more wood. Sitting at the table, the girl's hands were stilled for the moment, wrapped around a pewter cup of warmed-over coffee, her gaze faraway and sad. Hating to interrupt her rare solitude, Madeline feared she might not muster her courage again. She cleared her throat softly, her query barely audible.

"How, and where, does one go about . . . ah, washing . . . ummm . . . undergarments?"

Lucy's plain face mirrored her surprise.

"Ain't you never washed no clothes neither?" she asked, voice hushed, incredulous. "Your ma didn't teach you much of anythin' useful, did she?"

Madeline bit back a retort elaborating the social skills her mother had seen to it that she was taught. This was not the time or the place.

"Apparently nothing of use to me for the circumstances in which I currently find myself," she humbly admitted.

Lucy immediately took pity on her. "There's a wooden

bucket in the corner over there. You could melt some snow in it next to the fire—not too close, mind—to wash up in, 'n' rinse out your longjohns in after, if you've a mind.''

It was the longest speech Madeline had heard from the girl, divulging everything she needed to know—almost. Her voice went lower still as she leaned toward her informant.

''Am I expected to bathe here, before everyone?''

''There's the loft, miss.'' Her tone implied that this was the greatest display of ignorance of all.

''Of course, the loft. Why didn't I think of that?''

The loft proved surprisingly warm, even in her state of total undress. She discovered a chipped china washbowl and pitcher, and a comb and brush that had seen better times, on the floor in one shadowed corner beyond the children's fur pallets. Warm water and a bar of soap Lucy found for her sluicing over her body seemed like sheer heaven, lacking only a good hair-washing to make it complete. Madeline substituted a vigorous brushing, weaving her hair into a single braid to hang out of her way down her back. It wasn't until she rinsed out her most intimate lingerie that she realized, to her dismay, that she had nothing to wear instead until the garments dried. Dressed in only corset and a single, unwashable satin petticoat under her disgracefully tattered dress, Madeline felt shamefully, daringly naked.

With no conscious effort on her part, Madeline's thoughts flew to their host. What if he should discover her state of *dishabille*? It would take little more than his seeing her linens draped here and there, drying. She shivered, though the loft had grown uncomfortably overheated, refusing to dwell upon his possible reaction. Whatever he might think, or feel—or expect—was certainly of no interest to her, except that he would never, *never* have his way with her under any circumstance, insufferable brute that he was! The sooner she escaped his questionable presence and these crude and primitive surroundings for good and all, the happier she'd be.

Madeline deliberately hung her underthings in the main room upon a length of rope she found upstairs, stretched between the peg on the wall beside the fireplace, and another near the foot of the bed. In addition to making an adequate location for drying laundry, the arrangement also provided privacy, of sorts, with petticoats strung tightly side-by-side next to drawers and chemise. Standing back, she admired her handiwork, amazed at her satisfaction, though no one but she herself appreciated the enormity of her accomplishments. None of the children had even noticed. No doubt that awful Mr. Spencer would, upon his return, and comment upon her efforts in his usual caustic manner. For the time she let none of that spoil her euphoria, though the thought crept into her mind rather quickly that this precious bit of privacy was but a brief and temporary luxury. Her underpinnings soon would dry, to be worn again. Then what was she to do? Madeline nibbled on her thumbnail reflectively.

Were Mr. Spencer not so pigheaded, so stubborn, that he refused her the use of his quilt, she might have proper, permanent separation between living and sleeping quarters. Loathe to give up that simple amenity, she decided that as soon as the man returned, she would approach him on the subject, and in such a way that he could not possibly refuse her. Hopefully, by now, common sense had triumphed over that abominable temper of his. She occupied the remainder of the afternoon working at framing her request so he could not deny her the reasonable, practical solution to her very real need.

He still hadn't returned by the younger children's bedtime. Lucy cleaned up and put away, saving a portion of supper aside for her uncle, clearly worried and frightened.

Paul's pretended indifference did not mask the troubled concern in his blue-gray eyes. Both orphans' faces bore the burden of maturity beyond their years. Madeline could only guess at the adult responsibilities they'd shouldered thus far, though barely out of childhood. Panic swelled high in her chest, realizing that if Sam Spencer did not return, ever, the rest of them left behind here in his cabin had no hope of survival. Not if that survival rested on their youthful, frail shoulders. Or upon her own incompetent ones.

Much later, alone at last and wishing she dared utilize aloud the vocabulary gleened from Major Vance to curse the foul-tempered beast of a man for leaving them all in these desperate straits, Madeline pulled furs up around her chin on the lumpy mattress stuffed with something that rattled when she moved about and smelled faintly of pine needles. Seeking sleep's oblivion, she found herself instead praying for Sam's safe return.

An unknown time later, an enraged roar filled the darkness. Bolting awake, Madeline dared not move. Gigantic shadows twirled and twisted in the weak light from a banked fire, flapping huge, fluttering wings like some beastial creature of fable or fairy tale. Terror turned to indignation as she recognized the almost incomprehensible vocalizations spewing from the monster's mouth.

"Mr. Spencer, cease whatever it is you are doing at once. You'll wake the children. Mr. Spencer! I must insist."

At the rising sharpness in her voice, he stopped his ridiculous dance, if that was what it was, to stand perfectly still, wings hanging limp at his sides in a misleadingly docile stance, continuing to mutter foully under his breath.

"If you're finished givin' me what-for, woman, you'd better sure as hell get me untangled from this trap you've set before I—"

"Cease your empty threats, sir. I set no trap, for you or anyone—Oh! Oh, my!"

Understanding suddenly what she hadn't before with a mind fogged with sleep, and frightened half to death, Madeline started giggling and couldn't stop herself no matter how she tried. Sam Spencer, somehow disoriented in his own dark cabin, had stumbled into her laundry, within which he was now thoroughly entangled. What she, barely awake, had mistaken as menacing wings were no more than her own drying petticoats.

Sam roared. *"Get . . . me . . . out . . . of this mess, woman. if you value your hide. Right now!"*

His tone told her he was definitely not as amused as she. Madeline jumped out of bed, circling him with caution, found the candle on the mantel, and struggled with trembling hands to light it, until at last she succeeded, giving her a better view to assess the extent of his problem. He'd managed to so thoroughly wrap himself in her lacy underthings and sturdy rope, he could no longer even lift his hands from his sides. She couldn't help herself, she burst out laughing anew, no more in control than before. Titters from the loft above echoed her merriment. The twins, on their knees, peered down on either side of the ladder; in the shadows between them stood Lucy, both hands wrapped over her mouth, blue eyes bright with amusement. Madeline wasn't certain, but she believed she caught a glimpse of Paul as well before she doubled over, clutching the stitch in her side. Only Sam's pained roar and resumed flailings brought her to her senses—especially when his threats to the participants above sent them scurrying back to bed.

"Mr. Spencer, you have no call to spoil their small bit of fun, even if it is at your expense. The children were merely following my lead, for which I a-a-apologize." A tiny titter escaped at the end, and she had to swallow twice before she got control of herself. "Now, do stand still. You're only making matters worse, and I should hate to lose a single one of my scant few garments to your thrashing."

"Scant they might be, woman," growled the furious man, "but danged if they're goin' to let go of me on their own. Any time you're ready," he concluded, voice thick with sarcasm.

At first, she was conscious only of the twistings and turnings of rope and fabric as she tried to free him from his bonds. Eventually, as she freed one of his arms, and he commenced helping, she became acutely aware of him in a way she had not before, though she had seen him on several occasions without the bulk of his fur jacket, as now. The hide cloth covering his chest, shoulders, and arms seemed more taut over flesh and muscle than she recalled. Taller than herself by a head or more, he was not as broad and brawny as she thought, rather lean and sparse and firm to the touch. His heat warmed her hands; the wild, not unpleasant musk and out-of-doors scent of him sent a sensation swelling deep within, from her chest to . . . to those lower regions of which one was forbidden to think or speak. A fleeting, unexpected flicker of response in his amber-flecked eyes made her knees go weak and her cheeks flame. The last of his restraints fell at his feet; both of them stepped back at the same time.

With a rough clearing of his throat, he bent, then held aloft the tangled mass of rope and lingerie.

"What the hell is all this?"

Breathing erratic, Madeline retorted, "Must every sentence out of your mouth be laced with profanity, Mr. Spencer? If you have no regard for my . . . my sensibilities, please consider the susceptibility of your young charges, who must suffer through your foul utterances along with myself."

Giving him no time to retaliate—most likely with a choice selection of his most potent phrases—she responded to his original question. "For your information, you are holding what was intended to be my drying laundry, once more soiled and wrinkled. Tomorrow, I shall have to perform the chore all over again—and I'll thank you not to examine each item with such scrutiny. They are most private and personal."

He tossed a glance upward, obviously primed with a fresh batch of colorful words and phrases. Instead he sputtered and growled, and finally thrust the whole tangled mess at her without verbal retaliation.

Not finished with her tirade in the least, before he could disappear on them again, she demanded, "Where have you been all day? We—that is, the children—feared you had abandoned us."

Face flushed livid—that which was not covered in hair— he sputtered out one word only.

"Milk . . ."

"M-milk?"

He grabbed up a container from the table nearby, a round, bottomless, inflated sort of thing of suspicious origin.

"Needed milk for the baby, so I got some."

"But where? How? In this weather, when it is deadly folly to step outside even for a few moments? What if you had expired, frozen somewhere? What if—?" All the terrifying possibilities she'd dwelt upon all day spilled out in a rush.

He threw back his head and bellowed, "Enough!" Piercing her with a stare, he warned, "I'm cold an' tired an' half froze an' I just got welcomed home with a goldarned trap of female folderol an' got nothin' to look forward to

but a cold bedroll in a colder barn. One more word out
of your mouth, woman, just one more—''

His huge hands rose over her, fingers curled in such a
way that she had no doubt of his intentions. Silence prefera-
ble to strangulation, Madeline pressed her lips tightly
together. Hoping to placate him, she made a gesture
toward the table on the far side of the room, then made
further gestures representing eating from a bowl with a
spoon.

"What the h—what kind of fit are you throwin' at me
now?'' he barked.

"Food!'' she ventured the one word. He didn't smite
her, so she tried a couple more. "We left out a bowl of
stew . . .''

An ominous calm descended over him. "I told you never,
never to leave food layin' around.''

"I—I'm sorry, I forgot. I won't allow it to happen again.''

Actually, it hadn't been she who'd forgotten, but Lucy.
The girl would crumble under one of his rages, whereas
she herself would not, not even with the threat of death
hanging over her. She did manage, barely, to sound meek
and compliant, a fair imitation of Lucy's demeanor, if she
did say so herself.

Without retaliation, Sam Spencer let the matter pass.
She watched lines of sheer exhaustion etch away the angry
frown creasing his brow. Beneath his eyes she saw broad,
dark smudges. Weariness put a slump in his broad shoulders.

"Bears'll come callin' sure as shootin' if they get a whiff
of food. They ain't the best-mannered guests when the
scent of a free meal comes over 'em.''

"I'll remember. Shall I heat up the stew for you?'' She
wasn't sure if she could, but she was willing to try.

He waved away her suggestion. "Too tired to eat. It'll
do for me in the mornin' instead of porridge. Put it in

the cellar with the rest, an' this here milk, too. An' don't forget the fire.'' He thrust the container into her hands.

Before she could protest that he mustn't go to bed hungry, he quietly left the cabin. This time, the last word was Mountain Man Sam Spencer's.

Chapter Five

The wind struck him in the face like a fist, sucking the breath out of his lungs, numbing his chest. There wasn't a chance in Hades this latest storm was going to let up any time soon! And him spending another night in the barn, freezing his tail off while a whole passel of greenhorn flatlanders slept sound and warm in *his* diggin's, goldang it! Wasn't right! Plumb criminal, matter of fact, that he should have to suffer and they . . . So what was keeping him from marching right back inside and throwing his bedroll down on the hearth?

Nothing! Nothing but that woman taking over every square inch of the place. Her and her blasted laundry!

Sam's face burned hot, not from the wind but with shame, remembering.

Dammit, she'd made him a laughing stock in the eyes of his own kin, and him having to stand there like a danged fool 'til she set him free, all the while making fun at his predicament. Her and the kids, too! Dad blast it! How was a man supposed to be taken serious after something like that?

Red-hot wrath carried him all the way to the barn, fighting the wind-driven blizzard for every yard. He'd set the barn, small by a farmer's standards but plenty big enough for his personal use, in a hollow, surrounded by trees and brush. On a night like this one, all his precautions for keeping the unheated log structure protected from the elements hadn't done the job by half. It was maybe sufficient for hide-covered beasts, but sure as hell not for a puny human. Another darned good example of exactly who was in charge up here in the Rockies, winning handsdown the ongoing battle between man and Mother Nature. Didn't take much imagination to figure out which one of them it was this time around!

Buried in a mound of sweet-smelling hay, wrapped in his fur-lined bedroll and every last woolen horse blanket he could spare, he lay restless and bone chilled, knowing sleep wouldn't claim him any easier this night than last, galled to know who was to blame. And it wasn't Ma Nature!

His roan stallion, Red, and the pair of mules in the next two stalls snorted softly in sleep, taking turns so the sounds, familiar, usually soothing never stopped altogether. The nanny goat he'd traipsed over the mountains to the next valley through thigh-high drifts to fetch home for Baby's milk, uneasy in new accommodations, shook her head, the ceaseless clang of the bell around her neck making a damned annoying clatter. A steady icy breeze blew down his neck no matter which way he tossed or turned; likely the mud chinking had fallen out between a couple of logs. Bad luck holding, he'd chosen to bed down right underneath, too whipped to make the effort to move.

And, dammit, every time he closed his eyes, he saw laughing violet eyes and full, kissable lips tipped up in a teasing grin, showing off that one dimple, the heart-shaped mole, leaving him awake and throbbing in spite of his best efforts. Wasn't fair a fellow should suffer that particular kind of bodily agony—having no say at all in the matter!—whether or not there was any way of satisfying the need that came over him just thinking of her. *That aggravating, infuriating, high-faluting Preston female!* Maddie. Her name rolled through his thoughts like an avalanche gathering speed.

Sam groaned, loud and long. Red stomped, snorting protest; the nanny goat bleated; only the pair of mules slept on, unaware of their master's suffering, noses touching companionably, too dumb to know nothing could come of it. Stupid beasts! About as likely a pair of mules'd get together as himself and her highness. About as likely as a snowcapped mountain in hell!

Sam flipped from his stomach to his back, the images conjured up at the thought raising more than possibilities. Curling on his side, pulling knees to chest, Sam tried to focus on something, anything, else but Maddie Preston.

Emily's kids! What the bloody blue blazes did his sister think he was going to do with her five pups atop a mountain? 'Course, Sissy had no way of knowing what it was like—inhospitable at best, unforgiving at the worst. Killer weather, murdering critters, wild men, redskinned and white alike, desperate men with nothing to lose, ambitious men with no goal but the fortunes they left everything behind and came West for. Daily battles just to survive for an experienced mountain man, sure as hell no place for innocent kids and some spoiled, stubborn female without a lick of common sense. How she got this far without getting herself killed . . . Should of stayed in Luckless and married up with Cougar Calaway.

Hell, no, that good old hoss had already gone through a half-dozen robe-warmers! She should of . . .

"Damn blast it!"

Sam thrashed his legs furiously until he freed them from

the tangle he'd made of his covers, staggering to his feet, groggy with sleep and hopelessly sleepless at the same time. And madder than all get-out. He was letting wandering thoughts of that woman rob him of much needed shut-eye. Again!

Wanting nothing more than to let loose with a string of the choicest profanities at his command, he held to silence for the sake of the gentle, hardworking, uncomplaining beasts sharing their quarters for a second night with the ornery likes of him. He ought to be sleeping in the cabin instead of disturbing their rest.

Shoot! Trapper's oath, he'd do it.

Before he could talk himself out of it, Sam caught up his bedroll. The closer he got to his cabin, fighting the wind blowing crossways and bitter, the better a pallet beside his own hearth sounded to him. He slipped inside on silent moccasins, cracking the door open only far enough to squeeze through. From his corner, Wolf raised his head, acknowledged Sam's presence, and went back to sleep. Had it been an intruder at the door instead of him, man or beast, he'd have gone for the throat. Sam stood, thawing, listening, for a good long minute, the only sound a soft, steady snore coming from his bed off to the right. He grinned. Prim, proper Miss Maddie Preston snored. The idea of it plum tickled his funny bone, wondering how she'd like knowing that, probably no more than knowing he knew. Maybe he'd let her in on the secret come morning. For now he'd rather warm up, get a few winks, then slip back out to the barn for morning chores, and her highness none the wiser.

"Mr. Spencer. *Mister Spencer,* do wake up."

Her caustic admonition shattered Sam's dreamless sleep. "Huh?"

"Mr. Spencer, if you do not move away from the hearth, how can you expect me to stir up the fire to keep it going? Would you rather I attempt to work around you, possibly setting your bedclothes ablaze?"

Sam rolled over, taking his bedding with him, missing by a horsehair knocking the woman off her feet. A couple of hours solid, uninterrupted sleep had left him feeling generous.

"Have at it, then."

He made no mention that he himself had stoked it when he came in and it'd last a while yet. He wanted to see if she'd notice that herself, and what she'd do about it. Pretending to go back to sleep, he watched her under half-closed lids. No "thank you kindly," no silent, grateful glance. Shrugging her slight shoulders, she set the log she held back on the pile and caught up the kettle for snow to start the day with, never giving him a second glance. Should've known! Without a coat, she ducked outside, neglecting to shut the door against heat loss, and back in again with the kettle brimming full. No sense calling her on any of it, Sam settled for a smug jibe.

"You snore!"

Her hands stilled at the chore of setting the kettle onto its hook inside the hearth, and her cheeks went redder than heat-fired.

"You are mistaken, Mr. Spencer," she announced with all the nose-in-the-air dignity she could muster, profile to him, spine arrow-straight.

Ah-ha! He'd hit a tender spot!

"Heard you myself. Snorin', sure as shootin'."

She tossed him a quick, sharp look.

"Were it true, you, Mr. Spencer, are no gentleman for bringing it to my attention."

Vexed as she was, she remembered to hold her skirt well away from the fire. Maybe the woman would prove herself

useful after all. The thought of her maybe taking over the
burden of Emily's kids until he figured out what to do with
them lifted a weight off his shoulders bigger than a boulder
and made him willing to drop his deviling her about snoring. About to remind her he never claimed to be a gentleman, had no hankering to be one, he watched,
dumbstruck, as she went to move the kettle on its hook
deeper into the fire and dumped the whole potful of melting snow onto the glowing logs below. With a sizzling sputter, the fire winked out and died. His temper flared, fueled
by smashed expectations.

"You did that on purpose. To get back at me for men-
tionin' your snorin'. Hell's bells, woman, that's spiteful.
An' downright dangerous. Keepin' the fire going—"

Expecting her to come back at him as good as she got,
he primed for battle. She faced him with a violet-eyed look
laced with frustration and self-recrimination.

"—is of prime importance for survival, I know," she
finished for him. "I intended to demonstrate that I had
mastered this one task on my own, and all I succeeded in
accomplishing was to compound my chores by extinguish-
ing the fire you so thoughtfully maintained through the
night."

A sigh heaved her chest; she eyed the smoldering hearth
with genuine regret. Sam choked back the apology that
was her due for misreading her, clearing his throat with a
rumbling grumble.

"No harm done. Dumped a pot or two of water myself.
Fetch another an' I'll stir up the fire to melt it over."

Taking him up on his offer, Madeline hastened to comply, baffled by the man's abrupt about-face from teasing
to raging to kindness in mere moments. Perhaps there was
another, more reasonable individual under hide and hair
and stentorian bluster. A man who'd lived in solitude the
length of time he appeared to have might be expected to

forget the rudiments of basic social amenities, she supposed, especially at the unanticipated—if unavoidable—invasion of a number of diverse individuals into his private domain. A difficult situation at best for all concerned. As the only other adult in residence, she must force herself to do her part to make the ordeal endurable.

Madeline reentered the cabin, resolve high, to find the children up and breakfast preparations begun. The fire ready to receive her kettle once more, she managed to swing it in place without further disaster, hazarding a sideways glance to see if Mr. Spencer noticed and noting, with some disappointment, that he apparently had not. Seated on a three-legged stool on the far side of the hearth, he carved with a large, wicked-looking knife upon a short length of branch.

"May I inquire what you are making?" she ventured in a conversational tone.

He paused in his labors, threw her a glance, and resumed his labor.

"Peg. For my coat."

"I see!"

It would appear he had no intention of reclaiming the one she'd appropriated last night for her impromptu clothesline.

Pausing, he examined his handiwork; apparently satisfied, he brushed shavings off his knees and rose, offering, "I'll bring a couple of horse blankets from the barn to curtain off the bed. 'Less you like petticoats better."

The humor in his voice didn't quite reach his lips, camouflaged behind facial hair, but she caught a golden glimmer of it in his dark eyes. Much encouraged, Madeline dared offer a suggestion to which she'd given much thought during the waking hours of darkness before sleep claimed her.

"The quilt in the chest would be sufficient—to spare

your animals possible discomfort—if the bottom section were reattached.''

His face turned as stony and sharp-edged as his mountain.

"No!"

The finality in the single syllable brooked no argument. Still, Madeline determined to try. She opened her mouth to protest his heavy-handed refusal.

"No! No quilt! Hang your—your frilly stuff all over the damn cabin for all I care, but keep your hands off my quilt."

Turning on his heel, he snatched his hatchet from the mantel. For a fleeting, frightened second, she feared he meant to use it against her, and relief flooded through her as he used the blunt end to pound his peg into the log wall in two powerful, well-placed strokes. Reassured that he had not taken out his ire on her, she opened her mouth to pursue her idea.

"B-b-breakfast."

He swiveled on silent moccasins at Lucy's timid announcement, leveling Madeline with his usual glowering frown.

"Breakfast," he echoed.

"I only meant to suggest—"

"Gettin' cold—"

"Perhaps afterwards we might further pursue—"

"No!"

"You intend yours to be the last word on the matter?"

"One way or the other."

"Meaning?"

"Meanin', I can stand here as long as it takes, tradin' words with you 'til you run out, leavin' me with the last one."

"Very well!"

"Fine by me!"

"Sir, this verbal one-upmanship accomplishes nothing."

"Goin' to get me the last word for once."

"I—"

He growled, low and menacing, teeth bared. Madeline opened her mouth in protest, thought better of it, and clamped her lips together, tight and disapproving.

Menace at once turned to smug triumph.

"Let's eat!"

Circling the table, four wide-eyed children had followed their exchange—the twins identically open-mouthed, Paul's narrow face mirroring faint derision, Lucy covering her mouth with both hands, though her eyes were unexpectedly merry.

"So eat!" boomed their uncle.

Each jumped to obey, gazes riveted on trenchers. He grumbled wordlessly under his breath.

"You spoke?" Madeline queried sweetly, seating herself at the foot of the table on a second stool opposite the aggravating man at the head. He glanced up briefly; shoveling leftover stew onto a cold biscuit, he gestured with the resulting mix.

"Tellin' the girl I got milk."

He stuffed the entire biscuit into his mouth, chewing with exaggerated relish.

"Mr. Spencer, I—"

"I found the milk in the cellar, sir. Thank you."

Sam swallowed. "Name's Uncle Sam, not sir." He looked around the table, giving each niece or nephew a lengthy turn, resting finally on Lucy.

"Yes, sir . . . Uncle. Thank you kindly." Lucy spoke around Madeline's ready retort, ever the peacekeeper.

"Where . . . ?" Her courage failing, the girl lowered her head over her plate, biting her lower lip.

Sam answered anyway. "Got me a nanny goat, never mind where. She's in the barn an' primed for milkin'.

You"—he pointed at James—"know now how to milk a goat?"

With bravado, the seven-year-old squared his shoulders and thrust out his chin. "Yes, sir, Uncle Sam."

"You never milked no goat," his twin reminded him sharply.

James glared at her. "Makes no never-mind. Pa taught me how to milk a cow, same thing."

"Is not!"

"Is too!"

"Is not!"

"Is too!"

"Is not!"

"Is—"

"Enough!" roared their uncle. The room at once fell silent. "Eat up, you two. After breakfast, you, boy, can show me what you know. If you need more learnin', I'll do the teachin'."

Long minutes passed; Madeline reflectively chewed on a delicate bite of biscuit, swallowed, and spoke.

"His name is James, you know."

He spared her a brief glance. "Whose name?"

"The twin you insist on calling 'boy'. His sister is Jane. Paul is the next oldest; and the girl who works her fingers to the bone keeping house for you, and us all, is Lucy."

"I knew—"

"Did you, now?" she challenged, her ire raised for these orphaned children she scarcely knew. "You didn't know the baby was a girl, or—by the way—that she *has* no name."

"The kid's a baby, what'd she need with a name?"

"Mr. Spencer, infant she might be, but an individual nonetheless, deserving of a name identifying her as such. I should think even you could comprehend the significance."

Sam roared to his feet, tossing down the remains of a

sixth biscuit, toppling the three-legged stool he'd brought with him from the hearth.

"Woman, thanks to your ceaseless palaverin', I've gone an' lost my appetite."

"I would rather think five biscuits are to blame for that," Madeline countered mildly, taking perverse pleasure in placing the blame where it rightly belonged.

He glowered menacingly; she refused to cower. He turned on poor, hapless James.

"Boy, time to head for the barn."

James clamored off his seat on the bench, more eager than intimidated. Apparently he, like Madeline herself, suspected the man was more bluster than bite.

"Y-yes, sir . . . Mister . . . Uncle."

"An' you"—he nodded sharply, once, in Paul's direction—"better learn too."

Eagerly, the younger boy trailed his uncle, threw on his coat in a fair imitation of Sam shrugging his on, and swaggered out the door in his shadow. Paul followed more slowly behind, far less eager and willing than his little brother. With Sam Spencer out of the one small room, those who remained breathed more easily. Madeline scraped the dishes young Jane gathered, volunteering with newfound confidence to wash and dry them when she noticed how preoccupied Lucy'd become with the fussy baby, past due for a morning's nap. Jane declared she was going to watch the boys learn to milk the goat.

"Unattended in a blizzard? I do not believe that would be wise, Jane."

"It's not snowin' right now, miss," said Lucy from across the room where she changed the baby's diaper on the cot. "Uncle's made a good path 'tween here an' there. She'll not get lost. Look, miss, the sun's shinin'."

Madeline faced the window, noticing for the first time large breaks in the clouds, robin's-egg blue against mountainous white clouds with gray bottoms. Madeline's spirits soared with hope. Taking uncommon pleasure in her simple labors, momentarily alone while Lucy bedded down Baby upstairs, Jane having safely reached the barn under her vigilant observation, she spontaneously burst into song, a pleasure she indulged in all too infrequently.

Madeline loved music; her repertoire was unlimited, taking her through dishwashing and wiping up, attending her as she took wash and rinse pans outside to dump. Inspired by the glorious day, she allowed her voice to trill and warble, rise and fall to the full extent of her vocal range and volume.

" 'Tell me the tales that to meee were so dearrr, Loooooong, looooooong agoooooo; Sing meee the songs I delighted to hearrr, Looooooo—' "

The barn door slammed against the siding with the force of Sam's exit. Madeline's vocalizing broke off as he sprinted across the distance between barn and house like a man possessed, his face grim. Her first thought was for the children. She opened her mouth to ask after their welfare, but he caught her roughly by the shoulders, shaking her until her head bobbed on her neck.

"What's the matter, woman? What's happened? What's all the screamin'? Get yourself together, woman, answer me."

"Scream—?" He was addling her brain with his shaking. "Mr. Spencer, cease! You're hurting me. I cannot think." He paused, not removing his large hands from her shoulders, as if intent on resuming his ministrations without some forthcoming explanation on her part. "No one is in danger, or . . . or injured." She could scarcely bring herself to admit the truth. "I was singing," she blurted.

His hands dropped to his sides and his mouth fell open.

"Sing . . . singin'?" he roared. "By the spirits, woman,

that caterwallin's not singing! Screechin's more like it. Fit to wake the dead an' buried."

Madeline's face went hot. This was not the first time her attempts at song had been compared unfavorably, if less candidly, to that particular image. She tipped her head to look squarely into his fire-sparked eyes.

"The turn in the weather brought on a desire to express my pleasure in blue skies and sunshine after three days of storm, sir. I did not anticipate disturbing anyone's peace of mind."

"Woman, if I hadn't stopped you when I did, likely you'd've disturbed the mighty mountains themselves, bringin' an avalanche down on our heads about any minute now."

"And your shouting at me in that manner will not?"

His roar turned to a disgruntled growl between clenched teeth. He raised a fist close to her face to shake a pointed finger at her.

"Don't sing like that again. Matter of fact, don't sing again at all in my hearin'."

"Is that an order, Mr. Spencer?"

"Order or suggestion, take it any dang way you want, only *don't sing* out like that again unless your life depends on it. 'Til I find time to teach you to shoot the Hawken, it's the best protection you an' the kids got."

Her indignation faltered.

"Protection against what?"

A victorious glint turned amber flecks golden.

"Critters, four-legged an' two, frequentin' these mountains, least half more foe than friend."

"I—I assumed we'd become completely isolated here . . . because of the storm."

The mountain man's expression shuttered closed within the blink of an eye; he took a backward step, enforcing the distance between them.

"You found your way to my place durin' the blizzard, if you'll recollect. Ain't likely, but could be someone or somethin' else, out there lookin' for somewhere's to hol' up before it commences snowin', could find it too again."

Madeline's heart sank at his last words.

"Snow? Again? Surely the storm has passed."

"Passed, an' another comin' to take its place before nightfall that'll make the last one look mild in comparison."

Disappointment clouded her vision. The one thought that had inspired her flight into song was that soon, very soon, she'd be escaping the too-small confines of the cabin's four log walls, the indignities of no privacy, not to mention this man's insufferable presence, for the pleasures of civilization.

"Surely the foul weather has passed. It is a clear, beautiful day most suitable for you to take me to Fort Farewell."

He barked a humorless laugh.

"Not blamed likely, even if I was of a mind to."

Turned to lead, her heart felt as if it had fallen into her serviceable leather boots.

"You can't intend to keep me prisoner here?"

He glared.

"It's me that's the prisoner in my own diggin's, with a crazy, screechin', bad-tempered female an' five troublesome kids. No one'll be happier than me when I can finally haul you all back down my mountain an' be done with the lot of you. But it ain't goin' to happen today, woman, 'cause there ain't time to get as far as Luckless before the next big blow hits."

"But Major Vance cannot be expected to await my return much longer."

He stared as if she'd lost her mind.

"What the hell makes you think he's lingerin' in Luckless waitin' for you?"

"Why, to protect his investment, of course." She couldn't believe he was unaware of the circumstances regarding her journey into the mountains. "After all those weeks of traveling with the man, I came to know him well enough to know he would not wish to return the cash paid out to him by that—that man for my hand in marriage."

"Vance's long gone. Cut his losses, gave Cougar Calaway back his cash, left before me an' the kids did."

His words struck her like individual blows. Sudden tears threatened; she fought them back, attempting to cope with this latest disaster.

"Then I'm trapped here for the duration of this deplorable turn in the weather?"

"Don't set any better with me than you, but yes, that's the facts of it. An' the worst of it, to my way of thinkin', is that you're goin' to prove to be a whole hell of a lot more trouble than you're worth. On a daily basis. Singin' . . . Damn and blast! Who'd've guessed?"

Shaking his head, he turned to go. She stopped him cold with her furious retort.

"Mr. Spencer, I deeply resent your disparagement of my singing abilities, and resent even more being considered a liability. I fully intend to carry my fair share of responsibilities regarding household and child care."

He spun.

"*You* look after the kids? Hell, no! You can't even take care of yourself, let alone someone else. An' you keep your paws off anythin' you even suspect belongs to me. Seen for myself what you can do to a man's belongin's when he's lookin' the other way."

"I was desperately cold . . ." She bit back her words explaining her fateful act, refusing to belabor the point. "I can successfully perform any task given to my attention—with sufficient instruction, of course, if it proves to be something with which I've had no previous experience."

"An' why should any one of us take the time an' trouble to teach you what we can do better an' faster ourselves?"

"Because—well, because . . ." But she could think of no reason whatsoever. With her last shreds of pride, she tilted her head high and gave him her haughtiest stare. "We will simply have to endure one another's company to the best of our abilities until you are willing to take me to the fort, or until help reaches me from whatever source Major Vance has raised a rescue party."

Again that annoying, mirthless bark that passed for humor.

"Just so you'll know, 'round here, Vance's come to be known as 'Wrong Way' after he led a troop under his command at Fort Farewell east instead of west pursuin' the mauradin' war party they was trackin'. Honest mistake or cowardly retreat, Vance took an early discharge from the Army 'stead of demotion. Left in disgrace, an' good riddance far as everyone knew he was concerned. From the tales I've heard of late, he's no better at leadin' a wagon train an' gettin' it where it's goin'. If he does give you a second thought, woman, my guess is it wouldn't be with any idea of comin' lookin' for you an' stirrin' up folks' memories 'bout times past."

After the lengthiest speech she'd heard come from the man, he clamped his mouth shut with finality.

"Very well, then, since no rescue is imminent, I will attempt to repay your questionable hospitality by helping out whenever and wherever I can—at no inconvenience to yourself, of course. You need have no fear that I shall in any way intrude upon your busy schedule, Mr. Spencer, making certain I take all my queries to Lucy."

"You leave Lucy alone. She's got enough on her hands with the cookin' an' cleanin' an' seein' to the kids an' tendin' to the baby. Don't need you pesterin' her every few minutes with dumb questions, tryin' to help out. Your help's not needed, or wanted, woman. Got that?"

"You've made yourself perfectly clear. However—"

He growled a warning.

"Point taken, Mr. Spencer, although those bestial noises of yours are an inadequate substitute for words and fail to frighten me, or anyone else, I'd wager, due to the frequency with which you overuse them."

He bit back a growl mid-rumble and glared with a look intended to intimidate. When she allowed him to see she'd remained unaffected, he threw his hands up, spun on his heel, and stalked back toward the barn.

Following his retreat with an unwavering stare that tended to blur, Madeline heaved the shuddering sigh that had been building in her chest since he descended on her, mistaking her attempts to lighten her chore with melodic vocalization for cries of distress. Pulling the last shreds of dignity about her like a protective cloak, she ran trembling hands down her skirt front, then slipped back inside the confines of Sam Spencer's cabin.

Lucy, sitting on a stool beside the hearth, babe in arms, lifted a finger to cover her lips.

"I just got Baby to sleep, miss."

"Our quarreling disturbed her. I'm sorry."

"No, miss." She hesitated. "Wasn't the arguin', was— umm—your singin'. I'm sorry, miss, but I think Baby took it for screamin', like Uncle an' me."

Madeline briefly pressed fingertips to her lips.

"Sweet heaven, was it truly that bad?"

Lucy nodded, blue eyes apologetic.

Closer to tears than ever before, Madeline fled to the questionable privacy of the cot behind the furs draped over the rope, her latest bid for privacy. But as she attempted to shove her way behind the hangings, the sheer weight of them caused the rope to snap in the middle, dumping the whole onto the floor.

Self-pity instantly dissolved into indignation. She stomped her foot, furious and frustrated, with nowhere to go and no one to vent her ire upon, though it was that infuriating Sam Spencer with whom she was so enraged.

Every degrading assumption he'd voiced about her, his enlightenment concerning Major Vance, his refusal to let her so much as attempt to help, his deportment, his hideous grammar, endless profanity, growling and roaring— there was simply nothing redeeming about the man. She could bear his intolerable presence not a moment longer.

A desperate glance out the window showed clear blue skies with not a cloud in sight. Surely there was no chance at all there'd be another blizzard any time today. The despicable mountain man had lied to her about a coming storm to avoid making the trip to Luckless with her. The sooner she made good her escape, the better. And why not today? Why not right now?

Whyever not right now?

A thrill ran through her.

Oh, yes, she could get away this very day. And nothing to keep her. He spoke the truth—she was of little use here. Leaving, now, was the perfect solution to all their problems, especially hers. It might even be that in the lower regions of this mountaintop of Mr. Spencer's, the snow they'd experienced here had been nothing more than spring rain. More than likely—very probable, in fact.

In an hour or two, four or five at the most, she could reach balmy temperatures, grassy slopes turned green and blanketed in spring blossoms. Sweet, fragrant spring. Anticipation bloomed within her heart like the imagined flowers.

With hands trembling in eagerness, she searched through the pile of fallen furs, looking for something to provide warmth and protection until she reached the warmer climate below. Smothering a cry of triumph, she discovered a generously sized piece already bearing armhole slits properly positioned, as if it were a garment in the making temporarily serving otherwise. She threw it over her shoulders, finding it a perfect fit. Eager to begin her journey, Madeline headed for the door.

"Where are you going now, miss?" came a mild query from the hearth.

"What? Oh!" She'd forgotten all about Lucy in her haste. "I thought I'd stand outside the door in the sunshine for a spell."

Lucy offered no challenge to her weak attempt at subterfuge. Leaning her back against the plank door, Madeline stood on the stoop, studying the challenge ahead of her.

Obviously she could not follow the path etched in snow to the barn. Nothing left to do but push off through knee-high drifts in another direction, then circle back out of sight of the cabin. Leaving the stoop, following the log structure to the rear as close to the wall as she could manage, quickly Madeline set off on her homeward journey before her courage deserted her.

Chapter Six

"Where's Maddie—er, that woman?" Sam demanded of Lucy and Paul from the open doorway.

His sister's two oldest sat across the fire from each other on his pair of three-legged stools, heads together, unaware he'd come inside. They jumped when he spoke, looking guilty enough to make Sam figure they'd been comparing notes over their complaints against him. At Paul's feet, Wolf lifted his head, raised one eyebrow, golden eyes alert at his companion's tone.

Sam already had his answer, having seen the footprints in the snow leading around behind the cabin. Weren't his, or any of the kids, all accounted for. Only reason for asking was to find out from Sissy's kids if that dang fool female might've said where she figured she was running off to this time. Even giving her the benefit of the doubt, his personal opinion was he knew the answer to that one, too . . . she didn't much care, so long as it was away from him.

"She . . . she said she was goin' outside to stand in the

sun a while," the girl offered in that quivery voice of hers, like she all the time expected him to bite or something.

The boy, as usual, said nothing.

The lass looked so scared of him that he struggled to lower his voice and keep the tone reasonable.

"When?"

"S-s-some time ago. Ain't—isn't she out there?"

He glowered; she cowered; the boy glared. Clearing his throat, Sam pressed three fingers hard against the bridge of his nose where a throbbing ache had settled in.

"No, no, she ain't."

Lucy replied so softly that he almost missed the words. "I think her feelin's was hurt 'bout us not likin' her singin'."

He flashed a reassuring one-sided smile at his worried niece. *Girl's too tenderhearted for her own good.*

"About that, an' a few other words passin' between her an' me, I figure." He heaved a heavy sigh. "Can the pair of you handle things for a piece while I go haul her on back before she gets herself into trouble?"

"I—I think so."

The boy scowled. Getting real tiresome, that look; Sam decided he'd have to have a good long talk with the lad, real soon, to wipe it off the kid's face for good and all. For now, he ignored the boy.

"Don't bother holdin' supper. An' don't worry if it's late, or mornin' before I—we get back."

"All right, Uncle." She bit her lip, hesitating, then blurted, "B-b-be careful. An' . . . an' bring Miss Preston back safe an' sound. Please?"

"Safe an' as sound as she ever was, which ain't sayin' a whole lot," he agreed. "You comin', Wolf?"

Wolf arched a questioning brow in Paul's direction. The boy stroked the animal's big head with a feather touch. Laying his chin on crossed paws, with a sigh that heaved his chest, Wolf closed his eyes. The boy held his breath, watching for Sam's reaction. *So that's how it is,* thought Sam. His faithful companion of these past years had found someone else to attach hisself to, and the boy to the wolf. Seeing how Paul took to the ornery old nanny goat in the barn and now the wolf, Sam suspected he had a natural way with critters. Or maybe Wolf figured he was needed inside so long's the kids were here and Sam himself wasn't. Never could be certain of the workings of the animal's mind, no matter how long they shared diggin's. Either way didn't much matter to him; he might even get to like not having a wolf dogging his every step.

Missing the silent companionship of the hairy beast anyway, Sam left his warm cabin, turning his attention to the task at hand. Blasted crazy, stubborn woman! Looked like he'd be spending another miserable cold and sleepless night thanks to Miss Maddie Preston, damn her pretty little hide. When he caught up with her, he was going to—! He stopped himself, jaw muscles jumping. *If* he caught up with her in time, he corrected, picking up his pace.

Escape proved far more difficult than Madeline had envisioned. Plowing through knee-high snow was like walking in deep water, infinitely slow and exhausting. Drifts, often thigh-high, caused her to flounder, fall, struggle until she broke free.

Counting on the longer daylight of coming spring, she faced instead rapidly darkening skies foretelling the storm Sam Spencer had predicted. Drat him for being right! Again! Belatedly, she also recalled the "critters," four-footed and two-legged that he had warned lurked everywhere in the dense pine forests encroaching close on every side, stark blue-black against white. Endless white, hurting her eyes, confusing her sense of direction, numbing her to the bone though she felt overheated with exertion. Step by labored step, her heart grew heavier, as did her snow-encrusted boots.

Her desperate decision to leave the safe haven the cabin provided for this vast unknown suddenly seemed the unwisest of folly. To mind came nightmare flashes of the arduous, terrifying journey of a few days ago—was it only five? It seemed an eternity—and what a blessed sanctuary the one-room log structure had proven at the time. And was still, in spite of Mr. Sam Spencer's bluster and bad temper. If she'd but admit to it, only to herself of course, once again she might not have given sufficient thought before taking action.

It was not too late, however, to turn around and follow her own trail back, possibly before she was even missed. Another warmer, sunnier day she could, and would, attempt escape again. Meanwhile, biding her time, she'd make much more thorough plans, horde sufficient supplies, ask veiled but pointed questions of the mountain man whose hospitality she must suffer yet a while to aid her in her quest for freedom.

Hard as it was, Madeline reversed her steps, quickly realizing the wisdom in her decision as snow began to fall in earnest—large, heavy flakes, as if some great hand in the sky had torn open an enormous feather pillow. If she did not hasten, she would have no trail to follow. Panic pushed her onward as fast as snow-soaked skirts and boots allowed, determined to beat the storm.

From atop a plateau overlooking his valley, Sam watched the woman heading back for the cabin, retracing the winding, aimless route that would've gotten her nowhere but lost. Saving him the time and trouble of going after her—unless she got herself lost anyway. No sense of direction, not a lick. And none too bright, if her actions since he met up with her were any indication. Roundly cussing *that* day, Sam waited and watched until he felt positive that even mule-headed Maddie Preston could find her way before he scrambled down from his perch, hell-bent on beating her there.

It took her near an hour. Sam had just given in to the silent pleading in four pairs of eyes boring holes in his rawhide-covered back. His fingers had closed around his coat to lift it from its peg when the door cracked open. She slipped inside as if she hoped no one'd notice. Knowing the kids would be full of questions, he stopped theirs with one of his own, to pay her back for inconveniencing him and cluttering his head with worrying after her.

"Takin' a walk in the sunshine?" he asked, tongue-in-cheek.

She looked about tuckered out, blue with cold except for the flush of windburn on her cheeks, her springflower eyes turned purple with defeat.

"What? Oh, I . . . yes. I felt the need to stretch my legs a bit after the confines of the cabin. But the weather . . . turned inclement."

The woman had a hard time spitting out the words admitting he was right about the coming storm. They put a frown between her arched black brows and puckered up generous lips meant for smiling as if she were sucking on something mighty bitter.

"Kids figured you might've run off like you've a habit of doin' when the goin' gets rough," he needled.

That put a spark of life in her.

"I do not run . . ."

She couldn't say the words denying it, Sam saw, not when he'd been in Luckless to witness the truth with his own two eyes. She'd run out on Vance when he shackled her to good ol' Cougar Calaway; likely she'd run away from home before that for some reason or other without thinking it through, just like today. Sam doubted that her folks—if she had any—would've given their blessing to a highborn female such as her traveling cross-country with the likes of Eben Vance.

Now she worried her full lower lip between small, even teeth, her gaze flitting from one thing to another, looking to change the subject, if he guessed right. She caught sight of the handiwork that had filled his time while she took hers getting back to the cabin. Expecting complaint, he watched pleasure put roses back in her pale cheeks, a sparkle in her eyes. She pressed her hands together between high, round breasts. Watching the change come over her, Sam felt something flip-flop deep in his belly, like a spawning trout struggling upstream come spring.

"You've rehung my privacy curtain, Mr. Spencer, and made a much better job of it, too. Thank you."

The room went hot, and so did Sam's face. He mumbled something.

"What did you say?"

She leaned toward him, so close by that he caught her scent, all fresh air and female. He cleared his throat.

"Should've used new rope first time."

"I shall remember that for future reference."

She bobbed her head in a nod, fine features serious, thoughtful. That leaping-fish feeling rose up and arched at the base of his throat; danged if only a couple of kind words didn't make him hanker to see what else he could do to put that admiring light in her odd-colored eyes. She was giving him the once-over as if she were reconsidering her poor opinion of him, a damned uncomfortable sensation.

Sam shoved down the lump in his throat with a grumble.

"Supper's been waitin'."

Her gaze swam into focus, her thoughts clearly taking another, safer turn.

"By all means, let us partake, then. I am ravenous after my . . . my walk."

Seated across the supper table from the man, Madeline found it infinitely difficult to look Sam Spencer directly in the eyes—those coffee-brown, gold-flecked eyes which mirrored his every thought, without guile or the social subterfuges to which she had so long been accustomed. Had she not been too exhausted to do battle with him as usual, to verbally parry and thrust and cross swords at his every word, perhaps she might have missed this significant moment of realization altogether. No longer a beast in her estimation, by his simple act of restoring her needed privacy during her absence, he had attained for her a new status. A very solitary man of simple needs and desires forced by circumstances beyond his control to suffer unwanted, unasked-for, human companionship that complicated his life, often past enduring, turning him surly and snappish at best, but never hardhearted or mean-spirited. He had not succumbed to the intolerable behaviors she had observed in those other mountain men gathered together in the lawless town of Luckless. Her present fate, and that of the children, lay in better hands with him in this wilderness than in any other's; they were very fortunate to have him, hot-tempered eccentric though he was.

After an awkwardly silent meal during which not even Baby cried out for attention, Mr. Spencer left the cabin without a word, and a shuttered, unapproachable expression behind his overabundant thatch of hair and beard. What manner of features lay beneath—handsome, plain, or ugly—was left to speculation, Madeline having decided them to be marred in some severe way, else why would he camouflage them? Those mesmerizing eyes, so dark and rich in color—piercing, knowing, private, and stormy by turns—only began to tell the story of who he had been and now was.

At the man's abrupt departure, all the charitable fantasies she'd dwelt on flew out of Madeline's head with the closing of the door behind him. One might expect at least a mildly affable comment from him as to where he was going, and when—or if—he planned on returning. Deciding that she could not care less, Madeline rose from the dinner table to help Lucy clear. Before she could work herself into a state over Mr. Spencer's inconsiderate behavior despite her resolve, he returned, arms overflowing with freshly cut pine boughs, distributing a trail of snow and needles from the door to the center of the room, where he dumped his load.

"What're them for?"

Only irrepressible Jane proved bold enough to ask the question on everyone's lips.

"Snowshoes," her uncle muttered, his narrow-eyed gaze seeking out and finding his quarry. "You lads—Paul, James—shrug on your coats an' help me bring the rest of the things we'll be needin' in from the barn. We're goin' to have ourselves a snowshoe-makin' class here tonight, with me the teacher an' all of you my class, no exceptions but the babe."

Again, Jane alone dared speak.

"Miss Preston, too?"

"Especially her."

He stared pointedly into her eyes, challenging her to protest. Madeline said nothing. In truth, she could think of no objection to which to put voice. Any diversion from another endlessly long evening with nothing to do and nowhere to go while the others were otherwise occupied presented a welcome change in routine.

"What's snowshoes, an' how'd we make 'em?" James asked as the males of the household exited.

The answer cut off with the shutting of the door, Madeline responded to a similar query from Jane.

"I believe they are large, flat objects worn on the bottom of the feet to spread out one's weight, facilitating walking on top of the snow without sinking in."

Which seemed to satisfy both girls, though they frowned over some of her phrasing. She found it hard to communicate on their level after years of learned and practiced drawing-room conversation. She must make more of a conscientious effort to try hereafter, for the children, and for the man whose education appeared equally lacking if his vocabulary and grammar were any clue, if only to decrease the friction close quarters seemed to encourage.

Clearing the dinner dishes from the plank table for a work surface for their lessons, Madeline sighed, resolving, on her part, to keep peace at all costs, though it was bound to be a tremendous strain on her already frazzled nerves. If only she had made good her escape that morning, the effort would not be necessary. If she had had snowshoes at her disposal, she would not even be here tonight.

Madeline's hands stilled at their labors, a new thought bursting full-blown into her mind. Perhaps Mr. Spencer's sudden willingness to help them all make snowshoes was not the generous impulse it appeared. What if it were a less than subtle hint that he'd like nothing more than for all of them to strap the implements upon their feet and walk away down his mountain and out of his life for good?

If that were his ploy, thought Madeline, ire rising and former kind thoughts no more than a bitter memory, Mr. Mountain Man Spencer would soon attain his wish. For once, he and she were very much in accord. To that end, she would happily formulate her own set of plans, augmenting his, but upon her own schedule. And in the meantime, she would keep the peace, as earlier vowed, so that the man need be none the wiser. Far sooner than he imagined, he would find himself alone once more on his mountain top with not a single other living soul to disturb his precious solitude.

Inordinately pleased with herself and her deductions, Madeline hummed—very softly—while she gave the table's surface a final swipe with a damp cloth, finishing just as man and boys returned, setting on the table an assortment of objects, only a few of which she easily identified.

"Mr. Spencer," she chided, resolve forgotten, "you cannot mean to let the children handle those dangerously sharp tools?"

"No, ma'm," he agreed emphatically in a mock-serious tone she ignored.

"Well, thank fortune for that."

"Just the boys," he added.

"You'll do no such—"

"I know how to handle 'em," Paul interrupted rudely, face and stance defiant. "Been helpin' 'round the farm since I was younger 'n Jamie, here. Past time we're 'llowed t' do more 'round this place than fetch firewood."

"Let's have at it, then," agreed Sam, leading the eager boys to the pile of boughs with their tools of choice. Paul and James sat side by side, cross-legged on the dirt floor; their uncle squatted on his haunches nearby. "Need to strip off all them branches down to one strong an' pliable stick . . . 'bout so long." He extended both arms straight out from his sides. "An' no tryin' to burn the leftovers in the hearth," he warned one and all. "Fire'll flash into the room all over you with fresh-cut pine."

He spoke conversationally as they set to work, Madeline, Lucy, and Jane standing by empty-handed, much to Jane's displeasure if her out-thrust lower lip was any indication.

His lean, strong hands swift and skillful in their labors,

he explained, "Should be usin' ash, and would, if we had any handy, which we don't. Tough as oak, bends easier when heated up . . . smells like popcorn when smoothed down with sand. Ash's what the Indians use—"

"You know some real live Injuns?" James asked, young face upturned and hopeful. Sam nodded. "Crickey! Will ya tell us all 'bout 'em someday, will ya?"

"Someday," his uncle promised vaguely, continuing his lecture.

"When we have us enough sticks, two apiece—"

"How many's that?" interrupted Jane, impatiently shifting from one foot to the other close to her uncle's elbow.

Sam threw her a glance, thick salt-and-pepper brows drawn down toward the bridge of his nose.

"You figure it out."

Jane's face became mutinous. Madeline quickly intervened.

"That would be ten branches, twelve if Mr. Spencer were making himself a pair as well."

"Ten'll do. I got mine," Sam said briskly. "Looks like we got about that now."

Rising easily from a squat, he bent to gather together the striped lengths of pine. Madeline mentally counted as he did, holding her tongue until he straightened.

"I believe you have only eight there, Mr. Spencer."

Not looking her way, he barked, "You, Paul, trim up a few more." He turned his head, glancing over his shoulder, no light in his dark eyes. "Six enough?"

"More than enough. Two would be sufficient for a total of ten."

"Could be we'll need extras for makin' mistakes on. Got 'em? Let's get to work, then."

The thought flitted through her mind as they all sojourned to the table for the remainder of their lesson that perhaps Sam Spencer's formal education had been far more lacking that she'd first suspected; perhaps he'd had no schooling at all and suffered a silent shame over the lack. She stored the thought away for future perusal as the mountain man began his demonstration.

"Bend your branch around, so, end next to end. Take it slow, so it don't snap, an' don't let go've either end. I'm comin' around the table to tie your ends together with this here rawhide. Out in the snow an' damp, it'll shrink down tight, keep the ends from separatin' on you. Then we're goin' to weave us a center to stand on, using sinew. Sinew don't shrink when it's wet. The shape of a snowshoe depends on what's on hand an' the maker's personal preference; rawhide an' sinew, used like I'm tellin' you, always stays the same. Sinew for bindings tied around your toes an' lacing wrapped to the calf, too."

"What's sinew?" asked James, studying the pile of pale, dried strings in the center of the table, holding his bent branch tight, waiting his turn.

"Tendons," said Sam, not looking up. "These're moose."

"Moose? Crickey! What's tendons?"

Sam shrugged, catching the ends of James's branch as his grip loosened, thoughts elsewhere. "Holds bone to muscle. Dried, the stuff's tougher'n longer lastin' than rope. An' easier to come by, moose bein' near at hand if you know where to look an' are a passable shot. Good long-lastin' supply of meat, too, for roastin' an' stewin' an' smokin', an' a whole bunch of other necessities from rack to hooves. Leg tendons're the longest, like these." He nodded toward the pile, skillfully wrapping the ends to form an elongated oval with scarcely a glance.

"Crickey," breathed James in awe of Sam's continued revelations, pulling a single long strand from the pile for closer examination.

Madeline thought the whole concept rather grisly to dwell upon, but she could not reprimand the boy for his obvious enthusiasm, nor the man for imparting a bit of his apparently vast knowledge of mountain survival skills which might one day prove useful to herself as well. She did give a rather queasy moment of thought to what type of meat their supper stew tonight might have contained. Not that it mattered, she would have eaten both generous servings even so, and relished them just as much, she realized, for she had no other choice but starvation.

Sam had left James' side for her own, making her all too uncomfortably aware of his close proximity and the pleasant, pungent scent of pine clinging to his clothing. A sensation similar to the static shock of a woolen carpet in winter spread from tingling fingertips and toes inward through her limbs, converging mid-torso and enervating her to the point of breathlessness.

He lifted the oval hoop of pine from her limp hands with his capable, weather-browned ones, swiftly binding the ends together. She followed the progress of those hands as one mesmerized, watching muscle and bone and . . . and sinew undulate under the bronze of his skin, noting the blunt squareness of his nails, the stains of pitch on the callused, fleshy pads of his palms, the prominent bone and rich blue veins in his wrists where his fringed and cuffless rawhide sleeves ended. The room had become uncommonly warm, she thought absently, and let her gaze stray sideways to a narrow waist circled with a multicolored beaded sash. Not quite daring to peruse downward to that private part of male anatomy she knew of only through innuendo from giggling married friends, she inadvertently glanced upward to the deep open V beginning immediately above a fringed yoke, exposing an unanticipated glimpse of curling salt-and-pepper hair. One of his braids swung forward, brushing her cheek in passing, and then again, and again, as if deliberately. And she was, she realized, suddenly hot-faced to see his dark eyes sparkling with amused amber flecks very close to her own. Before she could comment, offer excuses, and without any of his own, Sam Spencer moved on to Lucy, turning his broad back on her.

Some minutes later, he completed his circuit around the table to stand at the head, looking from one upturned face to the other, until he came to her. He studied hers longer than any of the others, she was certain, then he winked, briefly, almost imperceptibly, but a cheeky wink nonetheless.

Still unwaveringly focused on her, he announced, "Hope you all were payin' attention when I came around to you, 'cause I'll be expectin' you to tie up the other one on your own. After that, you've each got the pair of them to string up before bedtime." There was a general groan. "An' I want you to draw around the shape of your hands on this piece of brown paper. Tomorrow night we're goin' to make mittens out of some rabbit pelts I've got stored in the barn." The glint in his narrowed eyes sent out a warning none dared challenge.

In a surprisingly short time—or perhaps due to absorption in the task at hand—every individual had successfully completed his or her own pair of snowshoes, even the youngest, the twins, with more than a little patient help from their uncle. For the first time, neither child protested climbing into the loft to their fur pallets, though they were heard halfheartedly quarreling over whose pair was best until sleepy voices dwindled to silence. Sam and Paul stacked snowshoes beside the door, not speaking, but without the usual tangible hostility, after which Paul, too, went upstairs to bed. Lucy changed Baby's wet diapers, fed her a biscuit softened with milk and syrup, and headed that way herself, babe in arms. At the bottom of the ladder-like stairs, she turned back.

"Uncle, if you have a wash tub anywhere around . . . Baby's needin' some clean clothes real soon."

Sam scratched his wiskered jaw thoughtfully. "Used to be one in the hayloft. If it's still there, I'll bring it over in the mornin'."

Lucy ducked her head. "Thank you, Uncle Sam."

With Lucy's departure, they were alone. He watched Madeline steadily, lengthily, like a hunter his prey or an observer studying some odd curiosity, but said nothing. Madeline returned his unwavering stare with one of her own, but turned away first, pretending to busy herself with restacking pewter dishes on their shelf. Because there were so few, and because it really was a needless task, she finished all too quickly. Running her hands nervously over the flour sack serving as an apron knotted at her waist, she faced him, refusing to look directly into his eyes, staring rather over his left shoulder.

"Well, then, I believe I shall retire also."

She all but ran across the room to the bed behind its enclosure, then sat on its edge, trembling, shamefully aware of the man on the far side, knowing sleep would be difficult to come by for a good long while, for reasons she dare not examine too closely.

Stretched out on his back on his bedroll beside the banked fire, arms crossed to pillow his head, Sam stared wide-eyed at the shadow patterns on the raftered ceiling, seeing in them the graceful swish of the woman's faded purple skirts, the imagined sway of raven hair unbound and cascading to her trim waist, a waist he could span with his hands and still lock fingers. His groin throbbed heavy and hurting as he lay without moving, listening to the quiet sounds behind the hide wall he'd rigged hoping to help him forget what was on the other side. She sighed, and again, tossing and turning the way he hankered to and wouldn't. Tonight, sleep came no easier to her than to him. Sam liked thinking it was for the same reason that kept him from dozing off, that her suffering matched his.

He'd studied her studying him when she didn't know it, sitting so close that he brushed up against her without half trying, the heat of her body reaching him clean through his rawhide and that ugly old dress of hers until he was near desperate to strip down to his loin cloth and hightail it outside to roll in a snow bank in a blizzard in the black of night. Might still have to do that very thing sometime real soon if he didn't stop wasting shut-eye hours mooning over that woman.

Sam sat upright, all hope of sleep gone. Sitting cross-legged Indian fashion, staring into hot coals until his eyes watered, he searched his spinning brain for a way to get a decent night's sleep, a minute's peace of mind, for as long as he was forced to share his cabin with her highness. Short of building a whole new one to stick her off in on her own, he couldn't come up with an idea for the life of him. And she was sure as heck going to be the death of him if he didn't get some sleep sometime soon.

He pondered a while longer before it struck him, making him shake his head in wonderment.

Didn't have to build her a cabin. All he had to do was build her a room of her own—or to share with the girls and the baby, if she'd a mind. The stack of rough lumber sitting in the barn intended for some long-forgotten project, would make a mighty spacious spare room, with a sturdy plank door with a latch, near the foot of the cot, his cot, soon to be reclaimed along with his sanity.

Rubbing his hands together in smug satisfaction, plumb pleased with his decision, he yawned widely, eyes heavy-lidded. Stretching out as before, he slept at once with the dreamless, worry-free sleep of the innocent youngun's overhead.

Chapter Seven

"Mr Spencer! How—how dare you?"

Abruptly awakened to the sound of hammering upon the outside wall to which her bed was attached, Madeline leapt from beneath her covers, having completely forgotten she wore nothing but her chemise. Her lawn and linen underthings had grown so fragile with overwearing, it seemed prudent to save wear and tear by sleeping in as few as necessary for decency. Spying Sam Spencer standing at the edge of her hide curtain, stare steady and candid, she pulled the scanty garment down over her hips.

Caught in the act, the mountain man possessed conscience enough that the exposed part of his face flushed red; hers flamed as hotly. Snatching up a petticoat, she whipped it over her shoulders like a protective cape, holding it together with both fists, though it scarcely reached the hem of her chemise, a fact which did not go unobserved by Mr. Spencer. His gaze traveled from her knees downward, his perusal slow and lingering, making her toes curl against the earth floor. Further vexed by this involuntary response, she chided, "You might have made your presence known."

Making no apologies, he admitted, "Ain't the first time I've seen a female without her drawers on. Figured you'd be up and about by now, it goin' on half past seven, an' what with all the racket."

"I could not fail to hear. I feared we were under siege by one or the other of those savage Indians and wild animals about which you go on and on."

Her conclusion crinkled smile lines into the corners of his eyes; one side of his mouth turned up the slightest bit, disappearing under the droop of his mustache, so she wasn't precisely certain she'd seen him smile or imagined it.

"Naw, just addin' on. Makin' you an' the girls a bedroom off by yourselves. Plannin' on cuttin' out a doorway, about there."

He pointed with the ax he held in a one-handed grip, stretching his arm straight out, exposing beneath rolled-up sleeves a bulging forearm and veins that stood out like corded blue ropes.

A shiver trembled through her, though she felt overly warm. Chin tipped high, she utilized high dudgeon to mask discomposure.

"Right now?"

He shook his shaggy head, his braids dancing against his bearded jaw. Reminded of that same caress on her own cheek last evening, she unconsciously raised one hand to rub the back of it just there. Her makeshift covering slid sideways, revealing one scantily covered breast.

The man's eyes took on a wicked gleam in their dark depths; he cleared his throat. Madeline's heart beat heavy and hard against her ribs.

"Not 'til me an' the boys get the walls up an' a roof

on," he answered her half-forgotten question, voice raspy. "Need to take some measurements. I can do it when you're . . . later."

He backed out, the hide robe dropping back in place behind him. Madeline waited, poised and listening, until the front door quietly closed. Scrambling hastily into her clothes, she made no attempt to put her hair up—she'd lost most of her hairpins anyway—and took only long enough to gather it at her nape with an appropriated string of rawhide.

Forcibly thrusting from her mind the embarrassing incident of the mountain man's having seen her so exposed and vulnerable, she concentrated instead on how best to help with the project at hand. Surely he would expect her to tell him what would most suit her needs, and those of her proposed roommates.

Ideas abundant now that she'd put her mind to it, she exited the deserted cabin to a surprisingly mild, if overcast, morning, following the sounds of hammer and ax and lively, youthful conversation around to the side.

"I want my own room," Jane protested loudly and repeatedly, the repetitions punctuated by the scrape of shovel against frozen ground. She and Lucy labored side-by-side to enlarge the cleared rectangle intended for the foundation, Lucy, as always, bearing the burden of the chore.

"Ssshush!" cautioned her older sister, pausing to push flyaway hair out of her face with both reddened hands, tossing a wary glance in her uncle's direction. "You ought'a be happy just leavin' the loft to the boys. You're all the time complainin' Paul makes noises in his sleep an' James won't leave off pesterin' you."

"I want my own room," Jane insisted, pouting unprettily.

Madeline spoke up. "I agree with Jane that there should be two rooms," adding in a rush of words, "but so that we females and the boys might each inhabit one, leaving Mr. Spencer the private retreat of the loft when our constant companionship becomes too trying for him. And,'' she continued over Jane's expected protest, "I further feel each room must have at least one window, possibly two, proper ventilation being imperative to healthful sleep, with each room having its own entrance, thus creating an adequate flow of air—"

A deep, warning rumble abruptly terminated her monologue, not through intimidation—she'd long ceased being impressed by the man's nonverbal threats, or his equally overused glare under furrowed brows—rather in genuine surprise. He leaned upon the end of his ax handle with overlapped hands, the steel head resting on the toe of one moccasined foot. Behind him, the wall bore the beginning of a long, narrow trench within which to set a new plank wall, as evidenced by the stack of cut lumber on the ground near at hand.

"Did you not expect that I would wish to contribute to the design of accommodations intended for my use?"

"By the spirits, woman, I'm only plannin' on puttin' you up a few more days . . . or couple've weeks, if the weather don't cooperate. What'd you figure I'm goin' to do with those extra rooms once you hightail it on home?"

"Why, the children shall continue to inhabit them, will they not?"

All eyes turned Sam's way, boring into him clear to the core, every younguns's as blue as a summer sky, same as their mother's, his sister, who was depending on him to see to her offspring now that she couldn't. The purple-eyed stare the woman leveled on him made him regret coming up with this idea in the first place. Should've left good enough alone, sweated out a few more sleepless nights 'til the weather lifted. Knowing he'd never make it, not after seeing her practically in the altogether, and his mind's eye going over and over the look of her high, round breasts, the slender, shapely legs and pretty, dainty feet. Not when imagination, and memories, filled in what lay between. Sam hauled himself back to the present, breathing too hard. Expression expectant, she awaited his answer to some question. What was it? Something about the kids, the room.

Not the time to mention he planned on taking the lot of them along with her as far as the fort, all the way back to Independence, if need be. Get them adopted, hired out. Atop a mountain with the likes of him wasn't no place for a passel of kids.

"Stayin' ain't likely their best choice," Sam countered in self-defense.

"Their choices are few, Mr. Spencer. A life with their crusty bachelor uncle, or at the mercy of some judge's decision. Possibly to end up as street urchins, starving, stealing—"

Put that way, Sam was at a loss for words to defend himself. He lifted one hand off his ax handle, palm out in defeat.

"Two rooms, then. But *no* windows. Ain't got no glass, an' no place to get some."

"Post store at the fort's got window glass. I seen it," the female twin piped up. "You could get some there after the snow melts."

"No windows." He hefted the ax onto his shoulder, needing to swing at something, anything. "Step back if you're wantin' to hang on to your head," he warned, contrarily satisfied that he'd put a touch of fear into the bunch of them when they scrambled back to their own tasks, and twice as pleased with himself when the woman disappeared into the house without another word.

* * *

Her few self-appointed chores completed, Madeline sat
on a stool beside the fire planning the pair of bedrooms
down to the last detail. She must suggest to Mr. Spencer
that one be larger than the other, the larger with two
double-sized beds—one for herself and one for the girls—
with perhaps a trundle beneath for the baby, and the
smaller with a pair of cots the size of his own for the two
boys. As Mr. Spencer himself would inhabit the loft, his
bed could be relocated there, giving more room to their
cramped living quarters. And, of course, she must further
attempt to get him to agree to windows, if not installed
during her brief stay, at least later on, for the children.

Marveling over her ongoing concern for the orphans,
the pleasure she derived from anticipating the new rooms
and the changes she envisioned, Madeline discovered a
domestic side to her nature she had not dreamed she
possessed. She further shocked herself with the admission—but only in the most secret recesses of her mind—
that she also thoroughly enjoyed the challenge of frequent
verbal battles with that stubborn Mr. Spencer and the triumph of occasionally besting him. Even more—and this
she dared but lightly examine—she especially relished
causing him to smile, whether with pleasure or in teasing,
and found most thrilling of all that certain expression—
appreciation, speculation . . . desire?—which came into
his fathomless dark eyes sometimes when he looked at her,
like this morning when he caught her in a state of *dishabille*.

Refusing to examine more closely that last bit of self-
realization, Madeline glanced about the one small room,
seeking release for her arrant, highly improper emotions.
And saw nothing needing her attention, Lucy being the
tidy, thorough housekeeper that she was.

Hands idle in her lap, Madeline sighed, dreading another long day with no better occupation than counting her own erratic heartbeats throbbing at the base of her throat, dwelling upon the unthinkable. Just when she believed she'd go mad with anticipated inactivity, the door banged open, admitting the subject of her dangerous flights of fancy, his muscled arms stretched around an enormous wooden tub. Squatting on lean, powerful haunches, he set his burden down near the fire. Rising, he jerked his lion-like head in a nod.

"Washtub."

"So I surmised after Lucy's request last evening."

"Told her I figured you could handle the washin' on your own. She's wantin' to keep workin' out with us men, an' we can use her. Could send in that little one won't stop talkin'—Jane—to help out." He looked hopeful until she shook her head. "Well, then, you know how to heat water by now without dousin' it, or burnin' the place down an' yourself with it, right?" He grinned, briefly, as proof he was teasing. "Good. Use that dish-washin' soap, but sparin'ly. It's all we got."

"And where am I to hang the results of my labors?" she demanded tartly, feeling the sting of his reminder of her past transgressions. "There are quite a few items in need of a thorough scrubbing." *Including a number of yours, to relieve them of that lingering pungency from the hides' original owners.*

He scratched his jaw, scanning the room, thick brows furrowed in thought.

"Reckon you can take down that curtain of hides for some of it. I can string up another rope on the other side of the fireplace. An' a couple of lines in the rafters upstairs if you think you'll be needin' them."

"Rest assured I shall. In addition, Mr. Spencer, I would suggest a nice, hot bath for each of us this evening before we don freshly laundered clothing."

He frowned. "Suppose you ain't partial to a jump in the crick an' a good rubdown with sand?"

"Bathing out-of-doors in a spring-fed stream? In this weather? Certainly not." She shivered at the mere thought. "How could you even suggest we court illness, even death, with such foolishness?"

"Been bathin' that way myself most every day long's I've lived in these mountains. Ain't never done me no harm."

"*I* prefer warm water, comfort, and *privacy* when I bathe, Mr. Spencer, as I am sure do the children. We will all have labored hard and long this day. Weekly, if not daily, bathing, I'm sure you'll agree, is imperative in the close proximity of these tight quarters. It should be a pleasure to look forward to, not a torturous ordeal to dread. Also," she hurried on over the deep rumble of his nonverbal protest, "if that all-too frequent scratching of your over-abundant facial hair indicates an exploration for living things, I further suggest that shaving might be in order."

"Woman," he bellowed, face florid, eyes glittering, "a man's chin whiskers're his business an' nobody else's. 'Specially not yours."

She stood her ground. "Indeed it is my concern, Mr. Spencer, despite your profane denial—all of ours, as we are the ones who have to look at you day in and day out, wondering each time you explore your beard if we are soon to be infested with the vermin therein."

"*I . . . ain't . . . got . . . bugs,*" he spat out, loudly enough to make her ears ring.

She made a tight moue of her lips and said no more, watching him struggle to get his temper in hand. Had she thought he would listen, she'd have suggested he try counting to ten.

"Goin' to the barn, for rope," he announced, teeth clenched, jaw knotted, and abruptly departed.

He appeared more in control when he returned some

time later, though obviously unwilling to join her in the lightest conversation. She ceased in her futile attempts to engage him to add another heated kettle of water to the others in the washtub. When she straightened, he was gone, and just as well. Faced with the busy day she'd planned for herself, she did not wish for Mr. Spencer to guess her intended thoroughness involving the task at hand until he first spied the results of her handiwork—his own clean, sweet-smelling garments. Happily anticipating his appreciation, his gratitude, his praise for her initiative and successful completion of the task at hand without mishap, Madeline examined the piles of dirty laundry on the floor surrounding her, gathered from various sources, segregated by color and fabric, as logic dictated.

"White things first, while the water is hottest and cleanest," she announced aloud, dumping the entire bundle into the scalding bath. "Whyever Mama's housekeeper complained so on washday, I cannot imagine. This is going to be easy."

Moments later, Madeline tapped a rapid tattoo with one foot, blistered forefinger thrust into her mouth, staring down into the tub where soap bubbles mixed with steam, surveying the evidence of her first mistake—a tub so full of garments that no room remained for the kettle of snow with which she hoped to cool the water sufficiently to dip in her hands. From that point onward each new difficulty, every hard-won solution, served to prove her hasty optimism wrong. Her hands grew raw and red, and so sore she could scarcely ring out the last few items. Her back ached the entire length of her spine, and her feet hurt as if her shoes were two sizes too small. Her violet merino gown had suffered still further abuse, possibly ending its wearability altogether, water-stained as now it was from collar to hem, and ripped out beneath both arms in her final descent down the ladder from the loft, having hung the last of the wash, Mr. Spencer's, there.

Day-long task completed at last, Madeline flung herself down on the bed, too weary to care that she had nothing to wear, too worn to respond to the cramping grumble of her empty stomach due to missing lunch. Upon a pewter plate on the table lay the forgotten cold, sliced pork and biscuits Lucy had left for her before returning out-of-doors for the impromptu picnic she declined to join. Never, in all her nearly twenty years, had she experienced this kind of exhaustion.

But, oh my, she could not recall ever having felt such a sense of accomplishment! And pride in her hard-won, if modest, success.

Madeline's euphoria, and her solitude, lasted a scant few seconds more. Door striking wall announced Sam Spencer's arrival even before he called out to her.

"Woman, where're you hidin'? I'm needin' an extra pair of hands."

The strident urgency in his voice sent her scrambling off the bed and out from behind her drying petticoats.

"I'm here. What's wrong? What's happened? The children—oh, merciful heaven, what have you done to yourself?"

He stood in the center of the room, one large hand wrapped protectively around the other, blood dripping into the earthen floor from between his fingers.

He gave her a wary glance.

"You ain't goin' pass out over a little blood, are you?"

"I—I don't think so." She swallowed hard and took a deep breath. "How seriously injured are you?"

"Not sure. Haven't looked up close. Hatchet slipped."

"But you're so skill—"

"I wasn't wieldin' it."

"Who—?"

"Never mind that. Need you to get me a pan full of snow to stick my hand into. Cold'll slow the bleedin', stop it altogether if I'm lucky. No, not the cookin' kettle, use a dishpan."

She hastened to comply, meeting up with a cluster of frightened children blocking the doorway.

"Is he bleedin' to death?" asked Jane with more curiosity than distress.

"Of course not. His injury is only a scratch, I'm certain. The greatest help you all can be is to pick up and put away your supplies and equipment. I'm sure we've all done enough work for one day. Go along now. Your uncle will return directly to supervise."

Surprised by her own steady voice and their prompt disbursal to do as she bade, she scooped up the cleanest snow she could find, her hands shaking so badly that she could scarcely keep from dumping it back onto the ground. Stomach churning, snow-filled pan balanced on one hip, she closed the gaping door behind her. Afraid he would hear a quaver in her voice, she silently set the pan before him as he sat at the table. He plunged his hand into it up to his wrist, scowling.

"Damn . . . cold."

Ignoring his profanity, she watched with grim fascination as pink stains spread throughout pristine white.

"How . . . how long before this works?"

"Might need more snow."

"I'll fill the other pan."

She returned to find him examining his wound, a gaping gash along the pad of his thumb, tip to palm, from which blood continued to seep. He held it up for her to see.

"It's stoppin'. Looks like I'll live to devil you another day." He winked and flashed a quick grin, grimacing when he inadvertently flexed his wounded digit.

"Well, thank fortune for that," Madeline retorted with forced light sarcasm.

His eyes lit at her attempted humor. "Bandages in the tin box on the shelf over there. Ointment too. Figure you can fix me up?"

"I believe I can manage the thumb, Mr. Spencer. As to your other imperfections . . ."

She left the rest unspoken, merely shaking her head, as she fetched him the tin and set out needed supplies. She applied a stinging salve, eliciting from him a sharp intake of breath and extended exhale, then wrapped the injured thumb as he directed, around and around, down and around the wrist twice before securing it, so intensely aware of the intimacy in the simple act that she could scarcely concentrate. Heat radiated between them, so close in proximity that she could hear his deep, steady breathing. The flesh of his hand was surprisingly smooth to the touch where not callused from a lifetime of physical labor. Madeline felt the structure of bone, the flexing of muscle, and her knees wobbled.

"You ain't goin' pass out on me now it's all over, are you?" he challenged, but companionably.

She tied the last knot, immediately stepping back.

"Over a minor injury such as that? Of course not!" Then, to change the subject, "How did you say it happened?"

He lifted his broad shoulders in a shrug.

"Didn't. My own fault for trustin' that boy with my hatchet."

"Which boy?"

"Paul. Kid's all thumbs." She winced at his attempted pun. "When it comes to handlin' tools, an' about the clumsiest young'n I've ever laid eyes on, all the time trippin' over his own feet an' droppin' everythin' I put into his hands, includin' my best hatchet. Shouldn't've tried to catch it before it landed in the dirt. That was my own danged fault.'' He shook his head ruefully, hoisting himself to his feet. ''Better be gettin' out there, show them kids I ain't breathed my last.''

At the door, he paused, raising his wounded hand. ''Thanks for the nursin'. Done good.''

Sam put off mitten-making lessons he'd planned for the evening until his thumb stopped throbbing some; not a single one of them objected, not even Maddie . . . that woman. One by one, fresh from their baths behind her hide curtain, they took themselves off to bed, eyes drooping closed, feet dragging, worn out with a good day's labor. Sam didn't have the heart to tell them tomorrow'd be another just like it, and the day after that until two rooms stood sound against the weather yet to come and ready to move into . . . the end of the week at the earliest. He'd push them harder if he dared, get those rooms finished and occupied so he'd have himself a decent night's shut-eye free of thinking, and dreaming, of Maddie Preston sleeping, and snoring, little more'n an arm's reach away.

He waited, listening, until he was certain sure everyone was sound asleep, including her, then filled the tub for himself in the light of the flickering hearth. Didn't hurt a fellow to indulge in a little hot water once in a while. He was especially planning on scrubbing hair and beard with strong lye soap, if only to prove to himself he wasn't infested. Dammit, he didn't have no critters living in his chin whiskers, no matter what *she* said. Scratching his beard helped him think, was all.

Before he climbed into the tub, he knelt before it, dunked his head in to the neck, coming up sputtering, muttering ''hot!'' He lathered well and dunked again to rinse, rewarded for his efforts by confirming himself bug-free with the absence of bodies floating feet up on the

water's soapy surface. *Knew there wouldn't be!* First thing
Three Fingers and Bertie insisted on the winter he stayed
with them was daily bathing, outside, in their own spring-
fed pond, no matter the temperature or weather conditions—a habit he had never broken himself of, and which
served him well now when thinking about that woman got
him all het up, in more ways than one.

Sam settled into the bathwater, knees to chest, head
bent beneath a curtain of hair, eyes closed, letting welcome
heat soak the soreness out of his muscles, trying to keep
his mind on something, anything, other than Madeline
Preston. He forced himself to plan out tomorrow's work
on the room, what came next, who he'd have help on
what.

His thoughts floated, like soap bubbles on the surface
of his bathwater, drifting away from the here and now,
recollecting now what that pile of milled boards'd been
intended for—the nursery he'd never got around to building for their baby, his and Hettie's. Always putting it off
for one reason or other, until there was no reason any
more to build it.

Sam lifted his heavy head, vigorously dry-scrubbing his
face, with his good hand, eyes closed, in an effort to rub
away bad memories threatening to cloud his brain. At a
slight sound, his eyes flew open. Maddie stood just in front
of her hide curtain, wrapped in a fur robe, unbound raven
hair spilling down all around to her waist, purple eyes
startled, like a doe caught in lantern light and poised for
flight. By the spirits, she made a pretty picture. His body
answered, growing taut and needy. Chest tight, he stared
right back at her. Waited.

"I—I heard a sound."

He cleared his throat.

"Just me. Takin' a turn bathin'."

"I didn't mean to intrude . . . Can I—get you anything?"

He answered without thinking. "You can scrub my back if you've a mind. Thumb's botherin' me somethin' fierce." He held up the injured digit, bandage soaked and unraveling. *Now, why the hell'd I say that?*

She took one small step into the room.

Sam held his breath.

She took another, her face alive with indecision. He saw the exact instant she made up her mind. Crossing the room, she knelt behind him. He handed her the bar of soap over his shoulder, taking short, shallow breaths.

"Lean forward, please."

He complied, forehead to knees, trying to keep his mind as blank as new snow. He heard the soft swish of her lathering her hands, felt the first tentative touch of those hands. He lifted an arm to swing his hair out of her way, glad for the abundance of it falling over his face. Her stroking hands moved across his shoulders, down to the waist, their touch firmer now, slow and exploring. *Thunderation, what's she doin' to me?*

He had half a mind to tell her to stop; the rest of him wasn't cooperating. All too soon, her hands fell away on their own. But she stayed put.

Sam swiveled, knees tight together to spare her the sight of his arousal. Her fur robe had fallen to the floor unheeded; the lacy bit of fabric covering her breasts, high and round and pebbled, had gone transparent with water. She didn't notice, maybe didn't care. The look on her face, all mesmerized and misty, set his stomach to quivering.

"Maddie . . . ? Maddie!"

He rose out of the tub, taking her with him, hands gripping her upper arms. In a single move, he stepped out in front of her, pulling her tightly against him. He buried his face in her freshly washed hair, breathing deeply of her own unique scent. She made a small sound, not of protest—of pleasure, he was sure—encouraging Sam to lift his head, find her lips, drink deeply of their sweetness. And, glory be, he found her as thirsty as himself.

The kiss lasted a good long time, long enough for his hands to trace the length of her spine, for hers to sink into the hair at the back of his neck and hang on. Long enough for him to urge her lips open with his tongue, and hers to mimic his explorations. She shifted a bit, her thigh coming in contact with his hardness, causing an involuntary jerk of the unruly member.

She leapt away as if burned, giving his manhood a quick glance. Her eyes went wide, confused first, afraid next. She tossed a frantic look around the room, everywhere and anywhere but at him and his.

"Now, Maddie—"

"Madeline," she spat out, but halfheartedly. "I—I'm sorry. I—I shouldn't have . . . I can't . . . oh!" Her hands flew up to cover her mouth. "Merciful Providence, what have I done?"

He caught her shoulders. "You—*we* ain't done nothing so bad as to get that worked up about."

"You are . . ." She darted an overall look at him, then herself, wet underthings leaving little to the imagination. "I—I'm . . . oh, no!"

She wrenched herself out of his grip and spun away, darting to safety behind her barricade.

"Damn!" said Sam, but softly. He looked down at himself. "All your danged fault, Ol' Hoss. Thanks to you, seems like we got ourselves a midnight swim in icy water after all."

She sat on the edge of her bed, scarcely breathing, heart hammering, until she was certain he'd dried off, dressed, and taken himself elsewhere. Then she curled into a tight ball under her covers, waiting for the throbbing in her lower regions to diminish, feeling shamed and shameless at the same time.

Why, oh, why had she looked out from behind her wall of hides? She knew it was Sam she heard, and what he was doing. She should have stayed safely in bed. Something beyond reason drove her to peek, something stronger still to respond to his invitation to help him bathe. Sweet mercy, his flesh had felt marvelous under her soapy ministrations, hard and soft, strong and smooth, the broad, muscled expanse so indomitable and vulnerable at one and the same time. The sensations evoked took her away to a place far beyond reason, to needs of her own so primal she could not deny them.

Nothing, not warnings, not innuendoes, nor love-inspired confidences, had prepared her for the reality of her responses to this man. She could no more have stemmed them than ceased the beat of her heart. Awareness surfaced slowly, all too slowly. She could not believe what his nakedness revealed, how large he was, how compelling, terrifying, his intent so clearly displayed.

And she had wanted . . . how badly she had wanted to learn more, discover more. Wanted him as much as he obviously desired her.

More frightened of herself than for herself, she had fled. And now she cursed herself for her cowardice. Her wantonness. The base humanness which would not have denied him again had he pursued her.

Long hours she tossed upon her tangled bed, dwelling upon possible future encounters, one question surfacing over and over without answer. Would she have the strength to turn away Sam Spencer should he approach her once more, especially as she was mortally afraid that he might be the one her misguided heart had chosen to love?

Chapter Eight

"What happened to your face, miss? Cat scratch ya?"

Jane piped up from the breakfast table the moment Madeline made her rather tardy entrance, having lain awake until almost dawn.

"Ain't no cat hereabouts," her twin scoffed in fair imitation of his uncle.

"Looks more like a rash, miss," Lucy ventured.

Madeline pressed her palms to her cheeks and felt a faint tenderness. "Perhaps from the soap with which I washed clothes yesterday. It was rather harsh."

Jane concurred with a brief, satisfied nod. "Your hands is all red, too."

At the table's head, Sam Spencer made no comment as he stoically scooped porridge from the bowl to his mouth, not so much as acknowledging her arrival by word or look. The matter was dropped. As the morning meal progressed, Madeline caught his frequent glances her way whenever he didn't think she noticed, saw the thoughtful frown then

creased his brow, uncertain what his reason might be, other
than that he regretted their intimacies of the previous
night. She knew he had slept as little as she. Shortly after
they ... their ... after she retired, she had listened to
his restless movements until he finally exited the cabin
altogether. Though he attempted to keep the sounds of
his labors to a minimum, she could hear him just on the
other side of the wall supporting her bed, working on the
addition until the first rays of morning.

She noticed immediately that the tub used for washing
and bathing had been removed from the cabin, grateful
she would not be faced with this tangible reminder of her
indiscretion, as if she could ever forget.

Like guilty, skulking cowards, neither she nor Sam Spencer made an appearance until the children had risen to fill
the room with their distracting chatter. Of all the tensions
suffered in each other's presence thus far, this was by far
the worst; for the first time in her life Madeline found
herself tongue-tied, shy. What did one say to a virtual
stranger after seeing him as naked as the day he was born,
after having willingly exchanged all but the final act of
conjugation with him?

What in the world had possessed her to look out from
behind her curtain of hides last night? She knew he was
bathing, had tossed and turned upon her lumpy bed trying
to block mental visions of him in the act of making his
ablutions, until she was driven to blend reality with imagination. The mountain man proved even more marvelously
built than she could have envisioned, every inch of him
lean and muscled, and that which she had seen on no man
before so fascinating, she could not force herself to look
away even after he spied her watching. With need far
beyond her control, beyond mere curiosity, she had
accepted his invitation to wash his back. Her soapy hands
freely explored the length and breadth of his back as far

as she dared go. Her married friends had never so much as hinted at the delightful sensations resulting from so humble an act, the memory of which remained alive and as potent with every reliving.

Sweet mercy, what was she to do now? How could she live in such close proximity with this man, with whom she'd grown so infatuated, without betraying herself further by word or deed? What must he think of her wantonness? And why should the good opinion of this crude mountain man be of any concern of hers, though she could not resist his physical attributes? Her last thought before sleeping after their intimate encounter—that she might have actually fallen in love with him—in the light of day she hotly, vehemently, denied. Impossible. The most unlikely match imaginable—for either of them. Were the time spent together in the crowded confines of this small place not destined soon to end, they would verbally slash each other to shreds in no time. She could no more live in his world than he in hers. Unimaginable. As intriguing as she might find the man on a purely corporeal level, a union on any other would be disastrous, absolute folly. Still, she found herself wondering, daydreaming of the impossible, hoping . . .

Madeline was more than a little relieved when, immediately after breakfast, Sam shrugged into his fur coat without a word.

James jumped up. "We goin' start workin' on the room, now?"

Over his shoulder, his uncle replied, "Somethin' I gotta tend to first. On m'own."

"What're we supposed to do 'til you get back?" whined Jane.

"Plenty to do, like takin' down them danged clothes before someone gets all tangl—" The rest broke off with the slamming door.

142 Pamela Quint Chambers

"Let's each of us gather his or her own," interjected Madeline to postpone further protest.

At once, Lucy took the twins in hand, suggesting making a game of being the first to complete the task. Paul rejected the idea with scornful silence, going to sit cross-legged by the fire, taking up a stick to poke a log back in place, staring moodily into the leaping flames. Elbows on knees, palms supporting chin, his rawboned features set in grim lines, he withdrew into himself, as was his all-too-frequent habit. In a flare of comprehension, it occurred to Madeline that he might be attempting to mask the pain of his recent loss, of change, of growing up, with deliberate, sullen separateness. Some impulse prompted her to pull up a stool beside him, to attempt to engage him in conversation.

"I find myself seeing stories in those dancing flames." He gave no indication he'd heard her. "Especially in the evening when there is so little to do, and nothing at all to read." His head cocked at a listening angle. "Reading is one of my favorite pastimes." He glanced her way. *Ah, now I have his attention!* "I'll read anything I can get my hands on, Mama says, including soup can labels if nothing else presents itself. Unfortunately, there's not so much as a single can of soup anywhere around here . . . I've looked."

The moody teen did not speak, or further acknowledge her presence for so long an interval that she almost gave up, leaving him to his brooding solitude.

"Had me a copy of *Last of the Mohicans* at the fort."

He startled her with the abruptness of his contribution, but she took hasty advantage of the small beginning.

"I so enjoy James Fenimore Cooper's novels. Did you bring it with you?"

Madeline's hopes rose, as thrilled with having reached the boy, if only in a very minor way, as with the prospect of something to read, or in this instance, reread. Paul shook his head, dashing her expectations.

"*He* wouldn't let me. Said books'd take up space best used for supplies."

"Surely one small book . . ."

She bit back her frustrated retort, loathe to undermine any further the tenuous authority his uncle had over the boy.

"Space is at a premium when supplies must be hauled in to the wilderness on one's own back. Have you read any other of Cooper's Leatherstocking series—*The Prairie, The Pathfinder, The Deerslayer,* or the first, *The Pioneer?*" He muttered a soft "no," bony cheeks flushed with more than heat from the fire. Embarrassment over literary shortcomings? Frustration of a budding scholar over the lack of a good book? Had she struck a tentative chord with the boy? Madeline dared not pursue it further, concluding, rather inanely, as she stood, "They are rousing good tales, one and all, fit for future reading. Well, I'd best help take down and fold the laundry."

"All done, miss," said Lucy from the table put in service for sorting garments by ownership.

"Oh—oh, well then. Thank you."

"How's come my blue skirt's got red spots all over it?" Jane held the garment up against her waist, looking from it to Madeline, an accusing grimace on her small face.

Dismayed, Madeline apologized, "I don't know how it happened, but I'm afraid a number of things came out of the washwater that way. I had hoped the spots would disappear when the clothing dried."

"Colored things'll run if the water's too hot, miss," said Lucy mildly. "It's usually best to be on the safe side, washin' blue with blue an' red with red, not mixin' 'em."

"I—I didn't know." Madeline's words barely whispered out past the sense of failure swelling in her chest.

"You'll do better next time, miss." An unasked question remained in Lucy's eyes.

"Is there more?" Madeline asked weakly.

Biting her lip, Lucy hesitated. "Well, miss, I don't guess no one told you about rinsin' . . . Gotta get the soap out, or it'll make you itch. 'Specially Baby's things . . . left-in soap'll give her a rash."

"I—I didn't . . ." Madeline's words choked off altogether, her eyes stung with tears she refused to shed before the youngsters.

"It don't much matter, miss," Lucy comforted her. "If Uncle'll bring the tub back inside, we can rinse 'em up real quick."

Madeline cleared her throat. "I'm sure I can manage that simple a chore unassisted."

"Yes, miss."

"What about Uncle Sam's stuff upstairs?" Jane demanded. "It's in the way."

"I'll deal with that, too." And better left to be done privately, in case some new disaster awaited her. "I'll also wash and dry the dishes, having already proven myself competent at that task."

James spoke up from behind the pile of folded laundry in his arms.

"So long's ya don't *sing* while yer at it."

Madeline flushed. "Rest assured, I shall not. At least not within anyone else's hearing."

From inside the only empty stall in the barn, Sam let out a string of cuss words that singed his own ears.

"Why the bloody blue blazes am I doin' this, anyway?" he asked his scowling reflection in the sliver of mirror balanced on a scrap of two-by-four nailed crosswise to a support post. His half-shaved image scowling back made no reply. "Ain't like that woman's likely to suffer any more scratchin' from this here beard of mine again any time soon. Likely never.''

He was sure as hell relieved that he was the only one recognizing those red abrasions on her cheeks for what they were! Twice as glad no one, including Maddie—especially Maddie—had any idea how he hankered after the woman. One damn fascinating female was Maddie Preston, never a dull minute with her around, challenging his every word, raising his hackles with every one of hers. She gave him notions he had no right to be thinking, all softhearted and softheaded in a way he never wanted to feel again, knowing how hurtful things could end. Double dang, why'd he open his mouth last night, invite her to join him? Damn-fool thing to do. Shouldn't've kissed her, leaving him still wanting her so bad this morning, he could taste her on his lips.

Sam cast a glance in Ol' Clyde's direction. The mule watched Sam's every move with those big brown eyes, placid and accepting, his head hanging over the shoulder-high wall between his stall and Sam's make-do barber shop.

''Should've given a might more thought to choppin' off my chin whiskers,'' he admitted at length to the companionable beast. ''No sense in mournin' the loss, beard'll grow back in no time. Can't leave it this way anyhow. Startin' to look like a stranger to you, ain't I, Clyde? To me, too. Ain't gone around barefaced since . . . well, don't remember when.''

That was a bald-faced lie. He knew the exact day, nearly to the hour, when he gave up daily shaving. The day he came home from a trip to Fort Farewell to learn his wife, his Hettie, had passed on while he was gone. After that, shaving didn't much matter. And shouldn't now, except for those red blotches on Maddie's tender cheeks.

''Ain't 'cause of her I'm doin' this, you know.''

Clyde snorted agreement, bobbing his head.

"Well, I ain't. It's just . . ." No reason came to mind. "Damn blast it! Women!"

He finished shaving himself clean, saving his full mustache on principle alone. A quick once-over and he chopped a couple of inches off the hair hanging down his back, leaving his braids untouched. His head felt ten pounds lighter. He studied himself, seeing a stranger, a man with all the boy worn off, weathered and wind-burned and hard-edged, like his mountain. He liked what he saw. Would Maddie? What the hell did he care? But, dammit, he did, more than he was willing to confess, even to Clyde—or himself!

Sam set his trimming shears next to his bit of mirror. "Time to face the firin' squad. Wish me luck."

Madeline guiltily broke off her soft humming mid-bar the moment she heard him scrape snow off his feet outside the cabin door. She turned from her dishwater, wiping soapy hands on her flour-sack apron, her request for the washtub on her lips to forestall anything else being spoken of between them. At his entrance, the question died unasked, her mouth fell open, and she openly stared. And stared. Absently grateful the children had gone outside to play and wouldn't witness her gape-mouthed discomposure.

Sweet mercy, clean-shaven, Sam Spencer was the handsomest man she'd ever set eyes on!

A strong jaw—jutting a bit too stubbornly—a wide, generous mouth—rather lopsided, cocked a bit to the right—long creases in his cheeks accenting too-prominent cheek bones, but making her hungry to see him smile.

Instead, that wonderful mouth—that she had so recently kissed—turned down in a frown.

"What're you starin' at, woman?" he growled.

"You . . . shaved."

The lower part of his face, considerably paler than the upper, turned red; he wouldn't meet her eyes.

"Shaved, 's all. Didn't grow two heads."

"Excuse my staring. I was simply so . . . surprised."

"How about pulling yourself together if you've stared your fill, an' tell me what you done with my other set of duds. I'm all over itchin' with hair clippin's down inside've these I'm wearin'."

Her hands clutched convulsively at her waist. "Oh, my, I'd planned to surprise you, have them all neatly folded for you now they've dried. I forgot."

The color drained from his face; his eyes turned to flame, his voice to ice.

"You *washed* 'em? *My* clothes?"

Without speaking, she nodded, apprehension building.

"Who gave you leave to do a dang-fool thing like that?"

"They were soiled. And had an odd, pungent odor, and—"

"Where'd you put 'em?"

"I haven't had time to take them down—"

"*Where . . . are . . . they?*"

"Upstairs."

He took the ladder two rungs at a time; an instant later his bellow filled the cabin, forcing her to cover her ears. An interminable silence followed, long and thick. She watched the ladder, breathlessly waiting, until his moccasined feet appeared on the top rung. He descended with back against the ladder, arms extended, clutching board-like shapes resembling the fringed hide pants and shirt he wore.

"What—what happened to them?" she asked weakly.

His chest heaved once, twice, before he spoke, tone even, without emotion.

"Deer hide don't take to water. *'Specially* not hot water."

"How . . . how then does one clean . . .?"

"Don't. Dress it by scrapin' an' stretchin', smoke it proper before makin' it into somethin' to wear, an' it'll stay soft an' water resistant practically forever. Don't need no washin'."

"But the odor—"

"Smell's natural. Can't take a good, natural stink now an' again, you don't belong out in the wild."

Wounded by the unexpected sting in his words, though the truth, Madeline gripped her hands together more tightly, lifting her chin.

"That, Mr. Spencer, is a conclusion I have also reached. Fortunately, we shall not have to endure each other's company once the snow has melted sufficiently to allow me to leave, hopefully soon."

He scowled heavily.

"Damned fortunate, woman. I ain't got time enough in a day—in a lifetime—to clean up after the messes you make an' the damage you do, helpin' out."

Fury bubbled up within her and overflowed.

"You ungrateful—ungrateful barbarian. Have you not a shred of gratitude for all my efforts? I have performed each and every task assigned me to the utmost of my ability, only to be criticized at every turn. I simply cannot sit idly by. You have no books, no writing paper, nothing at all with which to busy my hands. I—I would go mad with cabin fever if I did not find some form of occupation to fill the long days and longer nights."

"There's always plenty of mendin', socks an' the like," Sam interjected, his tone hopeful, faintly apologetic.

"I sew even more poorly than I do laundry."

Sam scratched his clean-shaven jaw, frowned, then ceased mid-scratch, as though the gesture failed to elicit the same results as prior to shaving. She watched him struggle with the problem, saw his frown ease with decision.

"I'll teach you to hammer an' saw, same's the kids. Your room, might's well put you to work buildin' it."

"A grand idea, Mr. Spencer. I would very much like to contribute to its construction."

"That's buildin'. *Not* supervisin'."

"Of course. I understand. You are completely in charge. May we begin at once? Oh, but what will you wear?"

Sam held the stiff deerhide aloft.

"These're fit for nothin' but burnin'."

Madeline saw his gaze flit to the humpback trunk, away, then reluctantly back again. Hers followed his, guilt flaring as always when she viewed that which contained his most private possessions—and the evidence of her violation.

"There's the homespun I arrived in these mountains wearin'," he admitted, resigned.

"Thank fortune for that!" Madeline agreed too heartily.

Fearing intrusion, she busied herself with completing her dish-washing, in water gone cold and scummy. Sneaking repeated glances over her shoulder, she saw him kneel, pause with head bowed, slowly lift the lid until it rested against the wall, pause again—this time longer—then reach inside as if the contents might scald. At last he began a methodical search, rummaging and sorting, taking so long that she wanted to scream because she could not keep her gaze from him to save herself, his profile as splendid and dear to her—in spite of the slight bump on the bridge of his nose and stubborn chin—as was all else about the man.

He set some items on the far side of the trunk; she couldn't see what they were. He laid several articles of clothing across his knees, quite a pile of them, then stirred around some more, clear to the bottom, bending almost head-first inside. Apparently he intended to perform a thorough job of it, once begun. At last, he rocked back, gently closing the lid. He ran a hand lightly over the scratches and gouges she had inflicted. Madeline bit back another apology betraying her having spied on his privacy. Rising in a single, flowing move, he looked her way. She quickly turned back to her labors. He came up beside her so quietly, she jumped when he spoke.

"It ain't purple, but it's clean an' whole. An' washable, when the fancy strikes."

She faced him, her soapy hands flying to her cheeks at what he held up for her inspection.

"Oooooh!"

Blinking furiously to clear away the mist clouding her eyes, Madeline stretched one wet hand toward the garment dangling from his fists at chest height, a simple dress of nut-brown dyed homespun. She pulled back her wet hand before reaching the fabric, fisting it with her other between her breasts, feasting her eyes on his miraculous discovery— a change of clothes for herself as well, clean and whole and serviceable, and approximately her size. Though the unfortunate color would turn her skin pale and sallow and fade the violet of her eyes, the mere thought of a change of clothing after months in the same dress, made these minor flaws inconsequential.

"If you don't mind hand-me-downs, that is. Been stored away more'n eight years. Past time for wearin' again, though it smells a might musty."

"I don't mind. Not at all."

He handed the garment into her eager hands, hastily dried on her apron. She clutched it to her as if it were the choicest of treasures. He would have left then without another word had she not stopped him, asking, "Whose—?"

Over his shoulder he said, "Wife's. Long gone."

"Gone?"

"Dead."

"Oh!"

He snatched up a pile of homespun from the floor beside the trunk and leapt up the ladder to the attic without so much as a backward glance.

Madeline sat down, hard, on the stool beside the table, what little he had said spinning in her brain. Sam Spencer had been married. Questions crowded in so fast, she couldn't put words to them. Unfamiliar emotions—jealousy to the fore—swamped her ability to think or reason. Before she could make sense of any of it, Sam came back down the ladder. He wore a shirt of the same fabric as the dress he had offered her, the warm brown color of it turning his windburned and sun-weathered skin golden. The shirt, unbuttoned at the collar to expose a glimpse of curling hair, he'd tucked into a pair of suspendered gray pants, also tucked in to his knee-high, fringed moccasins. Beardless, and with mane trimmed to shoulder length—except for the long, twin braids swinging against his cheeks—in homespun he looked more civilized by far than the wild mountain man of before. Contrarily, Madeline missed that untamed fellow.

Across a distance of less than ten feet, they stared at each other warily. Sam spoke first, with a toss of his head in the trunk's direction.

"Set out a couple of books I found inside. Yours to read come evenin', if you want."

"I—I do . . . I will. Thank you."

"After you change, I'll show you what needs doin' outside. Be sure an' wear that fur robe you favor. Nippy out this mornin' 'til you work up a sweat."

"I—I will. Thank—"

He was already gone, as was his habit.

On her way to her enclosure to change, Madeline picked up the stack of three books, reading the spines. *Pilgrim's Progress, Robinson Crusoe,* and the third not designated. Relishing the anticipation in waiting, Madeline promised herself to save discovering what the last volume contained until evening.

She stripped down to chemise, drawers, and petticoats, stepping out of a puddle of the remains of the violet merino, hopefully for the final time. She practically tore off the buttons of the separate top in her haste, dropping it beside the other, kicking both under the bed for later discarding, fit for nothing but burning. Madeline hoped she'd never have to set eyes on the offensive garments again.

Trembling with fear that it wouldn't fit, she stepped into the one-piece dress, slipping her arms into generous armholes, buttoning the row of irregularly shaped buttons from neck to below the shirred waist as fast as her fingers could work them.

Sam's unknown wife had been a woman of slighter proportions in bust and waist than herself, though approximately the same height. The resulting snugness outlined her upper torso shamelessly. She refused to deny herself the pleasure of wearing the plain, serviceable, clean garment even so. Tossing over it the sleeveless fur robe, she hastened to join the others outside, eager to contribute.

The day proved crisp and cold and gloriously sunny. Madeline knew better by now than to trust that sunshine meant an end to the blizzards that seemingly sprang up from one moment to the next. She vowed to relish this respite nonetheless, however long it lasted.

"Gracious, look at your progress!" she exclaimed at seeing for the first time the frame structure awaiting only siding and roof boards and interior finishing.

Sam and Paul glanced up briefly from the rough sketch scratched in charcoal upon a plank, quickly dismissing her arrival in favor of some construction lesson for Paul's benefit, clearly reluctantly imparted and unwillingly learned.

A surge of unreasonable disappointment marred her happy expectations of the mountain man's appreciation of her improved appearance. Vowing that she would hereafter feign indifference as well, Madeline turned her back on the unresponsive lout.

Lucy smiled a silent greeting, returning to her mother-hen attempts to restrain the twins from their snowball fight in favor of collecting and disposing of wood scraps for kindling.

"Can I help?" Madeline volunteered.

The girl's expression went from frustrated to grateful. "If you would, miss. The twins have been workin' right along like the rest of us, good as you please, but bein' youngsters, they tire real fast of all work an' no play."

"With all the progress that's been made, they deserve to indulge themselves for a little while. Though inexperienced, I am certain I can manage to determine the difference between usable lengths and waste." She couldn't quite manage to keep the sarcasm out of her voice, still stung over Sam's appraisal of her ineptitude.

"Thanks, miss. The two've us oughta finish pickin' up right quick."

No sooner had the work area been cleared of debris than Sam called to them all to gather about, twins included, and no more nonsense about it. He appeared annoyed, and Paul bad-tempered and rebellious. Whatever they'd been laboring over together had not gone well for either one.

"I figure after I teach Maddie the fine art of hammerin', I'll have her an' Lucy in charge of nailin' up the sidin'. I'll cut it to length, an' Paul'll be haulin' from the supply behind the barn back here."

With a glare all around, he dared anyone to disagree, resting his gaze the longest on Paul. The boy clamped his lips tight around some ready retort. With a parting glare, he stomped off over the trampled path to the barn, Wolf trailing behind.

"What 'bout us?" demanded Jane.

"Past time to clean out the animals' stalls."

"Barn stinks. I wanta help on my room," Jane insisted.

Sam's jaw jumped as he gave the child his undivided attention. "After you finish in the barn."

"I'm scared of them big horses an' things."

"Mules."

"Them mules is scary-lookin'."

He forced what resembled a smile, but was more a pained grimace. "You'd be funny-lookin' too if your mama was a mare—that's female horse, for them's don't know—an' your daddy a jackass."

"Mr. Spencer!"

"What's a jackass?"

"Male ass."

"Mr. Spencer!"

"What's a—"

"Mr. Spencer!"

"A donkey. Okay to say donkey, Miss Preston?"

"Quite all right, Mr. Spencer. Please remember hereafter that little pitchers have big ears."

"If that ain't one of the dumbest sayin's, I don't know what is. Scoot, you two." The twins scampered off, leaving Sam's singular attention for her. "You plannin' on spendin' the day jawin' or workin'?"

"Working, of course, once you have given me the proper instruction. Does one hold the hammer thusly?"

"Only if one's tryin' to drive the nail into her own forehead. Flat side out, claw in, works a whole heck of a lot better."

Sam's hand closed over hers to demonstrate, as she had secretly hoped—despite earlier resolve—when feigning utter ignorance. He fairly radiated strength and heat; Mad-

eline felt herself begin to melt beneath his touch, chill
when he backed off quickly. Paul arrived soon thereafter,
staggering under an armload of lumber. Boards clattered
down around their feet. Paul rubbed one shoulder as
though it pained him, but said nothing, eyes downcast.

"Easier on your back to bring fewer, make more trips."

Without comment, Paul stalked back toward the barn.

"Can't figure that boy out. What's he got to be so mean-
spirited about?" Sam raked the fingers of both hands
through the shorn locks at his nape.

"Perhaps anger is the only way he knows of expressing
his distress over the recent drastic changes in his life and
in himself."

Sam's hands stilled, then fell to his sides. She saw in his
expression that she'd struck a chord of understanding,
and that he found less satisfaction than she'd hoped in it.

"Longer we stand here palaverin', shorter the workday
for buildin' your room."

"Rooms."

"Rooms!"

"Let us not further delay, then, Mr. Spencer. I am eager
and willing to master whatever skills you feel necessary to
impart, and shall labor as hard and fast and long as the
rest of you to ensure rapid completion."

Hours later, she regretted those cavalier words, for he
worked her almost beyond enduring. Throughout, she
made no protest, offered no complaint, in fact thrilled to
take an active part in raising the walls, helping Lucy and
her siblings hoist long timbers onto the roof for Sam to
hammer in place, even after she wasn't certain if she'd
survive until Sam called a halt when it became too dark
to continue.

The day's labors had taken their toll on her. Exhaustion

too deep for sleeping, every muscle screaming protest, Madeline spent the evening sitting by the hearth, soaking a smashed and swollen finger in a cup of snow. Sam had excused her from the postponed lesson in mitten-making, volunteering to make her pair himself because of her injury. He and the children cut and sewed companionably around the table. On her lap lay the three volumes Sam had lent her, as yet unopened. The effort seemed almost beyond her, but curiosity to know what the unidentified book might be finally overcame listlessness. It could be poetry, a collection of sermons, possibly one of those missives regarding housekeeping so popular of late. Wouldn't the latter be fortuitous?

Eagerly, she opened the dark blue cover, instead discovering tidy, feminine handwriting crowding the page, the first words being, "Today Sam and me got married . . ."

Chapter Nine

Madeline's hand came down over the page, fingers splayed. She tossed a quick, guilty glance in Sam Spencer's direction. Absorbed with the children's mitten-making lessons, he didn't spare her a glance. Looking back to the page she'd hidden from view, Madeline struggled with temptation until she was forced to close the book, slip it under the other volumes on her lap, and open another in a futile attempt to resist. And could not concentrate on either Bunyan's prose or Defoe's when in her mind's eye all she could see was that simple phrase that said so much: *Today Sam and me got married.*

The date of that entry, as she recalled, was May 15, 1836, almost nine years ago. How long were they wed before she died, of what cause? Who was this mysterious narrator who had been Sam's bride? What was her name? Had he loved her deeply, devoted even beyond death? If so, why had he kissed her as he had last night? Unanswered questions barraged Madeline's brain until she could think of nothing else but seeking the answers within the blue covers of the journal.

Why else would he have given it to her along with the two works of fiction, if not for her to read?

But surely a private man like Sam Spencer would never allow a virtual stranger the freedom to invade his life so intimately.

Unless . . . unless he did not know the slender volume to be any different than the others. Probably had never even leafed through the pages between the indigo covers to observe that they were handwritten rather than printed. Because he could not read. And was incapable of seeking solace from the memories of his married life contained within those covers after his wife's untimely, and clearly lamented, demise.

Struck numb by this last thought, Madeline sat with hands idle in lap, staring reflectively into the dancing flames in the hearth.

If her conclusions were correct, now what was she to do with the small volume, and her knowledge of Sam Spencer's plight?

From across the room his voice boomed out.

"Done. That's the last pair, an' a good evenin's work. Time for bed."

"Do we *have* to go to bed?" protested Jane.

"If you want to get up bright an' early in the mornin' to finish up the outside work on your room, you do. Looks like someone's been dozin' already instead of readin' those books I found for her." He bobbed his head in Madeline's direction.

"Books?"

Hopeful expectation blossomed across Paul's usually sullen features, and in his unreliable voice. Conscience prickling, Madeline held up the two novels, ignoring Sam altogether for fear he'd see the nature of her contemplations reflected in her eyes.

"Pilgrim's Progress and *Robinson Crusoe.* Your uncle found them in his trunk along with his fresh change of clothes, and mine. You'll enjoy the latter, Paul, as adventuresome a tale as *Last of the Mohicans.*"

"What's that other'n?"

Madeline evaded. "Nothing nearly as exciting, and of little interest to a boy, I imagine. A woman's tale, of . . . of homemaking and such."

Truth and lie in the same breath, thought Madeline, uncommonly grateful when the lad accepted both without question, taking Defoe's castaway story from her outstretched hand and opening it immediately to the first page.

His uncle grabbed the book from his grasp. Slamming it shut, he placed it and the other two volumes he snatched from Madeline's lap on the mantel.

"Book readin' can wait 'til tomorrow evenin'. Mornin's goin' to be comin' around mighty early." He traded scowls with his rebellious nephew. "You got a problem with that, boy?"

A heavy pause stretched interminably long.

"No . . . sir," the boy grudgingly conceded at length. He spun away, stalking to the ladder and up without a backward glance.

Clearly, the line in the unspoken battle of wills between them had been all the more firmly entrenched, their many unresolved skirmishes foretelling some major conflict yet to come.

Madeline rose as swiftly as painful, protesting muscles permitted.

"By all means, let's retire. I for one am eager to finish the outside of the new rooms so we may begin on the interior."

Sam harrumphed.

"You heard Miss Maddie, off to bed with you all."

"Finish *my* room first, Uncle Sam," begged Jane.

"Ain't *your* room. You gotta share same's the rest've us," sneered James. " 'Sides, boys come 'head've girls. Goin' to finish *our* room first, Paul's an' mine—ain't ya, Uncle Sam?"

A warning sound rumbled in their uncle's throat, which the twins ignored.

"I'm goin' to have m'own bed. A big, big bed all to myself, ain't that right, Uncle Sam?"

"Are not! I heard Miss Maddie say you an' Lucy's gotta share. She gets a bed all to herself."

Another nonverbal warning from their uncle, this time louder, also went unheeded.

"I want a bed of my own."

"Can't have one," countered her twin.

"Can so if uncle says."

"Can *not.*"

"Can *too.*"

"Can't."

"Can."

The argument followed them into the loft under Lucy's gentle guidance, and beyond, dying down to sleepy whispers, drifting off at last to silence. With the children having retired, Madeline sought to fill the awkwardness between herself and the glowering mountain man with humor, if at his expense.

"Did I not warn you some while back that all those grumblings and growlings would lose their potency with overuse? I believe the twins have just demonstrated the truth of my prophesy quite pointedly. Wouldn't you agree?"

He cut off a rumble midway when she let him see her self-satisfied smile.

"That an 'I told you so' grin, woman?"

"Only if it doesn't jeopardize a big bed all to myself in the future, Mr. Spencer," she replied coyly.

"Wouldn't count on it."

"Then I herewith offer you my humblest apology."

"Hah! You an' humble bein' strangers, I ain't dependin' on your apology any more'n your willin'ness to let me have the last say."

"By all means, Mr. Spencer, say away."

"You got nothin' more to add?"

"Not a thing."

"Then how come you're standin' here jawin'?"

"I thought perhaps you were still searching for that elusive last word."

"This one's it. Go to bed, woman, before I gag an' hogtie you an' toss you there myself."

"Very well. I'm going."

"Go."

Reluctant to give up the game, Madeline swallowed her last rejoinder as his flushed face began darkening from scarlet to purple, secretly enjoying the ongoing competition for the final word nonetheless. She pretended indignation she did not feel, turning on her heel to march across the room and slip silently within her enclosure. She tried to resist having the last say this one time, listening to him move about, settle down in his bedroll beside the fire, but the temptation proved too strong.

"Good night, Mr. Spencer," she called sweetly. "Pleasant dreams."

No response. Either he had not heard, or he was pointedly ignoring her.

"Good night, Mr.—"

"Heard you the first time. 'Nother word an' I'm claimin' that bed of mine an' personally tossin' you into the draftiest stall in the barn. That worth the last word, woman?"

Ah, it was so tempting to come back with the pithy retort

already forming on her tongue. But what if he meant what
he said? Even for the last word, Madeline was not quite
willing to spend the night in an unheated barn upon a bed
of bug-infested straw in the company of large, malodorous
animals of uncertain disposition. She swallowed those
words, to relish and refine, as she quickly drifted off to
sleep, a smug smile on her lips, anticipation of their next
verbal encounter a warm spot in her heart.

Next morning, wearing Hettie's dress, with her black
hair braided and hanging to her waist, Madeline put away
freshly washed breakfast dishes. With her back to him, Sam
could almost imagine she *was* Hettie come back to life. Or
that Maddie'd been sent to his mountain cabin for the
soul purpose of taking Hettie's place—for the kids, and
for him. Dang! The woman was driving him loco, coming
up with that kind of crack-brained reasoning! Maddie Preston a mountain man's woman was about as likely as some
blue-ribbon, citified trotting horse taking to being used
for a pack mule. Sure'd be a challenge he'd like to give a
try, though . . . Maddie, not the horse.

Chore done, she spun around and caught him feasting
his eyes on her and grinning like a damned fool. All at once
shy and unsure, she looked away, over his left shoulder. Her
hands flew to her hair, smoothing down a few strays, then
to the back of her slender waist to untie her flour-sack
apron.

"Did you want something, Mr. Spencer? Oh, drat, I can't
get the knot out."

"I'll get it."

Two strides brought him face to face with her, real and
warm and reminding him so forcefully of what he'd been
thinking that his face went hot from the neck up. Her
cheeks were rosy red. She fussed with her apron in back,

those purple-flower eyes never looking straight at him. Maybe she'd been thinking of him, too, her thoughts no more pristine than his. The heat spread like wildfire all the way to his groin. Dang!

"Turn 'round!"

He hadn't meant to growl at her, it just came out that way. She did as he asked without comment or argument. Awful quiet and accommodating Miss Maddie Preston was this morning! Working away at the tight, wet knot at the small of her spine, Sam knew it wouldn't last. He'd say or do something she took exception to, and she'd be off and running with it, taking the two of them who knew where. Couldn't say he'd minded those trips all that much. Exchanging words with Maddie, competing for the last, brought something to the day he didn't even know he'd been missing.

The knot came free, but Sam hung on to the ends, dreading the end of this simple, pleasant moment between them, storing up memories for when she was gone.

"Can't you get it out, Mr. Spencer?"

"What? Oh, yeah. Just now. There you go."

Sam stepped back, whipping the apron off her as she spun to face him, presenting it to her, smirking like a brain-sick, love-struck fool. That 'love' word wiped the grin off his face right quick. She looked up at him squarely this time, steady and deep, a speculative frown pulling dark, winged brows toward her small, narrow nose. He figured he looked about as unhinged as he felt.

"Thank you, Mr. Spencer. I am now ready to lend a hand in completing outside construction of the rooms, if that's what you've come in to inquire after."

"No . . . I mean I didn't . . . That is I—er, we don't need you. Job's done."

"All done? So quickly? I'd hoped to be there." She sounded disappointed.

"Lots to do inside."

She cheered right up.

"Yes, there's that. Before we begin, however, I have some thoughts on the matter—"

"Have to keep 'til after lunch. We're takin' the rest of the mornin' off to make forts for a snowball fight."

"Snowball fight?"

"An' picnic. Nice day out. Sunny, not too cold. Whose side you wanta be on?"

She smiled, dimple rising just above heart-shaped beauty mark. *A mighty pretty sight,* thought Sam.

"The girls', of course. One would be rather foolish not to choose the winning side."

"Girls winnin'? Hah! Girls can't throw worth a—"

"I would pick my words carefully were I you, Mr. Spencer. It will be the females of this household who prepare that picnic lunch of which you anticipate partaking. I would also suggest you consider as carefully how accurately you take aim when firing your snowballs. An injury could possibly incapacitate one or both of those preparers."

"Yes, ma'am. Whatever you say, ma'am. I promise I won't hit a thing."

He raised one hand high, palm up, and pressed the other against his thumping heart, his grin gone so wide that his cheeks hurt. Thunderation, she made it worthwhile getting up in the morning just to see where her quick mind and ready tongue'd lead them next.

Words died between them, some things being best left unsaid, and with their passing, so went Sam's smile. He shifted uneasily from one foot to the other, cleared his throat, busting the silence with the first thing that came to mind.

"Be sure an' put on them new mittens I made you, fur side in. Sun's warm enough but snow'll give you frostbite if you ain't careful."

"I'll do that, Mr. Spencer. Thank you for making them for me."

"How's the finger?"

"My finger? Oh! Fine, fine. Fully recovered. How is your thumb?"

"That's fine too."

"I—I'll go get the mittens, then. And that fur robe . . . the one with the armholes . . . if you think I need to wear it."

" 'Til you get heated up some. I'll be puttin' those sleeves on it for you sometime real soon. Maybe tonight."

"I'd appreciate that, thank you."

"Be headin' on out then."

"I will join you—all of you—shortly!"

Took near a minute, seemed like, before either of them made a move. Sam mumbled something, didn't know what, and beat a hasty retreat. Somehow that woman turned him inside out and upside down whenever she was around. Made him wish, almost, she'd never showed up on his doorstep. Almost. Except now, dammit, he didn't know how he'd manage without her when she left.

True to his word, Sam Spencer's snowballs almost never reached their target. Actually, there were very few direct hits on anyone's part because the snow "wasn't good packing snow," to quote the man. Saving for a later date the battle between male and female opponents, Sam proposed instead that he teach the children and her how to use their newly constructed snowshoes.

"Ain't somethin' you can toss on your feet an' set off walkin' on when the need arises. Takes practice. Plenty of it."

Snowshoes were strapped on their feet and laced up around their ankles. Standing up while wearing them proved very difficult, walking in them seemingly impossible, occasioning many a tumble at the twist of an ankle only to discover that once down, one could not rise again without assistance. Sam guffawed over his students' awkward antics, frequently, loud and long, with a slap to his thigh or hands to knees, bent double. Rather than annoyed by his candid enjoyment at their expense, soon they all were joining in—even Paul, with a rusty, lopsided grin brightening his angular adolescent face. For the longest time, the lot of them attended to the lessons, rolling and playing in the snow and sun with all the abandon of a family of cats and kittens, more than actually developing a serviceable skill.

Sam's family, not hers, Madeline reflected soberly, and sadly, catching her breath after her latest spill. Resting her gaze on one happy face after another, lingering lengthily on each in turn, Madeline memorized the children's sweet innocence and Sam's rough-cut beauty for the time when she would no longer dwell among them.

"Need a hand up?"

Standing at her splayed feet encased in snowshoes, he offered her his bare hand. Hesitating, she finally slipped hers within his warm grip. He effortlessly pulled her to her feet, bringing them too close together for comfort. She dared not move for fear of falling; he apparently chose not to, for whatever reason. Some odd compulsion repeatedly found them thus, unable to speak or to be the first to put distance between themselves.

"I'm hungry!" said Jane, forcing notice, upturned face studying each of theirs in turn, demanding a solution.

Sam took a single backward step, forced a chuckle.

"I'd say Miss Preston's about ready an' willin' to give up snowshoe lessons in favor of preparin' you some lunch."

Madeline's chin went high at the inference.

"I can endure as long as anyone else."

"Not me. Not without somethin' nourishin' to fill up the empty corners of this here rumblin' belly." Sam patted the flat washboard above his waist. "I'm tuckered out with hoistin' you all up out of the snow one after another fast's I can make the rounds. How about you throwin' together picnic makin's, woman," he invited with a wink, "an' me brewin' up a batch of herb tea to take off the chill?"

"What are we supposed to do 'til the food's ready?" demanded Jane.

"Practice snowshoin'."

"I wanta—"

"Practice!"

He kneeled before Madeline to undo her snowshoe laces, a courtly gesture that made her feel as if a dozen butterflies had been set free to flutter about in her chest.

Or perhaps the sensation had only been occasioned by acute hunger. As she sliced, she nibbled at every sliver of the cold meat from last night's pot roast that she considered too insignificant for biscuit sandwiches. Sam dropped an assortment of dried leaves and twigs into the boiling kettle of water before joining her, stealing a large slice, biting off a generous bite, chewing with appreciative relish.

"Mr. Spencer, can't you wait a few moments more?" Madeline chided, because he stood far too close.

"Nope!"

He caught her by her elbow and swung her into his arms, favoring her with a long, hungry kiss with a roasted flavor. Her tongue flicked out to savor the taste. Immediately, he lifted his head, breaking contact, breathing hard. His hands fell to his sides, palms pressed against pantlegs.

"Been needin' to do that all mornin' long," he admitted huskily, catching her elbow again when she swayed. "Careful there, woman. Know my kissin's potent, but don't you go faintin' dead away 'cause of it."

His self-satisfied smugness struck her like a splash of icy water.

"Highly unlikely, Mr. Spencer, as I find myself altogether unaffected by your unwarranted invasion of my person."

His head jerked back as if she'd slapped him; an accusing frown drew his thick brows together.

"If that ain't a bald-faced lie, I ain't ever heard one," he spouted.

She drew herself up tall, tipping her head to meet his furious gaze.

"Are you calling me a liar, Mr. Spencer?"

"I sure as hell am, woman, an' I dare you to prove me wrong."

"Prove . . .? How?"

He leaned toward her, eyes glittering with wicked challenge.

"Kiss me again."

Trapped! And no way out of it but to comply.

"Very well!"

She squeezed her eyes closed, offered him tightly pursed lips, hoping her purposely unappealing appearance would deter him for the sake of her prideful denial, praying it wouldn't because she cherished his kisses, stored them away in memory for a time when that would be all she had.

Barking a brief *hah!,* he hauled her tight against himself, bosom to chest, waist to hip, thigh to . . . to . . . Before she had time to dwell on what pressed hard against her thigh, his lips crushed down on hers. No gentle, tasty kiss this, nor punishingly crude either. Into it he put all the intensity of emotion she herself was experiencing, had felt toward him for longer than she could now recall. And, sweet merciful heaven, she could not keep herself from responding in kind. Her arms found their way across his shoulders, around his neck, hands digging deep into his hair, tangling there and hanging on; his hands splayed, one across her shoulder blades, one just below her waist, pulling her closer, ever closer, until not a hair's breadth remained between them. His challenge became yet another lesson, his mouth opening, his tongue exploring, teasing hers into imitating its every gesture. A tingling began in her toes, climbing, swelling, turning to liquid fire at the juncture of her legs. Her lower belly exploded with growing sensation, almost beyond enduring. Madeline moaned, deep in her throat, hungry for more, more, fearing nothing could quench her need but to forever remain in this rugged man's arms. The firm, private object pressed between them jerked suddenly. Experimentally, she wiggled against it. Sam thrust her away as if burned, cheeks crimson, eyes like glittering black coals.

"Dammit, woman," he gritted out between clenched teeth. "Don't go askin' for more'n either've us are willin' to give."

Wounded, bewildered, Madeline found herself totally at a loss for words, a difficulty he did not fail to notice if the hard, tight-lipped smile were any indication. If only she could think of something to say . . . A persistent hiss broke through to her consciousness before anything came to mind.

"Your tea is boiling over."

"What?"

"Your tea. It's boiling over."

"Dammit!"

He spun toward the hearth, crossing the distance in two strides. Squatting, he reached out for the handle of the suspended kettle.

"No, don't!" Madeline cried out in alarm.

He pulled back just in time, offering her a sheepish, faintly apologetic grin over his left shoulder before turning to swing the kettle out from over the fire with the iron hook intended for the job.

Rising, he faced her.

"Tea's done, good an' strong. How about them sandwiches?"

"Ready in a moment."

As quickly as that, they moved beyond the encounter that left her so shaken. Her hands still trembled, and the butterflies metamorphosed into a flock of hummingbirds.

Running her hands down the front of her borrowed dress, she forced herself to speak of something she could not get off her mind.

"Mr. Spencer . . . ?"

He waited, watching her too closely for comfort, making her doubly uncertain that she should have begun at all.

"Mr. Spencer," she started over, "I feel a need to at least know the name of the woman whose dress I wear. If you don't . . . mind. . . ." Though of course her need went far deeper than mere curiosity.

He hesitated so long, she feared he would not speak at all. His face betrayed no expression, either friendly or hostile.

"Hettie. Her name was Hettie . . . Hester."

"Oh! I . . . Well, thank you."

"Them sandwiches ready?"

"What? Yes. Yes, they are."

"Let's get to eatin' them, then."

What else could she do but comply, though more unanswered questions—concerning Hettie, Sam and Hettie, herself and Sam—nagged her long after the picnic commenced, robbing her of her appetite, making her uncomfortably self-conscious.

With the conclusion of the picnic upon a cluster of horse blankets spread in the sunshine close behind the room addition, Madeline stood to gather up leftovers.

"What is the afternoon's schedule, Mr. Spencer?" she asked primly, busily avoiding looking at him.

"Figured we'd all head out behind the barn. Boys an' me'll be fellin' saplin's for bedposts; girls need to gather up pine branches for mattress stuffin'."

"Someone's gotta stay in the house with Baby," Lucy reminded one and all, her voice reflecting a silent plea for some volunteer to relieve her of the task.

"I'll stay with her," Madeline spoke up, trying not to sound too eager, for an idea requiring solitude had blossomed full-blown in her mind. "I'll clean up the kitchen, wash the dishes, and come for you when she awakens."

"Oh, thank you, miss."

Lucy's gratitude warming her heart, Madeline carried her heavily laden basket into the cabin. Greeted by the pungent aroma of scalded tea leavings, she left the door ajar. Her gaze immediately went to the diary on the mantel, knowing that if she were ever to have the opportunity to read it, now would be the perfect time. Throughout the impromptu picnic, she had dwelled long and hard on the dilemma of her growing affection for, and responses to, the rugged mountain man she was coming to love. Unable to understand whether his amorous pursuit of her was sincerely meant, or due simply to her availability as the only unclaimed female between here and Luckless, she wished fervently there were some other woman with whom to discuss her confusion, ask the troubling questions endlessly occupying her thoughts. Were she home in River Valley, there'd be Susanna and Thelma and Janet and Maureen in whom to confide, to possibly gain some clue as to the workings of this man's mind. Since she was not there, nor they here, the only female she could think of to help her work out her problems, though deceased these many years, was Sam's wife, Hettie. For surely in those pages of the young woman's journal lay exactly the infor-

mation she needed to better understand Sam Spencer, as
related by the very woman who would have known him
better than any other.

Time being of the essence, Madeline dropped the picnic
basket beside the open door and hastened to grab up the
diary and settle herself onto the stool beside the hearth.
And found it harder than she'd expected to invade Hettie
Spencer's privacy. At last, with a heavy sigh and conscience
not yet reconciled, Madeline opened the cover and began
to read what lay beyond "Today Sam and me got married."

Almost immediately, Baby awoke. Madeline lifted her
head and listened to the child's happy, contented noises,
hoping she'd soon go back to sleep, if only for a half hour
more. Unfortunately, Baby had finished with napping.
Before her sounds turned unhappy and her mood uncoop-
erative, Madeline brought the child downstairs, fed her a
late lunch of biscuits and honey, then set her down to let
her crawl about.

Finding it increasingly difficult to both read and keep
the curious, determined child out of harm's way, unwilling
to give up her privacy by calling Lucy into the house,
Madeline persisted in her quest, resolved to read beyond
the first few sentences come what may. Sam's Hettie spent
much time at first detailing the arrival at this cabin immediately after exchanging vows, and the new bride's enthusiastic itemization of its abundant contents, little of which
apparently remained. Hoping to get past trivialities before
her stolen time was up, Madeline hurried on to the second
page, attention unfortunately divided between the diary
and the child in her care.

"Baby, no!"

Madeline jumped up yet again to lift the persistent nine-
month-old down off the bed from which she'd already
fallen twice. As before when thwarted, Baby's lower lip
stuck out and began to tremble, and her eyes squinted

tightly closed in preparation for a wail of protest. Madeline held her close, the child's legs spread front and back across her hip, patting her back, speaking soothingly—silly talk, nursery rhymes, anything that came to mind in lieu of lullabies and other childhood tunes that would more likely agitate the restless baby.

Over the sound of her own voice came another from across the room, one which turned her cold and froze her in place where she stood. The menace in the low, rumbling growl made her tighten her grip on the child in her arms until Baby whimpered protest, squirming to be set down. Clutching Baby more tightly, Madeline slowly turned toward the door.

She smelled the enormous, long-fanged, sharp-clawed beast at the same moment she saw it, a gagging stench of wildness and death.

The bear had come in through the door she'd left ajar, to investigate the smell of food emanating from the picnic basket she'd dropped beside it despite Sam's many warnings. Clearly the beast did not want to share its find.

Baby burst into tears with a long, drawn-out wail, squirming vigorously to be let down, her cries and her frantic movements instantly enraging the invader. Rising on hind legs, towering over them but a few feet away, head brushing the rafters, the bear shook that massive head in anger, opening its slavering mouth wide and emitting a roar that reverberated through the small cabin.

His great paws swung this way and that, close enough to feel the wind of their passing, claws as large and sharp as Sam's hunting knife.

Moving with infinite slowness, Madeline backed up until her legs struck the edge of the bed, praying Sam would somehow become aware of their plight and not arrive too late to save her and her charge from being eaten alive.

Her desperate gaze flitted from one thing to another to

avoid looking into the jaws of this monster, searching for something, anything, with which to protect the two of them.

On the mantel lay Sam's knife; above it hung his long-barreled gun, the Hawken that was his pride—of use to neither herself nor Sam, should he come running to the rescue, for the bear stood between them both and those implements of salvation. If Sam should rush to their aid, it might be he the bear struck down and devoured first. And if—horrors of horrors—he did not arrive alone, four children would stand in the line of attack as well.

If she did not do something, and quickly, all those she cared for might die. And it would be her fault, for leaving the door unlatched, the leftovers unstored.

"Shooo! Go away!" she shouted.

The bear lurched toward her a step, proving her attempt a grievous error on her part.

Merciful heaven, without a miracle, she and Baby were going to die.

In a flash of desperate inspiration, she remembered Sam's warning her never to sing again unless her life depended upon it. But how to find voice with her throat tight with terror and mouth as dry as cotton? And succeeding, what if she only made the bear angrier? What else was there left to try? Offering up another hasty prayer, Madeline gave voice to the first song that came to mind.

"Sh-she'll be commmmmmming 'round the mmm-mmmmmmmountain when she commmmes . . ."

With each syllable, somehow her execution grew stronger, more full-bodied, ringing out loud and clear and almost totally on key. Baby screamed in chorus and the bear roared, shaking his head back and forth, clawing at his ears with his great paws as though they pained him.

As she swung into the second verse, the beast fell down upon all fours and bolted back out the door. Quivering like a leaf in a windstorm, Madeline managed to set Baby carefully on the floor, then race to slam the door behind him, prepared to bar the bear's reentry with a stout board slid into place.

Before her shaking hands could manage the task, the door burst inward. Madeline screamed, pushing with all her strength against intrusion, then screamed again when that strength proved insufficient and she tumbled backward onto the dirt floor, the door striking the wall beside her, leaving her no recourse but to clutch Baby to her and prepare herself to die.

Take A Trip Into A Timeless World of Passion and Adventure with Zebra Historical Romances!
—Absolutely FREE!

Let your spirits fly away and enjoy the passion and adventure of another time. With Zebra Historical Romances you'll be transported to a world where proud men and spirited women share the mysteries of love and let the power of passion catapult them into adventures that take place in distant lands of another age. Zebra Historical Romances are the finest novels of their kind, written by today's bestselling romance authors.

4 BOOKS WORTH UP TO $24.96— Absolutely FREE!

Take **4 FREE** Books!

Zebra created its convenient Home Subscription Service s
you'll be sure to get the hottest new romances delivered
each month right to your doorstep — usually before they
are available in book stores. Just to show you how
convenient Zebra Home Subscription Service is, we woul
like to send you 4 Zebra Historical Romances as a FREE
gift. You receive a gift worth up to $24.96 — absolutely
FREE. There's no extra charge for shipping and handling
There's no obligation to buy anything - ever!

Save Even More with Free Home Delivery!

Accept your FREE gift and each month we'll deliver 4 bran
new titles as soon as they are published. They'll be yours
to examine FREE for 10 days. Then if you decide to keep
the books, you'll pay the preferred subscriber's price of jus
$4.20 per title. That's $16.80 for all 4 books for a savings
of up to 32% off the publisher's price! What's more...$16.8
is your total price...there is no additional charge for the
convenience of home delivery. Remember, you are under
obligation to buy any of these books at any time! If you ar
not delighted with them, simply return them and owe
nothing. But if you enjoy Zebra Historical Romances as
much as we think you will, pay the special preferred
subscriber rate of only $16.80 each month and save over
$8.00 off the bookstore price!

We have 4 FREE BOOKS for you as your introduction to
KENSINGTON CHOICE!

To get your FREE BOOKS, worth up to $24.96, mail the card below. or call TOLL-FREE 1-888-345-BOOK

Take 4 Zebra Historical Romances FREE!

MAIL TO: ZEBRA HOME SUBSCRIPTION SERVICE, INC.
120 BRIGHTON ROAD, P.O. BOX 5214,
CLIFTON, NEW JERSEY 07015-5214

YES! Please send me my 4 FREE ZEBRA HISTORICAL ROMANCES (without obligation to purchase other books). Unless you hear from me after I receive my 4 FREE BOOKS, you may send me 4 new novels – as soon as they are published – to preview each month FREE for 10 days. If I am not satisfied, I may return them and owe nothing. Otherwise, I will pay the money-saving preferred subscriber's price of just $4.20 each... a total of $16.80. That's a savings of over $8.00 each month and there is no additional charge for shipping and handling. I may return any shipment within 10 days and owe nothing, and I may cancel any time I wish. In any case the 4 FREE books will be mine to keep.

Name _____

Address _____ Apt No _____

City _____ State _____ Zip _____

Telephone ( ) _____

Signature _____

(If under 18, parent or guardian must sign)

Terms, offer, and price subject to change.   Orders subject to acceptance.

KC0699

Chapter Ten

"Maddie! Maddie, open your eyes! Bear's gone. It's only me, Sam. Open your eyes an' tell me you ain't hurt."

His grip on her shoulders too painful to ignore, Madeline did as Sam told her. Her gaze swam into focus to find him bending close, fear and worry clouding the golden brown of his beautiful eyes.

"I am unharmed and shall remain so if you'll stop shaking me senseless."

His hold eased up, though he did not release her altogether, for which she was grateful. She still felt unlike herself, dizzy and disoriented. All the terrifying events of the last few moments poured over her in a flood, quickening her pulse, robbing her of breath as if she were drowning; nor could she master her trembling, in body or in voice.

"B-b-bear . . . In—In cabin . . ."

"Gone. Your singin' run him off just before I got here."

"B-B-Baby?"

"Fine an' dandy once I pried her outta your grip. Lucy's got her over by the fire. You kind've passed out for a bit."

Her relief so enormous that she could scarcely refrain from bursting into tears and falling into his arms to be comforted, Madeline instead sat more erect, pulling out of Sam's hold.

"I . . . I do not 'pass out'. I'll have you know, Mr. Spencer, I have never fainted in my entire life."

Sam chuckled.

"Then tell me how'd you get on this here bed."

Amazed to find herself there instead of on the floor, she could think of no response.

"Uncle Sam carried you," Jane piped up from the foot where the twins stood side by side. "James an' me figured you was dead, but Uncle said you wasn't. James an' me're awful glad you ain't dead, Miss Maddie. Ain't we, James?"

Deferring, as always, to his loquacious sibling, James nodded.

"Lucy an' Paul, too," Jane continued uninterrupted. " 'Cept Lucy an' me was hopin' not to have to share a bed if you was." She climbed up over the end to settle down beside her uncle. "Uncle Sam figures he can't fit two big beds in our little room anyhow. He's goin' to move this here one in there for you."

Madeline managed a shaky smile.

"I'm certain that it shall be adequate, as in the past." Unable to avoid confessing any longer, Madeline forced herself to admit, "I left the door ajar and the basket of food beside it, drawing that—that beast to its scent."

"Figured as much. Black bear's curious, an' not so shy of folks as grizzlies. Likely took the open door for an invitation, an' accepted."

"Baby and I might have died due to my neglect . . . possibly all of you as well. How could I have been so careless after your many warnings?"

Sam shrugged philosophically.

"Some lessons gotta be learned by experience. Sometimes learnin' comes too late. Dang lucky this weren't one of them times."

Her lower lip began to tremble; she was forced to cover her mouth with overlapped hands to keep a dry sob from escaping.

"You feelin' well 'nough to get on up so we can take apart the bed? Can't knock out a couple've doorways 'til it's moved outta the way," Sam informed her conversationally, though concern still etched deep lines around his mouth and between his salt-and-pepper brows.

Madeline's hands fell into her lap. "Already?"

Sam nodded. "We'll all be sleepin' in our new quarters by nightfall. If you're up to it."

Madeline scrambled to her feet, surprised to find her legs steady under her, and the experience with the bear diminishing to manageability. Her constitution was apparently even stronger than she had always believed.

"By all means, Mr. Spencer, let's get to it then, at once. As I see it, the doors should be equally spaced on the wall. And not too narrow for easy passage . . ."

Sam threw a gaze ceilingward, groaning, but grinning all the same.

"Hop to it, youngun's. Her highness has spoken . . . likely not for the last time before the doors are in an' up to her highfalutin notions of what's good an' proper."

Madeline's heart lightened in keeping with his playful mood. She lifted her chin regally to look down her nose at him.

"Keep my notions in mind at all times, Mr. Spencer, and you shall perform the task correctly the first time."

His grin widened.

"Yes, ma'am. You heard her highness, youngun's. Get movin'. Sooner started, quicker done."

By suppertime four beds stood foursquare and sturdy, nailed against opposite walls in the two rooms, with little space remaining for anything else. Upon them lay mattresses of stitched-together feed sacks from Sam's seemingly endless supply—Madeline suspected he seldom, if ever, threw anything away—and stuffed with fresh pine needles that brought a pungent fragrance reminiscent of all outdoors into the two windowless rooms, as well as Sam's loft overhead. Tempted to mention once more the advantage in windows for light and ventilation, especially in sleeping chambers, she refrained with difficulty. Sam had forgiven her a most serious transgression and quickly dropped the subject of the bear altogether; she had no desire to goad him into a characteristic display of temper by reintroducing the subject, not right now at any rate. Instead she lavished praise upon the clean simplicity of the spartan accommodations so easily and quickly maintained, and upon his skill at having created such handsome bedsteads out of the available materials.

He looked inordinately pleased with her compliments, perhaps because she'd bestowed upon him far too few during their brief acquaintance of but a week. Only a week, and Madeline could not recall at the moment a happier, more fulfilling time in her entire life. Facing death in its slavering jaws and defeating it had made crystal clear where her future lay. Now all she had to do was convince Sam Spencer that Providence had brought her into his life to stay, a task as formidable as single-handedly running off the bear. Renewed sense of purpose uplifting her spirits and wiping the twin clouds of doubt and confusion from her mind, Madeline returned to the present conversation.

"Furniture makin's part an' parcel of livin' off on your own," Sam was saying. "If a fellow can't make somethin' he's needin' or wantin' with his own two hands, likely as not he ain't goin' to have it at all."

"Fortunately for us, Mr. Spencer, your skills in so many areas have proven more than adequate. And doesn't the main room seem spacious without my—without the bed!"

"If you don't mind me crowdin' it up some again, I was thinkin' of bringin' in the rockin' chair that's been stored out in the barn since Het—for a good long while now."

Madeline clasped her hands over her heart.

"A rocking chair! How lovely. Please, do bring it in as soon as you're able." She eyed him curiously, recalling his bride's enthusiastic inventory of the bounty contained within this small structure. "Have you any more treasures hidden out there of which we might avail ourselves, Mr. Spencer?"

She instantly regretted her request at the sad, shuttered expression that settled over his rough-hewn features. Memories of his wife, Hettie, just might prove the greatest challenge of all to her new resolve.

"Maybe, maybe not," he evaded. "I'll look around, see what I can come up with, one of these days when I got time on my hands."

"The rocker will do for now, I'm sure." She then added knowingly, "I am certain the children will all want their turns rocking in it before I ever get mine."

The somber moment passed with his lopsided grin.

"An' knowin' our Janie, she'll probably be the first, mark my words. I'll head on out to the barn an' fetch it in right now."

Still smiling widely, Sam shrugged into his coat as he exited the cabin, never realizing his slip of the tongue that had set her heart to palpitating. "Our Janie," he'd said. Had it been only another instance of deplorable grammar on his part, or. . . ? What if he wished her to stay on here, with him and the children, after the snow was gone, as much as she wanted the same? If he were but to ask, she would quickly reassure him that Madeline Genevieve

Preston could indeed find happiness and fulfillment in the wilderness with only a crude, often rude, mountain man and his five charges for company. With or without the benefit of marriage, in spite of spring blizzards, endless hard labor, and the threat of future attacks from wild beasts and savage natives. If he but asked.

"Here it is," Sam bellowed heartily soon thereafter, bursting into the cabin carrying a chair of generous proportions, of milled and sanded wood, stained and polished to a warm walnut. "Where'd you want it, woman?"

Pleased beyond measure that he would solicit her suggestion, Madeline had no difficulty in pointing out the exact spot.

"Here, beside the hearth. What a delight it will be to sit and rock, working or reading by the light of the fire of an evening."

"Good place for rockin' babies . . . Baby," Sam agreed soberly, averting his gaze at his slip to set the chair where she'd indicated.

"A little more to the left . . . now back. Just there. Perfect."

"Me first, me first!" cried Jane, jumping up and down and clapping her hands.

Madeline and Sam shared amused glances.

"Figures," said Sam.

"Figures," mimicked James, with a knowing bob of the head.

Later, when the novelty of the chair had worn off and the children had disbursed earlier than usual to the luxury of their new rooms, Madeline appropriated the rocker, resigned to rereading *Pilgrim's Progress* for the third, possibly fourth, time—at least until Sam also retired to his pallet in the loft, when she could at long last resume her search through Hettie's journal, which might contain answers to her most pressing quandaries regarding the young woman's stubborn, volatile husband.

Sam went out to the barn a second time, returning with a stack of what appeared to be kindling.

"You could have sent one of the boys out for firewood," she commented as he dropped the pile beside the hearth.

He settled down on a three-legged stool across from her, picking up a short length of wood and holding it aloft to examine it for straightness with a practiced eye, the other squinted shut.

"Ain't burnin' wood, it's buildin' wood." He pulled a folding whittling knife out of his pants pocket, sparing her a glance.

"Oh? What have you in mind to create?" she asked, interest sparked.

He cleared his throat twice before responding.

"Bed. For Baby. With high railin's all around to keep her from havin' the run of the place when she oughta be sleepin'."

"What a blessing that will be, especially for Lucy. How fortunate you had on hand all the materials you'd need."

Sam's jaw jumped, his attention staying on his knife as he shaped the wood.

"Hettie was goin' on nine months with child when she died, takin' the unborn babe with her."

"I'm so sorry. I didn't—"

"Past is done an' gone, an' oughta stay there."

He bent at the waist, his hair swinging forward to cover his expression. Retrieving two more lengths of wood from his pile, examining each, he discarded them in favor of the first.

Their companionable conversation having reached an unfortunate conclusion, Madeline pretended to resume reading *Pilgrim's Progress*, covertly watching his strong, beautiful hands carving a delicate spindle out of raw wood.

She jumped when a log split in the firebox amid a shower of sparks. For a time, she watched the pattern of dancing flames, ever-changing in shape and color, too impatient to begin reading Hettie's little blue book to concentrate on Bunyan's moralistic tale.

Sam spoke out of a lengthy silence.

"Started snowin' again. 'Nother blizzard on its way, looks like."

"Oh, surely not more snow! How can that be possible after a beautiful day like today?"

Sam barked a laugh. "Sayin' goes, 'If you don't like the weather, wait a bit an' it'll change.' Same's true other way 'round. If you get to likin' the warm sun beatin' down on your back, sure as shootin' it'll turn nasty 'fore too long. You'll know winter's given over to spring at last when my valley's overflowin' with wildflowers all in bloom, an' not a day earlier. Wait'll you set eyes on springtime in these here mountains . . ."

She held her breath, anticipating the words inviting her to stay, then exhaled sharply when they were not forthcoming and Sam simply stopped speaking, turning his attention to the work in his hands..

"Perhaps some day I shall, Mr. Spencer, though it seems unlikely," she retorted, more bluntly than intended, daring him to contradict, willing him so to do. Her waiting pause availing her nothing, she invited, "In the meantime, why don't you describe it to me?"

His cheeks had taken on a flush, perhaps only from the fire, perhaps not. He spared her a quick glance.

"I ain't got no way with words, woman."

"Oh, but indeed you have, Mr. Spencer. You have proven most eloquent on many an occasion, whether in stating an opinion or giving necessary instructions. I would very much like to hear your thoughts and experiences regarding life in these mountains."

Sam's hands stilled in their labors. He stared contemplatively into space for a good long while.

"Summer's short in the Rockies, spring an' fall no more'n a couple've days between it an' winter on either end," he commented abruptly. "Higher you go, the shorter. Above the timberline maybe only lastin' six weeks or so. Sunny days, not too hot, an' cool sleepin' nights. An' a thunderstorm now an' again to keep things lively an' growin' green.

"First time I set eyes on my valley, spring'd just given over to summer. Flowers was in bloom, all kinds, all colors, spreadin' from one end to the other. Virgin pine an' snow-capped mountains an' clear blue sky all around, an' that rocky, spring-fed stream rushin' off to nowhere in particular slicin' straight through the middle. Earth so black an' rich, at the turn of a plow, a man could feed himself an' his family from one season to the next without never leavin' home except for huntin' and fishin' for fresh meat, an' that mighty plentiful, too. Just livin' off the land the way the Indians been doin' for hundreds of years, maybe thousands . . ."

He paused for breath, reflectively rubbing his thumb over the beginnings of a spindle coming to life under his blade.

"You make it sound like paradise, Mr. Spencer."

He glanced up.

"We both know it ain't. Except for sometimes an' some people. This here's my time, an' the place I plan to live out my life."

Madeline understood the words left unsaid as clearly as those he had spoken. If she herself did not speak up, now, when the moment presented itself, there might never be another chance to tell him of her change of mind regarding his valley and the Rocky Mountains in general.

"In spite of the deplorable weather we've been experiencing of late, I've come to appreciate your way of life here, which offers many of the same opportunities and challenges that entice men . . . and women . . . to venture even farther westward, as did I when Major Vance called for available female volunteers to go with him to California.''

Sam made a noise of pure disgust.

"I'd say it was more like the good ol' major trickin' a bunch of gullible females into headin' into parts unknown without no supplies or know-how. You'd all've been dead an' buried under three feet of snow by now if Vance hadn't stumbled into Luckless in the nick of time."

He'd missed the point entirely.

"One could see it that way, I suppose. On the other hand, perhaps Providence intended that we follow our foreordained destinies—"

"Life ain't about destiny an' Providence, woman, just luck—good luck, or bad, plain an' simple. That, an' what a man can accomplish with the brains he was born with an' his willin'ness to work hard all the days of his life."

Madeline bristled.

"That being the case, Mr. Spencer, why did you bother to speak to me of beauty and bounty, neither being within your control. What difference would it make where you— or anyone—resided, and with whom, attempting any accomplishments at all, if there were no larger purpose in an individual's life?"

Sam rose from his stool, towering over her.

"Woman, can't you never say nothin' straight forward an' unconfusin'? Shoot, you yabber on an' on 'til a man's head takes to achin', just tryin' to figure out your meanin' more'n half the time. Trapper's oath, I've had me about enough of it for one night. I'm goin' to bed."

He dropped the incomplete spindle onto the pile and stuffed the knife back in his pocket. Mumbling, " 'Night," he climbed to his room above, not waiting for any response on her part nor so much as glancing her way—fortunately, for she could not hide the pain and bewilderment occasioned by his deliberately cruel remarks. Once again he had failed to comprehend the meaning behind her words.

Long after he left, Madeline stared into the fire, unkind assessment of her arrested attempt reverberating through her mind, struggling to understand how it had come about. Was she to take his accusations at face value, that he'd become bored with the inconsequential "yabber" of a mere woman? Or was he telling her, perhaps without even knowing he did so, that he did not want her here in his wild, rugged world with him? That they were unsuitably paired, despite the passion in each other's embrace?

Either of those possibilities being the case, she would certainly be able to convince him otherwise with renewed effort and a careful guard on her words when she spoke to him. The third, which came to her as she regarded his wife's journal on the mantel nearby, she feared she might not. Maybe Sam Spencer had simply compared her to the woman he had loved enough to wed, whom he loved still, and found her lacking. Perhaps there never would be room in the mountain man's heart for someone else to take his Hettie's place.

The only way to discover which conclusion lay closest to the truth could be in reading this woman's words as set down in her own hand. If she were forced to stay up 'til dawn to read through from cover to cover, then that was precisely what she would do, if only to learn if someday, somehow, she'd be able to claim Sam's heart for her own.

Madeline left the rocking chair long enough to lay another log on the fire and grab up her fur robe from the peg on the wall beside Sam's to wrap around her shoulders against drafts. Settling in comfortably, she opened the small volume, better prepared for a long night's read.

15 May 1836. Today Sam and me got married.

Madeline skimmed over the bride's inventory of the
items with which she arrived to set up housekeeping and
those Sam supplied within their new cabin. She wondered
briefly what, if any, of all that bounty had been stored away
in the barn along with the chair in which she now rocked.
She must ask Sam at the first opportunity, suggest that
whatever remained be once more put in use.

No paragraphs broke Hettie's narration, punctuation
appeared infrequently, but her spelling proved passable if
often ungrammatically set on paper. Madeline followed
her finger down the remainder of the first page to the
middle of the second and the conclusion of Hettie's listing.
The next sentence reverberated through Madeline's head
as if spoken aloud.

*I know Sam dont love me. Not the way Ma and Pa do as
if there werent no other person but one to love that way.
But he needs me and Ma says thats just as important. She
says Samll most likely learn to love me like she did Pa with
time. I figure I can live with that for now. Sam and me got
a good long life ahead of us to share what with me being
barely out of pigtails and Sam only a couple of years older.
I can wait for Sam to love me like I already do him cause
I know Ma never tells me nothing that aint true good or
bad. And I can see with my own two eyes day in and day
out how much Pa and her love one another.*

Madeline lifted her gaze from the page, staring into the
fire to reflect on Hettie's brave words, marveling at the
wisdom in them, especially for a young woman of probably
no more than fifteen, sixteen at the most. Had her prophe-
cies, and her mother's, come to pass with time? Had Sam
come to love Hettie? Did he still?

Madeline pressed the fingertips of her right hand against

her lips, lingering on the memory of Sam's impassioned kisses. As lacking in knowledge about such things as she was, possibly she had mistaken that passion as being for herself, when rightly it belonged to another, gone but never forgotten.

Unsolvable quandaries were better left until later, when her spinning mind had sufficient time to sort them out, dwell on each in turn, hopefully reaching resolution. These precious private hours were better spent learning more about the young woman who might well, even in death, prove a very real rival for Sam's affections.

Im only going to write in this here journal when I got something important to talk about or some special occasion like Christmas. Sam aint likely going to want to fetch me another when this is filled up. He dont see why a bodys got to read and write long as he can make his mark need be. And cipher so he dont get cheated when cash money changes hands. I think the real reason he dont like to see me reading or writing is cause it reminds us both that he dont know how. Thinks it makes him look dumb I figure specially in my eyes. Dont matter that I told him and told him it dont. I tell him all the time how proud I am of him taking over when his pa died and him only ten working the farm and seeing to his ma and sister. Til his ma died and his sister got married he never gave a thought to what he wanted for himself like schooling. Told him Id druther have me that kind of a man for a husband than another one could read and write. Said Id help him learn like Ma taught me if it meant so much to him. He wouldnt have none of that though so I try not to let him catch me writing in this here book. He dont say nothing if he does but I know it makes him feel bad deep down. I love Sam a whole lot more than I care about writing about our life together.

Madeline paused, reflecting, before turning to the next page and the next entry.

Didnt mean to go on and on about Sam's not reading and writing. Was going to set down how Sam and me come to meet up and especially how we come to get married since like I said he dont love me in that way a man does the girl he picks for his wife. Well after his ma died and his sis got married Sam headed out west for these here mountains with some trappers he met up with at randayvoo to hunt and trap and live off the land. Went off on his own all puffed up with thinking he knew all there was to know about being a mountain man. Found out different when the first big snow swept in for a winters stay. Pa he was out hunting rabbits for supper and come upon him half frozen and brung him home to thaw out like any good neighbor would. Sam wintered with Pa and Ma and me learning how to take care of himself and make his way on his own. Picked himself out a valley come spring. We all helped build this here cabin for him. Guess he didnt care much for living all alone after wintering with us. Gets awful lonesome sometimes. So he up and asked me to marry him. Or maybe Pa or Ma asked him to take me on me being of a marriageable age. Right off after I told him yes sir and gladly we said our vows in the mountain way and here we are man and wife. Im happy as all get out about the way things turned out and I hope and pray to the Lord Almighty that someday real soon Sam will be too.

Hettie's next entry, in August of the same year, proved unsettling to its reader nine years later.

Sam and me is having a baby. Me and Ma and Pa is pleased as parsnips about it. Sam aint too sure. I figure hes scared he wont be a good pa to the youngun because he didnt get to spend much time with his own pa before he up and died. I keep telling him hes going to do just fine. I aint never been around no younguns either but I figure I can manage to be a good ma when the time comes. Ma says every body learns as they go so I aint worried. About that any way. Ma told me how birthing the baby hurts. Im a big baby myself when it comes to hurting. Hope I dont make a dang fool of myself screaming like a screech owl when the time comes. Ma and me is starting a quilt. Never made one before but Ma said she has quilt making being commonplace where she come from back east. This here one were making is a bride quilt on account of were going to put the date on it when me and Sam got married and her name and mine as being the ones making it. After that I'm going to stitch all around the edges the dates when our kids is born and when they get married like a regular story of our lives. Sam dont seem to give no never mind when I sit and sew nor notice my putting writing in with the quilting design and if he dont I aint going to tell him. Dont figure it to be lying if it keeps Sam from feeling bad about not being able to read and write.

In November and again in December, Hettie wrote of holiday celebrations she and Sam enjoyed with her parents. Apparently their living "in the next valley over" meant close at hand. Were they still living there? Had Sam remained close to them after Hettie died? He obviously owed Hettie's father—probably himself a mountain man—a great debt, his very life and future ability to survive on his own. Thank fortune for that, and for the fact that Hettie's mother had had education enough "back east" to teach her the basic skills of communication. Or else she herself would not now be reading this enlightening and informative missive. Eagerly she turned the page to read more, keenly disappointed at discovering she had reached the last entry in the book. Either Hettie had given up her journal altogether, or—more likely, as it was dated in May of the following year—the young wife of Sam Spencer had died soon thereafter.

Its a year today since Sam and me got married in the mountain way. And what does he go and do? Leaves me here alone and nine months gone with child. Said he had to head on down to the fort for something though its snowing up a storm. Wouldnt say what but I think he went to fetch home something nice for me. Maybe a length of calico so I can make myself a pretty new dress for when I get over being so big and fat. Ma says itll be soon and Ill have me a beautiful baby to hold in my arms and do for. Hoping for a boy for Sams sake. He dont say which hed rather have but a boy first to help around the placell make it easier on him. Told me before he left that I was to stay put in this here rocking chair he made me for Christmas til he got back. But I got things to do too. Got a couple more stitches to put in my bride quilt before its all done. Thats my surprise for him to celebrate our first year as man and wife. Im beginning to hope he might be coming around to loving me though he surely took his own good time. Think Ill come right out and ask him tonight that being the only way to pry something out of him. He dont never say much at all as a rule even less about what hes thinking and feeling. But I got to know before the baby comes and I got my hands full of tending him I forget to ask. Better set down this pencil for now if Im going to haul that quilt down from the loft where I been hiding it. Sam oughtta be here any minute.

Madeline closed the blue-bound book and held it close to her heart, both hands wrapped around it. Hettie Spencer's bride quilt, the very one she herself had violated so heedlessly with a few swings of a hatchet, had been one of the last things on the young woman's mind in this final record of her married life. Had it been her last day, her last few hours of life? How had she died? In childbirth? Not impossible, an all too common probability in such matters, she'd heard. Madeline prayed the girl had at least had the opportunity to ask and be answered regarding the concern uppermost in her mind. Had Sam come to love his bride, the mother of his unborn child, and had he told her? A double tragedy, losing mother and child together, and one from which Sam apparently had never recovered.

Could her being here begin the healing of his heart that had gone unmended these nine long years? She longed to try; it appeared it was her destiny, requiring only that he wished it as much as she.

Madeline yawned, her eyelids so heavy she could scarcely keep them from closing. After another quick reading of the precious few journal entries while she still had the opportunity, she really must get herself off to bed.

Chapter Eleven

Madeline started out of sleep, finding herself in the rocking chair where she'd dozed off beside the fire, now only a glow of hot coals. Hours had passed since completing her second reading of Hettie's journal. Some small sound woke her—that and the persistent shaking by hands clutching her forearm.

"Wake up, miss, please wake up," whispered Jane, her voice quivering with trepidation. "Lucy's sick. Awful sick. I think she's dyin'."

Jane's pronouncement brought Madeline as fully alert as if she'd been splashed with frigid water. She bounded to her feet.

"Merciful heaven."

Freeing herself of Jane's grip, she hastened to the bedroom, finding the older girl curled tightly on her side, attempting to smother her moans with a fist pressed to her mouth. Eyes tightly shut, she did not at first realize that Jane and Madeline stood over her.

"She's awful sick," Jane repeated in a fear-hushed whisper.

Lucy opened her eyes as if the effort tormented her; her words came out with difficulty, apologetic in tone.

"It's my monthly, miss. Never know when it's comin', an' first day's hardest. Makes my head hurt somethin' fierce an' my belly heave up if I move the least little bit. Gut's painin' me bad, too."

Madeline patted her shoulder awkwardly. With the sympathy of kinship for the indignities of this necessary, if inconvenient, rite of womanhood, she suggested that Lucy remain in bed for the day, speaking over her feeble protests.

"We'll manage, Jane and I. Between us we can see to meal preparations and care of Baby without you for a few hours. Rest. Don't worry. Have you adequate . . . ah, supplies?"

"Yes, miss. Thank you, miss."

"You're quite welcome. Rest now, and don't worry about us."

Already Lucy's eyes had closed. Madeline led Jane out of the bedroom, tiptoeing, forefinger over lips to still the little girl's questions.

"Lucy ain't dyin', is she?" Jane blurted as soon as permitted, her tone betraying hope and relief.

"She's not, and will be feeling much better with a day of rest. In the meantime, shall we get breakfast preparations underway before the others arise?"

Madeline sought to distract the youngster from further quizzing, loath to face attempting to explain the monthly flow that would one day, all too soon, be making an appearance in Jane's life as well. Luckily, Jane proved more interested in filling her stomach than in her sister's malady.

"How're you goin' make breakfast when you can't cook?"

"I have successfully prepared porridge on my own," Madeline reminded the child, "and am confident there are other staples in the cellar larder no more difficult to manage. Would you please collect a kettle of snow—clean snow, mind—while I stir up the fire?"

"Yes, ma'am."

Jane bounded away to pluck the iron kettle off the supply shelf. Staggering under its weight when filled, the youngster delivered it into Madeline's hands at the same moment Baby awoke with a wail she had come to recognize as meaning she was wet and unhappy with that state. Madeline collected the child before her cries roused Lucy from her sickbed, returning to the main room holding the sodden, unhappy infant at arm's length.

"I don't suppose you ...?" she offered a tentative request of Jane.

Jane shook her head solemnly.

"No, ma'am, Lucy don't let me tend to the baby no more after I dropped her that once."

"Dropped? Well, we certainly can't chance that. I am sure I can manage, if you will gather up a change of clothes for her. Don't awaken Lucy," she cautioned as Jane scampered off.

She placed the squirming infant on the floor before she herself dropped her. By the time she'd divested Baby of her soaked garments and dressed her afresh with only a few minor mishaps, the menfolk of the family were up and about. Informed that due to Lucy's feeling unwell today, Madeline was in charge of breakfast preparations, all faces took on grave expressions of doubt, including Sam's. Jane joined ranks with the rest, giving voice to their apprehensions.

"Your porridge's always thick an' lumpy."

"Or loose, like soup," added her twin, face crinkled in distaste at the memory.

Madeline bit back a tart retort challenging one of them to take over the task if any could manage more successfully. Throwing up her hands in defeat at the first obstacle was not the way to prove to Sam that she'd make the perfect wife for a mountain man, given the opportunity.

"I shall endeavor to create porridge this time that is neither runny nor stiff," she promised tartly, glancing at the man for support, only to find him struggling with barely suppressed mirth. "You have your doubts, Mr. Spencer? If so, please feel free to express them."

"Ain't that I don't trust your porridge makin', woman, it's come to be fair tolerable, lumps an' all. Least you don't scorch the bottom no more . . ." He paused for effect.

"Please complete your thought if you would, Mr. Spencer. We are all growing hungrier while awaiting your words of wisdom."

"Just picturin' the uprisin' you'll have on your hands servin' porridge breakfast, lunch, an' supper 'til Lucy's up an' about."

Madeline's chin came up.

"No one complained of the roasted meat sandwiches I prepared for our picnic lunch yesterday," she reminded him.

"Moose."

"What?"

"That roast. Moose."

Madeline swallowed hard.

"Moose sandwiches, then. We shall have cold roasted moose sandwiches again for luncheon, and for supper I shall—"

"Can't. Polished off the last of Lucy's biscuits at supper last night."

He looked so insufferably smug, she longed to put him in his place. But what could she say in her defense? Offer to bake more when she could scarcely boil water?

"Oh! Well, then, I—I shall simply whip up some of my own. I have been watching Lucy prepare hers for days now, and . . ." She saw that he was fairly bursting with the need to have his say. "If you must interrupt with some further comments of your own, Mr. Spencer, I would advise you to choose your words carefully and make them honey-sweet. You may be forced to eat them along with your evening biscuits."

Sam raised both hands, palm out, shaking his shaggy head and grinning widely, eyes alive with poorly concealed humor.

"Have you something to add?" she challenged.

"Me? No, ma'am. Not me. Not a word. Only . . ."

"Yes, Mr. Spencer?"

"Well . . . I was just hopin' . . . nice an' quiet an' all to myself so's not to get your back up . . ."

"Mr. Spencer!"

"I was hopin' your supper-makin' talents turn out better'n than your diaperin' ones."

"Me too!" chorused the twins, giggling.

Madeline spun in the direction indicated by a bob of Sam's head. The baby she'd left to play on the floor after dressing, had somehow managed to crawl right out of her diaper and now sat on bare derrière in the dirt, wearing the square of white cloth for a hat.

"Good gracious, Baby—" was as far as she got before she, too, giggled, but more quietly, hand over mouth.

Sam gave in to laughter with a full-bodied bellow; even Paul managed a chuckle or two, offering, "I'll diaper her for you, miss. I helped out a time or two when Lucy weren't around, an' Ma not feelin' up to it. You probably oughta watch how I do it."

"Thank you, Paul, you are a godsend. Can you cook, too?"

He looked his uncle's way, as if fearing he'd already said something wrong.

"That's woman's work," he informed her scornfully, with another wary glance toward Sam.

Sam, for once, did not lose his rare good humor.

"If there weren't no womenfolk for a hundred miles around, you'd be mighty grateful you knew how to fix yourself a plate full of good-tastin' eats on your own, boy."

Paul cast his gaze downward.

"Yes, sir!" His voice dipped and rose unreliably, as it always did when he became unsettled.

Madeline spoke up quickly.

"Perhaps, then, Mr. Spencer, you would care to demonstrate that skill for Paul here, and for all of us, by preparing the evening supper," she suggested sweetly. "Another lesson in wilderness survival, if you will, like snowshoe and mitten making."

He pretended to consider her suggestion most seriously, though he could not keep the laughter from his gold-flecked brown eyes.

"I believe I'll let you live up to your boasts tonight, woman, if it's all the same to you. Me an' the boys got us a day's worth of hard labor just clearin' a new path to the barn. Must've had us at least another foot of snow in the night. Figure us men'll be too tuckered come nightfall to manage more'n eatin' our fill of that grub you're plannin' for us."

He winked broadly for one and all to see, eliciting more giggles from the twins and a knowing exchange between Sam and Paul. If nothing else came of this little altercation, at least some progress had been made toward ending the hostilities between the lad and his uncle. Fearing she might be forced to eat her words come supper, Madeline conceded with a nod, so preoccupied already with pondering what she had sufficient skill to prepare, she failed to even attempt the last say.

Sam chuckled off and on all the way to the barn, tossing shovelsful of snow up as high as he could fling them atop the piles already to his shoulder. The boys he'd set to work making a clearing around the stoop and woodpile, so he had a few minutes to himself, a rarity these days that he'd thought he'd be missing a whole hell of a lot more than he was. A body could get used to almost anything, he guessed, including a houseful of kids and a bossy, know-it-all female underfoot day and night.

Breakfast porridge'd been just about perfect. Sam'd even remembered to tell Maddie so. And he resisted the temptation to remind her the bacon could've benefited from a might more cooking. Those thick, fatty slabs she served up took a lot of serious swallowing to get down, but he never said a word.

It turned out lunch wasn't all that good, but sure was filling. Biscuits harder than tack, scorched white gravy, and leather-tough fried moose wasn't his idea of good eating. But he kept his opinions to himself and gave Jane a kick in the shins under the table—not too hard, with his soft-toed moccasin—when she opened her mouth to complain, silencing the boys with a threatening glance at each in turn.

Despite the heavy uneasiness settled in his stomach for a good long stay, as though he'd swallowed ten pounds of lead shot, Sam felt pretty danged good this afternoon, about everything. Most especially about Maddie. Maybe she was right with all that talk of Providence directing her path to his door. Maybe she'd been sent to him on purpose, to fill up that deep-down emptiness inside he didn't even know was there until Maddie came along. *Dang! What a damn-fool notion!* If there was such a thing as Fate, it sure as hell had never worked in his favor before now, and he'd no reason at all to figure that'd changed. Except for Maddie. And them kids. And that funny feeling spreading wide and permanent around Maddie's lead-weight biscuits.

The notion took him that he oughta have a look-see out in the barn at all them house fixings he'd boxed up and stored in a dark, spidery corner in the hayloft. Whatever he turned up he figured Maddie could use to make chores a little easier and pretty up the place for the kids and him, especially those new rooms. Come spring he'd hightail it down to the fort for window glass, two each for bedroom windows, one for the other side of the front door, and another for his upstairs accommodations. Got pretty dang stuffy in close quarters and no windows, he had to admit. To himself, not to Maddie.

He scrounged around in the hayloft a better part of the afternoon. When the boys joined him, asking what else there was to be done, he set them to hauling boxes and trunks down to the barn floor, practically filling one stall. He took on the heavier oddments himself, naturally, including a couple of pieces of furniture Maddie's eyes oughta light up over—a chest of drawers and another rocking chair. His and hers, just like he and Hettie . . .

Sam stuffed thoughts of Hettie back down where he'd stored them away in the rear of his mind these nine long years. Trouble was, they wouldn't stay put. Nine years ago, May 15th, his wife had died 'cause of him. He as good as killed her. Wasn't something should be forgotten, not ever. It should be dwelled on, poked at like a rotten tooth, so as to be all the time on a fellow's mind, living day in and day out with the regrets of should'ves and if-onlys, so he'd never make the same sort of fatal mistake again.

A mountain man's life was supposed to be lived alone. That was rule number one. Number two—if you found yourself needing a woman so bad you couldn't stand it, you'd take yourself an Indian squaw, or borrow someone else's until the feeling passed—and don't never grow attached.

He broke both rules with Hettie, and now, darned if he wasn't going and doing it again, with Maddie and his sister's kids. If he wasn't the biggest piss-poor failure of a Rocky Mountain man, he didn't know what was. Feeling about as friendly as Maddie's furry visitor yesterday, Sam let out with a deep-throated growl when he heard her calling him from below.

"Hello? Sam . . . Mr. Spencer, are you up there? The boys said I was to come out, look at some things?"

"Down there. Right in front of your eyes, woman," Sam barked, planning on staying put in the loft, nursing his bad temper.

He made a lot of racket, as though he was working hard at putting things back in place. Fact was, there wasn't a heck of a lot to work with, most of it being down there, with Maddie rummaging around in it, oooing and ahhhing over every find.

"Oh, Mr. Spencer, such wonderful treasures. Do join me and have a look."

He wasn't going to take her up on the offer, but before he knew it, there he was right beside her, checking out the goods spread out all over the barn floor.

"You're makin' one hel—heck of a mess, woman. Gotta pack it all up again to haul inside."

She glanced up at him from where she knelt beside an open trunk, her cheeks flushed rosy, her purple eyes glittery with pleasure.

"I've told myself the same thing, Mr. Spencer, but I can't seem to stop." She clamped her hands together right between her high, round breasts; Sam swallowed hard, and it wasn't lunch this time putting the lump in his throat.

"And that chest of drawers, it's so . . . so magnificent. Did you make it?"

Swallowing again, Sam could only nod.

"A masterful piece of workmanship. Indeed, you could have been a furniture maker, you are so skilled."

He'd dreamed of it once, when he was a lad with his first new whittling knife, before Pa died, leaving him to work the farm.

"City fellow's job ain't for me," he snapped, not meaning to, especially seeing the hurt look in her flower-colored eyes before she turned away.

"Yes, well, you're right, of course." Her hands stilled in their treasure hunt, dropping to her lap. With a lengthy glance around her, she started packing up. "If you and the boys wouldn't mind bringing all this into the house, I'll sort through everything as I can." She brightened. "Won't the girls be pleased? We'll have such fun unpacking, finding homes for all this bounty. I even spied a length of flowered cloth for curtains, and a matching tablecloth, and . . ." She laughed lightly. "And for whatever else we women can come up with."

"Don't go makin' too many plans," Sam warned bluntly. "Ain't like you'll be stayin' on after the snow melts. Don't go tryin' to take over runnin' things like they was your own."

She stared away from him into the gloom of the farthest stall.

"You are right, Mr. Spencer, of course. Clearly it is none of my concern."

All the bright glow went out of her like the snuffing of a candle. Her hands shook all the while she stuffed things back into boxes every which way. She stood, dusting her hands on the flour sack apron protecting Hettie's plain brown dress that fit her too tight in all the right places, not looking him in the eye.

"Should you choose to allow us—me—the temporary use of your belongings, I would be happy to go through them for you after supper."

She picked up her skirts and skedaddled out of the barn as if those skirts was on fire.

Damn, he hadn't planned on hurting Maddie. But maybe it was for the best that she was madder than all get-out at him. Quicker she caught on there wasn't no future for the two of them, here in his cabin, the better. The kids, they'd grow up, move on; but Maddie, she'd just stick around forever if he let her, until one of them passed on. Shattering his heart into a million shards if she went first, like Hettie'd done. Better to make a clean break before he got attached.

He was afraid it was already too late.

Righteous indignation and hurt feelings sent Madeline racing for the cabin, but by the time she arrived at her destination, her resolve had returned full force. What could she expect from a man who'd become a virtual hermit, mourning the loss of his bride and unborn child, but that he would resist at every turn any changes inviting the possibility of further suffering? What he had to learn, and she to teach him, was that every soul alive faced the same probabilities. One did not simply shut oneself off from life's experiences because of it, a vital fact she must use whatever means of persuasion at her command to make him understand.

Supper proved yet another challenge, one she feared beyond her capabilities. There was nothing to do but repeat the noontime meal, but with a special treat as dessert, a creamy goat-milk bread pudding sweetened with honey, utilizing lunch biscuits grown otherwise inedible. She would rather it be a custard, or flan, as Cook had taught her when she was still in short skirts. Lacking eggs, she did the best she could, and, tasting, found the results most pleasing. She longed to demonstrate to Sam, and to the children, the culinary delights of which she was capable, custards and cookies, pies and cakes, taught her by one of the finest family cooks in River Valley. Her incurable sweet tooth, which had occasioned the lessons in the first place, now told her that this humble pudding would do her mentor proud.

While she prepared supper, Sam, Paul, and the twins brought in Hettie's household goods. First came the chest of drawers, to be positioned centrally between the two bedroom doors, then the rocking chair to sit opposite the other beside the hearth. The boxes and trunks were stacked off to one side for later perusal.

Lucy declined supper, saying she felt "a bit better" but not enough to relish eating. Madeline fairly burst with pride over moose steak that had not burned crisp at the edges and raw in the middle like the breakfast bacon, nor as shoe-leather tough as their luncheon fare. Nor would her supper biscuits break a tooth, being a tad undercooked in the center. The pudding, her special treat and a surprise, she watched those gathered around the table consume to the last spoonful scraped from a bowl with such delight it brought tears to her eyes. Sam's lavish praise was music to her ears.

"My specialty is mince pie, if I but had the ingredients."

"We'll have to see that you have them, then."

"But how? Where?"

His expression grew shuttered.

"Meant to say, be nice if we were able to get 'em."

"Oh, yes, of course."

After the supper dishes were washed, dried, and stacked, Lucy wandered out, wrapped in a blue knitted shawl, wane and weary but "much better now, thanks" and up to sitting in a rocker with Baby on her lap, watching Madeline and the twins begin the sorting process. Sam sat off by himself at the table, carving spindles; Paul, in the second rocker, pretended to read, pausing to watch more often than not. By bedtime, nothing remained to be done but tote the empty receptacles back to the barn. Wooden serving and mixing bowls, pewter flatware, and pottery crocks in assorted sizes graced the shelves over the table, as well as a second iron kettle and two smaller frying pans. A candleholder, identical to the one already in use, joined its mate. She found brightly patterned woolen blankets—Indian trade blankets, Sam called them—enough for one per bed, and linen towels for bathing and hand-washing. More than one length of cloth, patterned and plain, brought a cry of pleasure from Lucy's smiling lips.

Personal mementos of Sam and Hettie's life together Madeline carefully repacked into one box and surreptitiously slid under her own bed for going over later. She could not fight her need to know more about the young bride of the rugged mountain man she herself had grown to love, as though in understanding her, she could better understand him.

If only she could repair the damage to Hettie's quilt somehow, and by doing so, make amends for her heedless destruction of this labor of love and record of their life together.

Madeline lay awake long after the others slept, resisting tossing and turning the night away out of consideration for the three children sharing the room with her. Finally, when she could bear it no more, she threw her newly acquired blanket around her shoulders—much as she had the quilt that first day—and crept out into the shadowy, fire-lit main room. For a very long time, she stood over the humpback trunk by the door, staring at it, her hands locked in the folds of the wool blanket, resisting the urge to which in the end she succumbed.

Kneeling, she slowly lifted the lid, giving herself every opportunity to come to her senses. No longer neatly folded, the severed quilt pieces lay in a jumble near the bottom of the contents Sam had pawed through looking for a change of clothes. Madeline lifted them out with all the care and reverence the evidence of Hettie's inestimable skills deserved. How much this creation had meant to Sam's bride! What a wonderful future she'd envisioned recording upon it, never to be!

Madeline quietly closed the trunk, carrying Hettie's handiwork to the rocking chair that had—temporarily—become her own. In the flickering firelight, she examined in detail the fine workmanship, searched out and found the embroidered dates of which Hettie had scripted across the bottom-most edge of the scrap she'd chopped off, subtly worked into the quilting design:

15 May 1836, Samuel William Spencer wed Hester Susan Barnes. 4 August 1837, Hettie and Roberta Barnes begun making this quilt.

Though she looked, Madeline found no date for the quilt's having been finished. She vividly recalled Hettie mentioning in that last entry in her journal that she intended to fetch the quilt, a first anniversary gift for Sam, out of the loft before he arrived home, that she had a few more stitches to add—most likely the date of completion, as everything else, to Madeline's untrained eye, appeared done.

Had Hettie died on the very day of their anniversary, before she *could* stitch the date upon her quilt, before Sam came home? The thought sent a chill coursing the length of Madeline's spine.

If so, more than a labor, and a gift, of love, the homespun coverlet with a design of interlocking circles upon a muslin ground symbolized Sam Spencer's shattering loss of wife and child on a day meant for joyous celebration. A day intended to foretell many more such happy occasions, including the birthday of the couple's first child.

She had, if inadvertently, destroyed his most precious tangible reminder of the happy life that had been his for far too short a time.

Hands trembling, tears close, Madeline ran her fingers over the jagged edge separating larger from smaller piece a foot or so from the bottom. How heedlessly she had done this, never giving a moment's thought to the reason the quilt might have been locked away inside the trunk in the first place. Intent only on her own comfort and convenience when she took hatchet in hand, it had not even occurred to her that someone had lovingly labored over making it, that someone else had cherished it so greatly as to wrap and store the treasure away from harm.

How could I have been so heedless, so selfishly heartless? she asked herself, already knowing the answer. Because she had never been required to think of anyone but herself, nor beyond her own personal needs and wants. In all fairness, she could not bemoan the failings of the young woman she had been mere months ago and was no longer. That selfish, self-centered, immature individual had since experienced much and learned more—especially about love. The new Madeline Preston—Sam Spencer's Maddie—knew how to give as well as take.

"I must repair Sam's quilt," she whispered into the stillness broken only by the crackling fire. "But how," she argued with herself, "when you have never sewn a stitch?"

"I can help, miss. I sew real good."

Lucy spoke softly close at hand in the wavering shadows. Madeline started, glancing over her shoulder.

"Lucy. I didn't realize anyone was up. Did I wake you?" The girl shook her head.

"Got me too much sleep durin' the day, I guess. I can help you fix Uncle Sam's quilt," she repeated.

Madeline turned her attention back to the damaged fabric spread out on her lap.

"I fear what I've done is beyond repair," she admitted with a catch in her voice.

Lucy knelt beside her, gently fingering a ragged edge with knowing, work-roughened hands.

"We can fix this easy, miss, an' make new pieces, need be, with that cloth Uncle Sam found in the barn."

Still doubtful, Madeline reminded the earnest, eager child, "The patterns won't match."

"Easy 'nough to sew on new bits of cloth over top of some of the old ones here and there."

"Of course. That would work." Optimism bloomed in Madeline's heart. "How clever of you to think of it. And how kind of you to be willing to give your time and expertise to repair my foolish blunder in addition to everything else you're required to cope with alone because of me and my ineptitude."

Lucy meekly dipped her head, her fine, fair hair falling forward to curtain her face. Her hands characteristically came up to swipe it back as she looked with shy candor into Madeline's eyes.

"I don't mind the work, miss. Worked hard all my life, Ma bein' sickly's 'long as I can recall."

On impulse, Madeline stretched out a hand and lifted a wisp of fine hair off Lucy's fair, high forehead.

"You are a lovely young woman, Lucy, inside and out." Instead of pleased, the girl looked stricken.

"Me? Oh no, miss. I'm nothin' but a simple farm girl,

an' as plain as an old fence post. You're the beautiful one, Miss Maddie, an' talk so fancy, like a real lady. Wished I was more like you.''

'' 'Beauty is as beauty does.' You, my dear young woman, have an inner beauty far beyond the outward manifestations of attractive features and cultivated comportment.''

Puzzling over the big words, Lucy's pale blue eyes briefly brightened with hope before a flash of reality caused her to turn her gaze away.

''Hardly anyone ever notices inside beauty, miss, if the outsides ain't pretty.''

''Patience, sweetheart.'' Madeline placed fingertips under Lucy's chin, gently forcing her head upward at a proud angle. ''You have fine, delicate features in a face which shall blossom very soon into porcelain-like loveliness.''

''M'hair's all flyaway an' straighter'n straw.''

''Silky and lustrous. Only requiring taming until you are old enough to put it up. Here, turn around.''

Lucy obediently swiveled on her knees, presenting her back. Madeline caught back her hair, dividing it equally and swiftly braiding the plaits, tying them off with the strip of rawhide from her own hair.

''There now, isn't that better?''

Lucy faced her, one hand raised to lightly touch the results of Madeline's handiwork, pale eyes liquid with gratitude.

''Ever so much better. Thank you, miss. D-d-do you think I could learn to do that?''

Madeline laughed lightly.

''If I can, so can you. A trade, then, between us. Braiding lessons for quilt. Have we a bargain?''

Lucy's smile went wide and genuine.

''Oh, yes, miss. We surely do.''

''Tomorrow evening then, after everyone is asleep, lessons shall commence. Until then, I believe we both could use a little beauty sleep during what remains of this night.''

Co-conspirators, they folded and packed away Sam's quilt, then tiptoed off to bed.

Chapter Twelve

At breakfast, Sam announced that afterward he intended to teach the boys to use his Hawken. Madeline bit back a concerned protest over the dangers of firearms, especially in the untrained hands of two youngsters. After her ordeal with the bear, she realized the necessity of each of them being able to defend oneself by any means possible.

"We all should learn, Mr. Spencer."

"An' will, woman," Sam agreed readily. "But there's five of you to only one of me. Two green pilgrims is about all I can watch over at a time so's there ain't no accidents."

She refrained from suggesting that she, as the other adult, ought to be one of the first. With him and the boys out of the house until midday at the very least, she and Lucy could begin working on the quilt in the brighter light of day.

"Paul an' James ain't green, Uncle Sam," commented Jane seriously once she'd swallowed a generous mouthful of hotcake. "All us kids's skin's colored same's you an' Miss Maddie. See?"

She extended an arm over the table, barely missing her cup of milk. At her side, Madeline automatically moved it out of danger, saying, "Your uncle meant we are inexperienced. It is a colloquialism characteristic of men of your uncle's chosen vocation."

"Hunh?" Jane tipped her head questioningly, like a little bird. Frowning, she asked, "How come you talk so fancy nobody can figure out what you're sayin' half the time? Don't you know no easy words?"

James echoed his twin's sentiment. "Don't ya?"

Sam, Lucy, and Paul said nothing, but their faces told all. Sam crossed his arms high across his broad chest, his brown eyes bright with enjoyment at her discomfort.

"Of course . . . I . . . That is, I didn't realize . . . I shall endeav—I shall *try* to speak more simply hereaft—from now on." On second thought, she added, "At the same time, it would not hurt for all of you to learn to use a big word now and again where and when appropriate."

"How we goin' do that when James an' me ain't never even been to school?" asked Jane. "We don't know nothin' 'bout readin' an' writin' an' fancy talkin'."

"An oversight quite simple to correct. We shall begin reading and writing lessons tonight. One discovers a whole new world of information and enlightenment with those two skills alone, easily learned at any age. It will be most gratifying to me, too, to be able to contribute something of lasting value to you and your siblings."

She tossed a quick glance Sam's way; he avoided hers by staring resolutely into the cup of coffee he held midway to his mouth. She saw his jaw jump, but he did not speak up to refuse permission.

"What's siblin's?" the twins asked together.

"Ah, that can be the first lesson. Brothers and sisters are your siblings."

"You're a siblin'," Jane told her brother.

"No, you are," retorted James.

"You are."

"I ain't, you are."

"Children. You each are one. As are Lucy and Paul. All of you together are siblings."

"Oh!" Undaunted, Jane asked, "Are you one, Miss Maddie?"

"No, I don't have any brothers or sisters, though I always wished I had. I'm an only child."

"How about you, Uncle Sam?"

Sam, who had been watching the entire exchange with a bemused half-grin on his face, lost his look of good humor as quickly as the snuffing of a candle.

"Had. Died. Your ma."

"Oh." Jane's voice went small, her eyes misty.

Madeline sought a complete change of subject.

"Mr. Spencer, I've been meaning to ask you where Wolf has been keeping himself. I haven't seen him dogging Paul's steps or warming beside the fire in days."

"Visitin' a lady friend of his an' her newborn pups, likely," Sam responded rather too heartily, but at least he made the attempt.

"His pups as well, I imagine?"

"Probably."

"Oooh! Puppies. Can we bring 'em back here to live?"

Sam shook his head. Over Jane's protest, he stated firmly, "They're wild an' wild they'll stay. Their ma, an' Wolf wouldn't have it no other way. Me neither. An' don't go rollin' out your lip at me, youngun', ain't goin'a work. First thing you learn in these here Rocky Mountains is to let nature run its course without no interferin'. Got that?"

"Yes, Uncle."

Sam leveled a questioning stare at each in turn, as the other children echoed Jane's assent. That settled, Sam rose from his seat. He was once more garbed in fringed animal hide and had volunteered when he sat down at the morning meal that the garments had been well brushed and aired. His eyes, boring into hers, gave a clear warning to keep her hands off, and her opinions to herself. He might have been most surprised that, had she been free to comment, she would have told him how pleased she was to see him returned to his natural state, which suited him far better than wool and homespun.

"James, Paul. About time for them shootin' lessons."

Eagerly, James scrambled to his feet; Paul stood more slowly, with all the reluctance of a prisoner headed for the gallows. Clearly more scholar than woodsman, at least he understood the necessity of his uncle's lessons, though he made no secret of disliking them. He took his woolen jacket from its designated hook near the hearth and followed James and his uncle out the door.

Lucy sighed with relief. "Well, now we can get to our sewing lessons, miss."

Immediately, Jane's attention was piqued.

"What'cha makin'?"

Madeline threw a silent plea Lucy's way. Unabashed, Lucy responded, "I'm teachin' Miss Maddie how to do mendin' on her own. You wanta learn, too?"

The ever-curious child instantly lost interest.

"Naw! I'm goin' outside an' watch the shootin' lessons."

"You will do no such thing."

"Aw, miss—"

"Learning to handle a weapon capable of killing is not a game. Your bothers and your uncle do not need the distraction of your presence."

"But I wanta—"

Lucy, bless her, spoke into the fray.

"I figured you an' me'd make up a doll for you after I show Miss Maddie a couple of stitches an' set her to mendin'."

"I don't wanta sew."

"No sewin', just some cuttin' an' knottin' an' stuffin', just the way Ma showed me when I was your age."

"I want two dollies."

"If there's time. How 'bout makin' up the beds for me while I help Miss Maddie. Faster the work's done, the quicker you an' me can whip up a whole dollie family."

Jane ran off to bed-making with her usual exuberance. Lucy turned to Madeline with a knowing smile.

"That oughta keep her busy for a bit," she said, voice low. "I figured to show you how to practice your stitches on the mendin' 'til you can sew them all small an' even-like. Quilt-makin' needs the prettiest little stitches you can manage, Ma always said."

"A sound plan," Madeline agreed, hesitated, then spoke her mind. "Lucy . . . about your parents . . . their passing away . . . I want you to know how sorry I am for your misfortune, and compliment you on the fortitude you've shown in the face of all your subsequent difficulties. . . . You're a very resourceful young woman and . . ." She ceased lavishing praise upon the deserving girl when she realized she was causing Lucy increased distress with every word. "And now, if you would teach me to sew a fine stitch, I for one shall be out of your hair for the time being. Which, by the way, looks very nicely braided this morning."

Lucy flushed and bobbed her head.

"Thank you, miss. Took me half a dozen tries, though, 'fore I got it to stay put."

"A few more days of practice and it will take no time at all."

Lucy bit her lower lip, obviously gathering courage to say something more. Twice she made the attempt; the third

time she blurted, "I—I'm awful glad you're here, miss, to
. . . to help out . . . an' to talk to."

Her embarrassment acute, the girl dipped her head to
study interlocked fingers. Madeline cleared her throat
before she could trust herself to speak.

"I'm happy to be here . . . for all of you. I, too, love our
talks, especially since I have learned so much from you of
a practical nature." She attempted to lighten the mood,
and her tone. "However, I fear you exaggerate my role in
helping out, my blunders being of so conspicuous a nature
as they are."

At Madeline's continued praise, the girl offered a smile
that reached to her eyes, brightening her face quite ethere-
ally. For all her many inner strengths, she had a fragile
look about her that would one day turn into a subtle beauty
fit to turn heads wherever she went. She would need a
mother's guidance to help her choose wisely among the
numerous beaux vying for her hand.

If only Sam could be made to see Madeline herself as
capable of filling that void in the children's lives, and in
his own. Even if he did not love her yet in the way she did
him, perhaps he could yet learn—as she believed he'd
come to love his wife, Hettie, as evidenced by his ongoing
mourning, whether or not he ever told her so. Her first
step, then, appeared to be to get Sam to agree to let her
stay on after winter finally gave way to spring. As if reading
her thoughts, Lucy spoke again into the brief silence
between them.

"I—I wish you'd stay on for good, miss. The twins does,
too, an' Paul, if he wasn't too pigheaded to admit it."

Tempted to offer hope, Madeline did not dare raise
Lucy's, or her own, by putting voice to her thoughts.

"I believe he takes after his uncle in that," she commented wryly, stalling for the right words, failing to find
them, needing to fill the expectant pause. "With so much

to do and so many new lessons to learn each and every day, I find it difficult to plan beyond the next few hours to what time, and the spring thaw, will bring. Perhaps we'd best begin the task at hand before we find luncheon preparations upon us.''

Lucy smiled, but the light had faded a bit in her eyes with the return to reality. Her narrow chest, not yet in bloom, heaved in a quiet sigh.

''Always another meal waitin', mornin', noon an' night.'' She perked up, mischief lighting her serious face. ''I surely did like that puddin' you made for supper last evenin'.''

Madeline caught her new mood and smiled, teasing, ''Are you perhaps hinting for another sweet treat tonight?''

''Yes, m'am.''

''Then I shall have to think about what I might surprise you with, desserts being my specialty.'' She picked up the nearest item from the pile, a pair of James's woolen pants with a gaping hole in the knee. ''For now, you'd better show me how to salvage this disaster from the rag bag where I would have believed it belonged.''

Amiably, they settled into rocking chairs across from each other, laboring over the pile of mending Lucy had gathered. Madeline found sewing a fine seam a real challenge, and one she thoroughly enjoyed despite the many needle pricks she incurred. With repetition she picked up the rhythm of the chore so that she could dwell on other things, especially the repairing of the quilt. Across the room, Jane now struggled with washing and drying breakfast dishes by herself for the first time, standing on a stool over the washpans on the table.

Seeing that the child was totally absorbed in her task, Madeline ventured to ask in a low tone, ''What about the plain pieces of the quilt which must be repaired? I do not recall seeing any lengths of fabric among the stores from the barn in a similar pale beige shade.''

Lucy frowned, biting off the remainder of thread from a completed bit of work.

"Me neither. What we really need is muslin, like what was used, dyed the right color same's was likely done in the first place when makin' the quilt."

So far, she had not asked the significance of the quilt, and for that Madeline was grateful. She did not wish to betray what she knew of the matter to the girl; it was Sam's affair, and no one else's, especially uninvited.

"Muslin? I have two clean muslin petticoats I haven't been wearing any more since changing into this dress. Neither is in perfect condition, but there should be sufficient fabric using both."

"They'll do, miss, an' some left over for . . . for mistakes."

Madeline laughed softly. "Kind of you not to mention whose mistakes those would most probably be."

Lucy offered her lovely, if infrequent, smile. In the time remaining, with Jane distracted, she explained some simple dying techniques.

"Onionskin's one of the easiest, miss. Just boil up a bunch of dried outside skins 'til you get the color you want. Gotta keep an eye out, 'cause they'll yellow up on you real fast. There's other weeds an' berries an' such'd turn a better tan, but we ain't got none of those. . . . Then take 'em outta the water an' put your petticoats in. Watch 'em real close, too, an' pull 'em out fast when the color's close to matchin'. Rinse right away in cold water 'til your water's clear. You can set a couple've pans of snow to meltin' before you get started. Got all that?"

"I believe I do." Madeline repeated back to her the instructions as she understood them. "Vigilance—that is, careful watching, and haste, seem to be the most sig— important factors to remember."

Satisfied, Lucy nodded agreement. "I'll be showin' Jane

how to make her dollies now. Just give a holler if you need help.''

''I will.''

But Madeline fully intended to prove her capability at mastering the simple chore on her own. Both set to work. Madeline found it difficult to give her full attention to her labors, as dollmaking without sewing so fascinated her. Strips and squares of various fabrics, knotted and stuffed here and there, and Jane's family of dolls quickly grew in all sizes and shapes. Madeline did not let herself stray so far that she failed to elicit the perfect shade—as compared to the shorn end of the quilt she kept hidden close by for constant checking. The dye mixture and the dyed fabric were nearly identical to the quilt background, even given that the color would lighten with drying. Madeline felt inordinately proud of herself as she rinsed and wrung out her petticoats in preparation for hanging them in the bedroom to dry away from notice by the menfolk. At her request, Lucy came over to approve her accomplishment. Instead of words of praise, the young woman's voice held dismay equal to that in her troubled pale eyes.

''Oh, miss, look what you've gone an' done to your hands. You're supposed to use a stick for stirrin' an' such, not your hands, 'til you've gone through a half-dozen rinsin's.''

Madeline extended her hands, which appeared to have grown jaundiced from fingertips to wrists.

''Good gracious. Won't it wash off?'' Madeline's panic echoed in her question.

Lucy solemnly shook her head.

''It'll wear off.''

''How soon?''

''Never dyed nothin' but cloth. Don't know 'bout skin.''

''Oh, dear. How am I going to keep these yellow hands hidden from S—from prying eyes and curious questions?''

"Don't know, miss. I'm sorry, miss."

"It's not your fault, dear, and don't worry yourself over the consequences. Whatever they might be, I shall take full responsibility."

"Yes, miss." Lucy concurred, but continued to look doubtful.

At lunchtime, her hands were the first thing Sam noticed.

"Spirits almighty, now what've you gone an' done?"

Madeline tilted up her chin.

"I would rather not discuss it, Mr. Spencer. Sufficient to say, I have learned yet another lesson in wilderness housekeeping ... the hard way. A mistake I shall not repeat, rest assured."

The aggravating man, though he had the good grace to let the matter drop, chuckled off and on to himself throughout lunch, every time he glanced her way.

Jane wanted to learn to shoot after lunch. Sam informed her he was giving a whole day to teaching the boys and she'd have her turn along with the other females tomorrow. Jane contented herself with her dolls, playing happily on her bed after Lucy warned that the dirt floor would soil the new toys. Madeline, though itching to start on quilt repair, had to settle for more practice-mending, Lucy proving to be an exacting teacher. By late afternoon, her shoulders burned and her eyes blurred over the close work. She left her rocker to stretch and sigh.

"This sewing is putting me to sleep. I cannot continue without a few breaths of fresh air."

"You go on out, then, miss. I oughta be startin' supper stew about now anyway." She lowered her voice. "Tonight, late, we'll set to workin' on the quilt, your sewin's that improved."

"Thank you, Lucy, I'm relieved to hear it. Especially

after my error with the dying process. I'll return shortly to help with supper."

"Take your time, miss. Me an' Jane're goin' to play dolls for a while after I get the stew goin'. I promised her I would."

Madeline chose her fur robe from the outerwear hanging side by side on a row of pegs set into the log wall beside the hearth. Stepping out onto a clean-swept stoop, she inhaled and exhaled deeply, grateful that the vertigo from the thinner mountain air had finally become a thing of the past. Bracing cold and a cloudless blue sky greeted her. Welcome sunshine warmed her shoulders and her upturned face. At the far-off horizon, where mountain peaks speared the sky, gray clouds gathered, portending more snowfall. For the first time, she longed for a blizzard, one to last for days, postponing her departure until it no longer seemed an inevitability, until after she had somehow managed to thaw Sam Spencer's frozen heart so that she would never have to leave at all.

The shot from Sam's Hawken reverberating through his valley broke through Madeline's melancholy reverie. Resolutely, she set her steps on the path to the barn and beyond, whence the sound originated. With every crunching footfall upon the hard-packed snow, her determination grew to find a way to convince him to let her stay in his valley, atop his mountain, forever.

"Hell, boy, not like that. Tuck that stock in tight *below* your shoulder or the kick'll knock you on your butt for sure. Or worse. An' squint one eye closed to sight down the barrel. Can't hit the broad side of this here barn if you don't line up target an' sights. Dammit, boy, don't go pointin' that rifle at me every time you look my way. Never aim at nothin' you ain't plannin' to shoot."

From the mutinous glare in Paul's eyes, Sam was beginning to wonder if he forgot that particular reminder time and again purely by accident. Much as he figured his nephew hated him and anything to do with mountaineering, he had his doubts. Not only did the lad not want to learn to shoot, he weren't no damn good at it neither. Sam knew his heart wasn't in it; he'd rather have his nose in a book, sitting all cozy by the fire reading, than learn how to take care of himself in these here mountains.

Times like this, Sam was certain-sure book learning interfered with clear thinking. Didn't take no talent for reading and writing to figure out the necessity to bring down game to feed yourself or starve, and to defend yourself and yours against attackers, man or beast, need be.

Ciphering and signing your own name—what more did you need? And that wasn't envy talking for what the boy and Maddie, and probably Lucy, could do and he couldn't. Mountain men didn't need no book learning to get along, just common sense and good ol' mountain savvy. Maybe he oughta've told that woman she couldn't hold no lessons for the twins in the evenings. It'd likely prove their ruination. Maybe he'd do just that, come suppertime. Decision made, Sam turned his attention back to his own lessons, and his cantankerous student.

No sooner had he given Paul the go-ahead to pull the trigger than he caught a movement out of the corner of his eye. Damned if the boy didn't spy it too, and turn that way, pulling the trigger at one and the same time. Sam's heart stopped, seeing Maddie herself step around the corner of the barn, headed their way, a big smile of greeting on her face—never guessing she'd just become the boy's unwitting target.

His warning cry and the report of the rifle rang out together.

"Maddie, duck!"

Next thing he knew, she was on the ground, flat on her face. Safe, or shot dead, he didn't know. Sam took off running, with only a glance at Paul, his face gone sick and gray, standing frozen to the ground where he stood. No time to worry over the boy. If anything happened to Maddie . . .

"Woman!" he shouted as he sprinted toward her. "You dead or alive?"

He thought he heard her, could've been an answer, or a moan, or wishful thinking. Lungs burning, Sam ran faster. He fell to his knees at her side as she struggled to sit up. He grabbed her shoulders.

"You shot? Bleedin' anywheres?"

"I—I don't think so." She looked more bewildered than hurt. "What happened?"

Sam hesitated, not wanting to burden Paul with any more guilt than he knew he was suffering from already.

"Shot went wild. My fault. Was wool-gatherin' 'stead of keepin' my mind on lessons. Can't see no blood. Guess you got lucky." Relief too great to manage swelled over into unreasonable anger—at her. "What the *hell* was you thinkin' to go strollin' on in right in the middle of shootin' lessons? This here's damn serious business, life an' death. Hellfire, we ain't out here playin' no games, you know."

"I—I know—"

"You don't know *nothin' about nothin'* havin' to do with survivin' in these here mountains," he roared. "An' every time I learn you one way to take care of yourself, you manage to find half a dozen others to get yourself into trouble. Woman, I ain't got the time, nor the inclination, to keep rescuin' you. Sooner you're gone for good an' all, the better off we'll all be. 'Specially me."

The second he spat out those words, he wanted to grab them back. In a face gone all over white, her eyes burned dark purple, staring back at him with a hurting look more

wounded than if she'd been shot. Making him wish he'd
kept his big mouth shut on the subject. But he hadn't,
and likely that was for the best. Citified females like Maddie
Preston didn't belong in the wilderness; there was no getting around it. Could've told her kinder, though. Regretted
not telling her kinder. But not enough to bend his pride
and apologize. And dang glad he didn't, seeing the fire
of flaring temper douse the last of smoldering hurt in her
eyes.

She broke free of his grip. scrambling to her feet in calf-
high snow, round little chin out-thrust, hands fisted on
shapely hips under Hettie's homespun. Sam didn't know
whether to feel relieved or run for cover. She let fly in
that uppity way of hers that left him fighting mad and
frustrated all at once.

"Mr. Spencer, you flatter yourself. Whether I decide to
go or stay in the Rockies is not your choice, but mine. I
know for a fact that my successes these last two weeks far
surpass my failures, despite your belief to the contrary.
Yours is not the only valley, nor your cabin the only habitat
in these Rocky Mountains. Nor are you the only mountain
man with knowledge to depart. What I do after you have
expelled me from the premises with the passing of the
winter is absolutely none of your concern."

She turned on her heels, lifted her skirt to skim the
snow, and stormed off like a freezing blizzard sweeping
through his valley. Thunderation, she was mad. Didn't take
no lengthy pondering to figure out why, nor to know this
time it'd be a good long while before she got around to
getting over it.

And likely, that wasn't the worst thing could've happened. His words, blunt spoken, were the truth even so.
Kissing aside, wasn't nothing good about being stuck in
his cabin in the middle of spring snows with the likes of

her. And them troublesome kids. He'd be better off taking the lot of them back to Fort Farewell soon's he could.

Listening to his own pack of lies, he almost took them back. Truth was, he wasn't cut out to be a family man, never was. After what happened with Hettie because of him, the only thing a man like him deserved was to live out the rest of his life all on his own.

Shouldering the burden of past blunders, Sam crossed the distance between himself and Paul, all gape-mouthed and wide-eyed with shock on account of almost killing Maddie. And James looked little better after witnessing the accident that almost was. Going to take a heap of palaver and persuasion to get the lads over this one.

Dammit, if being a pa got this hard, likely he was better off not becoming one. Ever. Lucky no one'd have him. No one but Hettie. And look where that got her.

Chapter Thirteen

Madeline did not mention the near accident when she returned to the cabin and the girls already well into supper preparations without her. And she refrained from airing her grievances against the most aggravating man in the world, Sam Spencer. Her hands trembled, her heart beat fast and hard against her rib cage like a trapped bird frantic to escape, and her thoughts tumbled about in turmoil, so entangled with errant emotion that she could not seem to manage to bring them under any kind of control.

Uppermost in her thoughts, pursuing her in her mad dash for the safety of the cabin away from Sam's temper, had been that she dared not allow his hasty and oft-repeated words, declaring her unsuited for the wilderness and unwelcome in his home and his life, to deter her from her goal. Her only salvation lay in believing him completely, utterly mistaken. For if the irritating, irascible mountain man was right, she'd have to leave this place and these people she'd grown to love with all her heart, forever. And that she simply could not do.

"A way must be found." She whispered her determination as she hung her fur robe on its hook.

"You say somethin', miss?"

Madeline blurted the first fib that came to mind. "Only wishing aloud that Mr. Spencer would get around to putting some sleeves in my outer wear. My arms become so chilled with long exposure to the elements."

She extended her hands to the warmth of the fire in the hearth for a last few private moments. Though complete composure at all times had been schooled into her at an early age as an indispensable part of social upbringing, Madeline found it more and more difficult, with the passage of time in these unaccustomed circumstances, to remain mindful of that which she had been taught. Her emotions, more often than not, ran rampant within her, some so painful as to scarcely be borne, others so wondrous as to be cherished, relished, and shared. None seemed containable by, nor submissive to, willpower alone. And she had never felt so wholly alive. She could not, would not, leave. Ever.

Let that man bluster and deny her, even turn her out. She, Madeline Genevieve Preston, simply would not go. She'd prove him wrong about her suitability for mountain living. She'd show him how much she loved the children, how capable she was of assisting in their care and guidance. Above all, she'd convince him of her love for him, and his for her, though he yet did not realize it. Whether he knew it or not, Mountain Man Sam Spencer had met his match.

Feeling much more herself, resolute and with emotions once again in hand, Madeline took a deep, steadying breath, then two, in preparation for the challenges ahead.

The cabin door burst open, slamming hard against the log wall. Madeline spun.

"Mr. Sp—"

This time it was not the man, but the boy. Leaving the door gaping, Paul darted across the room to the one he shared with his brother, tossing over one bony shoulder a threatening glare from a pale, stricken face, defying any to follow. She heard his bed protest as he threw himself down on it.

Sam followed as far as the center of the main room, then stopped dead in his tracks at the look his nephew leveled upon him before disappearing.

"Damn!"

He raked a hand through the hair at his nape. Behind him, a cringing, concerned James carefully closed the door left open by his brother. He slipped around his uncle, never taking his worried gaze off him, to hang up his coat, only then turning an imploring glance Madeline's way.

"Paul an' Uncle Sam had a *big* fight," he whispered to her conspiratorially.

"So I gathered," replied Madeline softly. "I take it the— ah, shooting incident has not been laid to rest."

Shaking his head, James leaned closer.

"No, ma'am. Paul feels real bad 'bout 'most shootin' ya. Said he don't wanta shoot no more at all. Uncle said he had'ta 'cause he's gotta know how to 'fend hisself. Like fallin' off'n a horse, he gotta get right back on. Paul, he threw Uncle's Hawken down in the snow. Said he didn't need to know how to shoot 'cause he wasn't stayin'. Then he come back here, an' we did, too." Close to tears now, James begged, "Don't let Paul go nowheres, miss. I don't want Paul to go nowheres away from the rest've us. Ma tol' us to always stick together 'cause we're a fambly. How we goin'a stick together without P-P-Paul?"

"Paul ain't goin' nowheres, youngun'," Sam boomed, clearly having heard every word. He stepped before the small boy and laid surprisingly gentle hands on his shaking shoulders, his face troubled and kind and encouraging all at the same time. "Cain't, 'til the snow melts. An' by then, me an' Paul'll've smoked a peace pipe an' this misunderstandin'll be long forgotten."

James solemnly shook his head, no longer weeping but with eyes still leaking tears down wind-whipped red cheeks.

"Paul don't like shootin'. He tol' me so 'fore them lessons even started. Said he hated ever'thin' 'bout yer lessons." He leaned in, adding in a stage whisper, " 'Cause he weren't no good at none've 'em, not like me. He don't wanta learn 'bout nothin' but readin' an' writin' an' such, Uncle Sam. He's real good at them things."

The expression on Sam's face went from solicitous to stormy as quickly as the passage of dark clouds blots out the sun. Before the next words out of his mouth destroyed all the confidence James had built up in the man, Madeline interrupted.

"Anything new and unfamiliar that is difficult to learn can be fraught with failures before ultimate success, James. Paul speaks from having suffered one of those frustrating setbacks, I am sure." She immediately realized by the puzzlement on his face that her words had been more incomprehensible than comforting. She tried again. "I know how Paul feels. Look how many times I myself have made some mistake attempting something new to me. Including dying my hands yellow." She managed a light laugh around a compassion-constricted throat. She held out her hands the shade of her childhood pet canary's feathered belly for him to examine.

He studied them in all seriousness.

"They're mighty pretty," he assured her.

"And not at all something to dwell on, as Lucy tells me they will fade, as will the memory of my error. Others of my mistakes could have resulted in far more severe consequences, like leaving food out and the door ajar, inviting a visit from that bear, which might've ended very badly indeed, and did not. Any more than did Paul's, mistake, and mine, of today. Thank Providence all's well in the end, to be forgiven and forgotten. And learned from, so as to proceed more attentively in the future." Because Sam stood near at hand, she added, "I imagine your Uncle Sam could tell stories of the same sort of mishaps occasioned by his own inexperience before he became a seasoned man of the mountains. Couldn't you, Mr. Spencer?" she asked sweetly, with a smile, knowing full well, from reading Hettie's journal, that he had.

Sam Spencer frowned, muttered, "Gotta get somethin' from the barn," and took off out of the cabin like a shot from his favorite rifle. Whether or not he understood what she was trying to convey, to him as well as the children, she had no idea. But at least she'd gotten through to James, easing his concerns considerably, as evidenced by the bright, hopeful look on his young face. Surprisingly, she had struck a chord with Paul as well. He slipped from his room now his uncle was gone, shy with embarrassment but determined to have his say.

Venturing no further than the doorway, he admitted, chin defiantly outthrust, "I ain't . . . I'm not no . . . any good at shootin' an' buildin' an' such 'cause I don't wanta be no . . . a mountain man. I don't wanta live like this when I'm a man. I've got me plans to live in the city an' take up lawyerin' or doctorin' or teachin' or some such."

"Admirable professions, every one," she agreed. "As is becoming a trailblazer and pioneer in these wilderness mountains, as your uncle chose to do. Without men of either sort, our country could not have become the land of freedom and opportunity that it is today. We all can benefit by and learn from both sorts of men."

He conceded to her point of view only by his lack of rebuttal. Obviously unwilling, even then, to back down altogether, he told her, "I ain't . . . I'm not goin'a say I'm sorry . . . about before. Your fault's much's mine."

"Nor shall I, then, for I agree."

Madeline left him a few moments of reflective solitude, turning to face his bewildered sisters. Time later, over supper dishes, for explanation, she decided.

"Would you like me to set the table? Oh, I see you've already done it. I take it supper is ready? Good, I'm starved and dinner smells delightful. James, run out and tell your uncle . . . Ah, here he is now. Mr. Spencer, come join us, if you please. It's suppertime."

Grumbling who-knew-what, he set down a fur bundle he'd brought in from the barn and did as he was told, without a word or glance in her direction. Perhaps she'd given the man much to think about, or perhaps he'd already accepted that she was right about forgiving and forgetting past mistakes but unwilling to admit it. Either way, she felt certain Sam Spencer would not be so quick to judge her failings again, nor so hasty with his threats to "toss her out on her ear," if only to retain the respect of his recently acquired progeny.

Damn, if that woman didn't have him over a barrel, leaving him no choice but to go along with her. That, or ruin any chance of saving face. She knew it, too. Sam could tell just by sneaking looks all through supper at her sneaking looks at him and grinning like a catamount with a mouth full of blue grouse feathers.

Forcing a long bone needle threaded with rawhide through fur and leather, Sam sewed sleeves into Maddie's robe, only because Jane announced at dinner that Miss Maddie's arms " 'bout freezed off" doing without. Mulling over in his mind what he could've said or done any different, he didn't come up with a single thing.

On top of everything, danged if she didn't start her reading and writing lessons tonight. Tonight, goldarn it! Leaving him no escape from listening in but to hightail it to the barn on the bitterest, blusteriest night of the whole blasted winter so far.

She'd laid claim to almost every last scrap of his stash of brown wrapping paper and torn it all into squares. Drawing stick-like shapes, one pair per piece, she told the twins, "These are the letters of the alphabet, from which all words in many of the world's languages are created. We will first learn to recognize and to copy these letters, then go on to making them into words. But before that, let me teach you a little rhyme to help us remember all of the twenty-six letters in order."

She sang her "Alphabet Song" through so many times that, hours later, her off-key voice rang in Sam's ears. And dammit, he figured he'd see that teepee-shaped A and the small one—a circle with a slash on the side—in his sleep. If he wasn't careful, he was going to learn to read and write himself, whether he wanted to or not.

Would that be so bad? Sam wasn't so sure anymore. He didn't much favor the idea of the youngun's knowing more'n him.

Pa couldn't so much as sign his name, only make his mark. He'd set no store by reading and writing, calling it a goldanged waste of time better used for tending to business. Ma, though, could manage both, enough to get by. She told him once, private-like, that Pa'd tried a time or two and hadn't gotten the hang of it. Pa didn't take to the idea of his wife being able to master something he couldn't, so she pretty much gave up on book-learning. Told Sam, his being so much like his pa, he likely'd have no luck with it either, so why bother. He'd believed her right all these years, even giving Hettie a hard time about always

writing in that little book of hers 'til she probably burned
the dang thing.

Now he wasn't so sure about Ma being right. That A
stuck in his head real good, and that off-key nursery rhyme
was sure as heck running around in there, too, 'til he could
sing it himself, backward and forward. Maybe he oughta
hang around come evenings, learn what the twins did without anyone being the wiser. Never knew when a bit of
book-learning might come in handy—if only to prove to
that woman he knew a whole hell of a lot more than she
thought he did.

Madeline struggled with growing amusement throughout the evening, from the first moment she caught a
glimpse of Sam silently mouthing the words of the "Alphabet Song" during its third or fourth repeating. At first,
she had been more concerned with not singing so badly
as to be asked to please stop. Soon discovering that softer
seemed better, she gave herself over to the pleasurable
challenge of awakening young, fallow minds to the joys of
learning. The twins lapped it up, like kittens a bowl of
cream, and so quickly that she realized that in a week's
time she'd be able to teach them simple word recognition
and beginning printing. Later, when she caught Sam in
the act, she further realized that she must give careful
thought and attention to seeing that her lessons were
clearly available to him as well. She fervently hoped her
pilfered supply of brown paper lasted for the duration.

Paul sat in one rocking chair reading *Robinson Crusoe*,
already well into the story. Even given that Bunyan's *Pilgrim's Progress* would prove heavier, slower reading, he'd
soon consume all the available reading material, at least
until a visit to the fort became possible. She had thought

long and hard on the subject throughout dinner, and it occurred to her to suggest that Paul help out with teaching the twins, perhaps take over some part of the lessons altogether, particularly since he'd expressed an interest in perhaps becoming an educator himself someday. The troubled, restless lad desperately needed something constructive to which to devote his time and attention, something at which he could succeed.

Lucy, on the other hand, seemed perfectly content with her lot, as she sat in the opposite chair, gently rocking the baby asleep in her arms. What was her future to be, here in an isolated cabin in the middle of nowhere, doing selflessly for others with no life and no future of her own? And no young men from whom to pick an appropriate suitor, if the residents of Luckless were an example of those from whom to choose. It made Madeline's heart ache to think that this lovely young woman would never know the love of a man, nor hold children of her own in her arms as she now did her small sister. Something must be done, and somehow she must be the one to do it.

In Lucy's arms, Baby stirred and whimpered, eliciting a frown of concern on Lucy's part. Baby had been fussy all day, whining and crying, coughing and sneezing, ignoring the dollie Lucy'd made just for her, refusing nourishment, sleeping long hours. Probably teething, Lucy had declared, or coming down with the sniffles. From the troubled expression on the girl's face as she sat rocking the infant, Madeline could see she was no longer so sure that either of her earlier diagnoses had been correct. She placed a wrist against Baby's brow, then bent to press her lips against the same spot. She looked up, casting a worried glance between Sam and Madeline.

"Baby's burnin' up. I think she's sick. Real sick."

* * *

Many hours later, after Sam insisted the youngsters—
all of them—get some shut-eye, that Baby'd be just fine
by morning, Madeline sat in the chair Lucy'd been forced
to vacate, rocking the sick child. Across from her, Sam
pretended to work on another part of the crib now that
all the spindles were done, but his hands fell idle as often
as not, studying the restlessly unconscious infant, concern
etched deeply into his craggy, stubble-shadowed face.

"Have you any idea what might be wrong with her?"
Madeline asked.

Sam shook his head.

"Could be anythin' from teethin' to croup, or worse."

"How much worse?" her voice trembled.

"Symptoms for influenza an' diphtheria start out pretty
much the same as hers." Sam's tone and expression were
grim. "An' both'll spread like wildfire to the rest've us.
Diphtheria's what took her pa an' ma."

Madeline understood the implication at once, and felt
the blood drain from her face.

"Either one of the two is, as a rule, fatal to all who come
in contact with it."

Sam met her gaze, tight-lipped he merely nodded. Faced
with the staggering possibility of eminent death for them
all—herself, those dear, dear children, Sam—oh, please
not Sam—she went cold all over. Her throat constricted,
requiring her to swallow twice before speaking, giving her
needed time to gather her resources to deal with the reality
of their lot. She lifted her chin to look him squarely in
the eyes.

"Whether cold, or croup, or more serious, we must
somehow alleviate this poor baby's suffering if we can.
What can we do to ease her cough, bring down this fever?"
Madeline persisted. "I've heard high fevers alone can be

dangerous, especially in so small a child, no matter what their cause. And these bouts of coughing fairly shake her apart. Sometimes it's all she can do to catch her breath afterwards."

"No remedy I know of that I'd dare dose a youngun' so little with, most bein' poison if you give too much. I'll make up a poultice to ease the coughin'. An' we can keep some water boilin' for the steam, feed her a bit of honey as often as she'll take it in case her throat hurts. An' wait."

The night wore on slowly. Madeline tended the sick baby, and Sam began construction of the crib, which came together within the hour. He padded the bed with a soft fur and held out his arms for the dozing child.

"Let's see how she fits."

Madeline opened her mouth to protest.

"Maybe she'll rest easier. You can always pick her up again if she don't."

She relinquished her small burden reluctantly all the same, knowing she herself derived the most comfort from holding her, touching her. Sam took her gingerly, held her awkwardly—for the first time, Madeline realized. He held her quite some time, swaying slightly when she fitfully roused briefly, looking down into her flushed face, a sad, reflective expression on his own. Finally, he laid her in the crib and covered her with a soft square of flannel from his endless store in the barn. He studied Baby for a good long while before turning to see Madeline candidly watching him. He started to say something, stopped, then began again, as if he couldn't keep to himself any longer the thoughts long trapped within.

"M'own youngun' would've been nine years old by now. Bigger'n the twins, near Paul's size, likely."

Madeline chose her words with utmost care, speaking softly.

"How sad he or she never had the opportunity."

"He."

"Beg pardon?"

"He. A boy. Stillborn. Named him William, after my pa."

"I'm so sorry."

"No sorrier than me."

He sat in the rocker opposite her and rocked back so that his face lay in shadows.

"Sorry 'bout a lot of things."

She thought he might mean to apologize to her for his verbal transgressions against her earlier in the day, but his thoughts had taken another turn altogether.

"Sorry Hettie never got to see her babe, nor hold him. Sorry I weren't here to keep her an' him from dyin'." He rocked forward into firelight, leveling her with a steady stare. "My fault, their dyin'. Wasn't here when they needed me." His grim pronouncement seemed to hold some veiled warning for her as well.

She tried to come up with the best possible response to this unknown something, and failing, offered, "I—I'm sure you would have been here if you could have."

"Could've."

"Oh!" The one word came out in a whisper.

"Went off on a danged-fool errand down to the fort when I shouldn't've, knowin' full well a spring blizzard was comin' our way. Thought I could beat it. Didn't. Got stuck at the fort for days. Found her gone ... dead ... when I got home."

"In childbirth?"

"That, an' fallin' off the ladder outta the loft, probably when a birthin' pain come over her."

Madeline paled; a cold chill slithered down her spine. Vividly she recalled Hettie's last journal entry, and her intention to bring the bride's quilt down from the loft, despite Sam's warning against it before he left. Dared she tell him? Dared she not? Calling herself a million kinds of coward, Madeline postponed the inevitable with evasion.

"How . . . how awful for you."

"Worse for Hettie. Spare me your pity, Maddie. I don't deserve it. She begged me not to go. Told her I had to, havin' ordered somethin' real special for her to celebrate our first year together that needin' pickin' up at the fort. Damn stubborn fool, I paid her no heed and she died 'cause of it. All for a dozen fancy silver teaspoons decorated on the end with 'S' for Spencer."

Madeline's chest tightened. "Wh-what did you do with them?"

"Flung 'em over the first cliff I come to soon's I got the chance. Couldn't stand havin' 'em around to remind me."

She tried to hold her tongue, and failed.

"One of Hettie's spoons saved my life, Sam. If I had not found it half-buried in the dirt and leaves at my feet, I would never have seen the trail through the mountains leading me straight to your cabin and salvation from death by freezing or starvation."

She resisted the temptation to suggest Providential intervention once again because he looked so faraway in thought, his face so solemn, so sad.

"Did you keep it?" he asked after a time, tone low, hesitant.

"What?"

Her thoughts had already sped beyond her admission to the other which needed airing, coming back with difficulty.

"The spoon. You still got it?"

"I . . . yes." She patted the pocket in the seam of Hettie's dress. "I keep it with me at all times as a reminder of my good fortune . . . a talisman of sorts."

"Can I look at it?"

Reluctantly, with a nod she agreed, slipping her hand inside the folds of her skirt to retrieve the small item of

so great importance to them both, extending her offering
to him not knowing if it would be returned or pitched
into the fire. For a long minute he simply stared down at
it; and when he took it from her, he handled the silver
spoon as though it might burn his hand. Wrapping his
fingers around the stem, he thoughtfully ran a thumb over
the bowl. At last, he simply handed it back to her without
comment.

"M-m-may I keep it, then?"

He leaned back into the shadows.

"I don't need it to remind me of somethin' I ain't never
goin' to forget anyway. I was young, an' stubborn, an'
greener'n I knew in them days. Cost me everythin' meant
anythin' to me. Them kinda lessons stay with a man all
the way to the grave."

Tempted to offer words of sympathy, she knew instinctively they would not be welcome. She could ease his mind
a bit, though, if she had the courage. She could tell him
about Hettie's journal and what she'd read therein. And
yet, she dared not shatter the tentative companionability
between them with a blunt revelation. She rose to check
on the baby. The infant, round cheeks flushed, eyelids
blue-veined, so fragile in appearance, so vulnerable, did
not stir even when Madeline brushed back clinging damp
curls from her too-pale forehead. Slipping back into her
vacated rocker, Madeline attempted a roundabout approach to the subject that would not leave her alone.

"When we were sorting through boxes . . . I found a few
things of a personal nature, yours and Het . . . your wife's,
which I put all together in one. I have them stored for you
under my bed, out of harm's way. Would you rather keep
them elsewhere, in your room perhaps?"

After a pause. "Leave 'em be." A lengthier pause.
"There a book in them things? Handwritten? Had a brown
cover, as I recall."

"Blue. The cover is blue."

"You found it, then?"

"N-n-not during . . . during sorting. Earlier." He said nothing, and the silence between them grew ominous. "It . . . it was one of the three books you gave me to read a few days ago."

He barked a harsh laugh.

"If I'd've known how to read, would've known. Could've read it for myself after . . ."

There was another long silence, during which a burning log fell apart, sending up a shower of sparks. Madeline jumped.

"I take it you read it . . . Hettie's book?" His voice, surprisingly, held no rancor.

Shamefaced, Madeline nodded.

"I'm sorry. Yes. But not out of idle curiosity. Please believe it wasn't that. I—I felt a need to know . . . I hoped to learn more about . . . about you, a stranger with whom I was sharing very close quarters, someone I needed to believe worthy of my trusting with my very life. Especially after sharing . . . intimacies with a man who, you must admit, gave me more reason for apprehension than confidence."

"Did you learn anythin' to set your mind at ease?" he asked quietly, without emotion, his shadowed face revealing nothing.

She hesitated, thinking back over Hettie's journal entries.

"Yes. I believe I did. Reading her thoughts, seeing the husband she loved so completely through her eyes, I knew that she would never have given that love to a man without honor. She was very proud of you, Sam. And of this home you two shared. And so happy about the . . . the baby. If there were a flaw at all in her perfect life, it would have been that you never told her that you loved her."

Baby whimpered in her sleep but slept on.

"Never got the chance."

Madeline's skirts rustled as she rocked forward to study his shadowed features.

"Did you? Love her?"

He didn't answer at once, and she feared he might not at all. Then feared he might.

"Yes. Still do."

An ache settled deep within her, one she imagined would be there always.

"I—I'm glad. I think I would have loved her, too, had I known her. She'd probably have been a friend as valued as the ones I left behind at home."

"Then you oughta be happy to be headin' home once the way down to the fort opens up." Now an unaccounted-for anger tinged his words.

Disappointment, especially with the change in subject before she'd had her fill of the other, made her respond as bluntly.

"Mr. Spencer, you may as well accept the fact that I will not be leaving these mountains and that my future does not lie back East, but here."

"Here?" He bit out the word as if it had a bitter taste.

"Here in the Rockies. Perhaps at Fort Farewell."

"Doin' what? Married up with some bluecoat officer?"

She tilted her chin high. "Not an impossibility, though most probably as a tutor . . . or a nanny for the post children."

She waited with bated breath for him to challenge the idea, offer an alternative. Ask her to stay. With him. He said nothing, nor did he betray his sentiments by a change in his resumed impenetrable stoicism, as stony as his mountain. She searched her mind for some means of drawing him out again, and couldn't think of a thing. Having aired all her confessions, having listened to his, she should have felt some sense that the problems standing between them had been resolved, freeing them to love and accept love in return. That they had not was by far the most unpalatable pill she'd so far had to swallow. Another romantic fantasy on her part, as was the one that set her feet upon this folly-fraught journey in the first place. Foolish Madeline, heedless Madeline, lost in the middle of nowhere, in love with a man who chose not to return her love.

Tempted to run off to her room to hide, still she could not bring herself to leave lest Baby need her. The child appeared no better, possibly worse. Her breathing had grown more labored, her cough rattled thickly, and though her eyes seldom opened, she did not really seem to sleep. The heat of her small body radiated into the room. Heart aching with helplessness, Madeline raised her gaze to Sam's troubled one, offering no reassurance.

"You must give her a name, in case—"

Sam bolted from the chair, setting it to rocking violently. "Don't say it! She ain't goin'a die." He raked both hands through his already tousled hair, then scrubbed the back of his neck. "Been thinkin' on it. Figured to name her after her ma. Emily."

"Emily," Madeline repeated softly, uncertainly.

"What's wrong with it?" he demanded.

"Nothing, it's a lovely name, only that . . . the children . . . a reminder . . . it being so soon . . ."

"You got a better notion?"

"I . . . yes, I do. Faith. Faith Emily, if you will. Because faith is all that we have to go on—for her survival, and ours—without a doctor or medicine."

He offered no objection, his expression going from thoughtful to resolute.

"Call 'er whatever you've a mind to. But it ain't strictly true we gotta do without doctorin' an' medicine. I know where t'go for 'em both. I'll be headin' out soon's I shrug on my coat an' slap on my snowshoes."

Chapter Fourteen

"Don't go."

She watched him make his preparations to leave without speaking, but when he threw his snowshoes over one shoulder by their sinew straps and headed for the door, she could contain herself no longer. He hesitated, swiveling toward her, expression shadowed by the huge fur hood pulled protectively up around his face.

"Got to, Maddie, an' we both know it."

"How will I—we—manage?"

"Just fine 'til I get back. Warm an' dry, with plenty of food an' all the snow you could ever need for drinkin' and wash water."

His halfhearted attempt to make light of the situation did not mask the concern in his voice—for Baby Faith, for the other children, and for her. Madeline's greatest worries, however, were for him.

"What if a blizzard should overtake you . . . all alone . . . even with the snowshoes? It's a long way to the fort, miles to Luckless, snow higher than the trees in many places, as you yourself have frequently informed me, and impassable.'' She tried to sway with reason alone, but could not keep the fear out of her words. "What if you become ill like the baby, fevered, unconscious, desperately sick, far from home?''

He managed a one-sided smile.

"You goin' to worry 'bout me all the while I'm gone?''

Madeline had almost betrayed her feelings for him, though knowing his heart lay elsewhere. She stiffened, head high, responding with all the hauteur she could muster.

"Don't flatter yourself, Mr. Spencer. Under normal circumstances, you would be the last soul on earth for whom I'd spare five minutes of anxiety. Unfortunately, the safety and well-being of six others depends heavily on yours. I merely—merely—''

"Woman, you're one damned poor liar,'' Sam said quietly.

Two strides brought him from the door to her. He hauled her to him with an arm thrown around her waist, lifting her onto her tiptoes so that she had to cling to him or topple. Her arms encircled his neck and she clung while he kissed her deeply and long, a kiss she soon returned in kind, despite herself. Why resist when this embrace might very well be their last? She held back nothing nor, she felt certain, did Sam. Whether from the intensity of the moment, or true emotion, she did not know, and dared not hope.

When they reluctantly drew apart, breathless, she rested her forehead against his shoulder, hiding from him the naked emotion she knew he'd easily read upon her face. She felt his lean, angular jaw jump against the crown of her head, a sure sign of his own struggle for self-control, and took what small comfort from her knowledge that she could. All too soon, he broke contact, holding her away from him with firm hands upon her shoulders, his brown eyes, void of amber flecks, dark with concern, searching hers.

"I gotta go."

Tempted to turn her face away to hide rising fear, she kept her gaze steady, locked on his.

"I know."

"I'm goin' to be all right. So will you and the kids. And I'll be back. Give you my word on it."

She tried a reassuring smile, her lips briefly lifting at the corners in a brave grimace.

"I shall depend upon that promise, Sam Spencer."

He backed away from her to the door, raising a mittened hand.

"*Kla-hay-yah*, Maddie! That's good-bye, an' hello, in Indian talk. Meanin' the time apart's only temporary."

"*Kla-hay-yah!*" she repeated, along with the gesture, palm out. "I'll remember that."

Then, with a final peck on her cheek, he was gone, and she was alone, sole caretaker for a seriously ill child and the as-yet unaffected others. Panic rose up in her throat, drawing a breath becoming nearly impossible. She desired nothing more than to chase after Sam while yet she could, plead anew that he not go.

Baby Faith awoke with a start in a fit of coughing that sent Madeline flying to the crib by the hearth instead. Finding the infant red in the face, gasping for air, Madeline snatched her up from a tangle of covers, holding her upright against one shoulder, vigorously patting her back until the paroxysm eased with a wail, then a fitful whimper. Crossing to the rocker, Madeline sat, holding the child close against her bosom, receiving comfort as well as dispensing it with soft words of reassurance in lieu of a lullaby she feared might prove more unsettling than soothing, given her singing ability.

She held and rocked and whispered to Baby Faith through the remainder of the night, through periods of fitful dozing and alarming episodes of coughing. So fevered was the poor mite that Madeline soon became uncomfortable herself with radiated heat, but she dared not put Baby down in her crib even for a moment when only in an upright position did the small sufferer experience any relief.

As the first rays of dawn lightened the room, when Madeline could scarcely keep her eyes open, Lucy, sleep-tousled but dressed, appeared at her side, arms extended.

"Let me hold her for a while, miss."

"Gladly," Madeline responded softly, "if I can make my sleep-numbed limbs do my bidding."

The exchange was made without waking the baby.

"How is she? Any better?"

Lucy looked from her sister's small, flushed face to Madeline, hope in her question and in her eyes. Sleep-weary and emotions raw, Madeline bit her lower lip to keep it from trembling, shaking her head.

"Her condition has been unchanged throughout the night, restless sleep between coughing spells and a fever so high, the cool, damp cloths applied to her forehead seem to have little effect."

Madeline watched hope die, wishing for a brief moment that she had been less frank, realizing that Lucy would expect to be treated as an equal and an ally in the matter of the care of her small sister. Accepting the truth with characteristic stoicism, Lucy took Madeline's place in the rocking chair, babe in arms, while Madeline stretched out numerous kinks and aches.

"Why don't you go to bed, miss?"

"I couldn't sleep, not knowing how she fared ... and your uncle."

Scanning the small room in a glance, Lucy frowned. "Where is Uncle Sam?"

"He went for help—a doctor, medicine—from who knows where. He's been gone all night."

Worry came out sounding like impatience, and she was too weary to correct the impression, though she didn't fool the girl in the least.

"Uncle'll come back safe an' sound, miss," Lucy interjected quietly. "He got Baby her milk, didn't he? An' it was stormin' that time. Not snowin' at all this mornin'." She nodded toward the uncurtained window beside the door.

Madeline turned her head to see daybreak offering up a spectacular rainbow of color across a cobalt sky. The sight brought tears to her eyes and fresh optimism to her heart. She offered Lucy a weak smile.

"You're right." She sighed and rubbed the back of her sore neck. "It's lack of sleep making me so irritable, nothing more. A bracing cup of coffee is what I need—no, you sit still, I can make it. I've not watched you all this time without learning how to prepare an adequate pot myself."

But when, later, she sat across from Lucy, each sipping from a pewter cup, Madeline had to admit her coffee had turned out thick enough to stand a spoon in upright, and bitter, if bracing. She continued to sip long after Lucy set hers aside.

"Should I warm some milk for Baby Faith?" The slip of the tongue occasioned a silent query in Lucy's blue eyes. "Your Uncle Sam and I ... we named her last night ... because she is so ill. Subject to your approval, and that of your brothers and sister, of course. Faith with the anticipation that she shall weather this illness and soon be well again, and as a middle name your mother's—"

"Emily," she finished. "Faith Emily. I like that, miss." She kissed her sister's fever-damp forehead, then glanced up. "And so'll the others'll once they hear."

And they did. Faced with the seriousness of their infant sister's plight, each made an effort to be of help to free Madeline and Lucy of all but care for their small, ailing sister. James hauled in wood, and Paul stoked the fire without having to be asked; Jane set the table and stirred breakfast biscuits, and would have done more if Madeline had not refused to allow the youngster near the cooking fire, over Jane's usual, vocal arguments.

A somber meal followed a quiet morning, permitting the baby to rest whenever possible. Paul took himself off to the barn to feed and water the animals and milk the goat. Eventually, when their pleas became annoyingly frequent, Madeline permitted the twins to follow him there, with their promise to be careful and keep out of trouble, eliciting glib affirmations.

She should have suspected they had other plans after observing them with heads together all through breakfast, whispering and plotting, but she had not, too weary and too preoccupied with worry over Faith and Sam, to even recall the incident until Paul returned alone from the barn near noon.

"Where are the twins?" she asked over her shoulder as she set out pewter plates heaped with warmed leftover biscuits, white gravy, and crisp bacon.

Paul hung up his jacket, more attentive to the volume of *Robinson Crusoe* nearby on the mantel than his siblings' whereabouts.

"Ain't seen 'em since breakfast," he answered absently.

Cold apprehension settled in Madeline's midsection.

"I only allowed them outdoors because they promised to join you in the barn. Could they be playing outside nearby, perhaps hiding from you, expecting that you'd search?''

Paul shook his head, a frown drawing his light brows together.

"Without me hearin' them all mornin' long? Not that pair. Want me to go out lookin' for 'em?''

"If you will. But please don't wander too far. You should be able to follow their tracks in the snow leading to wherever they took themselves.''

The boy shook his head. "Sun's melted all them tracks around an' 'bout the cabin 'til you can't tell fresh from old.''

Madeline fought to still her rising fear, to reassure the youngsters, and herself, that nothing more than disobedience was involved, though she could not help but remember the bear. That large, hungry bear.

Paul reached for his jacket.

"I'll go circle the cabin, give 'em a holler. Don't fret none, ma'am, they'll come runnin' soon's they know it's time for eats.''

Lucy waited until her brother left the cabin before expressing her own grave concerns.

"I heard the twins whisperin' together this mornin', miss, 'bout wantin' to see them wolf puppies, though Uncle Sam told 'em 'no'.''

Madeline felt a sudden chill.

"Surely they wouldn't set out in search of them all by themselves?''

"Might've. Wolf goes visitin' every mornin' hisself. Maybe they figured on trailin' him . . .'' Her words dwindled, choked off by fear. She tried again, voice no more than a whisper. "Oh, miss, I'm awful 'fraid they've gone an' done just that an' got themselves lost out there in the mountains somewheres.''

"Let's . . . let's not borrow trouble. Maybe Paul has found

them by now no farther away than behind the cabin, building a snowman or a fort, engaging in a snowball battle with an imaginary foe . . ." Anything but what her fears conjured up. "I haven't heard him call out for them for a while now, certainly a good sign, don't you think?"

Both turned their heads toward the door as it swung inward, their rising hopes quickly crushed by Pauls' downhearted expression, his grim, tight lips. He looked from his sister to Madeline.

"Found me some tracks out back where the sun ain't reached yet. Looks like them kids took off after Wolf for sure. Just come inside to let you know I'm goin' after 'em."

"No, Pauly, don't!" Lucy cried out in alarm.

He glared at her. "Don't ya think I can find 'em on m'own?"

Madeline interceded to salvage his faltering ego. "That isn't it at all. Lucy and I, we need you here." Inspiration dawned. "You're the only one of us with any experience in loading and firing Sam's Hawken, which, thank fortune, he left behind for us."

He hesitated at the door. "Who's goin' to go lookin' for those kids if not me?"

"Your uncle. When he returns, any time now."

"I'll give him 'til mid-afternoon. He don't get back by then, I'm headin' out on m'own. Days're longer, but night still comes on right quick, and cold. Jane and James'll be scared to death out there all alone in the dark, even if they did find Wolf, or him them."

They ate the lunch Madeline had prepared in silence broken only by the sonorous breathing and intermittent coughing and crying from the baby. No one had much of an appetite, but all knew they needed to fortify themselves for whatever lay ahead in the hours to come.

The long afternoon hours were on the wane when Paul rose from the book he'd ceased pretending to read and crossed the room to retrieve his snowshoes from the stack leaning against the wall in the corner. He had spent the first hour after lunch showing Madeline how to load and aim the Hawken, though in the end she convinced him to take it, that they'd be far safer in the cabin with the bar dropped down over the door than he would be out in the woods on his own. Reluctantly, the boy agreed. Knowing how much he hated the weapon and its capabilities, Madeline had to admire the innate courage in the manner in which he accepted his unavoidable responsibilities.

Paul reached to take down the rifle from above the mantel; the cabin door burst open. Three figures filled the opening, blocking the sun. Backlit by its glow, their faces deep in shadow, they might've been anyone. Marauding renegades. Red-skinned or white.

Paul gripped the stock and swung, Hawken at the ready, pressed into his shoulder. The central figure took a step into the room, hand upraised in the sign of peace.

"Whoa, boy. It's me, Uncle Sam. Put that dang rifle back where you found it before you shoot some innocent—" He stopped himself, too late.

Clearly shamed at the reminder of having almost shot Madeline days ago, Paul did as bid, his face a stormcloud of dark emotions.

Sensing he'd not appreciate some placating comment on her part, Madeline restrained herself, resisting as well the impulse to race to Sam's side and cling to him for fear he'd disappear again if she let go. All her worry for him in his lengthy absence fell away, forgotten, at the reassuring sight of him standing there before her, big and bold and so handsome a sight in her eyes as to rob her of her very breath. Unspoken prayers of gratitude for his safe return swelled in her heart, and with them, so grew her love, acknowledged and denied in the same rapid beat. This was neither the time nor the place for arrant, unrequited emotions.

Rooted where she stood by willpower alone, she disregarded proper amenities and his traveling companions with the urgency of finding the missing twins before great harm befell them. If it hadn't already.

"Sam, the twins—"

He stopped her with an impatient gesture. "Maddie, this here's Bertie an' Nahios-si. Bertie's brung along her bag full of potions an' poultices aplenty for curin' the baby."

Stepping further into the room, encouraging his companions to follow, Sam ushered into his home two swarthy savages, dressed much like himself in rawhide and robes and knee-high fur-lined moccasins. Both wore beads and feathers in their braided hair as had Sam at first, the one called Nahios-si with twin black braids framing an angular, hawk-nosed face. The other, Bertie, had a single silver-streaked, braid down the back, like Madeline herself, who now found her gaze upon her, a bold, blue-eyed gaze. A woman, and a white one at that. Shocked into forgetful silence, Madeline stared openly, belatedly remembering her manners as temporary hostess in Sam's home.

"Welcome . . . welcome to you both."

The woman responded in English laced with a New Englander's twang. "Pleased to meet you, too, miss. Sam here says you got yourself a frettish baby."

"Yes, and thank fortune you've come. Nothing we've tried seems to help. Please excuse my initial rudeness, Miss—Mrs.—"

"Call me Bertie. Land sakes! Your welcome's friendlier than we come to expect. The pair of us make quite a sight, and I'm the first to admit it. Now, where's that sick little 'un?"

"Here, ma'am," Lucy responded without hesitation

from the rocking chair. She held the bundled baby up like an offering, tears gathering in her eyes. "Please make my sister well, if you can, ma'am."

Bertie carefully took the fretful, feverish infant into her arms, a kind smile for Lucy and soft words for the baby in a soothing foreign tongue. The baby fell attentively still. The medicine woman sat herself down in the other rocker, removing layered blankets with infinite care, never ceasing the flow of her sing-song words. Raptly attentive, Baby Faith stared into the woman's leathered face, unprotesting, as Bertie made a thorough examination, even when she placed an ear to Baby's chest, listening long and hard. The old mountain woman nodded twice.

"Hain't croup, nor diphtheria, nor influenza, or the poor mite'd be gone ere now. Bronchitis, most likely," she declared to one and all, then requested of her Indian companion, "Fetch me that there pouch, if'n you will. T'other'n, thank you kindly."

He retrieved for her the requested bundle from the pile at his feet, speaking quietly in his own tongue in a deep-timbred voice, nodding his head at her response. Bertie rummaged briefly through the contents of her bag, coming up with a small rawhide pouch and extending it to him. He reached for it, and Madeline was shocked to see he had no little finger on his broad, bronzed right hand, only an angry scar to show that he once had; and upon his using both hands to loosen the pouch's drawstring, she saw too that the man was missing the corresponding finger on the other hand.

Madeline quickly suppressed curiosity born of an overly active imagination for more pressing matters. While Bertie issued terse instructions to Lucy for boiling a measure of her herbs in water, Madeline moved to Sam's side, gripping his upper arm and tugging to regain his attention, for all the world like some possessive wife.

"Sam, the twins have been missing since before noon."

Something deep inside Sam's belly flip-flopped like a dying trout tossed up on a rocky shore. Quicker than the blink of an eye, the homecoming he'd dreamt about all those long, worrisome hours tramping over hill and valley to Nahios-si and Bertie's place gave up the ghost sure as that same danged fish. Expecting a warm welcome with Maddie's arms flung around his neck and hot kisses from her hot lips thawing his frozen ones, he'd come eyeball to eyeball with the business end of his own Hawken. Now this! Dang! If it wasn't enough to make the best of the mountain men throw up his arms in defeat, let alone a crusty old catamount like himself.

"No sign of them since?" he growled.

Guilt-ridden, and despite Sam Spencer's reverting to the surly demeanor he'd relied on to intimidate when first they met, Madeline forced herself to admit, "I sent them to the barn to play when they begged. Paul was tending the animals and I . . . I was so certain they'd run right out to him as promised. I had no idea they had an agenda of their own. Paul found tracks behind the house, Wolf's and two smaller, human sets. We fear they've trailed him to visit his mate and puppies. I should never have—"

Lucy spoke up from across the room, stiff-spined, voice quivering. "Ain't Miss Maddie's fault, Uncle Sam. I heard them whisperin' together 'bout the wolf pups an' paid it no mind. Knowin' the mischief them two can get into, I shoulda—"

Sam's nonverbal grumble interrupted.

"Nobody to blame but those two scalawags themselves. I know where the she-wolf's cave is. If Wolf ain't back, he's probably there. An' if the kids are too, he'll be keepin' an eye on them 'til someone comes searchin'." His ire burned itself out, concern furrowing his brow. He leveled upon Madeline his steady, dependably candid gaze, reassuring her. "Don't fret, Maddie, Nahios-si and me'll have those scamps back home before dark to devil you same as always."

"I'm goin' too."

Defiant, Paul by tone alone, dared his uncle to disagree.

Bertie spoke up. "Go along then, all of you. Best not to have menfolk underfoot when there's woman's work to be done anyhow. Sooner you set out, sooner you'll all be back, youngun's in hand."

For the second time, Madeline watched Sam head out on a quest of uncertain outcome, and little she could do but wait and follow their progress from the window until the trio disappeared from sight. Shadows of the towering pines surrounding the cabin stretched long across the snow with the afternoon on the wane. Night would come soon and swiftly. She offered up a prayer for a safe return for Sam and the others, and the twins home unharmed, fearful that she had already received her allotment of answers for one day from the Almighty. Believing with all certainty that without this man as well as each and every one of his inherited children, though she could somehow go on with the remainder of her life, she would no longer have the heart for it. Should Sam never learn to love her as she did him, she very likely would be faced with that eventuality.

"Honey?"

The old medicine woman said something to her she'd missed.

"I'll get it, ma'am."

Lucy scurried to comply. From her position by the window, Madeline watched the girl gather up the honey pot as well as a spoon and mixing bowl, while she herself wool-gathered. She should have been more attentive, more useful. Madeline pressed two fingertips between her brows, rubbing at the ache lodged there, resisting a heavy, self-pitying sigh with difficulty and reminding herself that she hadn't had so much as a few moments sleep since . . . since she couldn't remember when. Nor would she any time soon. Nothing mattered now but that the twins be found safe and sound, and Baby Faith be restored to good health. And that she herself make some useful contribution rather that stand uselessly by, mulling over maudlin self-recriminations. She watched, along with Lucy, who sat on a three-legged stool at Bertie's side, as the gray-haired woman of undeterminable age fed the baby a spoonful of a freshly decocted infusion of herbs and honey mixed together in a pottery bowl.

Squaring her shoulders, Madeline asked, "What can I do to be of assistance?"

Bertie glanced up, her keen blue eyes in a lined and weathered face missing little, Madeline was sure.

"Come set yourself down by the fire. You look plum tuckered out. Hain't nothing more to do afore it's time to dose this here wee one agin. Shouldn't wonder Sam'll've found them youngun's by then. He's an able lad, is Sam Spencer. Ayup." Sagely, she bobbed her head.

Madeline silently complied, afraid that if she said anything, she'd betray all, so raw were her emotions, so troubled her thoughts. She concentrated instead on listening intently as Bertie offered a bit of her seemingly vast herbal knowledge.

"Injun tobaccy's good for fever and coughs, and a mess of other complaints. Potent stuff. Some call it poison. Takes study and practice, and larnin' from someone what knows. Used proper, though, it'll save a life. For this sweet little mite, a teaspoon—mostly honey to make it slide down slick and tasty—by the hour oughter do it, if'n it's going to work at all."

"How soon will we know?"

"Should be seeing improvement in a couple of hours."

Already Faith appeared to have found some measure of

relief from one dose alone, for she slept more easily now than in the many endless hours preceeding. Or perhaps she sensed that the woman who held her possessed the healing skills to make her well. Maybe she merely took comfort from the soft sing-song in a foreign language that sounded to Madeline like a lullaby. Sam's medicine woman seemed a true miracle-worker indeed.

Refusing to sleep until the outcome for all the children proved successful, Madeline distracted herself by asking one of the numerous questions crowding her mind regarding this most unusual woman, hopefully one of the more tactful ones, garnering no offense.

"Did you learn about herbal medicine from your husb— from Na . . . Nayo . . .?"

Bertie broke off her gentle chant, chuckling amiably and rocking, baby to her shoulder, rubbing her back in slow, soothing circles.

"Nahios-si, meaning Three-Fingers was you wondering, and he's my husband sure enough, for more'n twenty-five year now. Calculate you have a whole mess of questions about me and him, hain't you? So let me ease your mind some with the telling of my tale. First off, I reckon by now you kinder figured out I hain't Cheyenne."

She accepted her listeners' rapt silence as assent, her eyes taking on a faraway look. "I was borned in upstate New York. How long ago hain't nobody's business but mine and my Maker's. Papa was a preacher. Married up with a preacher, too, Fred Barnes by name, a strapping, good-hearted young fella . . ." Lost in memories, Bertie's voice drifted to a stop. Sadness touched her leathery face, but fleetingly, before she drew herself back to her narration.

"Both of them, Papa and Fred, made it their mission in life to bring God's Word to the Injuns way out west of the Mississippi. Me and Mama, we come along, too, having both given our sacred vow in the Good Lord's house to stick by our men come what may." Bertie shook her head ruefully. "Had no idear the kinder trouble we was heading inter." Madeline involuntarily murmured agreement. "Ayup, see you knowed jest what I'm talking about. And I'm as eager to hear your story as you are mine, so I won't ramble on and on, but get right to the gist of it. 'T'warn't more'n a few days afore reaching these here Rocky Mountains afore them Injuns set upon us and our party of travelers like ourself and our guides, and when 't'was over . . . 't'warn't nobody left save me and my unborned babe. 'T'warn't for me being big with child, likely I'd not've been spared neither . . ." She paused, her voice liquid with emotion.

"If this is too difficult—"

"Not so hard, my dear, that I cain't finish the telling. As Sam's loved ones, you'd best understand all there is to about the company he keeps."

Madeline stored away for later the impulse to correct Bertie's misconceptions about herself, letting the older woman go on without interruption.

"I recollect how danged much I was wishing I'd been kilt right off, too, afore bringing to mind my soon-to-be-birthed babe. Them Injuns, five renegades amongst their own people, come to find out, carried me on back to camp hog-tied and tossed me inter one feller's tipi . . . that's what they call them cone-shaped houses, tipis, made outer poles and rawhide.

"Couldn't get myself free of my bindings no matter how I tried, and I'm here to say I tried my dangedest, right up 'til I knowed for certain sure my baby was acoming afore its time. Mebe from my struggling, mebe from the horrors jest past and expected yet to come. But that young 'n' was on its way, and not a blessed thing I could do to stop it, all trussed up hands and feet like a biddy hen ready for plucking. The pains was coming harder and faster, and I started hollering my fool head off for help. Weren't long afore I calculated wasn't nobody coming. I was all 'lone in my time of need, more 'lone than a body oughter ever be in this here old world." She paused, her hesitation intentional and dramatic. "Hain't telling you all this to unsettle you, but so's you'll understand what happened after."

"Please, continue," Madeline prodded.

Bertie roused herself like a waking sleeper.

"After I give this here babe another good dose, then I'll finish up my tale. The worst, and the best, is yet to come."

Chapter Fifteen

"Fever's down," Bertie announced soon after administering the second dose. "Oughter be near normal afore long. Coughing's quieted some, too. That there Injun tobaccy'll work wonders, if'n it don't kill a body first."

She chuckled, the sound much like a cackling hen, handed the baby off to Lucy, and settled herself more comfortably into the rocking chair beside the fire across from Madeline. She waited for Lucy to bed down the infant and pull her stool closer before picking up the thread of her story.

"Now where was I?"

"You were havin' a baby an' no one'd help," Lucy eagerly supplied.

"Ayup, ayup. And there I was, scared 'most to death what with being captured by Injuns meaning me who-knowed-what harm, and birthing my first baby not knowing how I'd manage all on my own. Having to push so bad I was near busting with holding back. They tell you giving birth's going to hurt, but not how bad—I guess 'cause if'n they did, you'd've kept your legs crossed in the first place." She chuckled. "Well, jest when I didn't reckon I could hold back no more, he come inter that tipi—"

"Na . . . Na-hios-si?" Madeline interjected, so caught up in the tale she forgot her good manners.

Bertie nodded vigorously. "Only he weren't Nahios-si, not then. Named Viho, meaning chief, that's how high his kindred's hopes was for him. Afore that night.

"Well now, he knelt down afore me, cut me free of my bindings, and went right to work helping me bring that young'n' inter the world, jest like he'd been doing it all his life. And without speaking nary a word to me. Stayed only long enough to catch my little gal in his own two hands when she come sliding outer me, then he were gone, as silent as he arrived.

"I dozed off after that, too tuckered out to keep vigil over my newborn babe and myself. Some while later, I woke up smelling food. It bein' still dark as pitch inside the tipi, I had to crawl around a bit afore I found a bowl with some kinder corn mush in it. Reckoned that same feller left it for me. Et down every bite and—I'm 'shamed to admit it—licked that bowl clean. Agin later, but still not morning, I heard a big ruckus going on outside the hide walls of my prison, men's voices—a half-dozen or more— shouting amongst theirselves. 'Course, I had no idear what about, not understanding a word of it, though I was some concerned it might be over me and my youngun' . . . what to do with us now I was done with birthing.

"Morning come, but no one bothered us all that day, not so much as to bring us food nor water. I reckoned them Injuns was planning on letting us die slow and hard of hunger and thirst. So I started plotting to escape, not sure how I'd accomplish it, still being all weak and shaky-like, and the little 'un depending on me 'cause there weren't no one else.

"That night, late, Nahios-si come back, his hands all wrapped in bandages, real crude, like he' a done it hisself. He made motion for me to rise up and follow him. When he saw I couldn't, he picked me up inter them strong arms of his—unmindful of his hurt hands—and carried me and that babe out of that Cheyenne camp clean over the mountains to safety. We been together ever since. And if'n you want to know more, you'll jest have to let me wet my whistle a bit, then I'll answer all yer questions I can."

They sipped cups of the honey-sweetened herbal tea Bertie had concocted in companionable silence. Baby Faith slept the deep sleep of healing, rosy-cheeked, with fading fever, breathing normally. Bertie let her go without her next dose, advising, "Wait and see if'n she needs more." Questions for the old medicine woman spun in Madeline's mind, each seeking predominance. Lucy beat her to the first when Bertie set aside her empty cup as a signal of the end of their brief respite.

"Your h-h-husband's own people cut off his little fingers?"

Bertie nodded solemnly.

"But why?"

"For helping a white woman?" Madeline asked in the same breath.

"For that, and on account of seeing me nekked, touching me. Cheyenne're about the most persnickety folks here 'bouts when it comes to matters of men and women . . . er, together. No touching, no talking to, hardly no looking at a female less'n she's your wife, nor a female a man less'n he's your husband. The big to-do I heard in the night turned out to be a bunch of camp elders arguing with Nahios-si over what punishment he deserved for helping me. Chopping off his pinkie fingers was what they come up with, marking him unclean amongst his people every-wheres for the rest of his borned days. He told me one of the few times we sat ourselves down for a good long gabber that next someone piped up with plans 'bout what to do with me, seeing's they'd found a wet nurse for my baby and didn't need me no more. Never had no intention of keeping me alive once I give birth, jest the babe to replace some woman's in the camp whose own'd died. Nahios-si never said 'xactly what them plans for me was, and I'm mighty glad he didn't or I'd be having nightmares to this day. Well, as I was saying, once Nahios-si found out what they were going to do, a fight broke out 'mongst the lot of them, and the next thing he knowed, one of them leader's sons—the one in charge of doing me in—was dead and the knife in Nahios-si's hand. Hain't nothing worse'n murder to the Cheyenne. Fact is, their word for murder's *he'joxones,* meaning putrid, the murderer being as dead and rotting away to one and all as the victim from that day on, and no redeeming hisself, not never. Knowing he was dead to the Cheyenne for all time, Nahios-si, he decides to come for me and the babe, take us far away into the Rockies where no one'd ever find any've us. And so we live, to this very day.''

"He must've loved you a whole lot to do all that for you," Lucy whispered, hands clutched together tightly against her breasts, a lovelorn light in her pale eyes.

Bertie cackled. "Not then he didn't, nor me him. 'T'was his responsibility, he figured, to save the life of the youn-gun' he helped bring inter the world, and mine too, since by touching and looking, he reckoned he'd spoiled me for all time, jest like hisself. No, missy, he didn't love me no more'n I did him. Not then. Sometimes love's a larned thing, not a falling inter one.''

She paused, reflecting. "Matter of fact, to this day, Nah-ios-si, being the man of few words that he is, he don't come right out and tell me he loves me hardly never. But I knowed it, here in my heart, 'cause he gave up everything for me, his home, his way of living, his people, not never looking back. And he hain't left my side from that day to this. Ayup, he loves me all right, and me him, though it come 'bout day by day, living all alone in our valley together, and not like some bolt've lightning outer the sky. That's how 't'was for us, might be for you, too, someday, so don't make the mistake've overlooking the possibility. And now I'm pretty much talked out, and my story's at an end. And jest in time for your men's return, if'n I'm not mistaken.''

They came bursting in on a blustery breeze. All of them, thank fortune, including the irrepressible twins, curiously eyeing Nahios-si's wife, eager to relate their adventure to Lucy and Madeline. Sam spoke up over their chatter.

''How's Baby?''

''On the mend, thanks to a couple've doses of Injun tobbacy,'' Bertie told him, to which Nahios-si nodded sagely.

Relief smoothed out the deep creases between Sam's brows and he gave the twins full rein with their storytelling.

James boasted, ''We followed Wolf's tracks, found his pups all on our own—''

Jane interrupted, ''They were sooo cute an' sweet.'' She thrust her lip out. ''Uncle Sam still won't 'llow us t' bring one home.''

At that, Sam made a warning, rumbling sound deep in his throat.

''That ain't all I won't allow. The pair've you ain't gettin' out of this here cabin again for a week.''

The more frustrated the man, Madeline knew, the worse his grammar; at least he'd learned not to bellow his displeasure. He ran his hands under the long dark hair at the base of his neck, massaging vigorously. She could almost feel that silky texture, the taut muscles upon her own palms and fingertips, remembering the intimacy of touching his warm flesh when they'd kissed—recalling, too, his strong, callused hands upon her, exploring, discovering every hill and hollow hidden beneath the many layers of clothing. An unforgettable tingling quivered below her waist, that perplexing sensation she could put no name to but found both delightful and frightening.

Occasioned by nerves, nothing more, stimulated by Bertie's story of adventure and love, by the repeated long waits for Sam's safe return—not with missing the man, wanting him. Loving him. Certainly not! She forced herself to ignore both thoughts and feelings to concentrate on Sam's recitation of the rescue while he paced, three steps in each direction, back and forth, the width of the small, single room.

"Lucky I had a pretty good idea where Wolf's lady was hol' up. It was darker'n Ol' Lucifer's black soul by the time we got there and found those two all curled up with the pups like they belonged, Wolf himself standing watch." He stopped in front of the twins, towering over them menacingly. "Could've been the death of the both of you out there with all them winter-hungry wild critters huntin' up a quick and easy meal. You could've been it." He shot out a pointing finger, stopping a fraction of an inch from James's short nose, then aimed for Jane's. "Or you. Don't you never, *never* pull a trick like that again or I'll personally tan your backsides 'til you won't be sittin' down again for a month of Sundays. We have ourselves an understandin'?"

The twins hastily nodded in unison, faces solemn, eyes large. But Madeline had the fleeting thought that behind their backs they very likely had their fingers crossed.

"Well, then, off to your rooms with you. You'll be gettin' no supper tonight."

Madeline bit back a protest that the punishment might

be too harsh, surprised when the two silently did as they were told, clearly too tired to argue, maybe even too tired to eat.

While the men smoked from pipes supplied by Nahios-si in companionable silence by the fire, and Paul read, off by himself, Madeline watched Lucy and Bertie cook up a feast of fresh, spit-roasted pork, generously supplied by Bertie and Nahios-si along with a number of other culinary delicacies, including fresh eggs. For supper, in addition to the meat, the two experienced cooks prepared a tuber vegetable, peeled, boiled, and mashed, which Madeline learned was the tuberous root of what she knew as Queen Anne's lace and Bertie called wild carrot. The pork proved to be beaver tail. Even knowing, Madeline intended to relish her portion, and seconds, just the same. Cornbread and herbal tea completed the menu, the bread served up with wild current preserves made by Bertie.

"It amazes me what bounty you have harvested from the land," she told Bertie, in awe, stealing a sample of preserves on the tip of her spoon and savoring the sweetness as Bertie mixed not one egg but two into her cornbread batter. "You must do a great deal of cultivated farming where you live to be able to share with us so charitably."

Bertie threw back her head and cackled until Madeline half expected her to produce an egg all on her own. At last, catching her breath, the older woman enlightened her audience of two.

"There's so much foodstuff in these here mountain valleys, free for the gathering, a body don't hardly have to raise nothing but a few chickens and goats for eggs and milk and eating when the weather's too foul for hunting and foraging—"

"Goats? Then . . . then Sam . . . Mr. Spencer obtained that goat for Baby's milk from you?"

Incredulous at the implications, and the possible extent

of Sam's betrayal, Madeline could scarcely get the words out. Her heart sank deep at Bertie's terse confirmation.

"Ayup!"

Madeline glanced toward the hearth and the two men peacefully smoking, silently contemplating the dancing flames. Reflected flickering firelight changed Sam's face from guileless to devilish and back again, shadow and light ever shifting among the angles and planes of his familiar features, supporting her sudden realization that even after living these past few weeks in such close proximity with the man, she still knew him not at all. Stricken, she searched Bertie's weathered, complacent face for understanding, finding none.

"He did not have to keep me here . . . against my will. Had he brought me to you for the duration of the storm, off his hands and out of his hair, I would not have shamed myself time and again demonstrating my inadequacies. All the countless mishaps and near disasters which could have been so easily prevented. He could have quickly, easily, freed himself of me, and me of him."

Bertie grinned widely, blue eyes twinkling in amusement.

"Now, Maddie, what'd be the fun in that, for either've you?"

Madeline's cheeks went hot, though she couldn't bring herself to lie to this kind and generous woman, who probably wouldn't believe her anyway. She brought to mind the snowball fights with Sam and the children, his teaching her to snowshoe, constructing those snowshoes with Sam's body pressed the length of hers. Touching Sam. Kissing Sam. Especially the kissing. Loving him. Against her will, but loving him nonetheless. Would she have wanted never to have loved him? No, unequivocally not. Even if he might never love her back, and probably didn't since he still mourned the loss of Hettie. Still, why . . .?

"Why didn't he bring me to you? Really."

Again that knowing shake of the head, Bertie's face reflecting her sober words. "Couldn't, being our friend. Wouldn't betray me and Nahios-si thataway. More as knowed our where'bouts, more likely it'd get back to them Cheyenne."

"They wouldn't be seeking vengeance against you after all this time, would they?"

"Not vengeance, Maddie. To their way of thinking, justice."

"He believes I would betray you." It was a statement of fact, not a question.

Madeline's eyelids prickled with unshed tears. After these last few weeks, Sam Spencer knew her no more than she him, and he did not trust her. Nor did he love her, never would. All too clearly, she understood that now. She was a convenient diversion for him, born of necessity, nothing more. She fell silent, unhappily dwelling upon her conclusions, until Bertie's suggestion broke through her maudlin thoughts.

"Come spring thaw, I'll head on back over here to help put in a garden . . . show you 'round in the woods so you'll know what to eat and what to leave plum alone."

"I'm sure Lucy will appreciate that." Bitterness laced Madeline's response. Lifting her chin, she hazarded a quick glance at Sam, who appeared oblivious, perhaps dozing, turned in profile toward the fire. "I won't be here once the snow melts. My decision to travel to Fort Farewell, then home, remains unchanged."

She saw Sam's pronounced jaw knot, unkindly pleased to see him not totally unaffected after all. She waited for him to ask her to stay . . . order her to stay. A breathless silence swelled within the single small room, indicating that the others waited with her. Paul's head lifted from his reading, Lucy twisted her flour-sack apron between her hands, Bertie's chopping knife poised midair over the wild onions she sliced for flavoring, and Nahios-si's pipe rested in his brown hand inches from his wide, thin-lipped mouth. The stubborn mountain man who, in the end, needed, wanted, no one in his life, moved not a muscle, nor did he speak.

Lucy broke the leaden silence first, asking too brightly, "How soon 'til dinner? Want me to be settin' the table?"

"Good idear. Be dishing up any time now."

Madeline, back ruler-straight, head high, with nothing more to say now that all that was necessary had been, turned to the shelves to lift down pottery serving bowls.

After a supper for the most part eaten in silence, whether relishing Bertie's succulent, abundant repast or from sheer exhaustion after sleepless nights and stressful days, Madeline found herself too soul-weary to speculate further. Dishes were washed and put away, evening chores in cabin and barn completed, followed by an early retiring for one and all. Sam gave over the loft to Bertie and Nahios-si, declaring over their expected protests that he preferred a bedroll by the fire for himself anyway. Like sleeping out under the stars. He'd keep watch over the baby in her crib near the hearth, should she need anything in the night.

"Which hain't likely after that last draught I give her. Closer to that Maddie-girl, I calculate, that's where he's of a mind to be."

Madeline overheard Bertie's whispered comment to her spouse and threw a quick, furtive glance in Sam's direction, hoping for the merest flicker of acknowledgment to give her hope. *Grasping at straws,* she silently chided herself, finding the man with his back to her, having poured a cup of warmed-over tea, sipping slowly and staring toward the black square that became of the window at night, aware only of his somber reflection.

Sam watched her watching him, saw her shoulders droop

and her gaze slip away as she turned to disappear into the bedroom she shared with the girls. Like a danged peeping Tom, he studied the shadow-dance of her silhouette on the far wall, undressing, slipping into one of Hettie's soft flannel nightgowns, sliding under her bed coverings.

Swallowing hard, he turned away, tasting instead of Bertie's sweet herb tea on his tongue the sweeter, remembered taste of Maddie's mouth, her skin.

Sam backhanded across his lips, attempting and failing to wipe off that memory that'd do him little good now Maddie'd made clear her intent to leave with the first signs of spring. Nothing he could do to stop her, nothing he could say. Likely the best thing all around anyway. Citified female'd never be happy in the long run isolated with him and five kids. Said as much tonight, telling Bertie—and any others with ears to hear, including himself—of her all-fired hurry to hightail it back on home. Well, let her. And good riddance. He wasn't about to do nothing to stop her. Didn't need her nohow. Didn't need no danged females in his life, except them little ones, and Bertie 'course, and that was that.

So, if that's that, how come I'm layin' here, dog-tired and wide awake only a couple've hours from mornin'? And my head so full of that woman, needin' her, wantin' her, I can't think of nothin' else.

Sam scrubbed his whisker-stubbled cheeks hard. Kicking himself free of his covers, he rolled up on his knees, planted a foot on the packed dirt floor, and rose like a rheumatism-ridden old man to check on the baby and finding her fast asleep. He stretched out a hand, folding all but forefinger in on his palm, brushing back a damp golden curl clinging to her forehead. It wrapped itself around his finger, near-white against his weather-darkened skin, and for a time, he let it stay. Pondering. Regretting. Speculating how it was going to be raising those five kids all on his own, how the bunch of them'd turn out without a woman's gentling guidance.

Paul, a real handful from the git-go, he'd probably take off soon's he could. Lucy'd stay, taking care of the twins and this little one 'til each and every one flew the nest, and stay on for him 'til she turned into some dried-up, long-in-the-tooth old maid. Better'n marrying up with some filthy, and filthier-minded and mouthed, old mountain man, he guessed, but not half good enough for a kind-hearted, hard-working youngster like Lucy, to his way of thinking.

And what of his future? No one to talk to when he was of a mind for a little grown-up palavering but Bertie and Nahios-si, no one at all to take up the challenge of trying for the last word. A grin tickled around the corners of his mouth, remembering those first couple've days with Maddie, battling away, him winning a few, and her the rest. Kind've made him wish things hadn't settled down so peaceful-like between them of late. His life needed a bit of stirring up now and again; so did Maddie's, if she'd own up to it. Being born stubborn, she wouldn't. By the Great Spirit, he missed her already.

He sensed Maddie close at hand before she spoke up from beside him.

"Did your wife . . . Hettie . . . know Bertie and Nahios-si?"

Madeline had watched him standing over Baby Faith's crib, his expression so reflective, so sad, for a good long while before she found the courage to approach, to ask the question uppermost in her mind, all but certain what his response would be from conclusions she'd drawn throughout the last several, sleepless hours. Not looking her way, he told her what she already knew.

"Ought to've. She was Bertie's daughter."

"I thought as much." He flicked a glance her way. "Sus-

pecting, as I did, that the ma and pa she mentioned so
frequently, and with such love, in her diary would have to
be the nearest other human inhabitants of these mountains.''

He showed no surprise that she'd reached the heart of
the matter as astutely as she had—in fact shared none of
his thoughts and emotions at all, his features as granite-
carved as his silent, stoic Cheyenne friend's. She could not
keep herself from prodding deeper.

"Had you been able to read, you would have known, as
set down in her own hand, how much she loved you as
well, hoping for you to soon declare the same, wishing you
every happiness. Her last entry alone related with what
joyous anticipation she was looking forward to your first
anniversary and the birth of—''

"Our son. Who never got to see the light of day, thanks
to me," he reminded her bitterly.

Guided by some instinct beyond her own understanding,
Madeline retorted, "Please, Mr. Spencer, spare me your
tiresome self-pity. The only way you could have prevented
your wife from ascending the ladder that day was to have
kept watch over her every waking hour and while she slept.
From what I read, that spirited young woman would have
found a way in any case to go up to the loft when you were
not around, to put in the final few stitches on the quilt
she hoped to surprise you with on your anniversary. Had
you so much as stepped outside to—to relieve yourself,
she would have attempted that climb.''

Sam's face went from stunned to thoughtful; finally, he
squared his shoulders as if a monumental weight had fallen
from them, and a bemused smile flicked across his desir-
able, well-formed lips. He leveled a bold, blue-eyed stare
upon her.

"You been givin' the subject considerable thought for
a while now, ain't you?"

"It bore reflecting upon, since your generally foul temperament seemed based upon some misconception or another, most especially this one. I merely hoped to alleviate the resulting discord so unsettling to the children—"

"Prairie patties."

"I beg your pardon?"

"Prairie patties is—"

"I know what they are, Mr. Spencer, having gathered my share while traveling westward. What, pray tell, does dried buffalo offal have to do with the subject of our conversation?"

" 'Cause that tall tale you're about to hand me as the truth is about as full of it as a campfire on some treeless stretch of ground in the middle of nowheres. Why you been pokin' into my business an' Hettie's ain't got nothin' to do with makin' things easier 'round here for them kids. If you set that much store by them, you wouldn't be runnin' off home first chance you get, as fond of you as they've become."

"So that you and I might nightly quarrel and bicker over them, or over something else? I think not. Not without—"

"Without what?"

She waved one hand like a trapped, fluttering bird, fearful the conversation had gone too far to redeem, desperate to try anyway.

"Without an extensive list of ground rules too numerous to remember, let alone follow. Not to mention our mutual lack of trust—"

"Plain to see *you* don't trust me no farther'n you can toss me—"

"Nor you me, as I was not even allowed to know the whereabouts of your nearest neighbors, with whom I could have sought shelter had you made good one of your countless threats to toss me out of your cabin into a snowbank."

He glowered. "Bertie told you how it was."

"She told me of the need for secrecy, yes. It was *you* who believed me unworthy of entrusting with that secret." She simply couldn't keep the quiver of hurt out of her voice, try as she might, though by biting her lower lip, hard, she stilled its trembling.

"Now look here, Maddie—"

"Miss Preston."

"See here, *woman*—Dang! Now I've gone and forgot what I was goin' to say."

He thrust both hands through his mane of salt-and-pepper hair with violence sufficient to pull it out by the roots. Madeline dared experience a glimmer of hope.

"An apology for misjudging me, perhaps," she suggested.

His eyes glittered like shards of ice reflecting a bold spring sky.

"Not danged likely. You ain't said nor done nothin' since you took up squattin' rights to my diggin's that I ain't come to expect from your kind've highfalutin female."

"Which would be . . . ?"

"Uppity. Spoilt. Jackass stubborn—my apologies to Ol' Clyde—without sense enough not to set out for home in a snowstorm, nor set a basket of vittles in the doorway invitin' some hungry bear to supper. An' a know-it-all what don't know nothin' at all've practical use here in these mountains."

He concluded his tirade by folding his arms over each other high on his broad chest and nodding once, tight-lipped and frowning fiercely.

Nothing had changed, especially his opinion of her. Madeline saw that now, and knew with absolute certainty that all her foolish hopes and dreams otherwise were nothing more than the wildest of fantasies. She spun away, all but running for the safety of her room.

"Givin' up?"

"One can do little else when one's opponent has begun to babble, Mr. Spencer," she retorted over her shoulder, not daring to expose to him her stricken face.

"Won fair and square. Can't take knowin' I'm right, that's what's eatin' you, woman."

She turned to look at him from the shadowed doorway.

She made no attempt to mask the defeat in her voice. "Perhaps, Mr. Spencer, for once, you are indeed right. Good night."

Unaware that he'd allowed her the last word without rebuttal, Madeline made good her retreat.

Chapter Sixteen

On moccasined feet, as quiet as a cat's paws, Sam came up behind her while she lingered over a second cup of morning coffee, standing before the cabin's one window and trying to think of nothing but the warmth of the sun on her face and the cloudless blue of the sky. She kept her back to him, even after he spoke.

"Look, Maddie—"

"Miss Preston. What is it you wish?"

"Now see here, woman—Dang! Forget it."

The door slammed, shuddering in its frame, with his exit, leaving Madeline alone with only the deepest regrets and a long list of should-have-said's and why-didn't-I's.

At her elbow, Bertie cackled her familiar laugh.

"If'n' you two lovebirds hain't the stubbornest pair I ever set eyes on, Nahios-si hain't got three fingers a hand."

Gaze averted, Madeline declined to acknowledge the 'lovebird' part of the old medicine woman's statement in favor of another.

"Mr. Spencer is the stubborn one, not I."

Again that cackle, which grew more and more annoying by the moment.

"How's that?"

Bertie cocked her head like a curious biddy hen, azure eyes candidly amused, but kind. So desperate was her need to confide in someone, especially another woman, that Madeline's words burst from her against her own volition. She faced her companion angrily.

"That man refuses to see that I have changed, that I am no longer the—the—"

"The highfalutin, citified female what took up squatting rights to his diggin's, not having the first idear how to git 'long in these here mountains?"

Madeline's cheeks went hot with shame. "You heard . . . yes, well . . . I am no longer that woman, but Sam . . . Mr. Spencer cannot seem to get beyond my earlier blunders, bringing them up at the slightest provocation."

"What you planning to do to make him see things different?"

"Me? Why . . . what . . . what can I do? I have tried, and failing to sway him, have decided to bow to his wish that I leave, which I intend to do, as soon as the way down the mountain becomes passable."

Bertie threw back her head, cackling loud and long.

"Passes been open for days, Maddie. Ever since that last thaw and no more snow after."

"Open?"

"Ayup."

"But he . . . he never . . . he not so much as mentioned . . ." Stunned, she could not grasp the implications.

"Kinder makes a body wonder how come he never brung it up, don't it? Mebbe that stubborn feller of yours don't want you to go no more'n you do. How to make him come 'round to admitting it, that's what you oughter be trying to figure out, afore you both 'llow that threat of your leaving you toss back and forth 'tween you to come 'bout, jest to spite 't'other'n.''

Madeline's shoulders rose and fell in a resigned shrug.

"I have contributed to the care of his home and the children in every way possible, whenever possible. Acquiring new skills daily, learning from my mistakes. I never repeat a single one," she assured Bertie earnestly, "but he will not forgive and forget."

She thought of the damaged quilt, which, to her mind, always remained tangibly, though unspoken of, between them, as real and as strong an obstacle as on that fateful day she took a hatchet to it. This she dared not confide in Hettie's mother, whose own stitches graced the bride's quilt, whose signature had been embroidered on its hem.

"What've you showed him you can do all on your own?"

"I—I don't understand. I have washed dishes and scrubbed clothing—even learning to rinse—made coffee and porridge and a few other things, with varying success, but more skillfully daily. I've—"

Shaking her head, Bertie declared, "Not special 'nough. What talent you brung to this here mountain cabin all on your own, one hain't nobody here'bouts already doing, and better'n you?"

Madeline lifted her chin at the challenge.

"Perseverance. Against all odds. I am not a coward, nor a fool. And I possess the intelligence to learn to survive here as ably as all others who come to them green and grow seasoned with time, including Sam—Mr. Spencer himself." Madeline saw by Bertie's expression that she had not given the answer she sought. In desperation, she added, "I can bake the very best mincemeat pie anyone in the entire Rocky Mountain range has ever tasted . . . if I but had the right ingredients."

Now Bertie grinned widely.

"Pshaw! That hain't no problem. Substituting, that's the key. Write down your receipt for me, and I'll show you what to use instead." She caught Madeline's arm when she moved to comply. "But furst, I want to hear in your own words that you love Sam Spencer 'nough to stay and fight for him. Not for my ears, mind you, for your own, 'cause if'n' you say it out loud there hain't going to be no question in your mind 'bout that fact, tempting you to run out on him when the going gits hard, which it will, mark what I'm saying. That feller's like a son to me, an honorable man and an honest one, or I'd never've married my only borned child up with him. It's writ plain on his face for anyone with the eyes to see that he's right took with you." She ignored Madeline's sound of denial. "And I won't help no one—'specially the one he's gone and fallen head over heels for—with a mind to mebe causing him more grief when he's had more'n his share of in this here lifetime already."

She pinned Madeline with a no-nonsense stare as constraining as the grip upon her forearm. Knowing she would release her from neither without an answer, Madeline complied.

"I love him, yes, but—"

" 'Nough said. The rest I can read for myself in your eyes, and hear in your words. You fetch something to write on. I'll head out to the barn to tell Nahios-si to go on home without me, I'll come 'long later."

Upon her return, bringing with her the scent of spring and its promises, Bertie studied the square of brown wrapping paper upon which Madeline presented her recipe.

"I have all the necessary ingredients for a flaky crust at hand—flour, salt, lard, and water. But where are we to find boiled beef when I have seen nothing but wild game served as long as I've been here?"

"You got venison. Saw it myself in the cellar. Gamier tasting, for certain, but if'n' you go heavier on the spices, won't nobody know the difference."

"Dried apples can be softened in water, but what of raisins and citron?"

"Brought you a pouch brimming with dried berries gathered from forest and marsh. Bound to be something what tastes near the same."

"Nutmeg, cinnamon, cloves, allspice?"

"Them too I can match, and better, if I give some thought to it. Anything else?"

"Wine?"

"Elderberry. Brought Sam his favorite, 'long with everything else."

"Bertie, you're a wonder."

Bertie grinned, large, even teeth white against dark, weathered skin, blue eyes sparkling like sunshine on rippling water.

"Hain't I that," she easily agreed, her smile going motherly, eyes reflective. "You're something special yourself, Maddie Preston. Come what may, and what oughter, you got my blessing, and Nahios-si's was he here to give it, on behalf've you and Sam."

Ignoring her usual restraint, Madeline allowed Bertie to pull her into her arms in a crushing bear hug, wrapping her arms around the woman's ample hide-covered waist, patting her back and lingering there until she'd sufficiently choked down unwanted emotion.

Then Bertie made selections for the substitute ingredients, leaving the actual labor to Madeline herself. While the resulting pie baked amid the coals of the hearth as Bertie had showed her, permeating every room with a mouth-watering aroma, the other occupants of the cabin—all conspicuously absent throughout—began to assemble for lunch, each searching for the source of the tantalizing scent.

"What smells so good?" Jane, as always, put voice to the question in everyone's questing gaze.

Bertie supplied a ready answer.

"Surprise. For supper."

"I *love* 'prizes. I want it now. I'm hungry," the child wheedled.

"Hain't done. Made some've my famous slumgullion for the midday meal."

Jane's small nose crinkled.

"What's that?"

"Stew. Made up of a little've this and a little've that, whatever's on hand. Whipped up dumplin's, too, light as air and chuck full've butter'n seasonin's fit to melt in your mouth. Only, don't go eating so much you don't have room left over come supper for Maddie's surprise."

Around the table, all heads turned Madeline's way, faces mirroring disbelief, then disappointment.

"Now, don't go jumping the gun," warned Bertie. "I had me a little sampling of that there surprise, and I'm here to tell you, it'll put my dumplin's clean to shame."

Appeased, if not convinced, the skeptics ate their fill of stew and dumplings, with seconds, soon departing upon their appointed chores out-of-doors, even Lucy and Baby Faith.

"Join us, miss," Lucy begged. "It's so warm out, the snow is startin' to melt, showin' grass, an' green growin' things in some spots. Come join Baby an' me on a blanket in the sun."

"After Bertie leaves and my p—my surprise is done," Madeline promised.

She hated to see the woman go, and told her so as she dressed warmly for departure. Bertie chuckled, and Maddie knew she'd miss the grating sound of it as well.

"Hain't like we live a million miles away, Maddie. Have Sam bring you on over to our place soon's you two git things settled between you. Bring them kids 'long too. Closest things to grandkids I guess I'll ever lay eyes on."

"I'm so sorry . . . about Hettie, and the baby who died with her."

Bertie didn't question how she knew; she nodded, sad but resigned.

"Sorry 'bout that myself, but that's the nature of living, dying when your time comes." She roused herself with a brisk change of subject. "Here's a couple've pouches of medicine herbs, and I slipped papers in each on how to use it. Pay no heed to my spelling, it's bad and I know it. Taught Hettie reading and writing, but spelling"—she shook her head—"neither one've us weren't no good at that."

"You've given us so much already," Madeline protested, taking the offered pouches anyway when Bertie shoved them into her hands.

"Neighborly thing to do. Same as Sam's done aplenty for us more'n a time or two. 'Specially when Nahios-si's laid up with the rheumatiz in his hands. Losing them fingers done more damage'n what shows. Changes in weather is mighty hard on him these days. I'll be taking my leave now, and you'd better see to that there pie, Maddie. Smells good and done to me."

Madeline sped to do as bidden. When she'd carefully lifted the pie out of the coals, folded towels protecting her hands, she rose from the hearth to find Bertie gone and the cabin strangely empty for her absence.

Later, while the pie cooled on the table, she sat and rocked, resting and reflecting, beside the fire for a while. The very wise woman had left her much food for thought in a visit of less than one day.

Primarily that Sam had not told her that the way down

from his mountain had become passable. Why not? Because he didn't want to see her go? That was not what he'd said time and time again, implied countless others by word and deed. Then why keep the knowledge from her that he'd changed his mind?

Of equal import, Bertie's insistance that he loved her. Which she doubted. He'd kissed her, true, frequently and ardently. He wanted more, she knew, naive though she was in her virginity. Lusted for her, if her married friends' giggled innuendoes were any clue. As she did after him, were she but to admit to it. But were love and lust the same? Or parts of the whole? Lust without love she could imagine. Loving Sam as she did, heart and soul . . . and body, she could not imagine love without that intense internal sensation, that *need*, unsatiated by kisses alone. Was it like that for Sam? Then how could he let her walk away, as she'd frequently insisted she would, without so much as speaking of it? Did he think she would simply let the snow disappear into the ground without so much as asking if the passage downward had cleared? An act of a cowardly man . . . or a proud, stubborn one.

And though her pie now cooling on the table was the most perfect she'd ever managed to create, bar none, she could not begin to fathom why Bertie had insisted on the baking of it. Change a stubborn man's mind? Madeline smiled lightly at that notion all the way to Lucy's spot in the glorious sunshine, upon a colorful Indian blanket in the snow. Problems in no way resolved, she put them aside to enjoy the pure pleasure of warmth on her shoulders and the sweet scents of spring's long-awaited arrival intoxicating her every breath, refusing to dwell on the possibility that, with spring, her days with Sam and the children could soon come to an end.

Still later, after supper, when her surprise was nothing more than a memory and a few scattered crumbs on the table's worn wooden surface, she received all the praise due her, by word and appetite, from all but Sam Spencer himself, though his generous portion had disappeared long before those of the rest. She rose from her place opposite him down the table's length, fisting hands on hips, demanding his attention with an unwavering stare. He dared grin at her, so widely that deep creases appeared in each close-shaven cheek. She wondered, fleetingly, if he had shaved just prior to sitting down to eat. Possibly bathed, naked, in the river cutting through his valley, swift and swollen with melting snow, for his hair that was not braided and hanging down along the lines of his familiar jaw, clung damply to his collar.

Ignoring the unsteady beat of her heart, the unfounded hope that his ablutions had been in honor of her surprise, she offered a pointed query.

"Well?"

He made a great show of not understanding, shrugging with arms spread and palms upturned, throwing the children, each in turn, a helpless silent appeal.

"How did you like the pie?"

"Tolerably well."

"Tol—"

"Bertie make it?"

"I'll have you know, Mr. Spencer, I myself made that pie with my own two hands. Bertie offered only suggestions for substitutions for ingredients not available."

"You sure you made it? All by yourself? No help from Bertie? None?"

"None whatsoever. I told you early on in our acquaintance that I had a talent for sweets and desserts, most particularly mince pie."

"You did?"

"Yes, I did. And I believe this masterpiece, of which you

partook of both your portion and mine, proved that point precisely."

"Damned best pie I ever et."

"Dam—the best? Truly?"

"Said so, didn't I? Well, that's that and evenin' chores awaitin' us." With a slap of the flat of both hands on the table, he rose. "Next time though . . ." He paused for effect, patting his flat stomach. "Make two. One ain't half enough to satisfy this ol' mountain man's sweet tooth."

Totally surprised, and inordinately pleased, Madeline forgot to so much as attempt a last word.

Madeline waited all evening and throughout the next day for Bertie's anticipated miracle of the pie, the transformation of Sam Spencer that would inspire him to declare his love and beg her to stay. Finally, she had to concede that her new friend had been wrong, terribly wrong. Hope waned and died, leaving Madeline downhearted despite spring's arriving by leaps and bounds. Or because of it. Soon, Sam would be forced to confess what she already knew, thanks to Bertie—that the way down the mountain lay open. Perhaps, she concluded, the time had come to prod him into that admission, if for no other reason than that she must—for sanity's sake—discover why he had not seen fit to mention it. She cleared her throat lightly, and as if waiting for her to speak, he looked up at her across the width of the hearth separating them, firelight dancing over his dear craggy face.

"I . . . I suppose that with the melting of the snow, the pass down to Fort Farewell might soon be open."

She forced her voice to remain steady, unemotional, not daring to make the slightest attempt to influence his response. His disconcertingly steady and speculative stare set her nerves so on edge that her apprehensions swelled within her like yeasted batter. She should have left well enough alone, waited for him to broach the subject.

"Not so soon's you'd think," he said at last, the sound husky with disuse.

"Oh?" she prompted, frustration rising.

He turned his gaze to the fire. "Thawin' brings floodin' an' slides. Mud slides is as deadly as blizzards an' avalanches to the unsuspectin' an' unprepared."

Bertie had warned her of no such possibilities. Madeline suspected yet another lie, and hope soared.

"So . . . then, you'd feel I should remain here for a while yet? Say, through my birthday?"

He glanced at her, then away.

"When's that?"

"In less than two weeks. May Day. May first."

"Later'n that likely."

Lie upon lie. Madeline ceased her pushing and prodding, sensing he'd only dig in his heels of stubborn resistance and make no confession of what she already knew to be the truth.

"Good," she announced briskly, fortified all the more when he glanced her way for an instant, expression echoing the hope born anew in her heart. "I shall have sufficient time, then, to resume the twins' reading and writing lessons, establish a schedule Paul should be able to carry on with at my departure, as he has expressed an interest in becoming a teacher."

He cleared his throat heavily.

"So long's it don't interfere with no one's chores." And cleared it again. "I'm thinkin' I'll likely set in on them lessons, too . . . never know when readin' an' writin'll prove handy. I've a mind to read Hettie's diary for myself . . . when I get around to it . . . durin' them long winter's nights."

Madeline kept her tone mild with effort.

"Reading can prove a satisfying diversion. Your presence will be most welcome, Mr. Spencer, and a fine example for the twins when they grow tired of reciting their ABC's."

"Already know 'em m'self."

His expression clearly showed he regretted the admission the moment the words were out of his mouth. His jaw jumped. Madeline covered his discomposure with a quick rejoinder.

"Excellent. Then you can assist with teaching the twins theirs."

He looked inordinately pleased, but responded with exaggerated indifference.

"Happy to, if I find the time, and have the inclination."

For the first few days after their evening's conversation, Madeline waited with bated breath for Sam to admit to his deception regarding travel to Fort Farewell. Days faded into a week, then two; the snow melted from mounds to patches, and was gone. Still he said nothing more on the subject. After a while it occurred to her that he might never again bring up the matter for the rest of their natural lives, as long as neither did she.

Preoccupied with the problem, it was well into the remaining few days before May 1st before she realized that everyone but she shared a secret. Frequently, she observed whispered conversations held among the others, excluding only herself and the infant, now fully recovered from her illness, thanks to Bertie's intervention. One did not have to be privy to what was going on to surmise that it most likely concerned her birthday; but though she hinted and pried, no one, not even chatterbox Jane, broke the apparent vow to keep it from her. Finally, she simply sat back, enjoying the mystery of it all, smug in the knowledge that their efforts were most surely on her behalf. On the Monday before her Thursday birthday, Sam made an announcement, studied in its casualness.

"Goin' to be gone for a couple've days, Maddie, if you an' the kids think you can manage without me."

She glanced up from the sampler upon which she labored to perfect her stitching for quilt-repair sessions while everyone but she and Lucy slept.

"Where are you going?" she asked, panic narrowing the passage of her words. *If he tells me down the mountain is traversable. I'll have to leave.*

"Gotta check my trappin' route. Should've got to it earlier but we . . . er, I been too busy."

"And this will take more than a day?" she challenged, the suspense of waiting daily growing so great, his confession at this point seemed less a torture than that this unspoken deception between them go on interminably.

"Weather conditions. Never know when they'll change, making gettin' 'round hard or dang-near impossible."

"And there are the floods and the mud slides. So you've said. Well, take your time then, and be careful."

He hesitated a moment. "Be leavin' come mornin'. Early. No need for you or the kids to see me off."

Vowing to take him at his word, she silently counted the days before his expected return. At the most, he'd still be home in time for her birthday. Feigning sleep in the morning, she listened to him go, missing him immediately as empty silence filled the cabin with the quiet closing of the door behind him.

"Dang fool's errand. If this ain't the double-darned damnedest notion I ever come up with, don't know what was."

After checking and resetting his traps in a matter of hours, Sam muttered a string of cusses to himself all the way downhill to Fort Farewell and halfway back, with a stop-off at Luckless and a couple've shots with the fellas.

Slipping down muddy slopes. Spending one stormy night hunkered up on soggy ground with his robe tossed over him, fur side in, as his only protection. And nothing to look forward to but another'n tonight by the looks of the gathering clouds and faraway thunder echoing through the surrounding canyons.

The notion had come to him, soon as Maddie told him her birthday was just around the corner, that if he got her something extra special, something to make the cabin more civilized in her eyes, she'd forget about leaving, leaving him. Windowglass for the bedrooms was what he came up with. Wasn't 'til he was all the way down to the fort that he realized she'd know he lied about where he was going soon's he handed over his gift. Lied about the way down being clear. He'd bought the glass anyways for the price of a couple of beaver furs; and in Luckless he'd bought Maddie back her ring left behind as payment for the supplies she took, as he found out. It was gathering dust on a shelf, of value to no one but Maddie.

How or when he'd dare give it back to her, he wasn't rightly sure. Maybe never, if she left someday soon. For the time being it rested in the small medicine pouch he wore around his neck. Hunkered down under his robe a second night while a cold wind and rain whipped around him, he fancied it gave off a warming heat all its own, that small bit of her residing there, over his heart.

When he'd given away a big chunk of that heart to Maddie, he couldn't recall, only that it was hers, and go or stay, he'd never get it back.

Climbing back up his mountain the next morning, he racked his brain for something he could give Maddie for her birthday without betraying where he'd been. Something special. Something she'd set store by, to remind her of him and the kids, no matter what. It came to him when he was almost home.

Them spoons. The dozen he'd bought for Hettie and sent flying over the cliff when he came home to find her and their son dead; and the one've them that had saved Maddie's life by pointing the way to his cabin. Funny the way things happened like that—lives lost, others saved by the same small something or other. Like life was a game of luck, or the playing-out of fate like Maddie believed. Either way, Sam figured he'd been given a second chance to love a woman. 'Cause whether he wanted it or not, he'd been dragged—kicking and clawing every step've the way, by fate, or luck, or both—right up to asking Maddie to marry him, if it came to that. If that was the only way to get her to stay.

It took near another day to find five out of eleven of the remaining spoons. Figuring an even half dozen was as good as a whole and one dang-good birthday present, shined and polished, Sam set his feet on the path to home, his strides longer and sprier the nearer he got.

Chapter Seventeen

" 'Mid pleasures and palaces though we may roam, be it e-ver so humble, there's nooo place like hooome ... there's nooo place like hooome!"

Madeline vigorously wielded the straw broom, gathering a growing pile of tracked-in dried mud, and headed for the door, warbling to her heart's content, confident she would not destroy anyone's hearing this bright morning— her birthday morn. The children had scattered early out of doors on secret errands of their own. Sam, too, had disappeared from the cabin immediately after breakfast, mumbling something about morning chores, perhaps only as a cover for some subterfuge pertaining to her special day.

She had worried incessantly over him during his three-day absence, lain awake two sleepless nights listening to the thunder and the wind-lashed rain, thinking of him and of his warnings of flooded streams and mud slides. Her imagination went wild, picturing in graphic detail each possible tragedy that might befall him, until panic all but drove her dashing pell-mell, out into the storm, in search of him, without regard to her own personal safety. Concerns for the children alone kept her from pursuing such folly.

Daytimes she cleaned house, washing every surface until all were spotless, airing bedding and mattresses, rearranging drawers in the bureau that needed it not in the least. The day before, eliminating dust motes from beneath her bed, she had come across the wooden crate containing Sam and Hettie's personal belongings. Tempted to while away the hours until Sam returned perusing the contents undisturbed, instead she added Hettie's diary to the box and asked Paul to carry it up to Sam's quarters in the loft before her resolution faltered.

". . . Be it e-ver so hhhhhumble, there's noooo place like hooome—"

She threw open the cabin door on a breathless exhale and inhaled deeply, preparing for the second verse while sweeping out onto the stoop, only to come face-to-face with Sam himself, blocking her way, wearing a huge grin.

"Chasin' away bears?"

"Mr. Spencer, you startled me." She feigned indignation. "Do you see any bears?"

"Nope." His smirk went wider still, and he winked. "That caterwaulin' of yours must be workin'."

She couldn't help but smile back. She was so happy to have him home safe and sound from his trapping expedition, so excited over anticipated birthday surprises, intended for her alone, to be disclosed sometime today— the sooner the better.

"Nor will you need worry that any will return so long as I am permitted free rein with my singing."

Sam shook his head slowly, frowning deeply.

"Ain't sure the sufferin's worth it, woman. Bear meat's

mighty tasty an' bear fur warmin' on a cold night. You chase off every bear in the county, what're we goin' to do come winter?''

"Why, Mr. Spencer, as proficient as you profess to be at mountain survival, I am certain you will devise some viable solution. Speaking of sustenance, are the children about finished with whatever they're doing to join us now for luncheon?''

She hoped to prod him into admitting a celebration on her behalf in the works, and imminent. His features remained guileless, though his steady, blue-eyed gaze glinted with scarcely suppressed amusement.

"More'n ready, likely. Anythin' to take 'em away from barn-cleanin' for a time.''

Not the slightest clue to tell her when, or if, there'd be a party in her honor. What if she were mistaken? Doubt dashed her happy expectations like a splash of icy water from Sam's spring-fed stream beyond the barn.

"Oh. Well, then, if you'll call them in, I'll set out plates. I thought perhaps we'd have cold smoked venison, sliced thin, on Lucy's fresh sourdough bread, if that's all right.''

"Sounds fine an' fillin'. I'll go fetch the kids.''

Madeline tried to remain philosophical and, she thought, inordinately patient, certain, for the most part, that Sam and the children had their own schedule for her birthday festivities. Yet, in spite of her persistent belief, the day proceeded ordinarily throughout lunch and the early hours of the afternoon.

Lucy remained inside to resume her weekly baking chore while Baby Faith napped in her crib. The infant, however, soon made known her wishes otherwise with increasingly frequent, piercingly loud wails of protest. Lucy, beating away at her batter in a large pottery bowl, glanced up, brushing a wisp of fine blond hair out of her face with a floury hand and leaving a streak.

"Miss, would you mind gettin' her up? Maybe take her outside to play in the sun? I got my hands full for a while yet."

Madeline set down her embroidery.

"My pleasure. I can't get enough of spring myself. Unless there's something I can do to help you—?"

"Mindin' the baby'll help out the most, thanks."

A couple of hours out of doors playing with—and chasing after—Baby Faith took all of Madeline's concentration and energy. The child, now nearly ten months old, scooted around on all fours almost faster than Madeline managed to keep up with her, and pulled herself into a standing position whenever she discovered something on which to haul herself up. Madeline entertained them both helping her practice walking, the baby's hands wrapped around her index fingers for support, echoing the child's glad cries and happy giggles of triumph at each faltering step.

When the soon-to-be toddler at last wearied of the lessons, Madeline caught her up in her arms. Lifting her high, then wrapping both arms around the warm, squirming body in an enveloping hug, she pressed her cheek atop a tangled crown of golden curls, breathing deeply of her sweet baby scent, experiencing a fleeting taste of motherly fulfillment in the loving embrace.

"I do love you, sweetheart, more than I ever thought myself capable of," she declared in a husky whisper. "And your brothers and sisters. And most of all"—her voice dipped softer—"your uncle. How shall I bring myself to leave all of you, if he does not ask me to stay?"

As if she understood, Baby Faith's plump little arms encircled her neck and clung. Madeline snuggled her closer and, ignoring doubts, imagined for this short, wonderful little while this baby as her own, and the cabin at her back, this glorious land of spring, spreading over snowcapped mountains and wildflower-carpeted valley as well.

"Miss. Miss?"

Guiltily, Madeline spun, fantasies flying away like wisps of passing clouds, to find Lucy standing in the open doorway, drying her hands on a flour-sack towel.

"I've finished my bakin'. Baby'd probably take that nap now, if you'll bring her on in."

Madeline relinquished the baby into Lucy's waiting arms, feeling the absence of the weight of her in her own with a sharp twinge in the region of her heart. Taking a fortifying deep breath, she followed the pair inside.

"Surprise!"

They cried out in chorus, Sam and Lucy and Paul and the twins, all standing behind the table upon which sat a cake on a pewter plate, a tall candle taken from one holder on the mantel stuck upright and lit in its center. Overwhelmed to the point of tears, despite her suspicions, Madeline approached slowly on legs grown suddenly wobbly.

"Blow it out. Blow it out," demanded the twins in unison.

"I—I had no idea . . . th-that is, I hoped—"

"Better blow out that candle, Maddie, or this fine cake Lucy whipped up for you'll end up tastin' of wax."

"Make a wish an' blow it out," cried James, adding a solemn caution, "only don't tell no one your wish or it won't come true."

No need to ponder, Madeline wished deeply and sincerely. Blowing out the flickering light, she followed with the silent plea. *Please, please let me stay in this mountain valley, with Sam and the children, forever and ever.*

"Presents. Open your presents," demanded Jane.

"Presents, too?"

She had not noticed the small collection spread out before each giver. Lucy picked up hers, of blue calico, which when unfurled proved to be a pretty, serviceable sunbonnet.

"Oh, Lucy, how lovely, and practical. You made this yourself?" She turned it over and over in her hands, studying the tiny, tidy stitching, looking up into Lucy's pleased, flushed face. "And the cake, too. How can I thank you?"

Embarrassed, shy Lucy ducked her head.

"Them's simple things, miss. See what Paul has for you."

Red splotches on his prominent cheekbones, Paul shoved a crudely wrapped, brown-paper package across the table at her. Within, she found three turkey quill pens, sharpened to a precise point, and a smaller wrapped packet of black powder.

"Mixed with water, that'll make ink," Paul told her. "Nahios-si showed me how."

"A perfect gift, and much appreciated, especially when lessons resume."

His entire face flushed crimson, he shrugged and glanced away.

"That's what I figured."

"Ours next, ours next."

The twins disappeared under the table, coming up together bearing the weight of a wooden bucket filled to overflowing with wildflowers, mostly blue ones with five white petals at their centers. Madeline knew them to be columbine, predominating in both the twins' offering and in Sam's verdant valley.

"So beautiful. Thank you both. You must have spent hours and hours collecting these."

"All mornin'. Ain't hardly none left's 'far's you can see," James agreed, his little-boy face alight with pleasure, adding an earnest reassurance. "Uncle Sam says they'll grow back, though, quick as weeds—which they ain't, Uncle Sam says."

Jane added, "If you keep the bucket filled with fresh

water, miss, Uncle Sam says they'll last a good long time. Can we eat the cake now?''

''Uncle Sam ain't given his present yet,'' her twin chided with an elbow poke to the ribs.

With all gazes focused on him, Sam shoved a bandanna-wrapped bundle across the table to Madeline.

''These ain't new, but I figure you'll like 'em,'' he muttered self-consciously, eyes averted.

She unwrapped the folds of blue cloth, hearing a faint clatter of metal, glimpsing silver, finally exposing five polished teaspoons, handles inscribed with a scrolled S.

''Oh! Oh, my!''

The shaky, inarticulate utterance was all she could manage before covering her mouth with overlapped hands, overtaken with sudden emotion. This gift represented so much more to her—to him as well—than a simple birthday offering. Of that she was sure. Sam knew what the one spoon already in her possession meant to her, what it represented. By finding for her five more, what did he mean to imply? The promise of a future shared? Concession? Commitment?

Sam spoke into the awkward silence.

''Found only those five out've twelve all told. Six, with the one you have, should do well enough. Run across 'em out checkin' my traps. Figured you might fancy 'em. Come all the way from St. Louis.''

So, after all her hopeful suppositions, he thought she'd fancy them, nothing more. Madeline roused herself from dwelling upon what might have been, replacing bitter disappointment with resignation, to take the knife Lucy offered her with which to cut the cake.

Enjoying the sweet treat—dried apple-filled coffee cake rather than layer—Jane and James bickered good-naturedly over the cake of choice when their birthday arrived in the fall.

"Chocolate," said James.

"White," said Jane.

"Chocolate with chocolate icin'."

"White with pink."

"Pink's for girls."

"I'm a girl."

"I ain't. I want chocolate."

"I'll make you each your own cake when the time comes," intervened Lucy, "so please hush an' let Miss Maddie enjoy hers."

Mollified for the moment, the pair changed tactics.

"Know what I'm goin' to wish for when I blow out my candles? A horse've my own, just like Uncle Sam's Red."

"You ain't goin' get it now, 'cause you told what it was."

"Don't count if it ain't your birthday, an' you're not blowin' out candles."

"Does so."

"Don't."

"Does."

"Don't"

"Enough!"

"Sorry, Uncle Sam," said Jane, with another change of subject. "Bet I know what Miss Maddie wished for. Bet she wished she could stay here with us an' never ever have to leave. I'm right, ain't I, Miss Maddie?"

Madeline sought out Sam; he watched and waited for her response as candidly as the children, but his expression, unlike theirs, betrayed nothing.

"I thought one couldn't tell, or lose the wish. How can you be sure I wasn't wishing Bertie and Nahios-si were here to enjoy our party?"

"Asked 'em," Sam admitted, clearly disgruntled at her evasion.

"When? While you were out checking your traps ... despite the still-hazardous conditions?" She could not keep from expressing her skepticism, if only by tone of voice.

He failed to rise to her bait.

"Couldn't get away. One of their nanny goats's fixin' on givin' birth any day now."

Whatever his motivation, the aggravating man had no intention of relinquishing his lie of adverse traveling conditions, at least not until some purpose of his own had been served, not even in light of obvious inconsistencies. But why? Unless he wanted her to stay and could not bring himself to ask. Too stubborn? Prideful? Fearful of hazarding a loss, as with Hettie? Madeline immediately rejected that possibility as the act of a coward, which Mountain Man Sam Spencer was not. She acknowledged his excuse for the older pair's absence with a brisk nod, suggesting another piece of cake all around.

The cake was gone, the dirty dishes stacked for later washing, and the candle replaced in its holder. Jane protested, loudly, that she didn't want the party to be over so soon.

"Oughta be games . . . an' prizes . . . an' . . . an' music."

"Ain't got no music," scoffed James.

"Could be we do, matter of fact," interjected their uncle. "If I recollect, there's a music box in that trunk over there. Whoa, there, you two. I'll do the checkin'."

He rummaged through the contents of the humpback chest, and with an *aha!* of triumph, came up with a small footed box, rectangular, of a gold-colored metal heavily embossed in a scrolled design. He returned to the table, setting his offering in front of Madeline.

"Give the key on the bottom a couple've turns, Maddie. See if that old thing'll still give up a tune."

It did indeed, once sufficiently wound. Madeline lifted the lid, disclosing under glass a revolving studded-brass cylinder and a row of brass finger-like strikers plucking out a lilting melody.

"How lovely. A waltz, if I'm not mistaken."

"I thought a waltz was a dance, miss," said Lucy.

"It is, as well as the rhythm you hear in this tune . . . *One,* two, three . . . *one,* two, three. Like that."

Madeline waved her hand as if holding a baton. On impulse she began to dip and sway, then dance and twirl, ending up before Sam on a deep curtsy.

"May I have this dance, Mr. Spencer?"

His face went from bemused to disconcerted to glowering in a flash.

"That kind've tiptoein' around's for citified pilgrims. Ask Paul."

The boy looked as thunderous as his uncle. Madeline suddenly regretted having mentioned at all the matter of dancing, apparently a subject of sensitivity for both.

"Ain't goin' to dance. Can't make me."

"My intention was not to force anyone to—"

Sam ignored her for Paul.

"Always got to be contrary, don't you, boy? Bet you'd stand out in the pourin' rain if I was the one to ask you to step inside."

Desperate to keep the confrontation, so unintentionally precipitated by herself, from accelerating, Madeline attempted a different approach.

"Mr. Spencer, there's no need to take issue—"

"Ain't nothin' that don't end up bein' an issue with this one, Maddie, an' I'm gettin' goldanged sick've it. Now's as good a time to get things settled once and for all."

"At my birthday party?"

"Music's stopped. Party's over. Boy don't want to dance nohow."

"Nor did you. However, I—"

"Ain't he can't dance—he won't 'cause I asked, see?"

"I do see, more than you—"

"Contrary, that's what he is. Right from the git-go. But all that's changin'—right now, matter've fact." Sam turned his glower on the boy, whose anger had been building as steadily and irrationally as the man's. "Boy, I'm goin' to give you a direct order, an' you ain't goin' to say boo about it, just do as I tell you. You don't want to dance, fine. From now 'til bedtime, you can chop kindlin' instead an' stack it in a nice orderly pile alongside the house. Without cuttin' off none of your own toes, if you can keep from it. Got that?"

Paul glared right back, muttering something under his breath that Sam apparently took for assent, if begrudgingly given, much to Madeline's relief. Man and boy parted ways, Paul to grab his jacket off its peg near the hearth, Sam escaping out of doors in two long-legged strides, neither conceding in the slightest to the other.

Madeline stood as if rooted in the hard-packed soil of the earthen floor, staring at the closed plank door, half hoping Sam would reconsider, be the first to bend, and return to make amends. What a disastrous ending to their happy festivities! And so unnecessarily. A tempest in a teapot. Once that man's temper had cooled, she intended to have a good long talk with him—

"Paul, no!"

Lucy's fearful cry rent Madeline from her musings. She spun first toward the girl, then the object of her alarm to find Paul wrenching Sam's rifle off its brackets over the hearth.

"You goin' a shot Uncle Sam?" asked James, both afraid and fascinated.

Paul tossed his brother a disgusted glance.

"Goin' to hunt me down a bear an' kill it dead so's he won't all the time take me for a fool an' a coward. I'll show him."

"No, Paul, that is not the way to favorably impress—"

Madeline took a forward step, but Paul backed away, out of reach.

"I'm goin'. Saw fresh tracks at the edge of the woods where the twins was pickin' flowers. Bear tracks. I'm goin' to get that bear 'fore he gets one've us. Uncle'll see then I ain't no'ccount."

"He doesn't—"

"Does. But he'll think different, see if he don't, once I haul home m'own fresh-kilt bear."

He darted past her and out the door. She followed as swiftly as impeding skirts permitted, but he had almost reached the barn before she called out from the stoop.

"Paul, wait. Come back."

The other children clustered behind her, echoing her pleas. Too late. He was gone. Into the forest on a quest so important to him as to deafen and blind him to all else, including the truth.

"What the hell's all the ruckus?" roared Sam, coming around the corner of the house from somewhere out back.

She turned on him in a flash, fists to hips.

"Paul has taken off into the woods with your gun, determined to kill a bear to prove his worthiness to you. I hope you're satisfied."

Frowning, Sam ignored her indignation in favor of her news.

"Boy ain't got no call to take my Hawken without askin'."

"That's *all* you have to say on the subject?"

"I suppose you want me to go runnin' off after the boy an' bring him on back. It ain't like he's goin' to find hisself a bear." He offered a weak imitation of his best cajoling grin. "You chased them all off this mornin' with your singin', if you'll recall."

"Apparently all but the one whose tracks the children discovered while picking wildflowers this morning."

Sam turned on the twins.

"Bear tracks? For sure? You'd know 'em if you seen 'em?"

They shared identical, solemn-faced nods.

"Paul's goin' to get hisself kilt, ain't he?" asked Jane.

"Double dang that boy, not if I can help it."

Sam spun and sprinted off in pursuit without so much as a by-your-leave or a good-bye.

Once again, Madeline waited, worrying, for endlessly long, lonely hours after the children were in bed and the cabin grown unbearably quiet. Would it always be that way should she stay? If so, from where would she gather the strength, knowing each time could be the last and could end very badly? Leaving her even more alone to face the great unknown all on her own.

Panic reared its ugly head, ran its course, and with its demise perseverance triumphed. She *would* survive, come what may, because she could not do otherwise. What did one do but fight the good fight? Lie down to die a coward's death? Not Madeline Genevieve Preston. She might fret and grow afraid, but in the end she would do what had to be done, and get on with her life, come what may.

The old clichés were small comfort while she waited, worrying nonetheless. She dozed, awakening to scuffling sounds outside the door. Sam returned? Or the bear?

"Who's there?"

Her voice came out strong despite her inner quaking. For endless seconds, there came no reply.

"Maddie . . . It's me . . . Sam. Open up."

She flew to the door and flung it wide. And gasped at the bloodied sight before her. Sam leaned heavily on the jamb, hair matted, face all but indistinguishable for the red rivulets pouring from long gashes in his scalp. Elsewhere, everywhere, she saw similar devastating damage; and in his arms, blood-covered as well, lay the inert form of the boy, unconscious or . . . or gone, she could not tell.

"Sam. Dear Lord, Sam. How—? Is he d—?"

"Not yet. Found his bear."

"You—you're both so hurt . . . What can I—?"

Her babbling ceased only because she didn't know what more to say or do.

"I . . . got 'im this far. Can make it as far as his room . . ."

Anything more seemed to require too much energy. He staggered across the room to the other, blood splattering into the earth floor in his wake. Following at his heels, Madeline could not keep her gaze from going back to the red drops turning brown, seeping into the hard-packed soil. Sam's life blood, and Paul's. How much more could possibly be left to sustain life?

He dumped the boy on the bed the moment she'd flung back the covers, then leaned heavily against the wall, braced on one bloody hand.

James stirred and awoke, crying out in alarm at the vague shadows filling the small corner. Madeline wasted no more time with preliminaries.

"Get up quickly, James. Sam and Paul are hurt. Help me get your uncle into your bed before he faints dead away."

"Ain't . . . goin' . . . to . . . faint."

Sam fell unconscious onto James's bed almost before the child vacated it, half on and half off. Madeline managed to swing his legs onto the bed, her hands coming away sticky and wet. Absently, she ran them down her skirt front, trying to muster her resources to know what to do next.

"Golly-gosh almighty, what happened to 'em?" James asked.

On a shaky breath, Madeline repeated, "Paul found his bear."

"Did he kill it?"

Patience gone, she retorted sharply, "What difference does it make? Merely having found it may cost your brother and your uncle their lives unless we do something, and at once. Light both candles—carefully—and bring them to me—and something to set them on. But first, rouse Lucy. And tell her to bring needle and thread. Her sewing expertise will most surely be needed."

"Yes, ma'am."

All the more frightened by her words and her tone, James sprinted away. Moments later, Lucy appeared in the doorway, a shadowy wraith in a nightgown.

"James and Sam have been gored by a bear," Madeline stated bluntly. "We will need to sew up their wounds. Quickly. They've lost so much blood already."

Upon seeing the inert forms on the bed, the girl clutched the jamb, swaying on her feet.

"I—I . . ."

"Please, Lucy, hurry."

"Miss . . . I—I . . ."

The girl slumped to the floor in a dead faint.

James and Jane staggered into the room in their nightclothes, each carrying a three-legged stool, skirting their sister on the floor with wide-eyed fascination.

"She dead, too?" Jane asked in awe.

"Lucy fainted. No one is dead, nor will be, if we're quick about it. James, the candles. Please. And Jane, please find the needle and thread I asked Lucy to bring."

"Yes, ma'am."

"Yes, ma'am."

"Then I'll need water. Lots of water."

"There ain't no snow to melt down," whined Jane.

"There's the stream."

"It's dark an' scary outside."

"Jane," Madeline spoke sharply, calming with effort,

"and James . . . there is no one but you two, and myself, left to deal with this. Our loved ones are counting on us to do everything in our power to save their lives, including facing our fears. Do you understand?"

"Yes, ma'am."

"Yes, ma'am."

Hand in hand, they ran off. Madeline stood alone in the room with the injured and unconscious, no less terrified than the twins for all her courageous words. Life and death lay in her incompetent hands. What to do first she could only guess, yet knowing full well she would do everything within her power to save these precious, precious lives. Beginning, first and foremost, with a plea and a prayer, and a promise. Madeline folded her hands at her waist, bowed her head, and went immediately to work.

Chapter Eighteen

Night became morning, but within the boys' room-turned-sickroom, two candles burned, and neither of the injured regained consciousness. Paul tossed fitfully, troubled by bad dreams; Sam lay as still and pale as death, only the slight rise and fall of his bandage-wrapped chest showing a sign of life. Madeline sat rigidly between them in a rocking chair, hands gripping the arms, not daring to rock for fear of lulling herself asleep. One or the other might need her, require sponging with cool water or covers replaced, pillows fluffed. Anything at all to make herself useful while they struggled with recovering—if they could—from their grievous injuries.

Both had suffered badly from the slashing claws of the bear, Paul at the back of his head and from shoulder to waist, left to right, following his spine. Sam had a series of swipes all on his right side from crown to jaw, across his chest, down his shoulder, arm, and hand—telling the story of the attack as clearly as words, of Sam's protecting the boy with the shield of his own body while trying to ward off the beast somehow. Paul's jacket, too, had saved him from worse injury, unlike Sam, with only the protection of a hide shirt, now in shreds. She could do nothing but further destroy his last remaining fringed shirt by cutting it off him. He was going to be furious with her over it when he awoke. If he awoke.

She dared not disturb their blood-soaked bandages once applied to see how their injuries fared, praying that her newly acquired sewing skills proved sufficient to bind them closed. There had been no one but she to deal with the urgency of the matter in any case; recovery, to whatever degree, or not at all, lay in hands other than her own.

Lucy quickly roused from her swoon, apologetic that she hadn't the stomach for the sight of blood, volunteering to tear and roll bandages in the other room. Madeline let her go; she had no other choice.

Then the waiting began, and so it continued, Madeline ever vigilant in the sickroom, and Lucy seeing to the children and necessary household tasks, as was her forte. Not daring to imagine beyond the moment, Madeline refused to think of the future if Sam did not survive, knowing somehow that she and the children would go on, yet not at all certain she'd want to, without Sam. Regretting with each passing second that she had not put words to the love for him in her heart while she could, promising herself they would be the first words out of her mouth when he opened his eyes.

She dozed off eventually, despite her best intentions, sleeping in fits and starts. It was dark outside when she woke, as she discovered upon emerging from the sickroom to deal with personal necessities. Supper was in progress. Worried gazes turned her way, three voices chorusing their concerns, Jane's as usual the loudest.

"How's Paul 'n' Uncle? Is they goin'a die?"

Tempted to offer up a reassuring lie, Madeline admitted, "Only time will tell."

"We're sure you done your best, miss."

"Thank you, Lucy, I promise you I have."

"Come sit with us. Have some stew 'n' biscuits. Won't do neither've them any good if you take sick."

Madeline did as she was told, but hurriedly, bolting her food without tasting it. Little had changed in her absence, she discovered when she returned to the sickroom, except that Paul appeared to be resting more comfortably, as if he had slipped from unconsciousness to sleep without opening his eyes. Sam had worsened, his breathing now shallow and erratic, his flesh on forehead and chest hot to her touch.

She stood over him, wringing her hands, panic rising. Speaking aloud, she kept her voice low so as not to disturb the sleeping boy behind her, nor alarm unduly the other children.

"Sam? Sam Spencer, can you hear me? You *will* recover from your injuries and live to devil me another day. I refuse to allow you to do otherwise. I—I'm going to give you some of Bertie's medicine, Sam. It broke Baby's fever, and so it shall yours." Her tone went sharp. "Do you hear me, Mr. Spencer? You are going to get better, if only to face me for this latest folly of yours, mark my words."

Her brave statements did little to ease her fears, but perhaps, if he heard, he'd take up the challenge she flung at him and fight to survive.

With Lucy's assistance, she prepared a weak tea of dried Indian tobacco, praying the infusion would not bring about, with improper dosage, paralysis or death—as warned against on the accompanying slip of paper. The girl ventured into the sickroom to help administer the liquid, by the spoonful to the unconscious man in the bed, trembling and pale throughout, escaping as soon as she could, her expression contrite.

"Call me when you figure it's time for another dosin', day or night, I'll come help, miss, I will," she insisted at the doorway.

"I know. Thank you, but I believe I can manage, freeing you to continue with the children and the chores, if you don't mind. Beyond that there's little else either of us can do but wait, and watch." Madeline forced a weak smile. "All will be well in the end. You'll see."

Lucy ducked her head.

"Yes, miss."

With her departure, Madeline resumed her vigil, the hours weighing heavily between times of medicating her patients. Madeline slipped out briefly, returning with the quilt. Hour after hour she labored meticulously over its repair, patching and stitching, ripping out any stitch that didn't please her to sew again and again until it did. In the last hours before dawn, she set in the last stitch with a quiet *ahh!* of satisfaction. On impulse, she scripted, in thread, at the bottom, "Damaged and repaired by Madeline Genevieve Preston, completed this 3rd day of May 1845."

Shortly thereafter, a weariness crept over her that she could not deny, arousing from deep, dreamless sleep in the early morning hours to find Paul happily awake and alert, complaining of pain and hunger. Fed thin porridge and weak Indian tobacco tea liberally laced with honey, he soon drifted off to sleep again.

Over breakfast she gave the children the good news that Paul was on the mend, their joy and hers tempered with the realization that Sam, as yet, was not.

Prepared for another endless nightwatch after supper that evening, and with little with which to occupy herself, Madeline took up one of her birthday gift pens, mixed a batch of ink powder and water in a cup, and gathered a half-dozen sheets of trimmed brown wrapping paper, intending to begin the frequently delayed letter to her parents. The effort proved futile, her concerns for Sam causing all else to flee her mind and destroy her concentration.

How long could someone remain unconscious, burning with fever, and survive?

Sam had now lain two days and three nights, unmoving, barely breathing. With the next dose of Indian tobacco tea, she upped the concentration of the herb by half, and again with the next. The only perceptible change being that he broke out into profuse sweating, whereas before his skin had been papery dry with heat. She sponged his bare torso wherever he was not bandaged, to the waist. Below that, still encased in hide britches, modesty forbade her venturing. It was one thing to see a man in the altogether while bathing and fully conscious, quite another to observe him thus vulnerable and unaware.

After a third dose, stronger still, perspiration turned to chills, racking his body and shaking the bed. Madeline pulled blankets and fur robe up to his chin, tucking them tight; still he shuddered, teeth clattering. She tossed Hettie's quilt over all, to no avail. At wit's end, she crawled in under the mound of covers with him. Mindful of his injuries, she wrapped her limbs around Sam in an effort to stop his thrashing, terrified he'd tear out her careful stitching and bleed as profusely as before. The man had no blood to spare for shedding by now, she felt certain.

Clinging to him despite his unconscious efforts to shake her off, Madeline grew uncomfortably hot and steamy herself; but her discomfort eventually seemed to ease his. His body warmed and grew quiet. His breathing settled to a slow, steady pace, as did his heart beneath her ear pillowed against his chest. Sensing a crisis had passed, Madeline

herself relaxed and drifted away into the sweet unconsciousness of sleep.

Madeline awakened slowly, languidly, aware at first only
of a gentle, repetitive stroking the length of her spine from
waist to nape and back. She tilted her head, coming face
to face with Sam, his blue eyes alert, if weary. Offering her
an imitation of his usually cocky smile, he spoke for the
first time in days, in a weak, rusty voice.

"*Kal-hay-yah*, Maddie."

"*Kal-hay-yah*." Perilously close to tears, Madeline swallowed twice. "So, you've returned to the living."

She broke free and sat up only because he was too infirm
to hold her. He appeared more puzzled than distressed.
Taking in the timbered walls of the room, he winced at
the slight movement.

"You're in the boys' bedroom. You have been unconscious for three days and four nights ... after a bear
attacked you and Paul."

"Paul?"

He turned his head, bandaged cheek pressing into his
pillows.

"Recovering nicely only a few feet away. Please, don't
move around so. You'll disturb all the stitches I meticulously—"

"You?"

Sitting there in the bed beside him, Madeline flushed
but held her head high.

"There was no one else. Lucy, it seems, is squeamish at
the sight of blood. I think you'll find my handiwork sufficient, Mr. Spencer. You are no longer bleeding all over
the bedding and apparently on the road to recovery,
despite your encounter with that bear. After all your warn-

ings against predators, in the end it was you yourself who should have heeded them, Sam Spencer.''

His fragile hold on her arm was all that kept her from pulling away and running off. Emotions held firmly in check all the desperate, lonely hours he lay unconscious swelled and spread throughout her—mind, heart and body—until she feared she could not hang on much longer.

His tired gaze never left her face.

"Paul . . . got his bear . . . Took its time . . . dyin's, all. Don't fret . . . Maddie . . . Be all . . . ri . . .'' He drifted off to sleep mid-word.

Madeline assured herself he was on the mend, nothing more, before scrambling off the foot of the bed in all haste. Frantic for some privacy before losing control altogether, she made it no further than a step away. Every tear unshed these last several weeks burst forth in an unrestrained flood, great sobs she muffled with her flour-sack apron pressed tightly against her mouth with both hands. After a time, she wept all the harder with overwhelming relief that her prayers had been answered. Sam, the love of her life, her whole life, would live. And so, now, could she.

Sam's recovery began, lengthier and far more painful than Paul's. There were times when Madeline—driven to distraction by her recalcitrant patient—almost, almost wished . . . She put no words to that evil wish, but oh, there were times.

Long after Paul was up and about, leaving him his privacy by moving into the loft with James, Sam suffered debilitating pain, frightening setbacks, once even tearing free Madeline's careful stitches with his impatience to quit his sickbed. His stubbornness cost her two more sleepless nights sitting up with him toward the end of that first week.

After that, Madeline laid down the law. He *would* lie still, and he *would* allow sufficient time to heal, or she'd wash her hands of him altogether.

"Then we'll see who feeds you and medicates you and watches over you, Mr. Spencer," she told him furiously, hands to hips, late one afternoon when he was being particularly trying.

He glowered. "Ain't like you can run out on us any time soon. Bound to be some time 'fore I can take you on down the mountain."

Immediately contrite, Madeline relented. "I'm in no hurry, Mr. Spencer. The children need me, and so, apparently, do you, whether you'll admit to it or not."

Relief flooded his countenance, which he tried to mask with a pale imitation of his usual bad-tempered frown.

"Dammit, Maddie. I can't take much more of layin' around with nothin' to do all day but count the rafters. I'm goin' plumb outa my mind."

He reclined against his pillows, half sitting for the first time since his injuries, his hands fisted around Hettie's quilt as if to keep himself from striking something in frustration. A full week had passed since first he awoke, but only a day or two since he'd been fever-free and able to sit up without passing out. She sympathized, but remained steadfast.

"Quiet and rest is what you most need right now, Mr. Spencer, so resign yourself to forced inactivity for however long it takes."

"I'll go loco, Maddie, if one've us don't come up with somethin'—*anythin'*—I can do from this here bed."

Madeline threw up her hands in exasperation.

"Only one thing comes to mind—"

"What?"

"I hesitate to even mention it—"

"Dammit, woman, what?"

"Reading and writing lessons. Nothing too strenuous at first, the alphabet, simply practicing—"

"No!"

"I *knew* you'd make an issue of it, though you did say you intended to acquire those skills—"

"No."

He turned his face away. She studied his stony features.

"I can think of one reason only. Pride. Stupid, stubborn pride. It's one thing to learn what you can by eavesdropping, and quite another to be the one and only student—isn't it, Mr. Spencer?"

"Dang, woman. You got beans for brains to come up with a half-baked notion like that."

"That being the case, *you* tell *me* the real reason, if you can."

His reluctant admission, a long time coming, surprised her. It came painfully hard as well, evidently something to which he'd given much troubled thought for a good long time.

"Could be I *can't* learn, woman. Could be, if I'm like my Pa, I can't never learn how to so much as pen my own name. He never did, no matter how many times nor how many ways Ma tried to teach him."

Sam's shamed admission stumped her, but only momentarily.

"On the other hand, Sam Spencer, perhaps you take after your mother who attempted to teach him. One would think that with all this leisure on your hands, it would be worth your while to discover once and for all which side of your family tree you truly favor, would it not?"

Reluctantly, yet with hope alight in his fathomless blue eyes, Sam agreed to give it a try.

"Ain't promisin' nothin', though," he cautioned. "An' you get to pushin' an' shovin' to get your way, like you tend to, an' I'm quittin' on the spot."

"We have a bargain, then, Mr. Spencer. I shall teach you—without pushing—and you will endeavor to master both reading and writing without falling back upon the excuse of some preconceived notion that you cannot learn."

Later, with paper and charcoal sticks for pencils spread out between them on Hettie's quilt, while Sam repeatedly, if disgruntledly, labored over *o*'s and *a*'s between lines Madeline had drawn, she complemented him on his rapid progress.

"A few more of each and we shall move on to *b*'s and *d*'s. To your knowledge, was there anything in particular your father seemed unable to understand?"

Sam gave the matter some thought, frowning in concentration and, remembering, barked a bitter laugh.

"Said the circles an' lines an' squiggles of the letters was all the time shiftin' an' changin' so he couldn't keep them all straight, tell one from another."

"And yourself?"

"Half wish they would," he grumbled, but appeared vastly relieved nonetheless. "Danged borin' makin' 'em 'xactly the same time after time after time. Ain't we done yet? That there *o*'s about as perfect as the human hand can come up with."

"Very well, Mr. Spencer. Pay attention, now. This is how we form the letter *b.* "

He grumbled expletives, but did as she'd instructed, over and over and over again for the remainder of that day and many more that followed during his convalescence, until he was able to read and write as well as his seven-year-old niece and nephew. The tedium of the simple lessons, as well as forced physical inactivity, had taken its toll on both of them by then. Sam turned stubborn, demanding something more challenging, though it seemed beyond Madeline's creativity to supply it.

"How about fetchin' me that diary of Hettie's you said I should take a look at." Madeline hesitated. "Somethin' in it you don't want me to see?"

"It's not that. It's—well, the diary is in writing, not printing."

"So, you'll help me over the hard parts. Go fetch it for me, Maddie. It's time. Past time."

Madeline returned from a quick trip to the loft carrying the box of items representing Sam and Hettie's brief marriage. Sam had cleared a place for it on the bride's quilt and was studiously studying the band across the coverlet's bottom. He glanced up when she set the box at his feet.

"There's writin' here."

"I know." She read aloud to him the words Hettie had set down, her name and her mother's, the dates when begun and completed, her and Sam's wedding date. "I—I contributed my own when I finished repairing Hettie's quilt. I hope you don't mind. See there . . . 'Damaged and repaired by Madeline Genevieve Preston, completed this 3rd of May 1845'."

He took the time to examine her repair down to the smallest detail, at last lifting his gaze to meet hers.

"You done a mighty good job here, Maddie, and I'm grateful to have it back the way it was."

"Considering that it was I who occasioned the need for repair in the first place, I am undeserving of your praise, Mr. Spencer."

"You're gettin' it anyway, woman, an' then that's the end of it. What's in the box?"

"Those personal items I told you I'd set away for you."

"What kind of things?"

He opened the box and dug inside with all the eager curiosity of a child. He came up with a gold pocket watch complete with chain and fob. He palmed it, rubbing its etched-scroll-design surface with the pad of his thumb.

"My ma's pa's watch. Never met him myself. Ma said he run a dry-goods store somewhere back East. Died before she got married. Said he was a good man. She give it to me when Pa died, said I was the man of the house an' deserved for it to be mine. You'll have to teach me how to tell time so I can carry it after this."

He set the timepiece on the bedcover, taking another bit of jewelry from the box. He held it out on an open hand for her to see. A porcelain cameo brooch of a sweet young woman whose face looked vaguely familiar.

"Hettie?"

"Her ma."

"Bertie? How pretty she was."

He agreed with a nod. "An' still is. Inside."

Madeline concurred with a murmur, lifting a pair of tiny beaded moccasins from the contents of the box.

"You make these for the baby . . . for William?"

"Nahios-si did. Don't know why I bothered to save 'em all these years."

Sobered by that find and what it represented, together they examined the remaining contents of the box. Sam's father's pipe. Bertie's Bible. A packet of steel needles and a silver thimble Hettie had probably used in the making of the quilt. Conspicuously absent was the one document Madeline had anticipated finding within. She had not found it anywhere else, though she performed a meticulous search. Sam and Hettie's marriage license was surely more valued than pipe and thimble and pocket watch. A question popped into her head, asked before she realized the words were out.

"What is 'married in the mountain way'?"

His head came up, and he offered a lopsided grin.

"Where'd you hear 'bout that?"

"Hettie's diary . . . Her opening sentence states, 'Today Sam and me was married in the mountain way.' Which aroused my curiosity to learn how it differs from say, a church wedding or one held in the family parlor.''

"Different as night an' day, Maddie. No parlor, no church, no preacher for that matter. Just two people, man an' woman, all on their own, promisin' in their own words to stick together come what may for all the rest of their days. Bertie an' Nahios-si married up like that, too, an' a good many other folks. Ain't no legal way to get hitched in the Territory, and can't always travel to where it is, so we take care of it ourselves, quick an' easy, an', and to my mind, as bindin'.''

He shrugged off the matter, but studied her face intently—waiting for censure, she supposed.

"A most practical solution, Mr. Spencer, and one particularly suited to these wild, unconventional mountains. Rather romantic, too, when one thinks about it. Two individuals giving their word, with nothing legal or ecumenical binding them together for life, nothing indeed but their own love and honor.'' She waxed eloquent, forgetting all but the imagery evoked, seeing not Hettie and Sam, but Sam and herself in her imagination. "I would prefer such a simple ceremony, given the choice.''

His large hand came down over hers upon the double-wedding-ring quilt, turning her to face him with a gentle nudge of his fingertips under her chin, his steady gaze probing.

"You askin'?''

"Asking? Asking you . . . to . . . to marry me? No . . . Of course not . . . That is . . . Yes, I believe I am.''

Suspicion furrowed his brow, chasing off fleeting pleasure.

"For them kids . . . or me?''

"You.''

"Why?''

"Why?'' Though she tried in vain to retain her compo-

sure, her ire got the best of her. "Why, because I have
learned to love you, stubborn, growling, grumbling man
that you are."

"Prove it."

"I—I already hazarded saying I hove you, not knowing
in the least how you fe—"

"Prove it, woman."

He pulled her into his arms with a pained grunt that
turned into a needful groan when their lips met. His hand
cradled the back of her head, making that kiss last until
they broke apart gasping.

"You accept, then, Mr. Spencer?" she asked primly when
she could breathe again.

He settled back against his pillows, smug with satisfaction.

" 'Xpect so, woman."

Madeline rocked back on her haunches, head tipped.
"Why?"

He groaned. "Goin' make me say it right out?"

"*I* did."

"That's woman talk."

"Nonsense. Confess, Mr. Spencer. Say the words. Rest
assured they will not unman you."

He lifted his shoulders in pretended indifference.

"Consider 'em said."

"Oh, no, Mr. Spencer. You'll not get off as easily as that.
The words themselves, Mr. Spencer, if you please."

His arm snaked out and his hand wrapped around her
wrist, hauling her up tight against him.

"Save them words for the weddin', woman. This kind've
medicine's more what I'm needin' right now."

He kissed her senseless, until she half forgot what they'd
been sparring over. Afterward, she snuggled against his
side, her head on his shoulder while he stroked her back.

"You've not fooled me, you know. I shall hold you to

your promise to include 'I love you' in your wedding vows, Sam Spencer."

His lips brushed her forehead.

"You're goin' to be givin' up an awful lot, Maddie, marryin' up with the likes of me, takin' on raisin' my sister's kids, along with our own."

She tipped her head to gaze into his troubled face.

"But I'm gaining so much more, Mr. Spencer."

He grinned, bemused.

"When you goin' to get around to callin' me Sam?"

"When you've finally ceased calling me 'woman,' I imagine."

His chest heaved in an exaggerated sigh.

"Guess I'll just have to get used to Mr. Spencer, then, woman. Maddie-of-my-heart."

"Ahha, you've said it."

"Have not."

"Have."

"Haven't."

His mouth crushed down hard on hers, long and lingering. After a lengthy, impassioned embrace he asked, thoughtfully, "What're your kinfolks goin' think've you marryin' up with the likes of me?"

It touched her that it mattered to him. Still she couldn't help a light laugh.

"Once you have met them . . ." She suppressed a giggle, beginning again. "When Papa met Mama, she was the daughter of a Southern aristocrat, raised on a prosperous plantation, who'd run off to become a stage actress, scandalizing and disowned by her family. And Papa—why, he was a farm boy from the East with aspirations to become a rich banker, and not a penny to his name. As unlikely a pair as you and me, I'd wager, who've been married twentyfive years to date."

"Your papa rich now?"

"Comfortable enough. Rich, no, except in friends and loved ones."

He fell silent, reflective, for a while, absently rubbing her back.

"Brothers an' sisters?"

"Me? No. After my birth, Mama suffered from some complications . . . She couldn't have any more children. There were only the three of us all these years. Seeing Lucy and Paul and Baby and the twins, how they are with one another when not giving each other grief, I realize I missed a lot." She ran her hands lightly over his bandaged chest. "I shall enjoy being a part of a large family."

"How large?"

"Very."

"Now see here, woman. Ain't I got no say in the matter?"

"I will consider your wishes, of course, Mr. Spencer, but I will have a half dozen nonetheless."

His hand ceased coursing the length of her spine, wrapping over her shoulder to pull her in for a lingering kiss.

"How's about startin' on 'em right now? Kissin' an' huggin' ain't half what I'm wishin' for," he asked, voice husky, yet hopeful.

Tempted almost beyond resisting, Madeline slipped out of his arms to scramble off the bed in all haste.

"Not until you are fully recovered."

"Aw, Maddie—"

"Not a word of complaint from you, sir, after what you put me through of late. When I am absolutely convinced you are whole and healthy, then and only then shall we . . . ah, act upon . . . our . . . our urges. And not a moment sooner."

Hot-faced, she spun on her heel to exit the room with all the dignity she could muster, giving him the privacy to cool his unruly ardor, and she, hers—his being clearly evident beneath his covers and hers in the beads of perspiration on her brow, the betraying, erratic thudding of her heart with imagining that promised pleasure yet to come.

May slipped into June, a short spring into full summer. Spring snow and rain gave way to summer skies of endless blue; the starkness of gray and black and white to all the colors of the rainbow. A feast to the senses, to sight and smell, taste and touch and sound. In the early morning on the first of the new month, Madeline and Sam stood alone together on the front stoop watching dawn's glorious arrival, all soft pink and peach. He'd come up behind her, pulled her tight against him, back to chest, his arms wrapped around her waist. She settled against him, appreciating the perfect fit, having given up protesting after the first few days that the children would catch them. There were few, if any, secrets in quarters as close as Sam's small cabin.

"I wish . . ."

"What?" he asked close to her ear.

"I wish . . ." She sighed. "I would really like a bath . . . warm and lingering and private, away from interruptions."

He hugged her tighter.

"All alone?"

"Actually . . . no."

She turned her head to give his cheek a quick little kiss, study his dear, expressive face gone thoughtful, then triumphant.

"Got the perfect place."

An hour later, the two of them stood on a ridge of a nearby valley big enough only for a spring-fed pool scarcely visible beneath clouds of rising steam.

"Hot springs."

"Perfect," agreed Madeline, and again when they'd selected a clear spot on the rocky banks to spread Hettie's quilt for the picnic lunch Lucy supplied. "How many a time these last several weeks I pined for this luxury."

"Goin' to talk or come on in?"

He worked the buttons of his homespun shirt free as he talked, pausing when she hesitated to do the same. An understanding passed between them without need of words, but he reminded her anyway.

"It's time, Maddie."

"Yes."

"Bathin' first . . .?"

"Yes. Please."

They shed their garments, each watching the other, candidly if shyly, without shame. Gazes roamed at leisure. Sam stood bold and unashamed, the florid scars following the contours of his right side, livid against illness-pale skin, but in Madeline's eyes, magnificent. His appreciative stare followed her every mound and hollow until she felt compelled to cover herself. He shook his head; her arms fell to her sides and her chin came up. If he saw no flaw, who was she to disillusion him by pointing them out.

He grabbed up her hand. Linked, they stepped into the hot water, walked into the soothing heat of it, to the waist, then shoulder-high. Facing each other, by silent consent, they continued their leisurely perusals by touch, with exploring hands and lips.

He gently scrubbed her flesh, and her hair flowing upon the water, with fine lake-bottom sand, until the feel of the slight, sensuous abrasion all but drove her to distraction. She dipped beneath the water, rising with a handful of sand to wash over his body until he arched with need, the evidence of which pressed hard against her thigh, throbbing, hot.

Groaning, Sam caught her beneath the knees, swinging her up into his arms, his mouth capturing hers. Without a word spoken between them, only the assent in locked gazes, he carried her on shore, laying her on the bride's quilt, stretching out to cover her. When he would have lingered over touching and kissing, she urged him on, instinctively opening a place for him, lifting her hips in welcome. He came into her with such infinite care that she clutched at his hips to pull him down tight against her, gasping at the brief, bright pain, feeling wetness spill down between her legs upon the quilt in christening. Soon she was insisting he go on with resumed movement of her own, until a firestorm exploded throughout every fiber of her being, the cry of Sam's release quick to follow, echoing off the canyon walls. They lay entwined, spent and at peace.

At length she ventured to ask, "Are we now wed in the mountain way?"

Sam slipped onto his side to face her, smiling.

"A little more to it than that, Maddie."

He rolled onto his back, stretching out an arm to retrieve his homespun britches. Sitting up cross-legged, he withdrew from his pocket something he held from view in a closed fist.

"Sit up."

She complied, legs demurely angled to one side.

"Give me your hand . . . no, the left one. There now."

In a flash, he slipped a ring onto her finger. Her birthstone ring, traded for food when she fled Luckless. She examined the treasure restored, hand extended, fingers spread, before giving him a quizzical glance.

"How . . .? No, tell me later. Please, continue."

He recaptured her hand.

"I promise to stay with you always from this day on 'til my time comes, an' after, if that ain't impossible."

"And?"

"And now you."

"Not until you say the rest."

A pained look crossed his craggy, scarred features.

"Won't let me out of sayin' I love you, even knowin' it's so?"

"No. Well?"

"I love you, Maddie Preston—have longer'n I knew 'til I give it some thought, an' will 'til the end of my days. Satisfied? Now you."

She cleared her throat, moved and amused, and determined to restore propriety to the most important moment of her life.

"I, Madeline Genevieve Preston, do solemnly promise to love you, Sam Spencer, and stay with you all the days of my life. Are we wed now?"

"Yep. *Kal-hay-yah,* Mrs. Spencer."

"*Kal-hay-yah,* Mr. Spencer."

He cupped her cheek with one broad, callused palm, his eyes alight with his love.

"You shine, Maddie, you purely shine."

"If I do, Mr. Spencer, it is because you are my sun."

He frowned.

"Sam. Name's Sam. No fair, I called you Maddie."

"All's fair in love and war—"

"Half the time a body can't tell with you which is which."

"Then always expect a little of both, Sam Spencer, a little of both."

"Got to have the last word, woman?"

"I—"

He growled and glared like a ravenous bear.

"Not this time, Maddie Spencer."

He hauled her into his arms in a crushing, possessive hug, but kissed her long and thoroughly, Mountain Man laying claim to his woman. Little did he realize, thought Madeline, returning kind for kind, arms wrapped tightly around his waist, that this first verbal skirmish of their married life was, in her mind, merely a draw by mutual consent. Sam Spencer had met his match. Oh, what magnificent battles lay ahead, and what deliriously delightful peacemaking.

"I love you," she told him later, much later.

"That what you was goin' to say before? Havin' the last word come what may?"

"The last? Oh, no! Not nearly, Mr. Spencer. Only with your final breath will you hear the last."

"Promise?"

"You may depend on it, Sam Spencer."

"Same here, Maddie. Same here."

Epilogue

Thursday, 28 November 1889
River Valley, in the Midwest

"Can she bake a cherry pieee, Billy boy, Billy boy? Can she bake a cherry pieee, charmin' Billy? She can bake a cherry pie, quick as a cat can wink her eye, but she's a young thing an' cannot leave her motherrr."

Madeline held one of her mincemeat pies aloft on the flat of her palm, trimming the extra dough off the top crust with a few swift swipes of the knife in her other hand. Warbling away in the solitude of her daughter-in-law's kitchen at four A.M. Thanksgiving morning, she figured there wouldn't be any hug-a-beds today thanks to the carrying sound of her voice and the scent of her cinnamon buns baking in the oven for breakfast. She'd already chased Sam out back to the woodpile, and she could hear him chopping away at the kindling with all the vigor of a man half his seventy-two years. Married forty-four years and still her heart swelled with love and need, picturing him with shirt sleeves rolled high above his elbows, swinging that ax, every sinewy muscle rippling across chest and back.

Fluting the edge of the crust, poking vents in the top with the tip of her knife, Maddie smiled with the sheer weight of forty-four years of shared memories, hers and Sam's. Private memories, and family recollections of raising two nephews and three nieces to adulthood, and five of the six children born to them—as she'd predicted on their wedding day—all but the second, stillborn Ann Mercy. Two sons and three daughters remained, alive and well and prospering this holiday season, and only two still single— though not for long, if she had any say in the matter.

Let Sam badger her all he would to stay plum out of interfering in their lives with her endless matchmaking. Her success record spoke for itself. As soon as she settled the situation here with Preston and Cordelia's daughter, Samantha, she fully intended to get back to the matter of finding suitable spouses for her own Quinten and Nina. Quint at thirty-six was showing too many signs of becoming a confirmed bachelor for her peace of mind. And Nina, at twenty-four only two years older than granddaughter Samantha—hers and Sam's surprise blessing when they thought they were all done—was in desperate need of someone to tame her wild and willful ways. Maybe one of those seven Morgan boys living right next door here in River Valley. Not the second oldest, Ben. She'd already set her sights on him for Samantha, and hopefully the matter'd be settled before she and Sam headed home after the holidays.

". . . and her shoes were number nineee."

Midway through Madeline's rendition of "My Darling Clementine," Preston and Cordelia's niece, Eliza, came in, rubbing sleep out of her eyes, setting out silver and china for breakfast without needing to be asked. Raised by Maddie's son and daughter-in-law since infancy, she was a shy, plain, skinny little thing who reminded Maddie of Lucy as a girl, though Eliza was in her early twenties and planning a New Year's Day wedding. One of those Morgan boys next door—she forgot which one—had discovered the young woman's inner beauty, as had—finally—another fine fellow appreciated Lucy's.

Cordelia came in through the swinging kitchen door behind Eliza, cradling her right arm in its sling with her left. A couple of weeks ago her daughter-in-law broke her arm, and with the holidays and a wedding in the planning all crowded into little over a month, had wired Sam and Maddie, begging them to come early to help out.

Of course they came, and gladly; but it seemed too odd to Madeline even after all this time to work away in Cordelia's kitchen where as a child she herself had learned to make puddings and pies and cookies and cakes from her parents' amiable cook. This house, left to Preston and his young wife, had enticed them to leave Colorado for the Midwest. Mountain-born, Preston proved to be a city-dweller in his heart, with a head for business. Of which his father-in-law Chester Gilbert took full advantage as successor to Madeline's own father at his bank, and Preston his when a heart attack took Cordelia's father while yet in his fifties. By Cordelia's manner of dress this morning, Maddie could see how prosperous the bank had become under her son's capable management, and though she missed her first-born daily, she couldn't fault him his choices in residence or occupation.

"'Morning, Cordelia. How's that arm feeling? Any better?"

One-handed, the petite, plump, and pretty woman smoothed back the rich, dark crown of hair coiled at her nape and adjusted her high boned collar of the royal blue satin morning suit she wore as regally as a queen. Of the

latest in bustled styles, the garment Maddie long ago would
have coveted and had copied was draped and flounced
and beribboned wherever conceivable, much too young a
style for a matron in her forties, but perfect for this particular woman whom Maddie had grown to love like a daughter
in spite of herself.

"No better at all, Maddie, I'm afraid." She sighed heavily. "I spent a very restless night, and without Eliza's help
dressing this morning I might still be abed."

"Samantha not up yet?"

"Not that I'm aware of, though she knows how much
there is to do, and me unable to help in the least." Her
tone went unbecomingly petulant.

"I'll be happy to give you something for the pain, if
you'd like, Cordelia. I brought along my medicine bag. A
tonic, too, to put some color in your cheeks."

Her daughter-in-law laughed without humor. "Thank
you, no. Maddie, you've been too long on your mountain.
You've forgotten that ruddy, wind-weathered skin is not
considered an asset here in the city. Nor would I care to
trust my delicate constitution to the vagaries of your rustic
herbs and potions."

Taking no offense, Madeline merely smiled and nodded,
marveling how much this woman reminded her of herself
when she'd first come to the Rockies and stumbled upon
Sam's one-room log cabin. So long ago. Remarkable how
much had changed for her, and how little in the world
she left behind and to which she'd never willingly return.

"I see you have everything well in hand already, Maddie.
If you'll excuse me, I'll go hurry Preston along. He should
be out there helping his father with that wood, not loitering
over his toilette."

Maddie chuckled. "Don't worry about Sam, he's doing
fine all on his own. Rather be outside than in here listening
to me sing."

Her daughter-in-law rolled her eyes toward the ceiling, but said nothing as she left the kitchen, another of the many who failed to appreciate Madeline's spirited renditions. She launched into a rousing good song, "She'll Be Comin' 'Round the Mountain." Let anyone in the entire house dare try to sleep through that one.

". . . when she comes," she chortled as Sam came in through the back door, knees bent under a towering load of kindling.

He tossed it in to the woodbox the moment she opened the lid, complaining.

"Keep down that hellaceous racket, old woman. You tryin' to raise the dead?"

With his crown of snow-white hair and full beard to match, and bold brown eyes slightly faded, to Maddie he was and always would remain the magnificent mountain man she'd tamed and married that day beside a misty lake. In their altogether, as naked as the day they were born, like Adam and Eve, in a mountain paradise all their own. And not a moment's regret since, on her part or Sam's, as he often reminded her in some small way by word or deed. Through hard times and harder, sickness and death and joy, for over forty years she'd willingly live all over again.

With a wink, her husband headed back out for another load of wood of the many more they'd need this day, preparing the Thanksgiving feast.

Above, through the heat grate between kitchen and the bedroom overhead, Maddie heard her granddaughter stirring.

"Samantha. Samantha Sarahannah Spencer, I hear you up there! Get out of that bed right now and come on down. Make yourself useful. There's more'n enough work for every willing pair of hands . . . what with your mama's having only one that's working."

"Coming, Grannie."

Maddie set about starting breakfast, with Eliza's help, cracking a dozen eggs into a large, hot skillet while she set out butter and jam and milk and made up a big pot of coffee. She was eager to see her favorite grandchild— though she never admitted it to anyone, not even Samantha herself, Sam's namesake and as strong-minded as he was, that she had a favorite. Time Samantha settled down and married a good man—Ben Morgan next door in particular. From what she'd observed over the years on frequent visits after Preston and James and Jane all chose to settle here with their families, they'd make a perfect pair, and apparently didn't even know it. In fact, Samantha had taken off for Chicago a year ago to become a reporter on some newspaper there, while Ben settled down in River Valley to teach. Thanks to Maddie's good fortune, Cordelia's broken arm, and Eliza's up and coming wedding, she'd have plenty of opportunity to help the two of them see the light.

Maddie put the matter out of her mind to enjoy Thanksgiving dinner around a laden table with most of Cordelia's many relatives, a good number of hers and Sam's, and all seven of the Morgan boys save one—from the oldest, Andrew, right on down the alphabet from Ben to Charlie— skipping Duncan, not among them again this year—to teenaged Edward and the little ones, Frankie and Georgie. And, unfortunately, not a one to match up with her daughter, Nina. Charlie and Eliza were engaged, and Ben clearly belonged with Samantha and she with him, though they pretended to have nothing to do with each other. As to the oldest, Andrew, he and Jane's daughter Olivia feasted their eyes on each other all through dinner instead of the food, like a couple of lovelorn fools. Jane had looked daggers at the two of them the whole while, announcing loudly—as was her way still—toward the end of the meal that, come spring, she was taking Olivia to New York City to find her a "suitable" husband among the rich or royalty.

Maddie wasn't sure if that was a warning for poor Andrew, or directed at herself and her well-known propensity for matchmaking. Sam raised his shaggy brows at her across the table as if to say, "See, I ain't the only one thinkin' you do too much buttin' in," but of course, she ignored him. What did men know of such things? Especially Sam himself, who had left it to *her* to do the proposing.

Getting ready for bed that night in her old room while Sam watched from the bed, as she exchanged day clothes for nightgown, with the same light in his eyes as on their wedding night, he offered a verbal warning.

"Don't you go messing in Samantha's love life. She'll pick out her own fella when she gets around to it."

"Fiddlesticks, old man. She's already picked him out and doesn't even know it. Samantha's as stubborn as you are. She'll take herself on back to Chicago and never say boo to Ben Morgan unless I step in and help them out a little here and there." She turned from brushing her hair, now more silver than black. "I've done all right by our children, every one of whom that's married is happily wed with the exception of Jane, who, as you'll recall, made her own choice and settled for that mild and mealy-mouthed traveling salesman, Noble Tyler, who lets her lead him around by the nose when he isn't escaping to parts unknown for his job. Wasn't even here for Thanksgiving with his family."

Sam grinned indulgently and shrugged.

"Ain't nothin' I can say'll change your mind once it's made up, Maddie, so forget the youngun's an' come on to bed. Take care of your husband's needs 'til mornin'."

Madeline experienced the same little shiver of delighted anticipation as on their first and every subsequent night together. Sam never ceased needing and desiring her, and letting her know it, for which she was endlessly grateful.

"Whatever you say, old man. But don't think you've distracted me for a moment from my goal. Mark my words, come morning, I'm making it my mission to open a certain young lady's eyes to that nice, available boy next door."

The next day, at a sewing bee to finish filling Eliza's hope chest, with all female relatives old enough to hold a needle gathered in the cozy back parlor, Madeline covertly studied Samantha more than she sewed. The girl couldn't sew a stitch, so help her, and sat off by herself near the window overlooking the back yard, ruddy brown-crowned head bent over a pad of paper, scribbling away. A body never saw the girl, from the time she was in pigtails on, without a pad and pencil, writing down everything she saw or heard or imagined. Until now, it had always been her greatest passion—her calling, she said. But Maddie saw her more often than not staring out the window, looking across the way to the Morgans' yard, where Ben and his two youngest brothers were building a snowman, her eyes the exact color of her hair, sad and thoughtful. Maybe the task of getting that pair together wasn't going to be as hard as she thought.

Minutes later, the girl slipped outside to join Ben and the boys at play, and saw the young man's face light up at the sight of her. *Ah, yes, this was going to be the easiest match of all.*

Samantha and Ben came in together later while the women were enjoying cookies and hot chocolate, acutely aware of each other, painfully so. *Good, good,* thought Maddie, handing each a cup. And when Ben left some time later, having charmed everyone in the room with his cheery good nature, Maddie couldn't resist a probing comment.

"Ben Morgan'll make a wonderful husband for some lucky woman one day soon, wouldn't you say, Samantha?"

Samantha's chin had come up, just like Maddie's own did when backed into a corner, and lied through her teeth.

"I . . . I hadn't given it a thought, Grannie."

Better and better.

But as the end of their visit, with Eliza's wedding a week away and Christmas morning dawning, Sam was all too frequently throwing her his "I told you so" glances, lips quirked up in that maddening, smug way he had. Madeline attempted to ignore him as she wrapped up one last package in brown paper and string.

"Still goin' to give the girl Hettie's quilt, woman? She ain't no closer to seein' the light about that boy next door than ever."

"So you keep reminding me, Mr. Spencer. Maybe she is, and maybe she's not, but maybe giving her the quilt will hurry her thinking along on the matter."

"Goin' to tell her the whole of it?"

"Not this trip. She needs to be married a while with a baby of her own on the way before she'll fully understand its meaning. I'm simply hoping to point her in the right direction." Her hands hesitated over her knot-tying. She faced Sam, asking him for about the tenth time since first bringing it up, "Are you positive this is all right with you?"

"Said so, didn't I, over an' over? Samantha's my favorite 's'much as yours—don't tell nobody I said so—an' the quilt's goin' to need a new home one've these days anyhow. Time to pass it on, I'd say, an' the story of it, too. When you givin' it to her?"

"As soon's I get it wrapped, old man."

"It ain't even dawn yet, old woman."

Madeline smiled thoughtfully.

"I have a feeling she won't be sleeping. Hasn't been since she and Ben had that falling out a couple've days ago."

Sam crossed his arms high on his chest.

"Told you your matchmaking wasn't goin' to work this time."

"Too soon to tell, Sam, far too soon to tell."

She gathered up her bundle and slipped out of their room into the upstairs hall. She knocked, once, on Samantha's door and didn't wait for a "come in" to enter. As she thought, the girl in the bed, propped up on her pillows, wrapped in some of Maddie's handmade quilts, had been crying. Heart-sore for her granddaughter's suffering, necessary as it was in the way of love and loving, Maddie forced a cheerful smile and brisk manner.

"Knew you'd be awake."

Dropping her bundle on the bed, she hiked up a hip and perched on the edge. Samantha eyed the package with a whole lot less enthusiasm than Maddie had hoped. Maddie patted it encouragingly.

"I've always meant for you to have this when I felt the time was right."

Curiosity overcame the girl's lethargy. She pulled the offering to her and began working on the knots.

"A Christmas present, Grannie? What is it?"

Maddie shook her head. "Not a Christmas present, my dear child, a coming-of-age present. For unless I'm very much mistaken, I do believe you're finally learning you are more than your writing. You've discovered your heart, how it can love and how it can hurt to love again."

Samantha pressed the flat of her palm over her chest as though it pained her.

"I wish I never had, Grannie. Life is so much simpler without the misery love brings."

Maddie squeezed the hand resting idle on the brown wrapping paper.

"Without that misery, how would you appreciate the exquisite joy? But never mind that now—open my growing-up gift to you."

Samantha threw back overlapping flaps of paper, revealing the double-wedding-ring quilt, lovingly worn and faded, still beautiful in its workmanship.

"It's so lovely. Did you make this as a bride?"

Maddie chuckled. "Not I. Sam's first wife. This was her bride quilt."

She enjoyed watching the girl's mouth drop open.

"Grandpa's first . . .?"

"She died very young. That tale—and a whole lot more—will have to keep for later. Look at the quilt more closely," she urged impatiently.

Samantha unfurled the quilt with a snap.

"Oh, Grannie, what a shame. What happened?"

She ran her hand over the mending stitches, resting briefly on the faded brown splotches left there on Maddie's wedding day.

"Someday I'll tell you the entire tale," Maddie promised. "As Sam's namesake, you'll appreciate the story more than anyone else, since you are blessed—or afflicted—with the same adventurous spirit as him, and me." She rose to leave the girl to her thoughts, hesitating at the door. "You do understand how much that quilt means to me don't you, Samantha?"

Clearly the girl didn't, not entirely, but she hugged the coverlet to her, nodding solemnly.

"Because I see how you value it, Grannie, I'll cherish this and pass along its legacy. Especially after I learn what that legacy might be," she hinted.

Madeline put a warning finger to her lips.

"Later, when you are a young bride yourself. Only then will you fully understand the story I have to tell."

"I won't—"

Maddie shut the door with a firm snap. Smiling softly to herself, glad and sad to have passed Hettie's quilt into other hands, she returned to her old bedroom, and Sam.

He waited for her, stretched out on the unmade bed, completely naked and far from sufficiently covered by one of her more recent quilts draped over his legs, his intent clear. Later on, she'd tell him how the quilt-giving went, and her intention to write down the whole story surrounding it as soon as they got home. Right now, unmistakable evidence indicated that a matter of more urgency required her immediate attention.

"Not up and dressed yet, Mr. Spencer?"

"Waitin' for you."

"Whatever for, Mr. Spencer?"

"Think you know, woman. My Christmas present."

"Under the tree with all the rest."

"You ain't goin' to want to give me this one I have in mind under the tree. This'n's private. Come here, woman."

Her clothing fell away to the floor, and she slipped back in bed with her husband, snuggling against his bear-scarred chest, squirming a bit until they were a perfect, comfortable fit.

"Merry Christmas, Mr. Spencer."

"Merry Christmas, woman, an' a hundred more, the spirits willin'."

Bemused, she tipped her head up to look at his craggy, seamed face, into his bold brown eyes unchanged by age.

"A hundred?"

She felt his shrug under her cheek.

"More or less. Mountain man's a sturdy breed an' so's his woman. I figure—"

"Leave your figuring to mathematics, Sam Spencer, if and when I get around to teaching you fractions. For now a kiss will do, and whatever else comes to mind."

"Oh, Maddie, my love, I got ideas along them lines fit to last a whole 'nother lifetime."

"Me too, old man, me too. I love you, Sam."

She knew that would shut him up quicker than anything else; saying those words back to her still came hard to him. Just when she thought she knew him better than she knew herself, he surprised her once again. Hauling her closer, face serious and intent, he told her.

"Love you too, Maddie. You're the best part of my life, are my life, you oughta know by now. I love you, Maddie Spencer."

His lips came down to cover hers, his kiss as passionate as the very first, and hers in return. One thing led to another, as good as always, too. Better. Later, much later, when Sam had gone on downstairs to let her dress at her leisure, she basked briefly in recalling her recalcitrant husband's unexpected eloquence. Belatedly, she recalled his smug grin, his cocky wink in departure. Sudden understanding made her smile, then chuckle.

Sam Spencer once again had had the last word.

This time.

There was, however, always the next time. And the next. And the next. For a hundred years, or whatever time remained of their life together in their mountain valley home-sweet-home.

"And I love you, Sam. I love you, too."

Whether or not he heard her, she considered that she'd had the last word after all.

ABOUT THE AUTHOR

To learn the future of Samantha Sarahannah Spencer, the granddaughter to whom Madeline Preston Spencer bequeathed the bride quilt, read *Samantha's Heart*, a December, 1998, release from Zebra Books.

I love to hear from my readers. You can write to me at:

Pamela Quint Chambers
890 76th Street SE
Byron Center, MI 49315.

Please include a self-addressed stamped envelope if you wish a response.

BOOK YOUR PLACE ON OUR WEBSITE AND MAKE THE READING CONNECTION!

We've created a customized website just for our very special readers, where you can get the inside scoop on everything that's going on with Zebra, Pinnacle and Kensington books.

When you come online, you'll have the exciting opportunity to:

- View covers of upcoming books
- Read sample chapters
- Learn about our future publishing schedule (listed by publication month *and author*)
- Find out when your favorite authors will be visiting a city near you
- Search for and order backlist books from our online catalog
- Check out author bios and background information
- Send e-mail to your favorite authors
- Meet the Kensington staff online
- Join us in weekly chats with authors, readers and other guests
- Get writing guidelines
- AND MUCH MORE!

Visit our website at http://www.zebrabooks.com

ROMANCE FROM JANELLE TAYLOR

ANYTHING FOR LOVE   (0-8217-4992-7, $5.99)

DESTINY MINE   (0-8217-5185-9, $5.99)

CHASE THE WIND   (0-8217-4740-1, $5.99)

MIDNIGHT SECRETS   (0-8217-5280-4, $5.99)

MOONBEAMS AND MAGIC   (0-8217-0184-4, $5.99)

SWEET SAVAGE HEART   (0-8217-5276-6, $5.99)

ROMANCE FROM FERN MICHAELS

DEAR EMILY   (0-8217-4952-8, $5.99)

WISH LIST   (0-8217-5228-6, $6.99)

AND IN HARDCOVER:

VEGAS RICH   (1-57566-057-1, $25.00)